Sherlock Holmes Never Dies

New Sherlock Holmes Mysteries

Collection Five

The Stock Market Murders
The Glorious Yacht
The Most Grave Ritual
The Spy Gate Liars

Craig Stephen Copland

Copyright © 2017 by Craig Stephen Copland

All rights reserved. No part of this book may be reproduced or transmitted in any form or by any means, electronic or mechanical, including photocopying, recording, or by an information storage and retrieval system – except by a reviewer who may quote brief passages in a review to be printed in a magazine, newspaper, or on the web – without permission in writing from Craig Stephen Copland.

The characters of Sherlock Holmes and Dr. Watson are no longer under copyright, nor is the original story *The Naval Treaty*.

Published by:

Conservative Growth

1101 30th Street NW, Ste. 500

Washington, DC 20007

ISBN-10:1973710307

ISBN-13:9781973710301

Dedication

To the members of the Toronto Bootmakers, the Sherlock Holmes Society of Canada. It was their announcing of a contest to write a new Sherlock Holmes mystery that got me started. Thank you.

Note to Sherlockians

These four novellas are *pastiche* stories of Sherlock Holmes. The characters of Sherlock Holmes and Dr. Watson are modeled on the characters that we have come to love in the original sixty Sherlock Holmes stories by Sir Arthur Conan Doyle.

The settings in the late Victorian and Edwardian eras are also maintained. Each new mystery is inspired by one of the stories in the original sacred canon. The characters and some of the introductions are respectfully borrowed, and then a new mystery develops.

If you have never read the original story that served as the inspiration of the new one—or if you have but it was a long time ago—then you are encouraged to do so before reading the new story in this book. Your enjoyment of the new mystery will be enhanced.

Some new characters are introduced and the female characters have a significantly stronger role than they did in the original stories. I hope that I have not offended any of my fellow Sherlockians by doing so but, after all, a hundred years have passed and some things have changed.

The historical events that are connected to these new stories are, for the most part, accurately described and dated. Your comments, suggestions, and corrections are welcomed on all aspects of the stories.

I am deeply indebted to The Bootmakers of Toronto (the Sherlock Holmes Society of Canada) not only for their dedication to the adventures of Sherlock Holmes but also to their holding of a contest for the writing of a new Sherlock Holmes mystery. My winning entry into that contest led to the joy of continuing to write more Sherlock Holmes mysteries.

Over the next few years, it is my intention to write a new mystery inspired by each one of the sixty original stories. They will appear in the same chronological order as the original canon appeared in the pages of *The Strand*. Should you wish to subscribe to these new stories and receive them in digital form as they are released, please visit www.SherlockHolmesMystery.com and sign up.

Wishing joyful reading and re-reading to all faithful Sherlockians.

Respecfully,

CSC

Contents

The Stock Market Murders 1

The Glorious Yacht 139

A Most Grave Ritual 225

The Spy Gate Liars 347

About the Author 451

The Stock Market Murders

A New Sherlock Holmes Mystery

Chapter One
Why Birmingham?

Paris has one. Parisians called it *Le Métropolitain*. The folks in New York City call theirs *The Subway*. Londoners, rather sensibly, refer to the network of trains that run underground as *The Underground*. Many of the clients who came to see Sherlock Holmes at 221B Baker Street traveled on the Underground, getting off at Baker Street Station and walking the short distance to Holmes's rooms. This has been somewhat more difficult of late as a result of the construction taking place at the station, where hundreds of workmen and machines toil to build the new Underground line that will connect Baker Street with Waterloo.

It may seem odd that I would introduce my account of one

of the most complicated cases ever pursued by Sherlock Holmes by reference to something as mundane as London's Underground. I do so because the Underground, and very specifically the Bakerloo Line, was directly connected to a series of brutal murders and one of the greatest commercial frauds ever perpetrated on the citizens of England. I have given the case the name *The Stock Market Murders* but it involved far more than a run-of-the-mill murder or two and, to this day, it has yet to be completely solved.

This unusual case began for me on the morning of Saturday, 15 September in the year 1900, the autumn of the first year of the twentieth century. I had been married for several years and my wife and I were living in a pleasant home not far from Paddington Station. The first floor of the house was occupied by my medical practice, which, I am grateful to say, had prospered and was providing me with a more than sufficient income; so much so that I had restricted the office hours to Monday through Friday, giving us the luxury of a full weekend of leisure.

On that Saturday, I rose early. It was a splendid fall morning and I took myself on a brisk walk around the Lagoon of Paddington Basin. The mist rising off the water, the warmth of the morning sun, and the sweet smell of the autumn leaves and flowers gave a lift to my soul, and I had to believe that my life indeed was blessed. So I returned to my home and sat on my porch, feeling rather settled and contented, sipping morning tea and reading the *British Medical Journal*.

At half-past seven, a hansom clattered up the quiet street

and stopped in front of my house. I was about to shout that my office was closed for the weekend and direct whoever was in the cab to Saint Mary's Hospital when the door opened and out stepped my dear friend, Sherlock Holmes. It being a Saturday morning, he was dressed casually in a riding jacket and open shirt and he waved and smiled as he approached my porch. It had been several weeks since I had seen him and this visit, while most welcome, was a surprise. I have to admit that I missed him. The adventures we had had in the past may well have been dangerous and at times foolhardy, but they certainly did stir my blood in a way that a full slate of patients with their oh-so-English complaints never could.

I smiled, rose and welcomed him, but with the premonition that my leisurely weekend was about to go the way of all flesh.

"Good morning, my dear doctor," he said. "I am so glad to have found you at home. I was quite hoping I would."

We shook hands and exchanged a few morning pleasantries, whereupon he gave me a good looking over and said, "Ah, but you are looking prosperous. Allow me to congratulate you on your new specialization in providing care for the veterans of Her Majesty's Armed Forces—a most admirable service."

Over the years I had come to expect that Sherlock Holmes could discern what to all others was hidden, and this was no exception. Still, I was utterly perplexed.

"All right, Holmes. There has been no public announcement of that news. There is no mud on my sleeve. My slippers are not burnt, nor is one side of my face more tanned than the other. There is no picture of Chinese Gordon for me to be looking at, and I have not even glanced at my war wound. So out with it, how in heaven's name did you know about my intentions?"

Sherlock Holmes has a way of smiling in a manner that, while friendly, is annoyingly condescending. He did so yet again.

"My dear doctor, whilst you have not put an announcement in the press, you have had a shining new brass plate affixed to your front door which reads *John H. Watson, M.D., Providing Particular Services for the Care of Veterans.* There was truly not a scrap of deduction required."

He nodded in the direction of the door behind me. I turned and noted the plaque that a workman had installed two days earlier and had to laugh at myself.

"And how, my dear Watson, is your good wife? Might she be up and around so that I may pay my respects?"

"No. She will be terribly disappointed to have missed you but she is away to Keswick for several days. Along with three friends from church, she is attending a conference of the Christian Suffragette Movement. She is serving as Secretary for the local chapter. They are calling themselves *The Daughters of Deborah* and are determined to be better judges of the good Lord's people than we men have been."

"That, I am sure," said Holmes, "would not be difficult. As long as they do not change their name to *Daughters of Jael*, you are probably safe from incurring a splitting headache." He chortled at his attempt at wit and I responded in kind, even though I had no idea what he was talking about.

"As your dear wife is away, I shall not have to apologize to her for dragging her husband and my only completely reliable friend off to help with a new case, shall I?"

I suspected this was coming and I must confess that I could not help but smile.

"I may have to miss mass one more time but I am happy as always to offer my services for whatever they are worth. When do we start?"

"Shall we say ... in five minutes? I believe that is all the time it will take you to pack an overnight case, and stock up your medical bag."

I shook my head in wonder, turned, and stepped back into my house.

"Five minutes it is then," I said.

"You might want some reading material as well," he shouted after me. "It's a bit of a journey. And kindly bring your service revolver along."

Five minutes later, I stepped into the waiting hansom. To my surprise, there was a young man sitting in the seat beside Holmes.

"Allow me to introduce my latest client," Holmes said. "Dr. Watson, meet Mr. Hall Pycroft, currently employed at Hichens Harrison in the City and the official guardian of two tomcats."

The young fellow smiled and extended his hand. "I am pleased to meet you, Dr. Watson. I am a devoted fan of your stories."

He was a comely young man, with a very fair complexion and sandy colored hair. He was seated, so it was hard to judge his stature, but he was not overly tall and of slight build. His hand was thin, almost delicate, with long fingers. His accent, however much he may have tried to overcome it, was still unmistakable and anyone could tell that he was born well within the sound of Bow Bells. I appraised his age at somewhat less that thirty and noted that his left hand bore no wedding ring. Judging from his appearance, I thought him more likely to spend his time in an art gallery or a theater than on the rugby pitch.

"Mister Pycroft," said Holmes, "is taking us up to Birmingham."

"Birmingham!" I exclaimed. "You did not mention Birmingham."

"Did I not? Dear me. Would you have joined me so readily if I had?"

No self-respecting Londoner voluntarily and enthusiastically visits Birmingham. I confess that when Holmes told me to pack for overnight, I was rather hoping for the South Coast, or perhaps the Cotswolds.

"Most certainly, I would," I lied.

Holmes laughed and we exchanged some bantering pleasantries for the few blocks to Euston Station. We boarded the train to Birmingham and, once we had started on our way, he turned to the young man.

"It shall be some time before we arrive there, so could you please relate to my friend all of the details of your concern. There is no need for brevity, but do be as precise as possible.

And kindly begin by explaining my remark about the cats."

The lad forced a self-conscious smile and with an unsure voice, began.

"Right, sir. I will do that sir. Yes, well, my friend ... my best friend, Kenneth Arkell, is from Birmingham. We were at Cambridge together. He has two cats that he cares about very deeply. He's always talking about them."

He seemed quite nervous and I sought to put him at ease, so I interjected a friendly question.

"A cat lover, you say. Brilliant. And do these two tomcats have names?"

"Ah, an excellent question," said Holmes. "A detail I had neglected to establish. Thank you, doctor."

The lad looked a bit sheepish but replied. "Yes sir. They do have names. One is Charles Darnay and the other is Sidney Carton."

Both Holmes and I laughed at the absurdity of naming cats after characters from Dickens.

"And just why," I asked, "would he so name his cats?"

"Because, sir, they are very temperamental."

"I beg your pardon? How does that have anything to do with it?"

"Well sir, Kenny says that ... well ... he says that they are the best of toms;   they are the worst of toms."

Holmes and I both laughed out loud and then groaned at the absurdity. Our reaction seemed to put the young chap more at ease, and he grinned and continued.

"Kenny and me got to be chums at Cambridge. We were both at King's and studying mathematics and seeing as we both come from working families and didn't fit in with the toffs, we become real close. Both of us did our Tripos and did well and I found a billet at Hichens Harrison and he got himself one at London and Globe."

"Pardon me," I interrupted. "You both studied maths, but then you went directly to work in the City."

"Well, yes, sir. We could see that numbers were numbers and you could either work with them at a poor desk in a university and be paid a few farthings, or you could work with them in the City and be paid hundreds of pounds. So we chose the City. I had a slow start but am doing very well for myself now, and Kenny was so diligent that they put him in charge of their office in Birmingham. That made him happy seeing as that is where he was from and his mum and da' and brothers and sisters are all there. But we kept up our friendship and once a week, every week, every Thursday that is, when he had to come to London to his head office for their weekly meeting, we would get together. He'd spend the day in the office in the City, and after work we would have a pint or two with some friends from school at the Cheshire Cheese. I'm not much of a one for sitting and drinking so I would not stay long. But Kenny would stay and chat and laugh until near closing time. Then he would bunk in at my place and sleep in the spare room. We were doing that now for the past five years. Never missed. We always looked forward to it. He would never stay any longer than overnight as he had to get back and look after Sidney and Charles. He chatted all the time about his cats and doted on them as if he was their mum.

"The week before this one just past, he arrived at my rooms around eleven o'clock in the evening, like he always did. But he wasn't smiling. He looked pale as a ghost. All he said to me was, 'Sorry. I'm not doing well. I'll just go to my bed. We can chat in the morning.' But through the night I could hear him. He was pacing back and forth and I heard him sigh and even speak a few oaths, which was most unlike him.

"At breakfast he was silent and hardly ate. But then he looked at me, and he had some tears in his eyes and he said, 'Hall, you are my dearest friend. And I have to ask you a favor, and I beg you not to refuse me.' He looked so desperate that I agreed straight away. And he then says to me, 'If anything happens to me, promise that you will look after Sidney and Charles. If they were ever to suffer, I simply could not bear it.' I asked him what he was talking about but he said no more and packed up his things and departed. He thanked me as he turned away and went out the door and again I could see tears on his face.

"Two days ago I waited for him at Ye Olde Cheshire Cheese. But he never showed up. I thought he must be delayed at his office and I went back home, seeing as I have to be up right early every morning to read the wires from New York. But by eleven, he did not show up at my door. So I walked over to the pub and looked for him. But he wasn't there. I asked the publican if he'd been in and he said that none of the chaps who used to meet there every Thursday evening had shown up. I sent off a telegram to him asking him to tell me if something was wrong. I had no reply. That's when I knew that something must be wrong. So yesterday, as soon as I was done in my office, I went to visit Mr. Holmes and ask his help. That is my case, sir. I know it may seem petty to you and nothing like all those I've read. But I just know that something is amiss."

Here he stopped and I could see the deep concern on his face. However, I must admit that I was surprised that Sherlock Holmes would take on a case that was about no more than a young man, a Brummie for that matter, who did not show up for work. Holmes, as I should have expected, read my mind and responded.

"You are quite correct, my good doctor. It is not the type of case that I would normally accept. And you know perfectly well that I have little use for household pets. Your failure to bring your bull pup to Baker Street many years ago was something over which I silently rejoiced. However, I have seen enough of people who are obsessed with their pets, utterly illogical though it may be. Men and women of that ilk will starve themselves before they allow their precious dogs or cats to go hungry. So I know that when anyone so inclined asks his friend to take care of them for him, something must be very wrong, and the premonition of untoward events about to occur must be sincerely and strongly believed. This case fits that pattern and thus we are off to Birmingham."

The train journey north into the Midlands was agreeable enough. England is a pleasant place in September and the succession of small farms and cottages we viewed from the train window had a quieting effect on my disposition. The vista changed as we entered Birmingham, the center of so much of England's industrial economy. One after another, the dark satanic mills that the poets objected to were passed, until we reached the heart of the city.

From New Street Station in Birmingham we walked the dozen or so blocks to an elegant mews that ran off Corporation Street.

"This is Kenneth's home," said Hall. He indicated a very respectable white terrace house. "He has the second floor to himself and his cats."

Holmes looked intently at the property. "Your friend has done well for himself. Even in Birmingham, a set of rooms in a neighborhood such as this one would require a gentleman's income."

"Kenny is very diligent, sir. His entire income is from his sales commissions and he has been very successful."

"And what," I asked, "does he sell that pays so handsomely?"

"Stocks, bonds, debentures and the like; all tied to the Wright group of companies. There is quite a market for them, what with all the news of the gold being mined in Australia, the Cape, and Canada."

We entered and ascended the stairs to the second floor. There was no response to our knocking. Holmes tried the door knob and the door opened.

"Hello! Kenny!" shouted Hall. There was no answer.

I glanced around the room. It was about the same size as our front room on Baker Street. The great difference was that this room was immaculate. There was not a speck of dust to be seen. Everything was neat as a pin. All of the books and *objets d'art* were lined up in perfect order. Every picture, plaque, and photograph on the wall was hanging perfectly straight. The carpets were clean and new and the hardwood floors were gleaming. This young man was quite obviously a fiend for neatness and order.

The only objects that were out of order were several articles of clothing, shoes, and socks that were strewn on the floor against the far wall.

Within a few seconds of our entering I heard loud mewing and meowing. Soon a large tomcat was brushing its side against my lower leg. Another was doing the same to Hall Pycroft. He leaned down and picked up the cat.

"Why hello there, Charles? Where is your master? Where has he gone?"

In reply to the inane questioning of a cat, Charles meowed very loudly. He did not appear to be in a good mood.

There was, I noticed a rather unpleasant smell in the room. It was due, in part no doubt, to the cats, but there was also an odor that was faint but all too familiar to me. I looked at Holmes and from his look I could see that he had noticed it as well. It was the smell of death.

There was a hallway off to the left side of the room. Holmes quickly glanced down it.

"That leads to his kitchen, toilet and spare bedroom," said Hall. He was otherwise absorbed with the cats and continued to talk to them.

Holmes next went to a door on the far side of the room and grabbed the handle. It was locked.

"That's his bedroom," said Hall, more to Charles than to Holmes.

Holmes knelt down until his eye was at the keyhole. As I watched him, I saw his eyes widen and a look of fear and horror sweep across his face. He quickly stood up.

"Watson, please. Hall, put that thing down and get over here," he said.

I moved quickly. Hall gently lowered Charles Darnay to the floor and sauntered over, still talking to the cats as he did so.

"Your shoulders. Now," said Holmes. He physically grabbed Hall by the arm and lined him up beside me. The door was a solid oak and the latch and lock appeared to be of unwelcome quality.

Hall was finally paying attention and looking quite perplexed but he did as he was told and on the count of three we rushed in unison into the door. It gave a responding crack but did not entirely open. Holmes stepped back and gave a strong kick to the plate below the handle and the door swung into the bedroom.

The next sound I heard was an unholy shriek of terror from Hall. In the middle of the room, with a rope around its neck and dangling from the ceiling was a man's body. The face had blackened, the eyes were protruding, and the tongue was protruding from the mouth. The entire body was naked and discolored in shades of purple, red and black. The stench in the room was sickening.

Chapter Two
Awful Evidence is Destroyed

It was far from the first time that I had looked at the terrible sight of a young man who had been dead for several days. Neither was it new to Sherlock Holmes. To poor Hall Pycroft, it was a terrifying shock. He descended into panic and rushed toward the body, grabbed it around the knees and tried to lift it.

"Get him down! Get him down," he screamed at Holmes and me. He kept shouting and attempting to raise the body. "Get him down!" he shouted again. The poor young man was beyond rational thought. Panic had overtaken him.

Holmes and I gave a look to each other and walked forward until we stood on each side of Hall Pycroft. Holmes firmly grasped one of his arms and I the other and gently but forcefully we pulled them back away from the corpse.

"Hall," said Holmes, "Kenny is dead. There is nothing we can do. He is gone. Now just let go and step back." He continued to repeat these words and we lifted the poor chap and dragged him back through the door and away from the ungodly sight. We forced him into the parlor and to the far wall so that he could no longer see through the door into the bedroom. When his back hit the wall his legs collapsed and he dropped to the floor and buried his face in his hands. He was crying uncontrollably.

We left him there and returned to the bedroom and the dangling corpse.

"Please," said Holmes, "do a quick examination of the body whilst I look around the room."

I nodded and began my unpleasant task. With the exception of a chair that lay toppled over by the wall, the room was every bit as neat and prim as the parlor. I was stopped, however, almost immediately by what I saw lying on the floor below the young man's feet. There was a magazine, a rather cheap one, with drawing or photographs on every page. The pictures were shocking. Page after page had images of young men, all in various states of being unclothed and all engaging in unnatural acts with each other. I was horrified and called immediately to Holmes. He came at once and looked at the magazine, but his face did not evidence repulsion as mine must have. He scowled and appeared deeply puzzled. His examination was interrupted by a voice from the doorway.

"I'm sorry, gentlemen. I lost control of myself," said Hall Pycroft. He was deathly pale and holding on to the door frame for support. "I'm fine now. I've recovered. What can I do to help?"

Before I could answer, I could see that Hall's glance had gone to the magazine on the floor. A look of fear came over his face and he rushed forward and grabbed the magazine off the floor and made as if he would stuff it into the inside pocket of his jacket.

"Hall," commanded Holmes. "Put that back. You cannot tamper with evidence. It is a serious crime. Put it back immediately. Here, now give it to me."

Hall Pycroft stepped back and pulled his jacket around his torso. Holmes stood and walked directly in front of him, extending his hand in a demanding manner.

"You can't! You can't!" Hall cried. His moment of self-control had vanished and he was again in panic. "You can't let people see this. You can't. It will be all over the press. I know his mum and his father, and his family. They will die. It would kill them. It will destroy them for the rest of their lives. You can't! Please. I beg you. No!"

Holmes lifted his hand and placed it on the young man's shoulder and brought his face close to Hall's frightened countenance.

"I am sorry, Hall. But you cannot remove evidence. The wheels of justice grind slowly and painfully, but they cannot be tampered with. It will be terrible for his family, but it cannot be avoided. I will not allow you to make yourself a criminal by attempting to do good. Now give me the magazine and go back to the parlor and sit and wait for us."

Holmes's tone was compassionate but determined and the magazine was handed over to him. Hall's face was contorted with pain and tears. He staggered back out of the bedroom.

"My dear doctor," said Holmes. "Would you mind taking the poor lad out of here and down to the pub on the corner? And have the publican call for the police. I will continue my investigation. You might take these miserable cats with you and see if the pub can find them any food. They do not appear to have eaten for several days."

I nodded, lifted one of the toms and gave him to Hall and took the other in my arm. I led Hall and we made our way back down to the street and to the local pub.

The publican promptly fetched saucers of milk and some morsels of fish for the hungry felines and a brandy for Hall. He sat quietly and sipped on it, leaning down to stroke the cats and muttering loving words to them. A police officer soon appeared at the door and I hastened to lead him back to Kenny's flat, babbling some information about the situation as we walked and not bothering even to introduce myself.

He was a large chap, the constable, and he had the puffy face and small eyes that tend to be associated with the Midlands. Londoners, somewhat smugly, refer to the look as *porcine*. This is unforgivably snobbish on our part but it accurately conveyed the chap's appearance. Upon reaching the room in which the body of Kenneth Arkell was hanging the constable stopped, stared and slowly shook his head.

"Ahh ... noo. It's Olive and Norm Arkell's boy, Kenny,"

he said, and paused. "Ahh, dear. Such a shame. He was such a bright light. Not many of our lads make it to Cambridge. We all had such hopes for him. It's so sad. So sad."

He walked around the body, giving it a cursory glance, and then stopped when his boot struck against the magazine lying on the floor. He picked it up and muttered, "Oh dear. We're not having any of this nonsense. Trash like this has to be burned." He stuffed the magazine into the inside pocket of his jacket.

Holmes looked at him, positively shocked. "Pardon me, constable, I believe that magazine is evidence and must be included as part of your investigation."

The large chap turned his gaze on to Holmes, gave him a hard look and said, "Magazine? What magazine, sir? I did not see a magazine, and as far as I know, neither did you, sir, if you know what's good for you."

Holmes had dealt with a great many police officers over the years and was not about to be cowed by a local Birmingham constable.

"I know perfectly well what is good for me, constable, and it is to give a truthful report to Scotland Yard about what I found here."

"Really, now. And what good would that do? It can't bring him back, now can it? Maybe that's what they do in London, Mr. Londoner, but that's not what we do here. This lad has a mother and father and family here in Birmingham and all they need to know is that their boy, this promising lad, had some tragic events in his life and chose to end it. That's what will be in my report, and Saint Peter himself couldn't be more truthful."

"And, pray tell," asked Holmes, "just what tragic events did he have?"

"Well, Mr. Londoner, he had a series of rejections in his love life."

"Good heavens, man. How could you possibly know that?"

"I know that because he's close on to thirty years old and still not married, so obviously his love life has not been successful. Like we say down at the station, you don't have to be no snot-nose Sherlock Holmes to figure that one out."

Holmes was not expecting that observation and was at a loss for words. The constable continued.

"And clearly he had a disappointing setback in his career."

"Constable!" Holmes sputtered. "There is no evidence of that whatsoever."

"Wrong again, Mr. Londoner. Kenny Arkell worked in finances. And we all know that anyone who is successful in finances gets promoted to the City. And he's still here in Birmingham, so we know that he must have had a painful loss."

The policeman took a glance around the room and continued.

"And I observed—and by the way you can learn a lot by just observing closely—that he has a bowl and saucer for a cat but there's no cat. So on top of his sad love life and failed career, even his beloved cat has abandoned him. That's the type of detail Sherlock Holmes would take note of."

"The cats," announced Holmes, "are at the pub on the corner and did not abandon him."

"Well that proves it, then. They preferred the company of the barmaids and left him heart-broken. So, sir, that is what's going to be reported."

He pulled a pencil and notebook from his belt and held it up in front of Holmes.

"Now, sir, I need to get your name and your friend here. First name first."

Holmes was silent for a moment and then replied, slowly and imperiously, "Snot-nose."

I left Holmes to deal with the constable and the local police station and returned to the pub to find Hall Pycroft. He was sitting quietly in the corner stroking the now contented Sidney and Charles. The two of us carried the cats to the station and boarded the train back to London.

Conversation between the two of us was limited but at one point I looked straight at him and said, "Hall. You do know what happened to your friend, don't you? Would you mind explaining it to me?"

The poor lad again turned ghostly pale. "Oh, please, Doctor Watson. Don't ask me to do that. Please don't ask me."

No more was said and we both continued to stroke the cats. Hall chatted with the feline in his lap. I did not. At Euston station I hailed a cab and had the driver take Hall to his flat and then me back to my home in Paddington.

Chapter Three
If It Happens Three Times

The following morning, I once again I neglected church and the state of my eternal soul and chose to wait in 221B Baker Street for the return of my cherished but peculiar friend. He appeared shortly after noon, greeted me with a nod, sat down, pulled his lower legs up onto the chair and closed his eyes.

Clearly he did not want to converse, but I did and had waited several hours for the opportunity.

"Such a shame," I began, "that the young man foolishly engaged in such risky behavior. He should have known better."

Holmes opened his eyes and looked at me in silence, but with unmistakable mild disdain.

"And just what," he asked, "do you think happened to him?"

"It's perfectly obvious, is it not? I do not think he took his own life. I believe the appropriate conclusion would be accidental death by self-strangulation. Surely you know about that. Cutting off your oxygen so as to enhance your erotic sensations."

"Good heavens, Watson. Have you bid goodbye to your entire rational capacity? He was murdered."

I was shocked by that statement and immediately challenged him to substantiate it.

He sighed and extended his legs to the floor.

"There was no question that he did not commit suicide. No one who is obsessed with the care of his cats would leave them to starve. And the mess of the clothes around the room is entirely out of keeping for one so fastidious. He was obviously not intending to die. As to its being an accident, I suggest that you review the literature on this unspoken but far from unknown practice. Those who engage in it do not stand on chairs and then kick the chair to the other side of the room. They take all possible precautions to make sure that if they do lapse into unconsciousness, their feet and knees relax and touch the floor. Add to that discrepancy the fact that the magazine was crisp and new, not dog-eared and stained as would be the case in one who engages in such actions. No doubt whoever killed him wanted it to appear that he died in the way you supposed him to, but the evidence points conclusively to murder."

I nodded slowly, once again chagrined by my failure to see

what had been so apparent to Holmes, but I had to ask, "If so, then by whom and why?"

"That, Watson, is what I now must deduce. I must admit that it has presented me with a challenge."

He once again closed his eyes and drew up his feet. I was quite sure that I would have no further conversation that day and prepared to depart. I was stopped by the sound of the door on Baker Street opening and closing and a set of footsteps ascending our stairs.

"Good afternoon, Holmes, Watson," said Inspector Lestrade as he strode into the room. He walked past both of us and over to the mantle, where he helped himself to a cigar and a snifter of brandy.

"If I have to work and pay you a visit on a Sunday afternoon, I do believe I'm entitled to some minor pleasures of the flesh, wouldn't you agree Holmes? Did your dear Mrs. Hudson leave any lunch out? I missed my dinner at home and had only a miserable sandwich at the station. Are you not going to offer me anything, Holmes?"

Holmes was giving the inspector a sideward glance bordering on hostile.

"I am quite certain that you did not just happen to drop in looking for a bite to eat."

"No?" replied Lestrade. A smug smirk had emerged on his ferret-like face. "And here I thought you might wish to be hospitable, it being Sunday and all. But if you insist, I will admit that I heard you had been up in Birmingham yesterday. A bit of a nasty and salacious thing going on there, what? So sad when fate and carelessness take the life of a young man who should have had a fine future to look forward to." He smiled, again smugly.

Holmes was not amused. "If you believed that his death was accidental, then you would not be here, would you, inspector?"

"Ah, ha. Right you are. I'll have to get up earlier in the morning, won't I, if I am to deceive Mr. Sherlock Holmes. You are, however, not entirely correct. I am here because earlier this week there was another tragic accidental death of a young lad who was also a Cambridge man. A fine young fellow named Arnold Bush. Must have fallen off the Tower Bridge, he did, and drowned in the Thames."

The change in Holmes's posture and his facial expression gave him away. He was interested.

"Do tell, sir. What happened?"

"All we know is that some folks nearby pulled his body out of the water just down from the bridge the next morning. He had a flask of gin in his pocket and so the local constable assumed that he was three sheets to the wind and fell off the bridge, didn't know how to swim and drowned."

Holmes was positively smiling. "And you would not be here telling me this if you believed that to have been what happened."

"Did I say he was a Cambridge man? Yes, I did, didn't I? Did I mention that he was on his college swimming team while he was there? No? And that he was wearing a winter coat on a mild fall night?"

Holmes had taken the bait and was drawn in, with no sign of objecting.

"Had he spent several hours at the pub and become inebriated?" asked Holmes.

"Seems he was an abstainer. Somewhat fixated on bodily health. I did say that he was a Cambridge man, right? Did I say that he was from King's College, graduated five years back with his Tripos in mathematics? No, well he did. Does that strike you as odd?"

"That is an interesting coincidence, inspector."

"Right, well I always say that if a tragic event happens once, it's happenstance. If it happens twice, it's a dreadful coincidence. But if it happens three times then it's a criminal conspiracy."

Holmes was looking more than a little annoyed. "I believe, my dear inspector, that is what *I* have been known to say. Not *you*."

Lestrade looked at me and gave an exaggerated wink. "I knew that would get his goat, eh, Watson?"

He turned back to Holmes. "Right you are, Holmes. And like I also say, we cannot jump to conclusions before we have enough data. So all we have is a coincidence. You're right."

He paused and looked around the room nonchalantly and then continued.

"I really would rather be home having my Sunday dinner with my dear wife, but I thought you might want me to tell you about that one. And the next one too. Another tragedy. A fellow named Geoffrey Delacroix went and shot himself in the head on Friday night. His landlady found him lying on the floor of his room. Still in evening dress. A revolver in his hand and a hole in his head."

Lestrade stopped, enjoying his little piece of theater.

"Keep going," said Holmes.

"Yes, another fine young lad. Still had his white gloves on and managed to shoot himself behind his ear without getting a spot of blood on them and not even a trace of gunpowder. It's been a bad week for these chaps from Cambridge."

"Cambridge?" queried Holmes.

"Oh, yes. I suppose that is significant. Graduated five years ago. King's. Did his Tripos in mathematics. Now, what was it you were saying about the third time?"

Holmes's eyes were now alive and he was rubbing his hands.

"I do not wish to be presumptuous, inspector, but is it possible that you are wishing to engage my services to investigate this coincidence that appears to have become a conspiracy? If so, I assure you that I could clear my schedule and devote some time to your case later this week."

"Wrong again, Holmes. I am not here to hire you to do anything later this week. I'm here because I want you to pack up straight away and get yourself up to Cambridge and find out what went on there five or more years ago that has resulted in three brilliant young men being murdered. If you get out of here within the hour you can catch the last train on a Sunday afternoon. And take your Boswell with you. I'll need full written reports."

Lestrade stood and turned toward the door. "And if you will excuse me, I am going home for my very late Sunday dinner. Here are some notes on the three fellows. Good day, Dr. Watson ... Good-day ... Snot-nose."

I'm sure he strutted down the stairs after that one.

Chapter Four
We Go to Cambridge

I gave Holmes a sharp look of disapproval, to which he responded by ceasing to rub his hands together in unfettered glee.

"My dear doctor, I stand reproved," he acknowledged. "Thank you for reminding me that the loss of life of three fine young men is a terrible tragedy. My pleasure in having a truly challenging case must needs be severely tempered by that awareness."

He appeared entirely sincere and I smiled in return.

"I am happy as always to assist you," I said. "And I do believe that I can be of more use than just taking notes for Inspector Lestrade."

Within an hour, both of us had packed a small valise, found a cab, and taken it to King's Cross Station. At four o'clock the train pulled in to platform number nine and we entered our cabin, located about three-quarters of the way up. Once settled, Holmes took out the dossier Lestrade had left us and began to read.

"Anything of interest?" I asked.

"Not much. He found some photographs of each of them. Those will be useful. We already knew whatever is here about Kenneth Arkell. The chap who drowned, Arnold Bush, was some sort of accountant with the Bank of England. Good family. Church of England. Hailed from Surrey. The boy who was shot in the head had a French name, Delacroix, but his family dates back to the Conquest. Old money. Minor nobility in his past. Attended Cambridge and did well but not terribly ambitious afterward. He was employed in the engineering department of the City of London. The only things they had in common were their age, and their studying mathematics at King's, Cambridge all at the same time. So reason tells us—as it did Lestrade—that we must begin in Cambridge."

"That does seem reasonable," I said. "And just where do we begin once we get there?"

"I have said, more than once," he said, "that when you eliminate ..."

"You have indeed," I interrupted. "Many times more than once."

"The immediate problem with this case is that the list of possibilities requiring elimination is rather longer than I would have liked," he said.

29

"Is that so? Very well, I'm listening," I said.

Holmes sat back in his seat and furrowed his brow. "It might be of use to me to have your comments, if only for their being so obtuse as to spark a contrarian insight on my part. Quite so. All right, let me begin at the top of the list. There is no family or blood connection among these lads, so we can safely rule out one of the most common causes of murder; issues of inheritance. The other common cause leading men to murder other men is jealousy over a woman. These were all young chaps in their early twenties and all with the uncontrollable animal instincts that accompany that age, so that is a possibility."

"Do you really think so?" I asked. "I can imagine one man killing another over the attraction to one particular woman. But if the object of your passions has already been courted by three other suitors, then I suspect that even the most inflamed of suitors would see that it is time to look for another lady."

Holmes smiled and nodded. "Once again, my friend, I bow to your superior knowledge in that department. We shall rule out jealous rages over the opposite sex."

"The *opposite* sex," I said and raised my eyebrow. "We *are* on our way to *Cambridge*."

"Ah, yes," replied Holmes. "Indeed we are, and so some connection to the love that dare not speak its name cannot be ruled out. An excellent insight, my good doctor."

I was feeling quite confident, having achieved success so far.

"Gambling?" I offered.

"Always a possibility," said Holmes.

"Anarchists?"

"The place is full of them."

"Spies? Possibly working for Kaiser Bill?"

"I believe that we are about to enter the prime recruiting grounds," he said. But then he added, "If they were working for the Kaiser and are now dead then our side must have done them in. Hmmm. We could be treading on Mycroft's turf. Best be careful on that one."

"Longstanding athletic rivalries?" I offered.

"A possibility. But these were all young Englishmen. They had good sportsmanship drilled into them since they could walk. If they were Italians, or Spaniards, I could see them holding a grudge over a lost match for several decades. But quite unlikely for a boy from our fine public schools."

My list had run out. Holmes made no other suggestions but moved on to our tactics.

"Time is of the essence, my friend," he said. "I must impose upon you to make some of the necessary visits and interviews without me and I will cover the rest. You shall have to trust me to give you an account for your records."

"And you," I said, feeling more than somewhat chuffed with his confidence in me, "shall have to trust me to ask the same questions and make the same observations as you would."

"I trust you completely to do your best."

I was not sure if I had been paid a compliment.

Upon arrival in Cambridge, we took a cab and checked into the Garden House Hotel, pleasantly situated alongside the River Cam. Over supper, Holmes gave me my assignment for the following day.

"It is nearly two weeks before the beginning of Michaelmas term. The faculty have all arrived but the students are still enjoying their summer vacations. The chaps we need to speak to should all be quite free to chat. So might I suggest that you investigate the gaming and gambling dens, and the fellow who is in charge of the theater troupe."

"The theater troupe? What in heaven's name for?"

"It was you, my friend, who brought to my attention the underground network of men who engage in unnatural romantic pursuits, and where better to find a concentration of them than in the theater? As to the gamblers, I recall from my previous visits to this great university town that gambling took place in every college residence and pub, but the only venue in which bets were placed of sufficient magnitude to lead to murder was in the back room of *The Eagle*. I suggest that you begin there. Meanwhile, I shall investigate leaders of the anarchists and spies. They should not be difficult to identify, as they all have tenure and offices with windows."

I rose the following morning at what I considered to be an early hour only to find that Holmes was already up and gone. I took breakfast on the terrace of the hotel and enjoyed the serene vista of the lawns, the river, and the swans. It seemed incongruous with my purpose in being there and I was somewhat certain that my peaceful morning would not last long.

It did last, however, for at least another hour as I elected to walk the half mile or so up the River Cam from Granta Place to the Bridge of Sighs and thence to the Cambridge Union Building, where the office of the Cambridge University Amateur Dramatic Club was located. The sight of swans floating by and young men in their rowing shells pulling hard against the current lifted my spirits yet again.

I was in a jolly mood by the time I knocked on the door of the office. The small brass plate on the door read *Godfrey Tollemache-Fiennes, Director*. From an inner room came a modulated baritone response.

"Who ... is ... it? Who dares disturb my morning before the rosy-fingered dawn has yet to flee the sky?"

Without answering, I walked in and found the fellow to whom the voice belonged. He was seated in a cluttered office, behind a cluttered desk, and dressed in a black suit with a black shirt. His feet, shod in sandals and *sans* socks, were propped up on the desk. I bade him a pleasant good morning and presented my card.

The feet immediately withdrew from the desk and the eyes went wide.

"Oh ... my ... goodness! Oh, be still my heart. The one and only, the divine Doctor John Watson? The *author?* The most popular writer in England? No, it cannot be!"

He had risen to his feet and was walking around the desk to accost me.

"Thank you," I said. "I fear you exaggerate…" But that was all I was permitted to say.

"Oh … my … goodness gracious!" he exclaimed, the volume increasing and his hands clasped together under his chin. "Oh my … what can I say? This is an honor … no… it is a blessing … yes … how utterly exciting … no not just exciting… truly *enchanting*. Yes, *enchanté*. And to what do I owe this faaaabulous visit, my dear man?"

He reached out his hand and I responded in kind. Instead of shaking mine in the manner to which I was accustomed, he turned my hand so that the back of it faced upwards and proceeded to pat it with his other hand.

Taking my cue, I gave a quick furtive glance around the room and then *sotto voce,* answered.

"Three young men, all from the King's class of 1894, have died in the past week. The official reports say they all committed suicide." Here I stopped and glanced around one more time. "Sherlock Holmes believes that they were murdered."

"Oh!" he gasped, placing both hands against his sternum. "You horrify me."

"Sherlock Holmes," I whispered, "may be in need of your help in solving the mystery. He believes that it is tied to something quite nefarious that took place here in Cambridge several years ago."

I had whetted his appetite and carried on. "Please take a look. These are the three young men. Do you recognize them? Were any of them involved in any way in the Dramatic Club?"

I laid out the images of Geoffrey Delacroix, Kenneth Arkell, and Arnold Bush. The drama director looked them over slowly and carefully.

"I remember these boys. Yes. They were at Cambridge a few years back and I seem to recall that they were all specializing in mathematics. Numbers boys, we called them. Not a dramatic bone in their bodies. I doubt they could do anything onstage except recite *pi* to the forty-ninth place or the first eighty-nine prime numbers. So, I am sorry, doctor, I wish I could be of greater assistance, but, sadly, I cannot." He sighed and looked at me with puppy-dog eyes.

I moved on to more delicate matters.

"If they were not directly involved in the theater, do you recall seeing any of them in the company of actors, or perhaps musicians. Might they have had a close friendship with anyone in the dramatic club?"

The warmth disappeared from the man's face and he gave me a hard look. All affectation was gone from his voice.

"Look here, Dr. Watson. I don't care if this is about murder and Sherlock Holmes. It could be about saving the bloody empire and matter not a whit. I will have you know that I do not tell tales out of school and I find it offensive that you would even hint that I might."

The man was visibly offended. I took a different tact.

"Oh, my goodness, of course not. Sherlock Holmes merely assumed that if any of the lads from the theater knew these boys well, they might have some knowledge of their political activities. You know, an interest in radical movements. Did they associate with anarchists? And if you were able to help us, and the mystery were solved, then I do believe both Mr. Holmes and I would be more than happy to express our appreciation by giving the Dramatic Club the rights to write and produce a splendid play about the story."

That worked. He was smiling again.

"Oh, yes. Why, yes, of course. But I still cannot help you, I'm afraid. All those lovely numbers boys simply do not have sufficient passion, sufficient charm or wit to be of any attraction to those other lovely young boys who give their hearts to the theater. The two play to audiences that come from separate universes."

He went on for several more minutes expounding on the passion required for acting and script writing and how it was non-existent on those who aspire to be actuaries and accountants. I listened politely and, when he paused for a breath, I interrupted and thanked him and excused myself.

Chapter Five
The Numbers Boys

The next stop was the *Eagle Pub*. It was only a short walk down St. John's and then Trinity Street. *The Eagle* proudly claimed to be the oldest pub in the town. During the school term, I was sure that it would be crowded with students, professors and the assorted hodge-podge of academia, but in the mid-morning of a weekday before the start of the term, it was deserted.

A loud "Halloa!" as I entered brought the publican out from his kitchen. He was a pleasantly round fellow who smiled at me, possibly suspecting that I was an inspector from the government and there either to inquire about his taxes or his serving of diluted ale. I bade him good morning and handed him my card. He looked at it, pursed his lips into a duck bill, nodded twice and gestured to me to have a seat. He smiled and I could see a bit of a twinkle in his eye.

"Aye, and did a murder take place in my establishment and no one bothered to tell me?" he said.

"Oh no," I said. "Nothing of the sort."

"Ah, now isn't that a shame. It would do wonders for business. Terribly slow when the lads are not in school. Do you think maybe Mr. Sherlock Holmes could arrange for one of his famous murders to happen here and you write about it in *The Strand*? I would be eternally grateful." He was grinning at me and having fun pulling my leg.

"No," I again answered. "But you are not too far off."

That got his attention. He sat back, tipped his head to the side and opened his eyes wide.

"Am I now? Well then, Dr. Watson, you best tell me about it. I wouldn't want to miss a chance to bring the curious and prurient all the way from London to come and have a look."

I explained to him the purpose of my visit and laid out the photographs of the three young men.

"Dead, you say. Ah, that is a shame. All joking aside, sir. That is sad news. I remember them. Of course, I do. All three of them. They used to sit at that table over there every Thursday evening. And if I remember correctly, there were five of them, not three. Numbers boys, they were. They would have their pads of paper and pencils out and be arguing about numbers, numbers, numbers. If I think for a minute, I might recall the names of the other two. One was Paul. No, not

Paul...Hall. Yes, that was him. Hall. He was the fourth. Now he did not usually stay long into the evening. Hall was a sweet lad who said good night and went back to his rooms to study."

"But you said there was another as well?"

"Yes. A red-haired lad. Nice fellow. He was also a numbers boy but a bit of a writer as well. He wrote a few articles for the *Varsity*. I remember reading them. He was quite interested in the world of business and finance and, if I recall, he had a flair for making sense of stock and bonds and dividends and share prices and all that. Some of the other lads used to ask him what they should be investing in, and he would always tell them to spend whatever they had on beer and barmaids and worry about the stock market when they were forty. He was friendly that way, he was. I'm glad to hear that nothing untoward has happened to him. And I can't imagine why anyone would want to do harm to these three you have in front of me. They were all such fine boys."

"The redhead," I asked. "Do you remember his name?"

He looked up at the ceiling for several minutes and then smiled again. "Simon. Yes. I always put a picture in my mind that helps me remember names. It is a good thing in this business to know the names of the lads. You never know when they are going to return. So this boy I pictured as meeting a pie man. You know, the nursery rhyme?"

"Of course. And any chance you did the same for his last name?"

The convivial fellow laughed. "Ah, now that is asking me too much. But if you call in at the office of the Varsity, they will have it in their records."

I was about to thank him and depart when I remembered the purpose of my coming to his pub.

"I am told," I said, "that a sportsman might be known to make a wager or two while sitting in *The Eagle*."

"Nooo. Who would have told you that?" The twinkle had returned to his eye.

"I must confess," I said, smiling back, "that I have been known to associate from time to time with such a deplorable crowd as those who wager on a good match. I'm not much for putting my money on the table with cards in my hand—which I am told might happen here as well—but on a game of rugby or cricket, or football … or perhaps a horse race. Well, we all have our human weaknesses."

"And I have one or two of the same, my dear chap," he said. "If the term were in session I would invite you back this evening to join the fellows at the table in the back room. It gets quite lively back there, it does. Some of these boys come from wealthy families and it is not unknown for a hundred pounds or more to cross the table. You'll have to return in two weeks when they are all back here, but before the examinations are close. Then the ones who are only pretending to be gamblers vanish."

"And the others?"

"The true gamblers? They gamble on their exams just like they do on their cards and wagering. Usually they lose all around. I don't suggest you join them." He chuckled and gave me a pat on the shoulder.

"And what about these lads I've been asking about? Did they do any serious betting? Were they known to hold a hand of cards through a game of whist?"

He shook his head. "No. Not that numbers boys don't like to play, but no one will play with them. Not after the first night. Those lads aren't gamblers. They're calculating machines. There's no passion. You can see them keeping track in the heads of every card that has been played and doing and revising the odds with every round. When they know the odds are against them, they might put up a farthing. When they know they are favorable, they make a modest wager. They seldom lose. But they are no fun to play with. They would never bet a fiver just on a hunch, or on a look in another player's eye. So, unless a player wants to end up owing them a fortune, they won't be welcomed at a table."

Interesting, I thought. I thanked him and chatted a bit more but, as it was now past midday, I ordered a sandwich and a pint of ale and he returned to his kitchen. The ale struck me as a bit on the watery side.

I dropped in at the newspaper office as advised and they gave me the name I asked for. Then I returned to the hotel and waited for Holmes to appear.

When he did, I recounted what I had learned and, to my relief, he did not belittle my efforts as he had done in the past. Instead he paid me a compliment but then it dawned on me that he only did so in comparison to what he had discovered in his quest, which amounted to positively naught.

"The resident leader of the academic anarchists," he explained, "is a tenured professor of Russian literature who therefore has the freedom to rattle on about Marx and Bakunin in classes that are supposed to be about Pushkin and Chekov. He knew who our lads were and dismissed all of them as capitalist swine. They appear to have been profoundly unsympathetic to the great lumpen proletariat no less than to long-winded Russian authors. There was not the least hint of their having been connected to any respectable set of radicals. As for being spies for the Kaiser, the chap teaching advanced physics, Herr Fischer, proclaimed that every one of our boys was too lacking in muscular masculinity to be of value to the Teutonic race."

"Anything else?" I queried.

"No," he said. "No, nothing. I have toiled all day and my nets are empty Yet there *must* be something. There has to be. Perhaps it is in the realm of divine retribution."

"Pardon?"

"Yes, we have seen it many times before. The sins of the father. Be sure your sins will find you out. It is possible that instead of looking back five years, I should be looking back much farther. It is possible that their fathers' or even their grandfathers' lives were intertwined and that something evil has continued to fester."

He took out his pipe and began to stuff it with tobacco. I thought about what he had just said and then responded with what to me seemed quite obvious.

"Have you considered letting your nets down on the other side?"

He gave me a sharp questioning look. I carried on.

"Why does it have to be five years in the past? Or fifty years in the past? Why could it not be something that is only five weeks in the past? These lads all seem to have continued to be friends. They continue to meet regularly just as they did at school; every Thursday, isn't it?"

Holmes had struck a match with which to light his pipe and he now held it in the air whilst he stared at me. He was motionless until the match burned down to the tips of his fingers whereupon he twitched his arm and tossed the stub to the floor.

"Watson," he said, "it is just possible that I have at times unfairly underestimated your intellect."

I was tempted to correct him and note that it was not just 'at times' but he continued with his small paean to my insights.

"Of course. It is entirely possible that Cambridge has nothing whatsoever to do with their deaths, except as the place where they first met."

He now lapsed into silence.

"Where," he said several minutes later, "did young Hall say that they met up?"

"Ye Olde Cheshire Cheese in the City."

"Yes, yes. That was it." He lapsed again into silence but after a few more seconds he suddenly sat up and grabbed for his watch. In a most uncharacteristic fashion he muttered an oath.

"We've missed the train."

"What train?"

"Back to London."

"Holmes, there are trains right up until later in the evening back to King's Cross. We have all sorts of time to catch one if you wish to return now."

"Oh, yes, Watson, of course. I know that. But we have missed the train that will get us back into the City before the offices close for the evening. But please, go and fetch your bag and meet me back here in ten minutes. We need to get back. And we need to get back before it is too late."

"Too late for what?" I demanded.

"Five of them met every week and they must have been on to something. Three are dead. I fear that the lives of the other two are at risk. Please, enough. Fetch your bag and let us be on our way."

I hurried to do as he had requested and within twenty minutes we were back on the station platform waiting for the next train to London. An hour and a half later we arrived back in London. Holmes was moving quickly.

Chapter Six
At Ye Olde Cheshire Cheese

At King's Cross, Holmes hailed a cab and gave the driver an address on Fleet Street. It took us a good half hour to work our way down Gray's Inn Road and into the City, but close to five o'clock we entered Ye Olde Cheshire Cheese pub and took a seat. A pretty young barmaid came up to our table. She was wearing one of those barmaids' dresses that has a very low cut square bodice into which her substantial breasts had been confined until they were ready to overflow. I suppose that this attire was proven to encourage well-paid young men from the City to spend more than they should at the pub, but I found it distracting all the same. Holmes was oblivious.

"And what may I bring to you two handsome gentlemen?" she asked as she leaned over to take our order. "No need for posh chaps like you to order at the bar. I am Lucy and I will be happy to attend to your every wish."

She was all smiles and flirts and clearly well-practiced in the art of legally relieving gentlemen of the contents of their purses.

She looked directly at me and then at Holmes and then stood up, the smile having departed from her fair countenance. In a whisper, she continued. "Are you Sherlock Holmes?"

"I am," Holmes replied, not entirely pleased to have been identified.

The comely lass brought her head close to Holmes's ear and she whispered into it.

"Are you here about the numbers boys?"

I could tell by Holmes's nearly imperceptible reaction that he was surprised. In a low voice, he replied, "Yes, we are, and your question tells me that you are likewise concerned about them."

She gave a suspicious glance around the room. "I have ten minutes of relief time coming up in half an hour. Could you please wait here until then? I have to talk to you."

Holmes nodded his assent and we ordered a round of ale and fish and chips as if nothing out of the ordinary had taken place.

Half an hour later Miss Lucy arrived bearing three generous glasses of what appeared to be whiskey.

"I'm sorry," she said softly, " but we can only fraternize with the gentlemen customers if they are buying us drinks, and they have to be select spirits not just ale. I'll pay for these, myself, but I could not sit here without them."

"Young lady," said Holmes, "you shall do nothing of the kind. It is an honor to share a drink with a lovely young woman and Dr. Watson has insisted that he will buy this round."

I gave a mocked look of shock and the three of us forced a laugh. We raised our glasses and each took a sip. Miss Lucy took a generous swallow.

"I know," she said, "who you are. I have read all about you. You've never been in this pub before, not since I've been here. But I read in the newspapers over the past week that three of the numbers boys had died. They said that it was accidents or suicides and that seemed hard to believe. And then you walked in and I knew. I just knew that something terrible must have happened. Somebody killed Kenny and Arnold and Geoffrey, didn't they? And maybe Simon and Hall are dead too. What happened, Mr. Holmes? What happened?"

"Please, my dear young lady. Enjoy your drink and allow me to ask the questions. You are doing your job wonderfully well, now please permit me to do mine."

She took another swallow and looked at Holmes. I could read the fear in her eyes.

"How long," asked Holmes, "had the boys been coming in here?"

She shrugged. "I have only been working here for the past two years and they were here when I started. Before that, I do not know, sir. I'm sorry."

"Nothing at all to be sorry for, my dear. Now give me their names and tell me what you know about each of them."

"Well, sir. All I know is their first names. There was Simon, he was sort of the leader of the group, or at least I should say that he was the loudest. A bit of a bragger, I guess you could say. Always trying to be funny but I only laughed because he was a customer. He worked for a newspaper, the *Financial Times*, so he did not have much money and I guess he had to make himself seem important to make up for that. A lot of the blokes who come in here are like that."

Holmes nodded whilst I scribbled.

"Then there was Arnold. He was the most handsome of the lot and I think he worked for the City of London. The barmaids all liked him because he was good looking and strong and even though he only drank lemonade or tea, he always paid as if he had been drinking cognac. He wasn't rich, but he was generous all the same. Kenny was a Birmie and the rest of them teased him about that but it was all in fun and all of them got on well. Never any cross words at all. Just lots of laughter. Geoffrey and Hall were always the best dressed. They had jobs in finance. Geoff was at the Bank of England and Hall at Hichens Harrison. Hall usually left early. I could tell you what they ordered for their drinks, if you think that is important."

"No, my dear. But you said they got on well. Never any arguments?"

"Never. They were usually loud and chatty, but during the past month they were all real quiet, like. They kind of huddled in close together after Hall had gone, because he always left early on, like I said. And they did not order nearly as many drinks. It looked as if they had something serious that they were talking about."

Holmes nodded again and again I scribbled.

"Was it always just the five of them? No others."

Here the pretty young woman leaned her head closer to the two of us and dropped her voice even more.

"It was always just them, sir. At least it was up until three weeks ago. And then again two weeks ago. Another chappie joined them. He was quite a bit older than them and I had a queer feeling about him. So did the other girls here."

"Indeed, please explain."

"I don't know if I can, sir. I'm sorry. But its just one of those things that a girl knows. And especially if you've been serving men for years, you get feelings about them. And we did not like this chap. None of us did."

"Please, miss, try to be more explicit. What was it about him that you did not like?"

She paused and looked ill at ease.

"It's hard to say, sir. But there's a friendly look that a gentleman gives a girl and you know that you can trust him as if he were your older brother. And then there's a look ...well, I don't know if I should say this, but behind the bar when we're talking to each other, we call it the three-legged look. Do you know what I mean, sir?" The young lass blushed as she spoke.

"I do, please continue. Did you catch his name?"

"No, sorry, sir."

"Not at all. But I am sure you can tell me what he looked like."

"Oh, yes. I can do that, for sure, sir. He was quite on in years, about your age, sir. And about your height, but much heavier. A bit of a tummy where you have none. He had grey hair, salt and pepper as they say, but a widow's peak. Dark eyes, and bags underneath them. And there was a gold filling on his left dog tooth. It was all gold, that tooth. Stuck out when he grinned at us. A bit creepy, if you know what I mean, sir."

"And have you seen him again, since?"

"Well no, sir. Those boys were not here last week. They didn't show up at all. We thought it a bit strange and were worried that we had said something to offend them and that maybe they had taken their business over to the Olde Cock. But that didn't make sense, because we know that our ale is two pence less a pint than theirs. And then I got to thinking and I knew, just the way a girl always knows, that something was not right and that it was tied to Mister Three-leg. And then I read about the fellows being dead and then you show up. So I know that something is not right. And I'm awful worried for Hall and Simon."

"As are we," Holmes confided. "As are we. Now, Miss Lucy, you have been exceptionally helpful. Please do not speak of our conversation to anyone else, unless an inspector from Scotland Yard shows up. But no one else. Can we trust you to do that?"

"Oh, yes, Mr. Holmes. You can trust me not to say a

word. But does that even mean my mum? She would be right tickled to know that I was chatting with Sherlock Holmes."

"Even your mum. Although I think it would be all right for you to tell her on Sunday. Can you wait until then?"

"I can do that, sir. Yes sir, I can do that."

I paid our tab, including the three select whiskeys, and we departed.

"Shall we call a cab?" I asked.

"No. The office of the Financial Times is only a block away. They have a newspaper to get out tomorrow morning and I expect that most of the staff will still be on the premises."

He was right. We walked through the door and found ourselves in a noisy beehive of activity. Framed copies of front pages, all in the well-known pinkish salmon color, adorned the walls. Everyone seemed to be too busy to even notice us and our initial attempts to make inquiries were flatly ignored. Then we observed a fellow on the far side of the room hand off some sheets of paper to a runner, who dashed away to the stairwell. The fellow then sat back, lit a cigarette and put his feet up on his desk.

"Excellent," said Holmes. "A reporter who has just filed. A perfect time to chat."

We walked over and Holmes handed him his card. The reporter looked at it, and looked at Holmes, and then at me. He appeared bewildered.

"You sure you're in the right place, mate? This is the *Financial Times*. We don't cover murders. Robberies maybe, but only *by* banks, not of them. Shouldn't you be over at the *Chronicle*? Bullets and bombs are their beat, not ours."

"I assure you we are at the right newspaper," said Holmes. "And it is very important that we speak to one of your colleagues, a young man named Simon Woodhouse. Could you point him out to me, please?"

"You're right. Simon Woodhouse is one of ours. You see that desk over there? The empty one? That's Simon's desk. But he hasn't been at it since last Wednesday. He said he was working on a stunner of a story and wouldn't tell the rest of us what it was about. So I hope he has something. Otherwise his editor will have his pecker in a press."

While I pondered the unpleasant metaphor, Holmes continued his questions.

"As I said, sir, it is terribly important that we reach him and quite important to his story and this newspaper. Might I bother you to ask if you have a staff directory listing the home addresses of your colleagues?"

The reporter took his feet off of his desk and opened the center drawer. He took out a spiral bound notebook and handed it to Holmes.

"He'll be in there. And if you find him tonight, tell him he better put in an appearance here tomorrow morning, or his editor will bust his balls."

"I will pass that message along," said Holmes. He quickly looked through the directory while I contemplated the potential injuries that were to be visited upon poor Simon's nether region.

Chapter Seven
The Arrogant Young Reporter

Simon Woodhouse lived on Grafton Mews in Fitzrovia. It was a well-to-do neighborhood and I concluded that he was still living at home with his parents in spite of his having completed his university years. Some young men are inclined that way.

It was now well past sunset and we approached the smart terrace house in the dark and gave a knock on the door. A maid opened it and Holmes announced that we wished to speak to Simon. There was not much light in the doorway but I thought I saw an apprehensive look come over the maid's face. She turned and retreated back into the house. A minute later a lady of a certain age approached us. She was nicely dressed and walked with elegant confidence. Her complexion was very fair and her hair was a rusty color. I imagined that in her youth it must have been closer to flaming red.

She smiled cheerfully. "You are looking for Simon? I am so sorry to disappoint you, gentlemen. Simon has gone to America. He departed on the weekend. A shame you did not come just a few days ago, you would have found him. But I shall be happy to let him know that you called. If you will leave your cards, I will put them in the envelope along with my first letter."

Holmes said nothing and handed his card. The lady read the name and gave Holmes a look of fearful recognition.

"I see, madam," he said, "that you know who I am. And I know for a certainty that Simon has not gone to America. He is not here because he fears for his life. My only purpose in this visit is to protect him. If you will tell me where I can find him, I assure you that both I and Scotland Yard will do whatever is necessary to keep him safe."

I watched as the color faded from the good woman's face, rendering her pale skin a ghostly white. Her hands began to tremble and she closed her eyes and took a deliberate deep breath.

"I am sorry if I attempted to deceive you, Mister Holmes. And, quite frankly, I thank God for your being here. Simon is in danger, you are correct. I begged him to go to the police but he refused. He said that he was about to write the biggest news story of the year and he feared that the police would let the news get out and some other reporter would print it before he could. So he insisted that I not contact Scotland Yard."

"Then if he spoke only of Scotland Yard and did not mention my name, you would not be betraying his trust by telling me where I can find him"

Mrs. Woodhouse smiled. "I cannot argue with your logic, Mr. Holmes. Although I fear Simon would not be pleased, it is all the excuse that I need. He is staying up in Holloway, not far from the prison."

"Is he with a relative of the family?" asked Holmes.

"No. He felt that would be too easy to trace. It is just a rooming house. Most of the tenants are men who have just been released from prison. It sounded terribly dreadful but he said it was the last place anyone would look for him. I will write out the address, and please, Mr. Holmes, do try to get him to stop being so pig-headed. I am worried sick."

"No need to worry, madam. We will find a cab and be on our way there post haste."

"Oh, thank you, sir. Thank you, Mr. Holmes. And you, sir. You must be Dr. Watson. Thank you, as well. You have brought such a relief to my heart."

We hailed yet another cab and hurried north to Holloway. The driver did not like being in the area after dark and had us pay him while the cab was still moving. He stopped only long enough for us to climb down and then laid the whip on the horse's haunches and sped off. At the end of the block I could see that great dark archway that led into HM Prison Holloway. Holmes had sent many villains and more than one villainess off to serve time there and I was hoping that none of them had been recently released to the neighborhood.

We knocked on the door of the house whose address we had been given. A large and very rough woman, who I imagined had been in prison for a decade for murdering a dozen men with her bare hands, greeted with in a manner that was lacking in any trace of civility.

In response to Holmes's asking for Simon, she told us, "That cocky little redhead twit is down the street at the pub. Doesn't like the food he gets here. Doesn't like the rest of the lodgers here, either. And he doesn't like me and the feeling is mutual. So you can go find the little blighter and tell him we'll all be glad to see the back of him and not a day too soon."

Holmes graciously thanked the landlady and we walked briskly in the dark to the Prince Edward pub. The patrons were a rough lot and I could see Holmes scanning the crowd, not wanting to encounter any of the criminals he had put away. I did not recognize anyone and apparently neither did he, so we entered and worked our way to a small table at the back. A young man with bright red hair was sitting at it writing busily. He had an opened valise on the table beside him and in it I could see a stack of pages that must have been three inches thick.

"Good evening, Simon," said Holmes as he pulled up a chair and sat down across from him.

The fellow looked up, startled, and quickly put the paper he was writing on into the valise and closed it.

"Who are you?" he demanded.

"My name is Sherlock Holmes and for your own protection I would like you to come with me immediately down to Scotland Yard. Your life is in danger and my only purpose in coming here is your well-being."

The fellow rolled his eyes and replied. "Yeah, yeah. So the great detective found me. Do I look like I'm running away like a coward? If you think I am going to hand over the biggest story to hit the London press in ten years to the coppers at the Yard, you're crazy, Mr. Holmes."

"You will not have to surrender your documents. But you will be safe."

"Oh, really? Is that so? And since when can Mr. Sherlock Holmes, amateur detective, guarantee what Scotland Yard will or will not do? Can you give orders to Scotland Yard? Right. Didn't think so. I'm fine where I am. So how about you just run along and forget you ever found me. By Friday this story will have hit the fan and be all over the world."

"It will do no such thing if you are dead."

"Right, well I'm not going to end up dead. You called on my rooming house, right? Do you think that monster landlady is going to let any thugs into the house? And behind her are six chaps who would happily eat you for breakfast. They're the best protection available anywhere. Tell that to Scotland Yard."

"There is no doubt," replied Holmes, "that your fellow lodgers are a fearful group and will protect whomever they *like*. However, I will wager that they do not like *you*."

That comment was met with a stunned silence as the fellow absorbed the implications of what he had just been told. Holmes continued.

"The one person who does care for you is your mother and you have placed her under terrible stress and worry. For her sake, if not for your own, please come with me."

That appeared to give the man pause and replied in a much more congenial fashion.

"I agree. I will go with you to the Yard. And I thank you for your concern. But I still have several hours of writing to do so I can turn in this story tomorrow morning. It will run every day for at least a week in the FT and will get picked up by Reuters and the AP and be all over the world. It will hit the City like an earthquake. Believe me, I am not exaggerating. Heads will roll and kingdoms will fall. I'm talking at least a million pounds. Maybe three million. It's the worst fiasco to hit the City ... ever. But I need to get it finished and I'll have to work through the night to do that. So if you can meet me at the house tomorrow morning at seven thirty I will go with you first to my office and then on to Scotland Yard. I promise."

Holmes sat back and folded his arms across his chest. "I assure you that I do not care a fig about your story. I do care that three of your friends have been murdered. I agree to wait until morning if you will tell me here and now who you suspect is responsible for those deaths. I work in complete confidence and I have no interest whatsoever in stealing your thunder or publishing one word of any reporter's story. I am interested only in bringing criminals to justice."

There was a stony silence between them for a part of a minute before Simon Woodhouse answered.

"All right, then, Mr. Holmes. I'll give you what I know. Is the name of the firm London and Globe known to you?"

"I have heard the name. I am not familiar with its operations."

"If you will look into it, you will find the people who have very good reasons for wanting my friends and me dead."

"And," asked Holmes, "might one of those people be a fellow with a gold tooth?"

Here the young man's mouth dropped open. "Why yes. How did you know that?"

"That, young man, is the part of my story that I choose not to disclose. I bid you good night. I will be at your door at seven thirty tomorrow morning."

We left Simon Woodhouse at his table in the pub and took a cab back to Baker Street where I bedded down for the night. I was weary from a long day and the travel that we had done and took myself off to my old room straight away. I left Holmes sitting in his usual chair with his pipe in his mouth.

At six o'clock the following morning I woke to the sensation of my shoulder being rocked.

"Come Watson, time to get back to Holloway."

"Good heaven's Holmes. It is only six o'clock. Could you not have given me another half an hour?"

"Perhaps, but I am feeling very apprehensive about our arrogant young reporter. Anyone could have gone to his mother and given her a card bearing my name and she would have revealed the location of her son. I fear we have no time to lose. Please. We can find coffee and breakfast after we get Simon delivered to Lestrade."

I was quite sure that all my early rising would accomplish would be a much longer time of standing on the sidewalk outside of Simon's door while we waited for seven thirty to arrive, but Holmes was insistent and there was no point arguing. So I rose and bathed quickly and by six thirty we were in a cab making our way through the early morning darkness back through Camden Town and into Holloway.

The cab turned off Camden Road and I heard the driver shout an abrupt stop. I quickly opened the door to see what had caused the obstruction, and then my heart died. In front of the rooming house that Simon Woodhouse was staying in were three police wagons. I feared the worst. Holmes followed me out of the cab and said nothing. He strode quickly up to the house and I tagged along behind him.

Emerging from the house was the familiar figure of Inspector Lestrade. He saw the two of us and looked honestly amazed.

"Good Lord, how in the name of all that is holy did you end up here? I only got the call twenty minutes ago."

"I fear, Inspector," said Holmes, "that our number of dead young lads who did their mathematics at Cambridge has just climbed to four."

"Not unless Cambridge is graduating large nasty landladies and monstrous ex-convicts. And those two in there are far from young."

Holmes hustled into the house. In the hallway and the kitchen were two bodies. Both had been shot several times in the chest and abdomen. The body in the hallway was that of the fearsome landlady. The one in the kitchen I did not recognize. Simon Woodhouse was nowhere to be seen. We scampered up the stairs to the rooms that had been let to lodgers. The door to Simon's room was open. The sweater he had been wearing the previous evening was draped over a chair. The valise that he had guarded so diligently was lying on the stairs. It was empty.

"So, Holmes, would you mind telling me what went on here?" barked a bleary-eyed Lestrade.

"I admit that I was wrong once again," said Holmes. "These poor souls apparently did try to protect the young man. They hardly knew him, and they did not even like him. Yet they stood in harm's way so that he could escape." He paused and sighed. "I can only hope that the Almighty recognizes true Christian sacrifice when it is standing in front of Him."

Between Holmes's account of the previous evening and the accounts of the other borders, Lestrade was able to discern that two men had entered the house just before midnight, immediately after Simon's return from the pub. They followed him into the hallway, but the landlady had blocked their passage. After a struggle during which she punched one of them in the face, they had shot her. Simon had been grabbed as he tried to ascend the stairs and one of the other lodgers had come to his aid. Simon was able to bolt up the stairs, but without his valise. The assailants had shot the nameless large tattooed fellow who had staggered back to the kitchen before collapsing and dying. Simon must have escaped through a window on the upper floor. Descriptions of the murderers were confused and contradictory. After seeing their fellow borders shot dead, the other inhabitants of the house took cover. No one attempted to get a closer look at or follow the killers.

Sherlock Holmes said nothing as we sat in the cab and returned to Baker Street. I occasionally looked at him and observed his expression change several times. I could see the look of steely determination and the hardened eyes that I had come to associate with his single-minded pursuit of the criminal. But twice I noticed that his face softened and his head shook slowly. He looked perplexed, as if having no idea what steps to take next. As we were rounding the park he turned to me.

"Do you know anything of this firm, London and Globe?"

I had heard of it and, in truth I knew a little. Thirty years ago, when I completed my medical studies I did not know the difference between a stock and a bond. What had changed over the past three decades was that both Holmes and I had become moderately wealthy men. My medical practice returned a gentleman's income, but the success of my stories about Sherlock Holmes had brought in surprising royalties, and it kept growing. I had, quite rightly, shared this income with Sherlock Holmes, on top of which he not only had his professional fees as a consulting detective, with the freedom to pick and choose amongst a long list of clamoring clients, but he had been the recipient of numerous rewards and awards. While I had, rather sensibly, left most of the decisions as to where to invest our assets to my wife, I did make it practice to scan the financial pages once I had finished with the racing news.

"It is," I said, "often in the news. Always announcing yet another discovery of gold somewhere, or an upgrading of their assay results. The driving force behind it is something of a character, but his Board of Directors is as blue ribbon as any mining company on the exchange."

Holmes pondered this information.

"How might we gain intimate knowledge of its operations?"

I thought about that and gave what I thought was a clever answer. "By becoming well-heeled investors. If we indicated that we, wealthy chaps that we are or at least can pretend to be, are interested in becoming major shareholders, I suspect we will be welcomed."

Holmes nodded and smiled. "There are times, my dear doctor, when I unfairly underestimate both your rational and creative abilities. An excellent suggestion."

I said nothing.

Chapter Eight
The Folly Under the Lake

T he next few days were uneventful. I returned to my home and medical services and enjoyed quiet evenings with my lovely wife. Holmes dropped by twice to keep me up to date and to see if I had managed one more time to develop new insights into the case, using my newly appreciated ability to be both rational and creative. I had not.

Simon Woodhouse was tracked to Southampton and was on his way to America. Lestrade had been to see Holmes several times to discuss the matters of the case but had made no headway on any of the five murders that were now in his docket.

Then, on Friday, the twenty-eighth of September a note arrived from Holmes. It ran:

```
Tomorrow afternoon, as I am sure you have
nothing pressing on your calendar, please
dress in the most impressive manner you
are capable of. We have been invited to
pay a visit to the most pretentious
estate in Surrey.

I shall come by at one o'clock.Kindly
implore your dear wife to join us as she
is far more convincingly elegant than you
are.
Holmes
```

My darling wife, Mary (née Morstan), was delighted to join us but declared that she would need a new fall frock and accessories if she were to play the part of the wife of a serious investor. Thus we found ourselves at ten o'clock on Saturday morning celebrating Michaelmas in a most unholy manner by enjoying the view of her in a mirror in a shop on Bond Street. Forgive my bias, but I could not help but be proud of being married to one of the most attractive women in all of London.

However, a minor financial disaster was rapidly approaching my pocketbook.

Mary and I stood side by side looking at ourselves in a large shop window. Her stunning appearance unfortunately rendered my habit dull and terribly uninspired by comparison. So off we went to Saville Row and I was outfitted off the rack with as fine a morning suit—"un-bespoken for" as the tailor explained—as could be secured on such short notice. It was not inexpensive.

At precisely one o'clock a handsome brougham pulled up

to our door and Holmes waived to us to join him. He was wonderfully attired and complimented my wife endlessly and me economically on our appearance. He had even brought along a photographer who took our likeness and promised that we would appear in the society pages of the Sunday newspaper. I, rather uncharitably, assumed that Holmes had bribed yet another editor.

We giggled our way from Paddington to Waterloo Station and found the South West Railway train for the Milford-Witley station in Surrey. Comfortably ensconced in a first class cabin, we rehearsed our lines and laughed heartily at the notion of our impersonating the twits and toffs that move idly through the lofty realms of England's parasitical rich. We tried to appear convincingly absurd and utterly snobbish.

"So, Sherlock," said my wife to our dear friend, "do tell. Who is this character that has invited us to tea in Surrey?"

Holmes smiled, removed his top hat, and leaned back.

"His name is James Whitaker Wright. He has dismissed the 'James,' reduced it to a mere 'J' and no one has called him Jim or Jimmy since he has been out of short pants. You are welcome to call him Whitaker or Whit. The word on the street is that he soon expects to be elevated to Sir Whit. He is a native of Stafford. His father was a clergyman and our man became one as well, but very briefly.

"His father passed on to glory when young Whit was twenty-five years old and for reasons that are unknown to any rationale being, the family emigrated and ended up in Toronto, Canada of all places. Young Whit was having none of that nonsense and soon decamped for the greener fields of

Philadelphia. Somehow, he discovered his true calling as a promoter of mining stocks and using rank bluster, enthusiasm and balderdash managed to convince a vast number of investors to buy the stocks in some mine in Colorado. He had his ups and downs in these ventures but ended up … *very* up, you might say. He married a lovely American woman and has a couple of fine offspring. A decade ago he returned to his own, his native land.

"He has continued to promote stocks and all sorts of other financial instruments that promise excellent returns on mining ventures in the wilds of Australia, South Africa, and the far reaches of British Columbia in Canada. In doing so he has made an excellent return on his efforts even if his many investors have not fared so well. He now commands an integrated group of companies, of which London and Globe is the leader. His Board of Directors are as blue blood as they come, and the chair is none other than a former Viceroy of India. He spent a fortune building the estate in Surrey to which we have been invited and it is reputed to be as stately as any of the god-awful pretentious stately homes in our fair land.

"That is a terribly short introduction to the man," Holmes concluded. "What have I neglected to disclose?"

"Why," asked Mary, "would a reporter try to link the fellow to the murders of those young men? He sounds like he has worked hard and has far too much at stake to risk any such criminal act."

"There are rumors," said Holmes, "that his empire is built on sand and might collapse some day, but no one knows and I have not been able to unearth anything that directly connects the fellow to the crimes. But that is not to say that any one or several of his minions, who would stand to lose their own small fortunes, might not have been involved."

"But is there anything," I asked, "*anything*, about his escapades that is against the law? I do believe that any man who would put his money into a get-rich-quick scheme is advised that *caveat emptor*."

"Right you are, doctor, and while there have been howls of complaints at his exaggerated promises, there is nothing to date that comes close to a violation of any statute. And your question reminds me to ask one of you. How much is each of us claiming that we are prepared to invest in these companies?"

"Fifty thousand pounds each," I said. Mary smiled and Holmes let out a low whistle.

"My dear doctor, I did not realize that I had anywhere near that much to my name."

Now I laughed. "Oh, you don't and neither do I. Our non-existent funds are tied up in oil and cows in Texas and it will take us at least three months to liquidate and bring them back to England. But he does not have to know that until he gets impatient for our deposits into his accounts."

"Ah, brilliant, doctor. Brilliant."

At three o'clock we descended the train at the Milford station and were met there by a gleaming brougham that brought us to the quaint hamlet of Witley. Just outside the village we passed through a magnificent set of gates. The arch overhead proclaimed, in large block letters of gleaming brass, that we were entering **LEA PARK.**

The landscape we encountered was like something out of the memoirs of Capability Brown. The gravel drive wove its way through copses of poplars, elms, oaks, and locust trees. Most were still small, seldom over twenty feet in height but all situated in locations designed to be pleasing to the eye. Intermingled with the trees were beds of flowering shrubs— camellia, hibiscus, juniper, honeysuckle and many more—and a wild delight of perennial and annual flowers. Every blade of grass had been cut to a uniform height and the lawns had the texture of bowling greens. At regular intervals along the driveway, Greco-Roman statuary had been placed. Here there was a discus thrower, there a headless Aphrodite from Milo, and farther along a Jupiter and an Achilles. Interspersed were many statues of attractive young men and women all minus their clothes. As we passed the second pond and entered an open expanse, I gasped. In front of us lay a small lake, on the far of which was an enormous manor house, perfectly framed with plants and fountains.

The estate not only announced fabulous wealth, but the freshness of it indicated that it was wealth that had been recently acquired. The established families of England tended to look down their noses on the *nouveau riche*, but, as Sherlock Holmes had observed, better to be *nouveau riche* than not *riche* at all.

I assumed that the driver would let us off at the front door of the stately home. To my surprise he stopped beside the lake where a walkway led out into the water. At the end there was a small island on which sat a glass gazebo.

"This way please, lady and gentlemen," the driver said, offering his hand to my wife as she stepped down from the carriage. "Please, follow me."

We did and walked along the narrow isthmus to the gazebo. Once inside the small structure, the driver requested that we follow him down a spiral staircase. The three of us looked at each, shrugged and followed until the dark stairs ended some forty feet below the surface of the water. From there we walked along a short tubular tunnel until we passed through a door into a room that was some sixty feet in diameter. I looked up and let my mouth fall open. The ceiling of the room was made entirely of glass, supported by steel arches. Above our heads floated schools of golden carp, rainbow trout, and scores of game fish. We were in Poseidon's lair under the sea. The sunlight filtering through the water and the plants gave a greenish light to the entire room. It was rather magical and yet eerie all at once.

"Please, be seated," a voice that emerged from an opening door said to us. "Kindly make yourselves comfortable." I turned and saw a gentleman of about my age and Holmes's height but several pounds heavier. He was well dressed in a rather bright blue suit and a brilliant red tie. His closely cropped hair formed a distinct widow's peak in his forehead and a salt and pepper mustache covered his upper lip. I shot a quick glance over at Holmes to see if he was doing the same as I was.

He was. Both of us were watching the fellow's face very closely, trying to get a glimpse of his dentures.

"Mister Wright will be with you shortly," the chap said. "May I offer you some refreshment while you wait? You must be weary after your long journey."

"Oh, no, not really," said my wife. "The drive through the lovely gardens was more than enough to refresh us." She gave the man her widest and warmest smile. He smiled back, exposing his canine teeth. They were not exactly straight and far from white, as is normal for an Englishman from the working class. But there was not a speck of gold to be seen. Both Holmes and I relaxed our gaze.

"I am delighted you enjoyed them. Permit me to introduce myself. I am Arthur Harry Pinner. The master of the estate refers to me as his Man Friday. One of my many duties is to meet visitors and ensure that they are well attended to. May I bring the gentlemen a cigar? We have some of the finest; the master imports them from Cuba. Nothing less will do."

Again we declined his gracious offer. It occurred to me that most fine establishments that offered a guest fine cigars were equipped with high windows that opened and permitted the smoke from the cigars to escape. I did not wish to take the chance that this chamber was so constructed.

"I am informed," the chap continued, "that you are interested in entrusting a small portion of your wealth to the Wright Group of Companies, with the completely reasonable expectation of expanding your wealth far more successfully than you might were you to leave your funds in a bank. Is that correct, gentlemen and lady?"

We nodded and grunted and otherwise indicated our agreement. Mr. Pinner carried on.

"I am also informed that each of you wishes to deposit an initial sum fifty thousand pounds and purchase stock in one or more of the mining enterprises that have been selected by Mr. Whitaker Wright. Is that correct? And might I ask you which of the Wright group of companies you are interested in?"

I confess that I had not expected that question and was not entirely familiar with the several companies that Mr. Wright apparently controlled. I gave a quick glance to Holmes and could tell by the look on his face that he was at as much of a loss as I. Fortunately, my dear wife came to our rescue.

"Sir," she said, "my husband and Mr. Holmes are too modest to admit it, but they follow the wise practice of diversifying their investments—not putting all your eggs in one basket, as they say. So we agreed that we would like to divide the investment amongst several of the companies. Some will be in the one undertaking mining in western Canada, some in the two Australian companies, and a portion in the new venture here at home that is investing in the magnificent new line of London's Underground. There are several others on their list, but those are the principal ones."

"Ah, a very astute approach," Pinney said. "We will prepare a recommended list with suggested divisions and have it to you by tomorrow. And when shall we expect to receive the funds?"

Here Holmes took over the conversation. "As soon as we can responsibly do so, sir. Once we examine the prospectus of each of the companies and request our brokers to sell some other investments that are doing rather terribly, the funds will be forwarded to you."

"Of course, of course," said Pinney. "That makes complete sense. I am sure that Mr. Wright ..."

That was as far as he got. He was interrupted by a booming voice from the door on the far side of the room.

Chapter Nine
Mr. James Whitaker Wright

"**M**ister Sherlock Holmes!" The sound filled the underwater chamber. "Doctor and Lady Watson! So great of you to be here! So great. Believe me, it's wonderful."

Coming across the room was a colossus of a man. He was several inches taller than Holmes and had a massive body. He must have weighed nineteen or twenty stone. I put his age at close to mine, although it was a bit difficult to tell. His balding head was partially covered by light brown hair that he had combed over from the side of his skull. His mustache covered his upper lip and spread out like sloping letter 'Js' on each side of his mouth. His wide smile was complimented with perfectly straight, gleaming white teeth. I thought that both Holmes and I had dressed rather well for the day, but his attire was the epitome of bespoke, and perfectly tailored and appointed. This, I concluded, was Mr. James Whitaker Wright.

We rose and shook hands and he inquired, quite sincerely I thought, concerning my children (of whom I had none) and my parents (who were long dead and gone). He claimed to be a fan of my stories concerning Sherlock Holmes and, as he was a writer himself, particularly appreciative of my talents. I thanked him for the kind words and mentally recalled that, according to the word on the street, Whitaker Wright had written more books than he had read.

"It's so great, so great to have you here this afternoon. Here. Let me give you a copy of my latest book. Hot off the press."

He wagged his index finger and one of the fine-looking young people who stood behind him rushed forward with three copies of a fine leather-bound book. He wagged another finger and a lovely woman who could not have been more than twenty years old rushed to his side and handed him a pen. He opened the covers of each book and scribbled on the title page. Then, with a warm smile, he handed one to each of Holmes, me and my wife. I looked at the title. It read:

How to Make England Wright Again   *by J. Whitaker Wright*

"It's a great book. Believe me. It's great. It's going to be the best seller ever. It explains all the terrible things that are wrong with this country and how I know they need to be made right. You get it, huh? You know. Right ... Wright." He uttered the last words with the somewhat short fingers of both hands pointing toward his chest.

"C'mon. Si'down. I don't want to make this meeting all about me. I want to hear from you. You're real famous. Real famous. They say you're one of the smartest guys in England. So let me hear from you, Sherlock Holmes. What do you think about how I'm doing?"

Holmes gave a very thin smile. "According to what I read in the press, Mr. Wright, some questions have been raised about your ventures. Some of the press consider you to be a rather high risk."

"The press? The press? Let me tell you about the press. Slime. Sleaze. Terrible people. Just awful people. But give them credit, I say. Give them credit for one thing. I do offer high risk. Why? Because, like I always say—no risk, no reward. That's part of what I call the Wright way. This country has too many weak people. I mean really weak. But guess what. In a few years, I might even take a run at being Prime Minister. I would be great at that job. Believe me, really great. I would make this country right again. You get that? You know. Right? Wright?" Again the small hands.

"That," said Holmes, "would make for interesting times. However, sir, we are not here to talk about your political ambitions, but more specifically about your venture concerning the new Underground Line from Baker Street to Waterloo Station. If we are to invest a portion of our assets with you, I must ask you for some data concerning it. Kindly be as concise and precise as you can be. What are the prospects for this undertaking?"

"It's going to be wonderful. Amazing returns on your investment. And it's already created thousands of jobs. And I mean thousands. And real jobs for hard working Englishmen. Not just for all those crazy Italians and Greeks that keep pouring into this country. Those chaps would just as soon cut your throat as look at you. Can you imagine how many people are going to save hours of their time taking my new line. I'm calling it the Bakerloo line. Great name, don't you agree. Thousands of people will ride on it every day. Millions maybe. All paying a fare and all making pretty good profits. Believe me, it will make millions. You'll love it. And it will be run by businessmen. Successful business men. Like me. Not any of those government employees. Those chaps are a disgrace. Total disgrace. And that whole line will look beautiful. Beautiful platforms. Beautiful cars. I love to build beautiful things. Believe me, it will be incredible. London will love it.

"You know, everybody is asking me why I'm doing it. I don't need any more money. I've got lots of money. I'm doing this because I care. I care a lot about the English people. People are saying that I should be recognized for my selfless service to the public. Lots of people are saying that the Queen should give me a knighthood. Not that I need one. I'm doing it because I believe in this country. And I know, I know what has to be done to make this country right."

"And I'm not doing this all by myself. No sir. I've got the best team in the business working with me. Advising me. You know who I have as the chair of my directors? Freddy Hamilton, the Marquess of Dufferin and Ava. You know that chap? Used to be Viceroy of India. Great chap. Lovely chap. Freddy's a good friend. A dear friend. And I've got Lord

Redesdale from up in Oxfordshire. Davey is a splendid chap. Has a lovely wife. Just lovely. And I'm sure that she and Dave will have beautiful children. But you can't imagine who I need on my board?

"Want to guess?" he asked, smiling at Holmes.

"I confess," said Holmes, "to being rather poorly educated concerning potential directors for such a venture."

"That's all right, Mr. Holmes. I love the poorly educated. So allow me to let you in on something no one else knows. I want Sherlock Holmes on my board. Just imagine it, Mr. Holmes. You've used your excellent mind ... and I know an excellent mind when I see one because I have one too ... you've used it for fighting crime. And that's great. Just fantastic. But now you can keep on fighting crime and join me in doing something monumental, something really great, something beautiful for the people of this country. Just think about it. I love to gather lots of smart people around me. If they turn out to not be smart enough then I fire them. But most of the people I bring on board are really smart, like me. That's why I want you.

"Some folks out there, they're scared. Not that I blame them. I would be scared about investing my money after what this government has done to this great country. A disgrace. A total disgrace. But if they saw the name of Sherlock Holmes as a director of the London and Globe Company, then they would know it was an incredible company. How? Because they would know that Sherlock Holmes would investigate everything there is to know about my companies and that you would deduce, that's what you call it, right? Deducing? Well, they would know that you could have deduced if there was anything at all wrong and you would get it fixed. What do you say, Sherlock? Will you join me and help me make this country right again?"

Holmes gave the chap another thin smile. "I am honored. However, you would have to furnish me with all the records so that I could take on such a task responsibly. If you can do that, I will review all the data and give you my response in two weeks."

"Two weeks? Sherlock, I'm getting old. I move fast. I get things done. How about one week? Deal?"

Holmes smiled. "Ten days."

"Deal," exulted Mr. Wright. "I'll have Pinney here look after all that. He'll get you all the data you need. Mountains of it. Believe me with ten companies all over the world, and believe me, I have been all over the world; with companies all over the world there is a huge amount of data. Believe me, it's huge. Pinney will have it delivered to your door by tomorrow. Now enough of business. Let me show you through Lea Park. It's not quite as fancy as my friend, Nate Rothschild's place, but not far behind. In a few more years, it will be the best. Believe me, it will be even bigger and better than it is now. Even more beautiful."

The remainder of the hour was taken up with Mr. Whitaker Wright giving a tour of his magnificent home complete with running commentary on the beautiful architecture, the fabulous artwork, the fantastic furniture and similar superlatives for every other aspect of the manor house. Along the way he constantly stopped to say a complimentary word to his staff, addressing every one of them by name. They appeared to be quite fond of working with him.

Two hours later we found ourselves on our way back to the station in one of Wright's many landau carriages. My wife shook her head and laughed.

"Oh, my. That really was quite something, wasn't it?"

"It was indeed," said Holmes. "Quite incredible."

"Well then, Sherlock" she continued, "are you going to become an esteemed corporate director? Join the St. James Club? Or White's? Will you still have time for us poor common folk?" She laughed and enjoyed giving a tease to our Bohemian friend.

"Somehow, I think not," replied Holmes. "I will, however, review all the data that I will be provided with. It might prove to be very interesting. And I do not believe that I have told you about what I discovered about the lads from Cambridge, have I?"

"No Holmes, you have not?"

"The fellow from Birmingham, Kenneth Arkell, was employed directly by London and Globe to sell shares to the people of the Midlands."

"I knew that, already, Holmes."

"Ah, yes. Of course you did. Our young friend, Hall Pycroft, works for the brokerage house of Hichens Harrison."

"Yes, Holmes. We know that."

"And did I also mention that Hichens Harrison was one of the brokerage houses that had the account to sell the bonds of London and Globe?"

80

"No, Holmes. You did not tell us that."

"It must have slipped my mind. And the young lad, Geoffrey Delacroix, that worked at the Bank of England. He was in the regulatory division, the one that oversaw the reports of the companies listed on the London Stock Exchange. It appears that his portfolio included the inspection of the filings of London and Globe."

"We now have a coincidence, do we not?" I observed. "And if I remember correctly, was not the young journalist chap, the one from the Financial Times, working on a story about London and Globe? That makes it a criminal conspiracy, does it not?"

"Excellent, Watson. You excel yourself."

"But what of the fourth chap, the lad working for the engineering division of the City of London. What could he possibly have to do with international mining ventures?"

"Young Arnold Bush," said Holmes, "had been assigned the responsibility as the representative of the City of London government to oversee the construction of the new Bakerloo line."

"Ah ha!" both my wife and I blurted out. It all fit together.

"And just how," I asked, "do we tie them all back to Mr. Wright. He did not impress me as the type who would resort to murder."

"I have to agree, with John, Sherlock," said my wife. "He was utterly full of himself and the greatest braggadocio I have ever met. But I cannot imagine him deliberately harming anyone. Believe me."

Holmes chuckled. "No, but I would not be surprised to find that there were others whose fortunes are tied to his that might."

Chapter Ten
Convincing a Crown

Another week had passed without my hearing from Holmes. So on the Sunday morning, I returned the visit he had paid to me, quite certain that he would not be warming a pew of any church.

Being so familiar with 221B Baker Street, I opened the door, climbed the stairs, and let myself into the parlor. At the best of times, Sherlock Holmes was an untidy man, and it was immediately obvious that this morning was far from being the best of times. The room looked as if a bomb had been dropped on it. Everywhere, on the sofa, the side tables, the floor, the mantle, there were files, papers, newspapers, ledger books, and ashtrays in need of being emptied. The only clear space was immediately in front of the hearth. In that space there was a large cat, curled up and asleep. Another cat was curled up on one of the chairs that normally belonged to the table. Seated at the table where I had enjoyed so many of Mrs. Hudson's meals, were Sherlock Holmes and Hall Pycroft.

"Ah, Watson. Wonderful to see you. Pull up a chair, and we shall try to explain what we have been up to. Yes, just tip the chair forward and dump Sidney on the floor and come and be seated."

I glared at the chair and looked at Master Pycroft.

"I couldn't just leave them all alone in my rooms. Not after all they have been through," he said.

I bit my tongue and brought the chair to the table. Holmes lifted several files from the place in front of me and added them to a pile beside him that already resembled the leaning tower of Pisa.

"What we have," said Holmes, "is a copy of the filings with the Bank of England for all of the firms in the Wright Group of Companies for the past year, as well as every prospectus issued, and their complete bank records."

"Good heavens," I said, "how could you possibly have obtained their bank records? Those are not made available to the public."

Holmes did not answer me. He just looked around the room and began to hum some tune from that infernal nonsense *Pinafore*.

"Ah yes," I said. "You called in Mycroft."

He shrugged. "That is a possibility. Nevertheless, we

have made some startling discoveries. I could not have done it without the assistance of our friend Hall. The young man really does know his stuff."

Hall blushed and smiled. "It is not all that difficult if you have to look at these things every hour of every day."

"Would you kindly explain to Dr. Watson what it is that you have discovered?"

"Yes sir. I'll do my best, sir. It's a bit complicated, but beginning almost a year ago, not long after the construction began on the Bakerloo line, some strange things began to appear in the records."

"Did they?" I said. "And what were they?"

"Well doctor, the Wright Group has twelve different companies. See, here's the list. There's the Imperial Minerals Exploration Company. It's doing work in South Africa. And here's the Yukon Mining Company and they're doin' work in Canada. And the Imperial Gold and Silver Company is concentrated in the Cape. And the rest of the list is just like that. Now all of their statements that they file with the Bank of England or issue to their shareholders and bondholders look as if every one of the companies has lots and lots of cash and other assets."

"That makes sense," I said. "They are all engaged in mining and all bringing out gold and silver and diamonds and precious metals, so yes, that makes sense."

"Well, not exactly, doctor. You see the Wright companies do not actually own the mines or do the mining. The mines are all owned by other shareholders, of which Wright is just one. The Wright companies mainly buy, and promote and re-sell the shares. Now that is quite acceptable and everything should be all just fine. But at the end of September just past, they were supposed to issue dividends and interest payments and they didn't do it. They told everybody that they were retaining the capital so that the mines could be further capitalized and made more productive. Now companies can do that, but their investors usually aren't too happy about it. But what with all those blue bloods on the board and Mr. Wright being who he is, nobody raised a fuss. There was a short article in the Financial Times, but nothing else was said."

"Very well, I fail to see the problem."

"What we saw in the bank records was that no money ever went to the mines. At least, not much. Instead I could see that on the twenty-ninth day of every month, or if that day were a Saturday or Sunday, then on the Friday before, one of the companies would loan money to another company."

"That is permitted, is it not?" I asked.

"Yes, of course. But it takes several days for the transaction to be completed and recorded on the books of the receiving company. So what happens is that the loaning company records the loan as bein' receivable and that is what is says on their statements at the end of the month. But the receiving company doesn't show it on their books for the same month because they haven't got the money yet. It's still on the way. Well, sir, like I said, it started about a year ago with just one company loanin' money to another. But after three months there were four companies doing it. And by last month all the companies were doing it."

That did strike me as odd. "How much money has been moved around?"

"That's what we've been working on. It's not real clear because he uses ten different banks. Six are here in London, three are on the Continent, and one is in New York. And each company might have accounts at more than one bank, and by last month each of the companies was making loans to two or three of the other companies, not just one."

"Very well, what is your estimate of the total amount being loaned," I asked again.

Hall paused and looked at the columns of figures he had written on the ledger sheet in front of him.

"It's not all that easy. You see starting about six months ago they started making the loans in shares of the mines and shares of the company and not just in cash. So I've had to go back and find the value of all of those shares at today's rates."

"And what did you find?" I pressed.

Hall shook his head slowly. "It looks as if those shares have been overvalued on their books by a factor of at least five, and up to ten. So the value of the loan receivable in cash is much less than what appears, since it is the claimed value of the stock."

"Come on then, lad," I said. "Give me a number. How much money is on the books but really is not there?"

He looked again at his ledger sheet and then looked up at me and whispered. "It's more than two million pounds."

I was shocked. "Two million pounds?"

"Yes doctor. It's hard to believe, but when you add it all

up, the company loans and the inflated stock values, that's what it comes to."

"Where, in heaven's name, did the money go?"

"That's a bit complicated as well. Some of it, several thousand pounds was transferred from companies that are publicly listed and over to those that are privately held."

"Held by Whitaker Wright?" I asked.

"No. Held by his wife and children. His son is only fifteen years old but he owns one hundred percent of the shares in International Ventures Corporation. And then it looks like that company paid out in dividends in cash to the boy. And the same for the company his wife owns, and the one his daughter owns. But that's only part of it. Most of the money has been moved over to the company that is financing the Bakerloo line. I can't tell if it was all used honestly, but the expenses for everything they have done is a long way over what was expected. And it has all taken much longer than what was planned. So, their payroll is going to be several times more than they planned, and their cost of blasting is more. And same for the steel that's used in shoring up the tunnels and for the track. It would just be a wild guess on my part, but it looks like the line is going to be three times more than was budgeted and it will still be at least two years before it is completed and begins to bring in revenue from the sale of the tickets. That company has already passed the credit limit that Barclays' set for it, and so it has been receivin' loans from the other companies. It is not a nice picture, sir. I don't know how they can go on much longer."

"Master Hall," said Holmes. "Please take a moment and

review your numbers and give us a reasonable estimate of how much longer the companies can continue."

"It'll take me another hour to do that, sir."

"We are patient. The cats are content. Pray proceed."

I walked over to the bookshelf and took down a volume to read. Holmes lit a pipe. On my way back to my chair I glanced at the work the young chap was doing. His pencil was moving at lightning speed scribbling down numbers in column after column. What was utterly amazing was that it appeared that he was adding, subtracting, multiplying, dividing and assigning fractional figures entirely inside his head. Obviously he had an aptitude for this task and his education had not been in vain.

An hour and a quarter passed and he put down his pencil and looked up at Holmes and me. His eyes were quite wide and he was shaking his head in disbelief.

"Six weeks at the most. They cannot survive past the end of November."

I looked over at Holmes. "Perhaps you might wish to postpone becoming a director. Pity, I was looking forward to lunches at White's."

Chapter Eleven
The Empire Falls

On the fifteenth of November the headline in the Financial Times read:

WRIGHT COMPANIES ARE IN TROUBLE

The byline said that the story had been written by Simon Woodhouse and filed from New York. I was not surprised that it failed to disclose the shifting of funds through inter-company loans. Instead it claimed to have investigated several of the mines whose shares had been promoted by London and Globe. The mines, while not at all fictional, were producing ore at a volume far below their potential. When contacted by the reporter, they claimed that they had never received the funds from the sale of their shares, or if they had then it was not nearly enough to allow them to upgrade their operations and increase their production.

The first story promised subsequent accounts of each of the major mines that had been promoted. Readers would be taken to Australia, and the Cape, and even as far as British Columbia. They would read the heartbreaking stories of hardworking men who had been crying out for years for better equipment and access roads, and enough capital to pay decent wages. They would hear about the miners who were not paid enough to support their wives and children, and about children going hungry and begging in the streets of Pretoria. Even white children were begging. Could anything worse be imagined?

Holmes read the story and smiled. "Our arrogant young reporter is safe in New York, relying on his memory, and no doubt thanking God for the transatlantic telegraph. I do not doubt the accuracy of the stories but they are a far cry from exposing criminal behavior. They will depress the value of shares, but soon they will be worthless anyway. It is a good thing that we never managed to forward our funds to Mr. Wright."

On the first of December, as predicted by Hall Pycroft, the Wright Group of companies collapsed. The front page headline of every major newspaper screamed about the multi-million-pound debacle. The companies had filed for bankruptcy. Thousands of shareholders, some of whom had invested their life savings, were immediately impoverished. The press hounded the Marquess of Dufferin and Ava and the cartoonists had a field day with humiliating cartoons of him. When asked for a statement, Mr. J. Whitaker Wright proudly claimed that he had done nothing whatsoever wrong. Those who invest in mining in the colonies knew they were engaging in a high-risk enterprise. "No risk, no reward. *Caveat emptor* and all that, my boy." Investors took a risk with the hope of vastly increasing their wealth and lost. Tough luck; try again. Take it like a man. He had lost money too, but he wasn't crying about it.

Of course, Mr. Wright was still a hugely wealthy man. His estate was protected and his personal investments were in blue chip companies.

On the fifth of December, Holmes, Hall and I paid a visit to the offices of Scotland Yard at their new headquarters on the Embankment. Inspector Lestrade and two younger inspectors sat around the table as Holmes and Hall tried their best to explain all of the complicated ways that London and Globe and its related companies had shifted their assets and cash around and falsely made it appear that they were solvent.

Lestrade shook his head. "Holmes, a jury will never understand it. Wright will hire some fast-talking pettifogger and confuse the daylights out of the jury. I can't even understand it and you're trying to help me. There's no chance of ever getting a conviction."

"My dear inspector," said Holmes, "you know for a certainty that a massive criminal fraud has been visited on hundreds of citizens. Surely you must do something about it.

You know that what took place was against the law."

"Look, Holmes. It doesn't matter what I know. All that matters is what we and a crown prosecutor can prove in court beyond all reasonable doubt and do it well enough to convince a jury. Criminal intent with malice aforethought is the dickens to prove. This doesn't have a chance. And who knows but Wright may be right. *Caveat emptor* as they say. There is not a snowball's chance in hell of the Yard's securing a conviction in any criminal court in any assize in the country. So I'm not touching it."

Holmes was glaring in anger at the inspector. He spoke in slow, deliberate words.

"I find it difficult to believe, Inspector Lestrade, that you, of all people, would be willing to ignore a case that is tied to five unsolved murders and a massive fraud. Frankly, Inspector, I find it unconscionable."

These harsh words, delivered to a senior inspector in front of his underlings, were enough to destroy the amiable friendship that had been slowly built up between Holmes and Lestrade over the past decades. I fully expected Lestrade to politely but firmly tell Holmes to vacate the office of Scotland Yard and not to return, ever. But the response that took place was not what I expected.

Lestrade leaned back in his chair and smiled at Holmes.

"Mister Sherlock Holmes," he said, "All I said was that *I* would not be touching it. I did not say that I was letting *you* off the hook. The Yard cannot help you, so I'm sending you over to the Royal Courts of Justice. They deal in matters of corporate malfeasance and I suspect that if anyone can mount a case against Mr. Wright and his confederates, they will. Their bar for proof is lower than our criminal courts. So once they have convicted and sentenced him, I can work with them and put his arse in a wringer and suggest that he might get off with a reduced sentence if he would implicate any of his foot soldiers who were involved in the murders. I suspect he knows all about it. And then I can act. That, Holmes, is my plan."

Holmes smiled back at him. "Forgive my harsh words, inspector. I spoke too soon. And, pray tell, who is it that I am supposed to speak to at the Royal Courts?"

"His name is Rufus Isaacs. He's a young Jew, but he is smarter than all of us in this room put together. He'll be able to see through everything you say this Wright chap has tried to pull. So I'll let him know that you will need several hours of his time early next week. And I might even find the time to come with you. I rather want to meet this fellow. He's going places, as they say."

Over the next few days the newspapers continued to cover the story on the front pages. Many titled people in England had lost thousands of pounds. Pension funds and charities that had trusted Mr. Wright with their investments had seen their portfolios reduced to ashes. The Financial Times continued with Simon Woodhouse's stories about the overstating of the value of the shares in the various mines around the world, but these stories were old news.

Now the attention was turned on the highly respected members of the board of directors of the London and Globe Company. How could they have been so incompetent?

And our large friend, Mr. J. Whitaker Wright, was being pummeled daily. He met each accusation with bluster and aggressive attacks in return. Mining was a gamble, he kept reminding the public. You win some and you lose some.

"And real gamblers don't weep into their tea," he was quoted as saying over and over again.

The furor had not diminished at all by the following Monday, when Holmes, Lestrade, Hall Pycroft and I met on the Strand outside the entrance to the Royal Courts of Justice.

"Inspector," said Holmes to Lestrade. "Who is the Isaacs chap that you have us meeting with? Please tell me about him and do try to be concise and precise."

Lestrade ignored Holmes's haughtiness and delivered his short lecture.

"He's certainly not like one of those toffs from Oxford or Cambridge. To begin with, he's Jewish. His father was one of those fruit merchants in Spitalfields. He attended the local primary school like all the boys from that part of the city. He had high enough marks to gain entrance into University College School and after that he entered the Middle Temple and studied law. Worked his way through the Temple by selling fruit and being an office boy at the London Stock Exchange. Called to the bar in 1887. Again, unlike all those twits from Oxbridge, he did not join a rich law firm but became a Crown. And a good one. Just a couple of years ago he got his QC. They say he knows every statute and every case for the past one hundred years and can run circles around most defense lawyers. I have not dealt with him, but some of my friends in the Yard have and they warned me that we had better be on our toes. He has a reputation for not suffering fools. So be ready, Holmes."

Holmes was smiling. There were few things he enjoyed more than matching his enormous intellect and wit against a worthy opponent.

An orderly appeared and we were led through the musty corridors and into the office of Mr. Rufus Isaacs, Crown Prosecutor.

He was not a particularly impressive man to look at. He had a high forehead and a straight hairline that had begun to recede. His eyes bulged somewhat but his jaw was firm and square. As expected, his nose was unmistakably from the line of God's chosen people. His attire was unremarkable and, given that he spent much of every day wearing a robe and a wig, this was also not surprising. The office was modestly furnished but the entire right-hand wall was packed with books, many of which had small scraps of paper extruding from their pages with handwritten notes scribbled on them.

He rose as we entered and gestured toward a small meeting table in the corner of the office. Once we were seated, he joined us and began immediately into the matters at hand, not bothering even to introduce himself or request that we do the same.

"Good morning, gentlemen. I am frightfully busy and I have only a few minutes to discuss this matter with you. Before you say anything to me, I must warn you that what you have stated in your letters to me had better have some substance, otherwise you leave yourselves open to accusations and successful actions against you for libel and slander. This

Whitaker Wright chap may be a blowhard, but he is exceptionally wealthy and will not hesitate to crush you and bankrupt you if what you have accused him of is without substance or merit. And, quite frankly, Mr. Sherlock Holmes, your popular reputation will not count for a speck of dust in such a lawsuit. As for you, Inspector Lestrade, you are apparently seeking to have my office secure a conviction that you have failed to even attempt, with the hope of then bargaining with Mr. Wright to give evidence against his colleagues and employees. That manner of dealing with criminal cases strikes me as contemptible and unseemly and I cannot guarantee the cooperation of my office. Please, now. State your case. Mr. Holmes, pray begin."

I could see that gleam in Holmes's eyes as he began and I was ready to kick him under the table if he started to rub his hands in glee. He was, however, entirely prepared and very sure of himself.

"Sir," he began, "we are claiming that the Wright group of companies, all twelve of them, have intentionally committed massive fraud. Rather than examine all of them, I will concentrate on only one. We will follow the money and show you how this one company has engaged in nefarious deception. If you are not satisfied with what we present, then we shall desist and not bother you again. If, however, you agree with us, then we shall move on to show you how all twelve companies colluded and twenty banks, stock exchanges in six countries, and over a thousand investors have all been deliberately misled and defrauded."

Holmes, with assistance from Hall, produced one page

after another and demonstrated, in a manner that I and even Lestrade could easily follow, what had happened to the money that should have been paid out to investors. The few minutes Mr. Isaacs had granted us soon stretched into thirty. Without giving any direct indication of his being convinced one way or the other, he asked endless very specific questions that I was very happy Hall Pycroft was able to answer. As they were both men who had cut their teeth in stock exchanges, they spoke each other's language.

After an intense three hours, Rufus Isaacs put down the file he was holding along with his pen and addressed Holmes directly.

"Very well, Mr. Holmes. You have convinced me. I am ready to take this case forward. There is, however, one outstanding matter."

Holmes knew he had been successful and was trying not to appear overly pleased. So he answered with feigned sincere interest.

"And what, sir, is that?"

"What is your position in this matter? Are you an interested party? Are you an investor? What standing might you have on this matter before the courts?"

Holmes nodded and replied. "I have none. I have refrained from investing a single farthing in any of Mr. Wright's companies."

"Well, sir, that was wise from a business point of view, but useless from a legal one. I need to bring this case forward on behalf of investors who have been defrauded, and you are not one. So I must ask you to find me several fools, now parted from their money, who are willing to admit their stupidity and swear that they were defrauded by Mr. Wright. Find those chaps and we can move forward. The ball is now in your court, sir."

The four of us gathered again on the pavement of the Strand after departing from the Courts. I was at a loss as to how to proceed and suggested that we might begin by putting a note in the agony column of *The Times,* and perhaps in several of the other daily papers.

"Doctor, sir," said Pycroft, "that will not be necessary. We have records at my brokerage of many of the institutions who invested and, if Scotland Yard will allow me to inspect the papers and effects of Kenny Arkell, I am sure that we can find the names of many working people who also bought shares and who will not be too proud to come and testify."

By Friday afternoon we had selected some twenty-two parties who all appeared to have invested their funds into the Wright group of companies. Some had lost thousands of pounds. One widow from Birmingham had lost a hundred. Her mite would be as important to a jury as the riches of a wealthy lord.

On January seventh in the year 1901, charges were announced against Mr. James Whitaker Wright. He was accused of many instances of fraud and false filings and could, if convicted, be sent to prison for up to twelve years. Again, the press had a field day and the story was all over the front pages. He was everywhere.

Chapter Twelve
Escape to Paris

Unfortunately, Mr. Wright was nowhere. When Lestrade accompanied an officer of the Royal Courts to Lea Park, he was informed that Mr. Wright was no longer in England, but a message could be forwarded to him if he were to make contact with his staff. So far, he had not done so.

I sent a note off to Holmes asking, "Where has he gone?"

A reply was returned almost immediately, stating, "Ask me again in three days."

And so I did. This time the answer was more specific.

"France. High probability of Paris."

My curiosity got the better of me and on the weekend I made a point of dropping in to visit Holmes quite early on a Saturday morning.

"Come. Now, Holmes," I said. "The man has the means to go anywhere in the world. How did you conclude Paris?"

"While Lestrade and his subordinates at Scotland Yard may be lacking in imagination, they are highly reliable when it comes to grinding, slogging, methodical police work. Within three days they had reviewed the passenger manifests of every ship that departed from Southampton, Liverpool, London and all other major ports where people embark for overseas locations."

"That must have been thousands of passengers," I exclaimed.

"Not in the first class cabins," said Holmes. "If Mr. Wright did not depart for overseas, then his most logical choice would be a ferry to the Continent. I cannot imagine a man of his tastes wanting to spend a day in Spain or Portugal, or even an hour in Greece or Turkey, so the most logical place to assume is France. And assuming France means assuming Paris, and further assuming one of the select hotels."

"Can you find him there?

"It should not be difficult."

"Will the French gendarmes send him back?"

"That may be a problem," Holmes said. "The French, as you know, do not care what a person does as long as he pronounces it properly. Our only hope will be their taking grave offense at Mr. Wright's bastardization of their sacred language. However, I should be able to track him within two weeks. I will let you know, and perhaps you would fancy a short journey to the City of Light."

Two weeks later I found myself standing beside Sherlock Holmes on the ferry from Dover to Calais. He quietly puffed on his pipe while fixing his gaze on the rolling hills of the French horizon.

"Our man is staying at the Hotel du Louvre," he said. "I sent twenty packages by post to each of the select hotels in Paris. All were addressed to Mr. Wright and all bore instructions to be returned to sender if the addressee was not a current guest. Those directed to the Ritz, Le Meurice, the St. James, the Scribe, and Le Crillon all arrived back within the week. Some of the less diligent took several more days. However, as of yesterday all had been returned with the exception of the one I sent to the Grand Hotel du Louvre. By process of elimination, that is where he must be staying."

I did not realize that my friend had acquired such an intimate knowledge of the fine hotels of Paris and must have given away my wonderment by the look on my face.

"My dear, doctor," he said. "Whilst studying coal-tar derivatives in Montpellier, I discovered that there is nothing that is intellectually satisfying to do there on a weekend. Hence, I made many jaunts into Paris and became acquainted with every possible hotel to which our Mr. Wright was likely to have patronized."

"But you have alerted him," I said, "to your pursuit, have you not? Will he not just flee the coup?"

"I am inclined to think not. That would be the sensible thing to do, but it is contrary to his enormous personal pride. I am convinced that he will not be able to resist sitting across from me, smirking, and claiming victory. He knows that France will not agree to send him back to England for defrauding the gullible English investor. He will be treated as somewhat of a celebrity and praised for tweaking the English nose."

From the port of Calais we boarded a train and traveled quickly through the snow-covered farmlands of Picardie. By the end of the day we had arrived at the Gare du Nord and secured a cab to the first *arrondissement*. The magnificent Hotel du Louvre was located immediately across the street from the famous museum and I indulged a thought that if we had a few hours to spare I might pay a visit to the famous smiling lady or perhaps find a quiet café and enjoy a *madeleine* dipped in tea.

Sadly, those pleasant possibilities vanished the instant Holmes approached the registration desk. He was handed an envelope, which he opened and read. I could see by the scowl on his face that he was not pleased with the contents.

"I have over-estimated my adversary's pride and under-estimated his cunning. He departed from Paris this morning," he said, and he handed me the note. It ran:

```
My dear Sherlock:
You cannot imagine how sorry I am to have
missed the opportunity to meet with you.
```

> A pleasant dinner of fine French cuisine together would have been such a delight. My only suggestion is that next time, buy gold.
> J. Whitaker Wright

Holmes stuffed the letter into his suit pocket and took a quick glance around the ornate lobby.

"Come, Watson. There is no reason for us to remain here. By now he is on board a ship to America, I imagine. We may as well return to London." He turned and started walking to the door as he spoke.

I sighed and followed him. Mona Lisa and my memories of Proust would have to wait.

On the return ferry Holmes did not stand serenely against the rail and enjoy his pipe. Instead, he paced up and down the deck is obvious anger and frustration.

"Come, now, Holmes," I said cheerily. "America does have an extradition treaty with England, does it not? What with all the evidence you have assembled, they will send the fellow back, won't they?"

"They will," he said. "But the wheels of justice grind very slowly and it may take months. It may take an entire year."

Chapter Thirteen
The Wheels of Justice

It took three years.

Whitaker Wright had managed to shift most of his wealth into cash and gold and move it to banks in America. He hired some of the most skilled lawyers and fought for every possible delay in being extradited to Great Britain. His generous donations to the Republican Party and the successful campaigns of Theodore Roosevelt may have been useful. Throughout these years he continued to live lavishly in New York and Philadelphia. His estate at Lea Park was managed by a skeleton staff and no more elegant events were hosted in the folly under the lake. Construction on the Bakerloo Line was halted. No investor had any interest in "throwing good money after bad."

Fortunately, Mr. Rufus Isaacs was every bit as skilled and tenacious as Mr. Wright's phalanx of Philadelphia lawyers and responded astutely and quickly to every roadblock that they placed in the way of extraditing him to England. Unfortunately for Mr. Wright, he was born in England and remained a British subject. Doing so was very useful to him when he had returned to his native country over a decade ago. It would now prove to be his undoing.

Sherlock Holmes, of course, was far from idle during these intervening years. He took on many new cases and was able to use his unique and extraordinary abilities to solve the majority of them. I wrote and published the story of what has become his most famous accomplishment, *The Hound of the Baskervilles*. It was published in both England and America and sold unprecedented numbers of copies. Both Holmes and I became increasingly famous and wealthy.

Yet there was no comfort to be had. Five people had been murdered during the early days of this terrible adventure. Three promising young men who had somehow discovered the duplicity of the Wright empire had been killed and their deaths were still officially recorded as accidental or suicide. Two otherwise unassuming working people who happened to be in the wrong place in the wrong rooming house at the wrong time had given their lives in an instinctive effort to protect a fourth young man who had come to know too much.

Every few weeks Holmes would pay a visit to the Royal Courts and converse with Rufus Isaacs. When I joined my friend for one of our irregular meals or quiet chats, he expressed his frustration at the delay, but couched it in glowing admiration for the brilliant young Crown prosecutor.

On December 28, 1903, the headline in *The Times* read:

WHITAKER WRIGHT BROUGHT BACK TO LONDON

Mr. Wright, however, had no intention of returning in the manner of a captured criminal, slinking back to England with his tail between his legs. He had no sooner landed than he announced a splendid reception at Lea Park for all of the nearby residents. They were thrilled to see his return, knowing that there would be restored opportunities for employment both on the estate and in all of the local shops and inns that fed off the estate activities.

Wright was a master at playing the press and he immediately launched a counter-attack on his accusers, calling them every name in the book and claiming that they were trying to scapegoat him for their own lack of business acumen. It worked. Popular opinion, which should logically have deemed him a pariah, was now divided. His bluster and bravado won over many citizens who shrugged and decided that the rich investors had been taken down a peg or two. Right up to the start of the trial, Wright proclaimed over and over again that he had done nothing wrong and that the mines would have turned a handsome profit if only the greedy vultures had not panicked.

On 11 January 1904, the trial began with Mr. Justice Bigham presiding. Hall Pycroft, Sherlock Holmes, my wife,

Mary, and Inspector Lestrade all had seats in the crowded courtroom. As the room filled to capacity I chanced to look back into the group of those standing at the back. I gave a poke to Holmes.

"That's Wright's Man Friday back there, is it not, Holmes?"

He turned around and looked at the gentleman to whom I was referring.

"Yes. Arthur Pinner, if I recall correctly. But who is the chap beside him. The two look remarkably alike, as if they were brothers."

Indeed, the man standing next to Pinner was of similar stature, coloring and facial features.

Holmes stared at the fellow for some time and I knew what he was looking for, but could not see.

He turned to my wife, Mary. "My dear Mrs. Watson, do you see that chap back there with the mustache, and grayish hair?"

"Yes. Oh, the one standing beside Arthur Pinner. What about him?"

"Would you be so kind as to go and see if you can make him smile for us?"

For a moment she looked at Holmes as if he had come undone but then she herself broke into a glowing smile.

"I'll see what I can do."

Mary stood and worked her way back through the crowd until she was standing beside Arthur Pinner. We watched as she bumped into him and then in convincing feigned surprise greeted him as if he were a long lost friend. He smiled and introduced her to the fellow beside him. We watched as Mary smiled and laughed and elicited a friendly grin from the fellow.

The gleam of a gold canine tooth was unmistakable.

Mary returned and sat down again beside us. "It's his brother all right. Freddie is his name. Can't say as I liked the looking over he gave me. Will there be anything else, gentlemen?"

We laughed and thanked her. Whereupon Inspector Lestrade, who had not been part of the escapade, turned to us and demanded to know what the joke was. I explained it to him, causing him to turn and look directly at the two men who had so recently been accosted by my wife.

A cloud immediately swept across his face.

"Who did you say they were?" he demanded.

"Arthur Pinner." I said. "Wright's Two I C, and the chap beside him is his brother, Fred Pinner."

"The deuce it is."

That caught Holmes's attention. "Obviously, you know them, inspector."

"Bloody right, I know them. I should know them. I sent both of them to Holloway twice for three years at a stretch. They're none other than the Beddington brothers, Jack and Bill. Both of them inveterate thieves and cutthroats. You say that one of them was working for Wright?"

"Working very closely," said Holmes.

"Well then, Holmes, I think we now have found our prime suspects for the murders."

Lestrade turned and looked intently at the two men. The one who had given his name as Arthur Pinney happened to look directly back at Lestrade and we could see him grab his brother's arm and lead him out of the courtroom.

"Are you going to follow them?" I asked Lestrade.

"No. My men can always find them and we have nothing to charge them with at the moment; not until the trial is over."

"How will that make a difference?"

"If it goes against Wright, which I suspect it will, he will face a long prison sentence. We'll put his nuts in a noose and see how long it will take before he agrees to play along and spill the beans on his thugs."

The visitors, spectators, and press were all seated and chatting when Mr. Rufus Isaacs and his colleagues entered. He was followed a minute later by Whitaker Wright and crew of lawyers. Wright was impeccably dressed, not at all underfed, and smiling confidently. I heard a low mutter of displeasure coming from Lestrade.

"Is something wrong with Wright?" I asked.

"No, not Wright. His barrister. He's hired Edward Marshall Hall. He's the best in the country. The press calls him the Great Defender. He's very good a swaying juries. Brilliant. Our man, Rufus, has his work cut out for him."

The jury then entered and again I gave a nudge to Lestrade. "They look rather like common folk," I said. "Not what I expected at a trial involving complicated high finance."

Lestrade whispered back. "For a trial like this they do not have chaps from the City on the jury. Too many of them or their clients lost a fortune by betting on Wright and would be biased against him. So to be fair, they conscript the common man."

Chapter Fourteen
At Last, the Trial

John Charles Bigham, the judge, then entered the court as we rose out of respect. He called the proceedings to order and went through the opening formalities. A long list of charges was read and the defendant was asked how he pled. Before his barrister could answer on his behalf, Whitaker Wright bellowed out "Absolutely not guilty! One hundred percent innocent of every one of those ridiculous false accusations."

The courtroom erupted in laughter and chatter, leading the judge to bang heavily with his gavel. Once order had returned he glared down at Wright and Edward Hall.

"Sir, you will instruct your client to control his outbursts. I remind him that mockery and laughter in a court of law are punishable by up to six months in prison. Mr. Wright, do you understand that?"

Wright leaned back in his chair and gave a wave to the judge. "Of course, I do. A most reasonable condition. Without it entire juries would be imprisoned. Wonderful law, yes, wonderful."

Again the room burst into laughter, followed by a round of applause. And again the judge demanded order and gave a tongue lashing to Whitaker Wright. He wisely said nothing in response but appeared to be hugely enjoying himself.

The Crown prosecutor was called upon to present his opening statement. He refrained from getting into very specific numbers and transactions and pointed out to the jury that thousands of people had lost their savings in the collapse of the Wright group of companies but that Mr. Wright, his family members, and close employees continued to live in luxury. He announced that he would not only prove that the actions taken by the companies were intentionally fraudulent, but that the damage done to individual lives was tragic. The jury would meet and hear from some of those who were so terribly affected. He promised to provide "chapter and verse" to prove all of his accusations but closed by claiming that the privileged condition of Wright and his ilk and the suffering of those who trusted him spoke for itself. This was a case, he reminded the court, of the established legal principle of *res ipsa loquitur*.

The judge turned to Wright's lawyer and asked, "Sir, is it fair to assume that your client is familiar with the legal maxim of *res ipsa loquitur*?"

Edward Hall leaned over and conferred with his client and then rose to respond.

"Your honor, my client assures me that in the bars and brothels of Philadelphia they talk of little else."

Again the courtroom broke into laughter and I watched as the members of the press scribbled furiously, with two of them pausing to slap their thighs in glee.

Rufus Isaacs announced that he would begin his case by calling a selection of the many stockholders who had signed the complaint against Wright. The first was an elderly lady who walked slowly to the witness stand, supported by a cane and somewhat bent over in posture. She identified herself as Mrs. Ruth Anderson, a widow from Camberwell. In reply to Mr. Isaac's patient questions, she confirmed that she had taken one hundred pounds of her savings out of the bank and invested it in the London and Globe Company. She did so because she was having a very hard time getting by and she had listened to Mr. Wright give a speech and read about him in the press and she trusted him to help her double her meager investment within a year. When the companies collapsed her hundred pounds disappeared. Now she did not know how she was going to get through the remainder of the winter. She did not even have enough to spare to buy feed for her pet budgie, Gladstone. She pulled out her handkerchief from her cuff and dabbed her eyes.

I could see the reporters attempting to stifle their laughter. One of them held up his notepad to another with the words "Gladstone Chirps No More" hastily written in bold letters. They really were a cynical lot.

They were, however, nowhere near as ruthless as Edward Hall, Wright's lawyer. He began his cross by expressing his deep condolences for the dear lady and especially for poor Mr. Gladstone. He asked a few sympathetic questions and then, seemingly out of nowhere, he asked her if she knew a Mr. Bartholomew Bishop. The lady looked perplexed and answered.

"Yes, I know Bartholomew Bishop."

"In what capacity are you acquainted with this man?"

"He is the spirits merchant in Camberwell."

"Is he now? And how often during the course of a month would you chance to chat with him?"

"Once a week, every Thursday," she replied and I detected a worried expression coming across her face.

"Once a week, you say. And where does this chat take place?"

"In his shop."

"In his shop? Indeed. And why, my dear Mrs. Anderson, would you happen to be in Mr. Bishop's shop once a week. Are you one of his customers?"

"I am."

"And what do you purchase in Mr. Bishop's shop once a week."

"A small bottle of spirits which I require for medicinal purposes. My doctor has advised me to do that."

"A small bottle of gin for your health, of course. But perhaps you could define what you mean by *small*. You see, I have a copy of a receipt from Mr. Bishop's shop that says that last Thursday you purchased two bottles of gin and they were both the twenty-six-ounce size. Is that what you consider small, Mrs. Anderson?"

He did not give her time to answer. "And it appears that you make a similar purchase every Thursday. And that during the past year you have spent over one hundred pounds of your pension and savings at his shop. Is that correct, Mrs. Anderson?"

The woman was terribly flustered and quietly muttered, "I suppose it is. I have not kept track of it."

Mr. Hall looked as if he were prepared to ask more questions, but then he smiled graciously and announced that he had no further inquiries and politely asked the widowed lady to step down and return to her seat.

I admit that I found what just took place disturbing. I glanced over at Holmes and Lestrade and was surprised to see that their faces were impassive, as if nothing untoward had happened.

The next shareholder of London and Globe who was called to bear witness was a young nobleman, a Lester Deleon, the Marquess of Horseley. He was an exceptionally attractive young man with pale skin, bright blue eyes and wavy blond hair. He was dressed in the latest fashion, bordering on the dandy in my opinion, but certainly a comely witness who would, I hoped, inspire a more sympathetic response from the jury than the previous one.

Rufus Isaac led the young chap through a series of questions that brought out a very clear picture of an innocent young man who completely trusted the honesty and integrity of Whitaker Wright. He had inquired concerning supporting documents before investing in the company that claimed to be successfully mining for gold in Western Australia. He had been shown extensive financial and assay reports. He had, conscientiously, taken copies of them to his father and his uncle and had their opinion and support. There was nothing he had not done by way of due diligence. He was now of the firm opinion that he had been lied to and deceived by Whitaker Wright.

The final question from Rufus Isaacs asked him to tell the court how much he had lost.

"Three thousand pounds," he said quietly.

"I'm afraid, sir, that I shall have to ask you to speak up so that the entire room can hear you. Would you please state again the total amount that you entrusted to Whitaker Wright?"

"Three thousand pounds," he said, clearly and distinctly. There were gasps throughout the room. A gentleman's income for an entire year did not often exceed three hundred pounds. Even if this lad came from a titled family, he was undoubtedly swindled out of a small fortune. The room was murmuring loudly and again the judge demanded order.

Edward Hall approached the witness, smiling, and began his cross. He was shaking his head and he strolled forward.

"Three thousand pounds. My, now that was a terrible loss. Just terrible. And yes, you were, indeed, very diligent.

Very diligent before putting such a sum at risk. I admire your diligence. A very responsible young man."

"I thank you, sir."

"Yes very responsible. Now could you tell the court what you as a responsible young man were doing this past July. On the twenty-fifth to be exact. The last Saturday in the month. Do you recall where you were that day."

"I was at Sandown Park, in Surrey."

"Ah, you have an excellent memory. What was taking place that you remember so clearly?"

"The Eclipse Stakes race was being run."

"And you were there observing?"

"I was."

"Alone?"

"Several of my friends were with me."

"And were you merely observing, or might you have wagered a pound or two on the race?"

"I did place a bet."

"On which horse?"

"On Ard Patrick."

"Bit of a risk, I must say. Wasn't that horse injured after the Epsom Derby the year before?"

"He was."

"What were the odds? Must have been quite high, given that he had been injured and had not run all season."

"They were twelve to one to win."

"And you bet on him? With those odds against him?"

"I did."

"How much was your bet?"

The young lord paused for a moment as if trying to remember. "I believe it was one thousand pounds."

There were gasps again throughout the room, and several quiet rounds of applause could be heard. Justice Bigham banged on his gavel.

"Well now," continued Wright's barrister. "You are a brave young gambler aren't you? Wagering a thousand pounds on a risky horse and taking home twelve thousand."

"I was very lucky that day."

"Are you always so lucky?"

"No, sir."

"What club do you belong to?"

"The Reform Club."

"Ah, yes. Phileas Fogg's club if I recall. It has quite the reputation for attracting those who like sporting adventures."

"I suppose some would say so."

"Is there not a room in the back of the club where a sportsman might play a friendly game of whist now and again?"

"There is."

"And have you ever played cards there?"

"I have."

"Have you now, and when was the last time you played a round in your club?"

"On Saturday evening."

"Oh, quite recently?"

"Yes, sir."

"And did you win anything on Saturday evening. Maybe a pound or two."

"No. I lost."

"Ah, so sorry to hear that. And by the end of the evening, how much had you lost?"

Again there was a brief pause before the Marquess answered. "A thousand, five hundred."

"A thousand five hundred what?"

"Pounds."

Again the chatter erupted in the court, and again order was called for.

For the next half hour the questions were relentless. The young lord had lost six hundred on a polo match, won four hundred on a cricket test, lost three hundred on rugby and then won it all back again. He had laid down two thousand on the Grand National and came away with his original wager plus another five hundred. I was jotting down numbers and it was soon apparent that this young gambler had over fifty thousand pounds pass back and forth through his hands in the past year. I looked around the court and observed the reporters gazing at him in rapt admiration. Two young women were flushed and looking all goats and monkeys at the fellow.

He most certainly was an adventurous soul if ever there was one, and a disaster as a witness.

The judge called for a brief recess and we shuffled out onto the pavement so that Holmes could indulge in his habit of tobacco.

"That was a disaster," I said. "How could Isaacs have not known what those witnesses were going to say? They were no help at all."

Holmes looked at me and gave a condescending smile. He then gave a glance to Lestrade, who offered a shallow nod and a wink. Apparently they knew something that I did not.

Before the day ended, two more shareholders were brought forward as witnesses and were again thoroughly discredited. I was entirely certain that Whitaker Wright was going to walk away scot-free. Holmes bade me good day and said that he would see me tomorrow. My wife and I walked all the way back to Marylebone and talked of nothing else but the fiasco we had witnessed. My mind was not so much on those folks who had lost money investing in the ventures of Whitaker Wright but on the five people whose lives had been snuffed out over three years ago, and for whom no justice had yet been obtained. What I found inexplicable was that Holmes did not appear to be in the least concerned.

Chapter Fifteen
It Does Not End

The following morning the newspapers were full of the first day of the trial. The jokes were given many lines of ink and the cartoonists had their sport making fun of the prosecutor and even poking a bit of fun at the judge. I had picked up three of our morning papers on our way back to the Strand and angrily read them while waiting in my seat for the day's events to commence. Holmes sat down beside me and I could not resist voicing my displeasure.

"That Isaac's fellow," I said, "reminds me of some sort of bumbling fool out of the pages of *Punch*."

"Does he now?" replied Holmes. "I would say he reminds me more of Sidney Carton and Charles Darney."

"Good heavens, Holmes. The cats? What are you talking about? Please, I do not see this as a time for frivolity."

I have already reminded the reader that over the years I have noted many times Holmes's habit of smiling at me in a condescending manner. He did so yet again.

"Elementary, Watson. Have you never observed how a cat at will play with its prey for as long as it wants and then grab it by the neck and shake it to death?"

He turned away, leaving me at a loss for words.

The first person to be called to the box that morning was Mr. Wright himself. He stepped, with a bit of a bounce, up to the front of the room, turned and gave a wave to the assembled spectators and reporters. Several waved back at him.

After being sworn in, he sat down in the witness box and smiled at the assembled people in the room. Rufus Isaacs approached him and opened with several standard questions.

"You have given the court your name. Might I ask you to state your date of birth?"

"The ninth day of the month of February."

"What year?"

"Every year."

The room laughed and Wright smacked his hand down of the ledge of the witness box. Justice Bigham immediately reprimanded him and Wright feigned a look of contrition.

Isaacs continued. "And do you agree that your appearance here this morning is pursuant to your having been charged with several instances of criminal fraud?"

"Nope. Don't agree. My appearance this morning is exactly like it is for any business meeting. I'm wearing my suit and a clean white shirt. How about you?"

This brought forth a round of applause and Wright smiled broadly and waved at the reporters. Yet again he was reprimanded by the judge. He assumed a look of shock and surprise. "Your honor, I was just answering the question truthfully, wasn't I?" He shrugged his broad shoulders and spread his hands, palms up.

Rufus Isaacs quickly interjected before the matter was allowed to go any further.

"Mr. Wright."

"Yes, Mr. Isaacs."

"I am assuming that you are an intelligent and honest man."

"Why thank you. I would dearly love to return the compliment, but unfortunately I am under oath."

This brought forth howls and hoots from the courtroom. The judge raised his gavel but put it down slowly and smiled. He turned to Rufus Isaacs and said, "You did rather set yourself up for that one, Barrister Isaacs."

Isaacs returned the smile. An air of frivolity had swept across the room and everyone seemed to be enjoying the sporting exchange.

Isaacs had one of his assistants erect a large easel that had pages of paper attached to it. He took out a grease pencil and walked over to it before turning to speak to Wright.

"One of your companies has been responsible for the

financing of the new Underground line from Baker Street to Waterloo station, has it not?"

"It has. That was our Imperial Victoria Company. I named it in honor of our dearly beloved queen. Wonderful woman. May she rest in peace. I said we were going to build the finest line in England. The most beautiful. Most modern. A true monument to the dear woman. So, yes sir. That is the company."

"And you issued bonds and debentures to finance this venture. Is that correct?"

"I did. One of the most successful issues of new bonds in the past decade. Very successful. Incredibly successful. Completely subscribed. Oversubscribed. Had to turn away hundreds of investors."

"And which brokerage firms did you use to handle the bond and debenture issues?"

"Two of the best. Fine firms. Hichens Harrison and Mawson and Williams. Love working with both those firms. Good men. Smart men. Honest men. We work well together."

"Ah, you consider them to be honest and competent."

"Like I said. Fine fellows. Smart and always honest. That's why we get along so well. Honest men trust honest men."

"Do you happen to recall how much available cash your bond and debenture issues brought in for use in the constructing of the new underground line?"

"Hey, now c'mon lawyer man. That was five years ago and a lot of water has gone under the bridge since then and I have done dozens more deals. Dozens more. Maybe a hundred since then. Big deals. You can't expect me to remember exact numbers. But believe me, it brought in a lot. Big time pounds, and dollars, and even francs. Big time."

"Of course," said Isaacs. "According to the records the court has received from the two brokerages, the total sale of the bonds and debentures amounted to three hundred and seventy-five thousand, two hundred and six pounds. If we take away their commission that provided you with three hundred and thirty-seven thousand, six hundred and eighty-five pounds for use on this construction venture. Does that sound correct, Mr. Wright."

"I already told you, there are far too many things, many many things, that I've done and built for me to remember specifics."

"Here is the report from the two brokerage houses, sir. You have said that they are honest men and so will you agree that these are honest figures?"

He handed a set of pages to Wright who looked at them and shrugged. "If that's what it says, then that's what it was."

"Very good, sir. Now I have here the accounts submitted by your contractors for the construction of the stations and the tunnels and the rails and every item that has been spent to date on this line. I must say, it has not been a cheap venture."

"We went first class all the way. First class. That's what I always insist on. First class. I wanted to give to people of London a line they could be proud of. A beautiful line.

Beautiful stations. So it has not been cheap. Nothing I build is ever cheap. Always first class."

"Very commendable, sir. But it looks as if the Baker Street station alone has already cost more than one hundred thousand pounds. Could that be correct, sir?"

"Yeah. It was a big one. Had to go deep, real deep. There were four lines already meeting there and we had to go under all of them. But it's gonna be a beautiful station. Fabulous. Really important to the people of London. It'll cut their time in half getting to Waterloo. Thousands of them have said they can't wait for it to be finished. We're so proud of what that station is gonna be."

"As you should sir. Now the station at Regent Park, well, that appears to be far more economical."

"Yeah. No other lines. Just an entrance to my new line. So you can get on and off right at the park. People are gonna love it. Everybody is saying what a great idea it was."

"I'm sure it will be enjoyed by all," said Mr. Isaacs. "However, the remainder of the stations—Oxford Circus, Piccadilly, Charing Cross, and the Embankment—each have cost you more than fifty thousand pounds already and they're not yet finished."

"Yeah, well, that's because we had to go deep again to get under the lines that are already at those stations. But that's what will make it so convenient. So great for the people of London. That's why I'm building it. For the people. They're gonna love it."

"I am sure they will. But it also appears that you had to dig your own new tunnel under the Thames to get to Waterloo Station."

"Do you know any other way to get under a river?"

The spectators and reporters chuckled at that response.

"No, Mr. Wright, I do not. But it appears that the tunnel alone cost you over half a million pounds. Can that be true?"

"Sure, it's true. I had to make it safe. Beautifully safe. You go cheap on a tunnel, you're asking for trouble. So you gotta ask yourself something, Mr. Isaacs, like, how long can you tread water?"

Again more chuckles and Isaacs again smiled in return and walked over to his easel and began to write down numbers for the jury to see.

"Mr. Wright," he said once he had finished putting a column of numbers on the board, "do correct me if I am wrong, but it appears that at the time the construction was halted on the Baker Street to Waterloo line, you had already spent over one million pounds paying for it."

"So? Building something beautiful gets expensive. Have you seen our stations? Beautiful. Real artistic. Are we have lovely artwork in the stations. Beautiful art. And when it is finished, thousands of Londoners are gonna use it every day. And they'll be happy to pay for it. Great investment. Beautiful investment."

"So you spent over one million pounds, but you only brought in about three hundred and fifty thousand in capital. Please tell the court where the rest of the money came from?

It appears that at least seven hundred thousand pounds was provided to the Imperial Victoria Company. Where did it come from?"

"I loaned it from some of my other companies. Perfectly legal. Normal smart business practice. If you got more money than you need in one company and less than you need in another, you can do a loan. Companies do that all the time, don't you know?"

"I do know that, sir. But they do so with the reasonable expectation of getting the money back some day, do they not?"

"Which they will with interest. Fabulous investment."

"Will they? Not according to the predictions of the City of London. I have a report prepared four years ago by the engineering department of London and it shows that your stations cannot support more than a seven-carriage train and that the highest possible level of ridership for your line will never exceed two million riders. Unless you charge every one of them a pound per ride, which would be prohibitive, you will never do much better than break even on your annual operating costs, let alone ever pay back those loans."

"Claptrap, sir. Pure claptrap. What do engineers know about running a business? I'll tell you how to run a business. You give the customers what they want and you do it better than anyone else and you have a business. A beautiful business. That's what we are doing. That's what's called business. It's gonna be a great investment. So great."

"But now those other companies have no money. And they closed their doors and went bankrupt. Funds that were supposed to be used to expand the mines were used for the

Underground. And dividends that were due to your shareholders were never paid."

"That's business. You know what people say in America? People say 'Some days you win. Some days you lose. Somedays it rains.' They're talking about baseball but it applies to business. And if you can't stand the heat, get outta the kitchen. Business is a tough game. You gotta play hardball. That's how I play and that's why I've been such a success. An incredible success."

"Indeed you are, sir. You are a fabulously wealthy man and your estates and investments are secure. So what do you say to all those people who trusted you with their money? Not only other wealthy investors, but churches, charities, widows, working men? All those ordinary folk. How is it that you are sitting high and dry whilst they are impoverished."

"That's called being smart."

"Ah, so if you're smart, all the others who trusted you are stupid. Is that what you are telling the court, sir?"

For once, Whitaker Wright had no immediate response. I could see the reporters scribbling madly. The laughter and chuckles in the courtroom had vanished. Mr. Wright seemed quite uncomfortable.

Rufus Isaacs did not give him a chance to recover. He returned to his easel and began to write more numbers on the paper.

Slowly and laboriously he forced Whitaker Wright to walk through the filings and accounts of one of his companies after the other. Each time the chicanery and obfuscation of the loans and share transfers between the companies was exposed. The painful process continued for the rest of the day.

And then it continued for two more weeks. The only defense that Wright could offer was to continue to declare that everything he had done was entirely legal, and just normal smart business practices. If a company failed, it was a shame but that was business.

The stories in the press took on a different tone. Rufus Isaacs was doing a masterful job of making the clandestine machinations of the Wright group crystal clear to the jury, the spectators, and the reporters. The press in turn copied his explanations and printed story after story informing the public of just what all had transpired. Mr. Wright slowly became a monster in the eyes of the citizens of England.

Edward Hall, Wright's barrister, did his best to defend his client, but the facts were stacked against him. High sounding orations about the need for visionary titans of business could only be repeated so often before they were falling on deaf ears.

On the morning of the twenty-fifth of January, 1904, the trial was concluded and the final presentations were made to the jury. The twelve true men retreated to their jury room and we returned to our homes, not knowing how long it would take them to reach a decision.

To my surprise, I received a note from Holmes early the following morning informing me that the jury had reached their decision and would be making their report at ten o'clock. We hastened back to the Strand and to our places in the courtroom. The room was packed to the rafters and there must have been another fifty reporters standing outside the door.

The jury returned. Not one of them looked at Mr. Wright. The judge asked the foreman if they had reached a decision.

"We have, your honor."

"And what is your decision."

"We find the defendant guilty as charged on all counts."

A chatter erupted in the room and Justice Bigham demanded order. He then thanked the jury for their service and ordered a brief recess prior to his announcing a sentence.

The Crown argued for a severe sentence of at least ten years, owing to the magnitude of the crime and the long history of Whitaker Wright's enriching himself at the expense of those who trusted him. Wright's barrister pleaded for a much more lenient sentence, noting his client's wonderful history of public service, his generous support of many charities and his record of being an admired employer and neighbor.

All of us sat in silence as Justice Bigham called for the defendant to rise. Slowly he read off the charges and then placed the list on the bench in front of him.

"Mr. James Whitaker Wright, I hereby sentence you to seven years in prison."

He made a few more remarks and then declared the case closed and dismissed the court.

Wright maintained an impassive face and sat down. The reporters scrambled over each other to race out of the court and back to Fleet Street to file their stories. The rest of us slowly made our way out to the lobby.

"What happens now?" I asked Holmes and Lestrade.

"We will wait," said Lestrade, "for the Crown and Mr. Wright's lawyers and arrange a time to meet and start to do some hard bargaining. I suspect that the last thing Wright wants is seven years in Millbank or Holloway or wherever they stick him. I would be willing to settle for three or maybe even two years if he helped us convict the Beddington boys of murder. Would you agree, Holmes?"

"It is far from what he deserves, but if that is the way the game has to be played then so be it."

Rufus Isaacs joined us and together we waited for Wright's retinue. When they approached we clustered together but before any talk got underway, Wright spoke to the officers of the court who were accompanying him.

"Pardon me, gentlemen, but I must excuse myself for just a moment. There are some bodily necessities to which even an innocent man is subject." He nodded his head in the direction of the WC. It was an entirely understandable request and the officers stood back and let him depart.

"Oh, Mr. Wright, sir," called a younger member of his legal team who was carrying an armful of papers, pens and other accessories. "I have your watch here. Do you want it?"

Wright smiled back. "No, but thank you. I really do not need it where I am going." He continued on his stroll to the WC.

133

As it was not appropriate to carry on making the intended arrangements, we all stood in silence.

Five minutes passed. Then ten minutes. And then fifteen minutes.

"Did he take a newspaper in there with him?" asked one of the court officers, attempting to break the silence.

Edward Hall turned to the chap and said, "Perhaps you could go and check on him and see if he needs any assistance."

The man nodded, said nothing, and walked over to the men's WC and entered.

A few seconds later the door burst open and the court officer came rushing over to us. He eyes were wide and his mouth was gaping open.

"He's dead! He's dead. He's lying on the floor in there and he's dead."

The group of us, minus my wife, all rushed into the WC. There, in the middle of the tiled floor was the large body of James Whitaker Wright. He was prostrate on his back, fully clothed, and with his hands clasped behind his head as if to form a pillow. I immediately dropped down beside him to check for his pulse.

There was none. Holmes knelt by his head and leaned over to his face and sniffed slightly. He looked up at the rest of us.

"Cyanide. Mr. Wright has taken his own life by swallowing cyanide."

Lestrade did a quick inspection of the suit pockets and extracted three large capsules. He also pulled out a Webley

Bulldog revolver. Having found it, he laid it back on top of the body and departed. We could hear his whistle summoning the nearest police officers.

Pandemonium broke out in the lobby. Most of the reporters had already fled to Fleet Street but those who were still on the scene pushed and shoved and tried to enter the WC. They were restrained by several burly police officers.

In fairly short order an ambulance wagon arrived and the attendants loaded the body of Whitaker Wright inside and drove off.

The crowds dispersed and we were left standing on the pavement in the wintery, bleak afternoon of 26 January, 1904. For no reason I can remember, we walked slowly and in silence south through the Temple Gardens until we were standing on the Embankment, looking out over the dark, cold Thames.

Lestrade spoke first.

"Somebody else will sort out the estates, the shares, the bankruptcies, and the unfinished underground line. Those matters are not my concern. But four years ago, five people were murdered and they were all connected to this case. My plan for arresting and convicting the killers disappeared in the WC. Dead men tell no tales."

Here he paused and gazed out over the water. He then turned to Sherlock Holmes.

"I will vow," he said, "to work at this case until justice is done. May I count on your assistance, Holmes?"

"Yes," said Holmes. "You may."

Did you enjoy this story? Are there ways it could have been better? Please help the author and future readers by posting a constructive review on the site where you bought your book. Thank you.

Historical and Other Notes

James Whitaker Wright is a historical character and the events of his life and suicide described in this story are more or less in keeping with what actually happened. He has recently been called "the Bernie Madoff of his day." The murders associated with his fraud and exposure are fictional. If Sherlock Holmes assisted the Royal Courts and Scotland Yard in bringing Wright to justice, it has not been recorded in the official accounts.

The characters of Justice Bigham and Rufus Isaacs are drawn from the numerous records of the trial. Both had highly commendable careers beyond the trial of Whitaker Wright. Edward Marshall Hall was the most famous defender of the day, but he did not serve as Whitaker Wright's lawyer.

The pubs, *The Eagle* and *Ye Olde Cheshire Cheese* were in operation in 1900 and still are. One of The Eagle's many claims to fame is that is was the location in which Francis Crick announced to his Cambridge colleagues that he and his partner, James Watson (no relation), had discovered the double helix of DNA. Ye Olde Cheshire Cheese has been patronized by many famous political, literary, and other characters during its centuries of service on Fleet Street.

Whitaker Wright did not carry out a Ponzi scheme. The mines whose stocks he promoted were legitimate operations in Deadwood, Colorado, Rossland, British Columbia, and various places in South Africa and Australia. His wealth came from retaining much of the money paid for the stocks for himself and forwarding too little to the mines to pay for the capital costs of extending their production. He managed to get away with doing so for several decades until his disastrous venture to finance the Bakerloo Line brought about the collapse of his empire, subsequent flight to France and then America, and eventual conviction for fraud.

The *Varsity* is the student newspaper of Cambridge University but did not commence publication until several years after the time in which this story is set.

The *Hotel du Louvre* was a fine hotel in Paris at the time of this story. It still is. It was the location to which letters to Hugo Oberstein, the villain of *The Bruce-Partington Plans*, could be sent.

Hichens Harrison & Co. is the oldest brokerage firm in The City and continues to this day to be a respected financial institution. It is now owned by wealthy Indian financiers.

The Bakerloo Line originally ran from the Baker Street Underground station to the Waterloo railway station. Construction was halted when the Wright companies collapsed and subsequently completed several years later. The line has been expanded on both ends and it now stretches from Harrow and Wealdstone in the north to Elephant and Castle in the south. It is used by millions of passengers.

The platform in King's Cross station should not need any explanation.

The Glorious Yacht

A New Sherlock Holmes Mystery

Chapter One
The Night of April 15, 1912

"Come my friends," said Sherlock Holmes, " 'tis not too late to seek a newer world. Push off, shall we?"

"My dear Holmes," I said to my old companion, "you tempt us, but it is just not practical. And poetry will not help."

"When was any adventure practical? A year in America would be a splendid experience for you and your wife."

"Please, you and I are both now over sixty years of age and I confess that spending a year in Chicago with you is just too overwhelming a change to consider. I fear I do not have the zeal that I would have had thirty years ago."

"Ah, Watson. Tho' much is taken, much abides; and tho' we are not now that strength which in old days moved earth and heaven, that which we are, we are;   One equal temper of heroic hearts, made weak by time and fate, but strong in will to strive, to seek, to find, and not to yield!

"Are you certain," he continued, done with Tennyson, "that I cannot convince you? I am setting aside my little property in Sussex and will be on my way in a month. It will not be the same without you."

"Oh, you go," I said, "and be Ulysses and touch the Happy Isles. Mary and I will keep the home fires burning until you return. You haven't even told us what you will be doing there."

"It is somewhat secretive;   an assignment that has been requested from Washington and Whitehall. Some international skullduggery tied to whatever Kaiser Billy is doing in Germany. I fear that is all I can tell you at the moment."

"Oh, Sherlock," said my dear wife, "then you go and have the time of you life. And do remember to write. We shall miss you terribly."

Sherlock Holmes leaned back in his chair. He had been our guest for dinner, as he was at least once a month. On this Saturday evening, the sixteenth of April in the year 1912, he had informed us of his most recent calling, arranged by his brother Mycroft on behalf of the Empire. He was off to America and I would miss him awfully, but my life now was far too settled to consider uprooting it.

So we chatted some more and enjoyed our dessert and tea and reminisced, as we often did, about some of the more unusual cases that we had participated in during the years that were now behind us. My adored wife, Mary, tolerated hearing our stories yet one more time and appeared to love us both all the more every time one of the most foolhardy was repeated. At the end of the evening, after a final cigar and brandy, Holmes took his leave.

"I would greatly wish to say that I will write, but most likely I will not. Writing is your department, my friend. But I shall think of you often."

"As we will of you, my beloved old friend," I replied.

We shook hands affectionately. Mary gave him a lingering hug and he made his way out of our home and into the chilly air of the evening. There had been a frost the night before and my wife chided him about not dressing appropriately. He smiled, pulled his hat down over his ears, and departed.

We retired to our bed, chatted briefly about our unique and much-loved friend, and fell asleep.

At six-thirty the following morning, we were awakened by a loud knocking at the door. It was still dark outside and I pulled on my dressing gown and rushed downstairs, thinking that there must be some sort of medical emergency amongst my patients. I opened the door only to find Sherlock Holmes standing there. He was casually dressed but unshaven and looking distraught.

"Good heavens, Holmes. What is it?"

"I am dreadfully sorry to disturb you, but I am afraid that my emotions, such as they are, have got the better of me. Would you mind terribly if I came in? You are the only true friends I have in London and I felt I had to be with someone on this terrible morning."

"Sherlock," said my wife, who had also donned her dressing gown and come down the stairs. "What is wrong?"

He said nothing but removed his coat and sat down at the table. From his pocket he pulled out the early edition of *The Times* and spread it open. We gasped in horror at the headline.

TITANIC SINKS
OVER 1500 FEARED LOST

"Oh, dear God, no!" cried my wife. "No. It's not possible."

I was speechless, totally stunned by the terrible headline. In silence, the three of us huddled close to each other and read the story. The details were still scarce but reports sent by wireless from ships that rescued the survivors indicated that the worst maritime disaster in history had taken place on the night of 15 April. On its maiden voyage, the "unsinkable" *Titanic* had struck an iceberg off the coast of Newfoundland and had gone to the bottom of the ocean. Over fifteen hundred souls had perished. The reports were still preliminary but there was no doubt that a disaster of unspeakable horror had happened.

Without speaking, Holmes turned the page to the passenger list. The names of those reported to have been rescued were at the top. Those missing and presumed drowned followed. Holmes placed his hand at the top of the latter column and slowly ran it down the list. Many of the names of the first class passengers were familiar. They were names that the general populace recognized from the business and society pages of the press; the great majority of them being those of men. Most of the women and children in first class had been rescued. Several of those who had perished had been clients of Holmes in years past.

We continued through the second class. Every so often I recognized the name of one of my former patients, or of a member of a patient's family. Holmes paused his finger tips many times at names he knew, his encyclopedic memory for people he had met or investigated was now a source of distress, not of utility. As we reached the third class section I could hear my wife starting to sniffle and I turned and noticed tears streaming down her graceful face.

"Dear God," she whispered. "There are so many. So many of them. And the mothers and children are all there too. It's terrible."

When the horrible task of reading through the names was over, my wife put her arms through mine and Holmes's and held us both tightly. We remained that way for some time. Then Holmes reached out his hand to the page in front of us and placed his index finger on a name in the first class list of victims.

"Do you remember Victor?" he asked me. His finger had landed on the name of Victor Emmanuel Trentacost of Donnithorpe, Norfolk.

I thought briefly and yes, I remembered Victor Trentacost. It had been over thirty years, but I remembered him acutely well.

"He was your friend from your college days," I said. "The chap who took us sailing."

"Yes, that was he," said Holmes. "I have had several thousand acquaintances over the years, but other than you, he was the only man I could truly call my friend. And, I must say, that our sailing venture with him was rather memorable."

"What!" exclaimed my wife. "You two? Sailors? That is just too much to believe."

Holmes smiled. "My dear Mrs. Watson, both your husband and I promised Victor we would never speak of it. It would have humiliated him beyond words and destroyed his career. And your astonishment at hearing of our unlikely venture at sea is proof that your stalwart husband kept his word as I did mine."

"John," she said, looking at me with some degree of accusation in her glance. "You never once mentioned this. Come now. Out with it."

I did not answer her directly but turned to Holmes.

"Did Victor have any family?" I asked.

"No. He was an only child. His mother, you may recall, died tragically whilst he was a toddler and, like me, he was a confirmed bachelor. We met once or twice a year at his club for lunch and he assured me that his horses, his tenants, and his constituents were all the family he ever wanted."

"Are we then," I asked, "released from our vow, if he has now gone to his eternal reward?"

Holmes pondered for a moment. "I do suppose we are, and it might take our minds off this terrible tragedy if we could have a morning tea and you tell your dear and long-suffering wife our tale. It would be a fitting eulogy to Victor. He was a generous soul and I am sure he would approve. I assume that you remember it."

"As if it were yesterday," I said. "I distinctly remember that over the course of three days I was swept overboard, nearly drowned, had a pistol jammed against my head, and was knocked silly by a swinging boom. I came closer to death in those three days than in all my time in Afghanistan. So yes, Holmes, thirty years may have passed but I cannot forget a minute of it."

Chapter Two
A Morning to Remember

And so it was that the three of us, on that terrible morning in April 1912, attempted to pay our tribute to Victor Trentacost, a true gentleman, and put the tragic news of the day out of our minds for an hour or two.

I recounted the tale of *The Glorious Yacht*.

Later that day, I took pen to paper and put the story on record. What follows are my memories, assisted in places by Holmes's, of what took place thirty-two years ago, in the glorious summer of 1881.

Holmes and I were much younger then, and much poorer. We had met the year before and decided to share lodgings on Baker Street in hopes of stretching our meager incomes. He had achieved some success in solving a handful of cases and I had written the story of one of them, *A Study in Scarlet*, and succeeded in getting it published, but to a disappointing paucity of notice and sales.

In late July of 1881, we both found ourselves with little to do. During the summer months the average Englishman is too concerned with his holiday plans either to take sick or to engage in crime. So it was a welcomed occasion when a note arrived from Holmes's college friend, Victor Trentacost. If my memory serves me correctly, the note ran, more or less:

```
My dear Sherlock:
I am desperately hoping that this note
finds you well but unencumbered. Next
week is Cowes Week along the Solent and
my irascible father has insisted on my
joining him there whilst he and his
equally insufferable friends race their
cutter in the annual regattas. I cannot
abide such frivolity and the prospect of
a week in their company appalls me. If it
is at all possible, could you and John
Watson come and join me? I will joyfully
cover all of your expenses if you will
only agree to offer conversation beyond
the endless repeating of tales of the
sea. Awaiting your reply, with earnest
hope,
Your friend,
Victor
```

Holmes and I looked at each other, shrugged our shoulders, and in unison said, "Why not?"

The Solent is the channel of water on England's south coast that separates the Isle of Wight from the mainland. The town of Cowes occupies the northern tip of the island, and across the channel and somewhat to the east sits the city of Portsmouth. In the Solent, being sheltered from the ocean, the waves are not overly large but the currents and tides can be treacherous due to the intersecting of the flow from the Southampton waters and the powerful currents of the great open expanse of the English Channel.

Every year, for several decades now, a week of regattas and festivities, Cowes Week, has been held in the town and on the mainland. Hundreds of boats of all classes come and race, and parties continue well into the night. The culmination of the week is a magnificent display of fireworks. I had only been to sea two times in my life, those being my journeys from England to India and back again when I served in the fighting in Afghanistan. My voyage out was pleasant and hopeful. The return voyage, aboard the *Orentes*, was a dreadful experience that I have tried unsuccessfully to forget. Any prospect of spending time on board a ship again was distinctly unappealing. The opportunity, however, of a midsummer week during which I remained firmly on shore, watching the colorful races whilst sipping chilled gin and engaging in pleasant banter was most attractive.

I confess that I was rather thrilled with that prospect.

Victor met us at Portsmouth Station on Sunday afternoon, 31 July. He was an exceptionally striking young man whose tall, thin body towered over me and even somewhat over Holmes. He had a fair and flawless complexion and a full head of wavy blond hair.

He was beaming from ear to ear.

"Thank you, Sherlock. Thank you, John. You cannot imagine how grateful I am that you agreed to come. The thought of a week in the company of my father and his raucous friends was giving me perfectly awful fits of angst."

"Oh, Victor," said Holmes. "Your dear father is not such a bad chap. I met him whilst we are at college. He is jovial and dotes on you terribly."

"Oh, I know, he loves me dearly and has been mother and father to me for my entire life. When we are alone we get along famously. But when his four friends join him they become entirely unbearable. They drink copious amounts of rum and tell the same stories of their adventures at sea over and over again. Some of them are inexcusably lewd and lead me to blush. They flirt shamelessly with barmaids and sing songs that should never be permitted in decent society."

"They sound like a rum lot if ever there was one," said Holmes. "I cannot wait to meet them."

"Oh, you will, soon enough," Victor said.

He hailed a cab for the three of us and we trundled along a few blocks until we reached a small inn in Southsea.

"Father knows the folks who run this place. They are relatives of the Italians he met in Brooklyn. They call it Bush Villas but that, I fear, is only to make it appear to be an English establishment and not run by immigrants from Italy. I do hope you will find it acceptable. We are only here for one night before we cross over to Cowes tomorrow."

"I am sure," I said, "that it will be perfectly acceptable. Is your father here now? I am rather looking forward to meeting him. He strikes me as a somewhat colorful character."

"No. He is in one of his favorite haunts about a mile from here. The good citizens of Portsmouth recently opened a Sailors' Home, something of a club for men from the navy or merchant marine who are stranded between ships. The founders hoped it would be a mission for seamen and contribute to the improvement of their immortal souls, but the sailors soon disabused them of that fallacy."

"Might we," asked Holmes, "walk over and join him there?"

"Really?" said Victor. "Most certainly we could, if you are sure you want to."

"I have found," said Holmes, "that the men of the sea offer a vast depository of insights into the human condition."

"If by 'human condition,'" replied Victor, shaking his head, "you mean the depraved mind, then I agree entirely."

We chuckled as we departed from the cab and entered a substantial house on Elm Grove. As soon as we had crossed the threshold, any doubt of the national origins of the proprietors vanished as we were welcomed by the pleasant odor of garlic and other spices. I began to look forward to dinner.

After leaving our valises in our individual rooms at the inn, we strolled the mile or so to the docks and found the recently opened Sailors' Home. It was an attractive but not ornate red brick building situated two blocks back from the water. The air inside was thick with tobacco smoke and the spacious bar was crowded with men who all looked as if they had spent their lives at sea. Many of them sported full beards and mustaches that did not quite succeed in obscuring their missing and misshapen teeth.

I was somewhat surprised to hear foreign tongues and one or two obviously American accents, and asked concerning same.

"They welcome all sailors here," said Victor, in response to my question. "It matters not what flag you come in under, all are accommodated. But come, let us find my father and hope that he will not do anything to embarrass us whilst we are here."

We shuffled and excused our way through the patrons of the bar and over to the seating area.

"There is my father," said Victor, nodding to a table by the far wall. "In a place like this, he prefers that I address him as Captain, rather than father. I do so to humor him. It keeps the peace."

"We shall do likewise," said Holmes. "He is looking a few years older than I remember, but then so are all of us."

Sitting against the wall, under a large portrait of Sir Francis Drake, was a man whose age I would have placed at around sixty. His hair was still full and dark, with some streaks of white just above his ears. He had heavy eyebrows and something of a Mediterranean look to his countenance. On his head he had a captain's cap, complete with the appropriate gold braid on the brim. In the few moments we stood looking at him, three other men came over, held pieces of paper in front of him to sign, shook his hand, and moved away.

"Is he signing up a crew?" I asked.

"No," replied Victor. "He has already hired three local boys to help him and his friends on the boat. He is recording bets on the schooner race."

As soon as he saw us, Victor's father waved away the other men who were standing in line to talk to him and rose to his feet.

"Ciao! My son, and Signore Sherlock. Wonderful to see you again. Please, please have a seat. Let me order you something to drink. The vino here, as it is all over England, is not fit for monkeys. But they do brew a good beer. And the food is fit only for cattle compared to what they serve on the Continent.

"A round for my son and his friends!" he shouted to the barmaid.

"Forgive me," he said, smiling, "but I lived with Italians for too many years in Brooklyn and I was spoiled with Chianti and prosciutto. But enough of my complaints, you must tell me what you have been doing since I saw your last, Master Holmes."

Holmes, who was not particularly accustomed to speaking about himself, quickly shifted the conversation to the publication of his monograph on tobacco and to observing that the various brands and countries of origin could be identified not only by their ash, but also by their peculiar aromas.

Already, he had noted some sixteen varieties here at the sailors' home.

The Captain chatted amiably for a few more minutes and then graciously excused himself so that he could return to the business he was conducting.

The three of us had had enough of suffocating in the smoke-filled interior of the building and pushed and bumped our way out on to the patio. We struck up several conversations with some of the fellows outside but once they learned that we were neither sailors nor gamblers, their interest in us quickly faded.

Taking our leave, we walked down to the water and then along the quays, past the old harbor, and then all the way down the esplanade to the Southsea Castle, before returning to the Bush Terrace for supper. I had assumed that the Captain would be joining us but he did not appear and I thought I heard him finally return sometime close to midnight after the three of us had gone to bed.

The next day, we walked to the docks and boarded a coaster ferry that took us from Portsmouth across the Solent to Cowes. Victor led us to an elegant inn that looked out over the water and I stood on the porch briefly before entering, enjoying the sunshine and the sea breeze, thinking that this had to be one of the finest places on God's good green earth. I rather felt that I was truly a fortunate man to be here and enjoying it.

There was a bit of a queue at the registration desk. In front of us were three quite impressive chaps that I remembered seeing the day before at the Sailors' Home. I overheard them speaking to the innkeeper and their speech immediately betrayed them to be Americans. I pointed to them in silence and gave a questioning look to Victor. He leaned in close to my ear and whispered.

"There are at least a hundred Yanks here for the regatta. It is quite the rivalry. The fight over the America's Cup has become a replay of the American Rebellion and it has spread now to the Cowes races. But all in good sport. And father says that some of them are jolly good sailors and even better gamblers. He says that he and his pals sailed many races against them in Boston and New York years ago and they could always be counted on for a wager of a hundred dollars."

When it came our turn to check in, Holmes, Victor, and I were assigned a large room on the third floor, with a delightful balcony looking out over the sea.

"I do hope you do not object to our all bunking in together," said Victor, somewhat apologetically. "Rooms in the town are scarce as hen's teeth, so we will have to share. I promise not to snore, but if you hear me crying out in my sleep, just ignore me. Just another nightmare. I seem to be prone to them."

Holmes and I assured him that we could be counted on to ignore him completely.

Tea, we were told, would be served at four o'clock and Victor gave us due warning that his father and friends would all be there, so be prepared to be appalled.

"Gentlemen," said Victor as the three of us approached

the end of the parlor where a group of men were sitting, "Allow me to introduce my friends. Sherlock Holmes was a classmate of mine whilst we were in college. And this is his friend, Dr. John Watson."

Victor's father stood to greet us. He was a full head shorter than his son and considerably stouter, but in his captain's cap and finely tailored jacket he looked as if he was used to commanding respect.

"Ah, delighted to see you again today, Sherlock. And you too, Doctor. Wonderful that you could come and join us for the week. As a group of old navy men, we are having a round of rum together. What may we offer you? Something to help you relax so that by tomorrow you will have given leave to your common sense and joined us on our boat?"

"Oh, really, father," said Victor on our behalf. "They are here as my guards to make sure that you do not shanghai *me* onto your boat."

The fellows laughed and we sat down to join the merry lot of them. They all appeared to be around sixty years of age and in rude good health. Some might have profited by losing a pound or two, but none was overweight and all were casually but not cheaply dressed.

"This fine gentleman beside you," began Victor's father, "is Senator Thomas Madison. Originally from Bedford. Elected to the legislature in the golden state of California many years ago, and now back in his home and native land where he belongs. And the one beside him is the Reverend John Wesley Jefferson, at one time of the Methodist Church of Virginia. A fine circuit preacher if ever there was one. You know those chaps, don't you? They all rode in circles, thinking they were big wheels, but were usually well-spoken."

The men laughed at this old saw and raised their glasses to the clergyman in their midst.

"If the reflection off the dome of Sir Monroe Quincy is blinding you, we can always draw the shades," he continued, pointing to a large man with a thick torso and a gleaming bald head.

"And that long, skinny drink of water on the end is Dr. Jackson Harrison. But don't ask him to cure whatever ails you, he's a doctor of philosophy who taught at Princeton until he saw the light and made his fortune along with the rest of us in the great American West."

He asked us to introduce ourselves further and I complied, noting my military service and current occupation as a general practitioner. Holmes announced that he had recently established himself as a consulting detective. This elicited claps and chortles of approval.

"Oh no," cried the Senator. "There goes our chance to bribe every judge on the course. Now what are we going to do?" Again, there were guffaws and laughs and some absurd suggested alternatives.

A young barmaid approached the sitting area and asked the group of us to place our order.

"And what's your name, my dear pretty one," asked Sir Monroe.

"Molly, sir," she said, with a bright smile. "My family name is Snow and I am known around here as Miss Molly and

I do not mind if you wish to call me that. Everyone else does."

She could not have been more than sixteen years of age, and was a mere slip of a young thing, but seemed quite sure of herself. As she turned around to leave us Sir Monroe gave her a firm slap on her backside. "Oh my, but God was good to you. Would you not agree, Reverend?" he said.

The young woman gave him a sharp look and continued on her way to the kitchen. She returned a few minutes later with a tray of pints of ale, glasses of rum, and a couple of chilled gin and tonics. She graciously distributed all of them until she had only a pint of ale left on the tray. She turned to Sir Monroe, who had ordered the pint, and began to walk toward him when she suddenly stumbled, sending the entire pint sloshing into the chap's startled face.

"Oh, I am so sorry, sir," she said, looking him directly in the eye. "But aren't you glad it wasn't a pot of hot tea?" She then walked on past him, leaving the empty glass in his lap.

It dawned on all of us at the same time that what had happened was no accident and there was a round of applause, even from Sir Monroe.

"Captain," he said, turning to Victor's father, "if I were you I would get my son to marry that girl tomorrow. She's going to give some young man the ride of his life."

The conversation continued amidst laughter as another round of drinks was served and sandwiches were consumed. When the tea was over, Holmes, Victor, and I excused ourselves and gathered out on the porch.

"Quite the merry band," I said. "How in the world did they end up together?"

"At the Royal Navy recruiting station," said Victor. "I believe it was in 1841. They all served on the same ship and have stayed friends for forty years. After they sailed around the world and had done their term, they agreed that America was the land of opportunity and off they went. Every one of them did wonderfully well and made a small fortune. And, being sailors, they would meet every summer in New York or Boston and take part in the boat races. My father was the most knowledgeable yachtsman, so that's why they call him Captain. *Sir* Monroe is most certainly not a knight here in England. He did some service and made generous donations to the Order of St. John, and they made him a Knight of Malta. Senator Tom was elected in California and served two terms. Doc Jackson managed to get himself enrolled in college and I'm told he taught at Princeton, but he does not act in the least like an egghead. But Reverend John Wesley is indeed a rather sober fellow and I've never yet seen him touch a drop of strong drink."

"Where are their wives?" asked Holmes.

"They are all bachelors, claiming that no good woman would ever put up with them, what with their running off with each other to stakes races, and rugby matches, and sailing regattas. My father was married for only a few years when my mum died. He insisted that he was blessed with his first marriage and was satisfied with his joyful memories. So they are all jovial irredeemable bachelors. I would not doubt that they have mistresses aplenty and have sired children in various ports all across the globe, but I am the only offspring that is acknowledged."

Chapter Three
Cowes Week

On the following morning, the Captain and his mates were on the water by seven o'clock along with the three local lads they had hired to crew for them. The gleaming cutter, the *Indefatigable,* was untied from its mooring and drifted gently away from the shore and out into the open water. All that the local boys had to do was hold on to the end of a line as tight or loose as they were told, and not let go. They did well and would be remunerated handsomely for their efforts. The large cutter moved gracefully through the waves, the two foresails and the large mainsail filling out and catching the winds. In my field glasses I could watch every member, the five older sailors and the three local lads, all performing their tasks like clockwork. When they came in for lunch, Holmes greeted them with small flutes of champagne and proposed a toast. He cheerfully raised a glass to Dr. Harrison and gave what I assumed was an appropriate Latin toast of *ire ad infernum*, smiled, and tossed back the drink. The learned doctor also smiled and did likewise.

At one o'clock on the Monday, the regatta was formally begun. There was a full card of races for varying lengths and types of boats. Small open dinghies, sloops, cutters, ketches, and yawls all would compete around several marked courses. Most were triangular but some required the yachts to race all the way down the Solent to the west, pass the Needles beyond the narrow passage at the far end, circle a buoy out in the open channel, and return.

The final race, the finale, would take place on Saturday. It would be the schooner race down the Solent to the east, out into the English Channel, circumnavigating the Isle of Wight, and returning to the finish line from the southeast. Betting on the result had reached a fever pitch.

On the first day, several of the shorter races were held for the small open dinghies, both sloop-rigged and cat-rigged. Some of these were just for the youngsters and we cheered the boys and girls on, all under the age of sixteen, who skillfully tacked and reached and ran free around the triangular course. It was a delight to see a team of a brother and a sister take the first race.

The Indefatigable had an excellent day. It was not the newest boat in the regatta by a long way and those that were newer, sleeker, and lighter had a distinct advantage, but our old sailors knew their stuff and performed well. We cheered them on. At the end of each day they brought the boat back into its mooring buoy and joined us for a pleasant evening.

All was going well, except that every so often I thought that Holmes was acting rather odd. I had no explanation for his behavior, except possibly that he might have been touched by the divine in such a pristine and beautiful natural setting.

He started whistling tunes, something he had never done much of before. I would have brushed it off as behavior inspired by the sublime location except for the fact that all of the tunes he whistled were vaguely familiar to me as hymns that we had sung in chapel when I was a school boy. On the Tuesday it was *Soldiers of Christ, Arise;* on Wednesday he was fixated on *O for a Thousand Tongues to Sing;* and on Thursday he serenaded us with *Love Divine, All Loves Excelling.* By Saturday, the whistling had ceased.

The entire week was idyllic. The weather was sunny, and a light breeze blew constantly. The races were colorful events as were the jugglers, actors, and musicians who performed for us. Several of England's better company bands were present and gave concerts from the band shell. At the close of each day, the crew the Indefatigable rowed in from their boat, slapping each other on the back, and laughing about their accomplishments and failures of the day. I had to note that they appeared to enjoy each other as much as any group of men I had known. That they had been doing so since they first enlisted in the Navy forty years ago was truly admirable.

The afternoon of the Thursday was hot and sultry and upon returning to the dock, two of the chaps, the reverend and the knight, unbuttoned their shirts, tossed them aside, kicked off their shoes, and dived into the refreshing water. I confess that I followed their example and did likewise. They were strong swimmers and I was able to keep myself afloat. After paddling around for at least fifteen minutes we climbed back out feeling utterly refreshed, with our skin and muscles taut and smiles on our faces.

Saturday was the cup race around the Isle of Wight for schooners only. None of our men was participating and we had a delightful day sitting on the lawn by the main dock. At eight o'clock in the morning we watched as forty graceful schooners skillfully crossed the line in a flying start. Their first leg was to east, down the Solent and out into the ocean. The winds were behind them and to the starboard, so the two large sails were let out and the boats sped off. Once they rounded the south corner of the island they would have to come about and then tack their way into the westerlies that blew up the channel. Before long they had passed out of sight but watch-posts had been set up in twenty spots around the circumference of the island, all connected by telegraph, and reports were cabled in to the judges stand. A large board with bold letter cards kept the assembled spectators informed as to which boats were in front and by what margin.

Holmes, Victor, and I did not wander far from the stands, but I was surprised that neither Victor's father nor his pals were with us. From time to time I spotted one or more of them chatting with some of the other boat owners and I assumed, knowing them, that a ripping set of wagers was being placed. However, I also noticed them speaking with some of the regatta officials who, I hoped, were not accepting bribes.

The race took the full day. Cheers went up from the crowd when the reports came in of the first boat to pass Ryde, and then to round Seaview, and then head out into the open Channel. Another cheer came when the first yacht sailed past the great lighthouse at St. Catharine's Point. In the late afternoon, a sign was posted telling us that the leading yacht had arrived at the Needles headland and entered the home stretch back to the finish line. Many spectators who had wandered off during the day now came back and resumed their vantage points close to the shore. Not far from where we now stood were our five old sailors, surrounded by at least twenty other gentlemen who had the look and body contours of the boats' owners.

The hour of seven in the evening had just passed when the first sail was spotted off in the distance to our left. Again a cheer went up and we were on our feet as one by one the beautiful schooners sailed across the finish line, running free with the evening breeze behind them. Soon the prizes would be awarded and the fireworks would begin.

The sun set at a quarter to nine and at least a thousand sailors, owners, and spectators were gathered. Before the first prize was announced, the regatta 'Admiral' called for attention.

"Ladies and gentlemen, sailors all," he shouted. "This has been a glorious week and we have held one of the largest and finest regattas in the history of England."

A cheer went up. He continued.

"Before we hand out all of the prizes, we have a special announcement. It concerns an event that has never before taken place in the history of sailing in Great Britain. There are so many splendid boats and wonderful sailors gathered here, in this one location, that an opportunity has presented itself. A group of boat owners has proposed a truly great sailing race; one that has never happened before. It will be an open race. Any boat may enter. The Black Friars Distillery in Plymouth, the makers of the fine Plymouth Gin, is offering a prize of a thousand pounds. Are you ready to hear what has been proposed?"

Shouts of "aye" and "yes" along with cries of "get on with it" were heard.

"Tomorrow morning all boats are invited to take part in a race down the Solent, through the Needles, down the Channel and out into the Celtic Sea. From there they must sail to the south coast of Ireland and round the Fastnet Rock. The finish line will be in the Plymouth Harbor. Already over one hundred boats have said they will take part. The race around the Fastnet will be one of the greatest sailing races of all time!"

He went on to give further details, but the crowd was all abuzz. Even as the prizes were awarded and the fireworks set off, the talk was all about the Fastnet race, *the great race. The greatest race ever.* It would take most boats almost three days and they would have to pass through some of the most treacherous waters in the nation. Truly, it would be a superb test of sailing prowess.

When we finally returned to the inn, at close to eleven o'clock in the evening, Captain Trentacost and the four old sailors were gathered in the parlor waiting for us. They were all full of the great race and indeed gave themselves some credit for having helped to propose it to the regatta officials. I could see that they were quite serious about the venture, so much so that they were drinking tea instead of rum. They announced that they would soon be off to bed so as to be ready at first light to prepare for the race to Fastnet and back. No doubt many bets had been placed.

Holmes retreated out on to the porch to have a final pipe and look out over the water before retiring. I joined him and enjoyed the sublime view of the moon over the waters. My serenity was interrupted by a cluster of men at the base of the stairs who were chatting, unaware of our presence. I could not hear what they were saying but I recognized them. There were six in total. Three were the local lads who had been hired by our friends to help crew the Indefatigable. The other three were the imposing American chaps that I had stood behind whilst in the registration line earlier in the week. Something about their meeting so late and secretively caused me concern.

"You don't suppose," I said to Holmes, "that those American fellows are trying to poach our local crew? Our men are counting on them for the great race tomorrow. I don't like the look of what's going on."

"Neither do I," said Holmes, "although I doubt whether they are being hired for any other boat."

"Why do you say that?"

"Because those Americans do not have a boat."

He said no more and turned to climb the stairs up to our room, then retired to his bed in silence. I did the same. Victor was already in his bed and fast asleep.

Chapter Four
Recruited to the Indefatigable

At five thirty the following morning, I was awakened by a loud "Wake up lads!" and the turning up of the gaslight. The first glimmer of dawn was slipping in through the windows and my sleepy eyes could make out Captain Trentacost and Sir Monroe standing over us.

"Good heavens, father" said Victor. "What is it?"

"Sorry to do this to you, boys, but something has come up and we need you."

"What's come up?" asked Victor.

"Our local crew has deserted us. They must have been given a better offer. All we got was a note saying that they had fulfilled their obligations to us for the regatta and would not be working for us any longer."

"Well," said Victor. "Where are they? Can you not find them and make them a better offer."

"We can find neither hide nor hair of them. Gone. All three of them."

"What are you going to do?" asked Victor, as if the presence of his father and Sir Munroe waking us up was not an obvious answer.

"We're recruiting the three of you. Now up you get and get dressed, and meet us downstairs for some breakfast before we take you out and show you what you have to do. Hurry. Jump to it."

"Aye, aye, gentlemen," said Holmes, to my surprise. "We shall be as true and loyal as Suleiman was to the Knights. You can count on us."

Holmes's strange behavior never ceased to perplex me. But Victor was having none of it.

"Faaaather," pleaded Victor. "I cannot abide sailing. You know I can't."

"For the next three days, you can learn to abide it," came the reply. "Now get moving or my boot will be up your arse. See you downstairs."

I looked at Holmes and saw that he was already out of his bed and getting dressed.

"Are you honestly going to get on a boat and sail with them?" I asked.

"I suspect that they need us in more ways than they know," he replied and shuffled off out of the room. I shrugged and reminded myself that I was not a bad swimmer and so was not likely to drown. Three days at sea I thought I could manage, and most certainly our men were in a pinch and we were needed.

Whilst I was dressing, Victor came up to me and sat down on my bed.

"Doctor John," he said. "I don't know what to do. It's not just that I do not like sailing. For some reason it terrifies me. The prospect of three days on the ocean frightens me to death but I can't disappoint my father. This race will be the last great hurrah for him and his pals. You wouldn't happen to have anything in your medical bag that I could take? I know there's nothing that can make me brave, but maybe something to render me almost unconscious so I don't have to think."

He looked at me and I could see the desperation in his eyes. I sat down beside him and put my hand on his shoulder.

"The only way," I said, "to get over a paralyzing fear is to conquer it. It's just like falling off a horse. You have to get up and keep going. You can do it."

His lower lip began to tremble. "Oh, please, John. I can't."

I thought for a moment and then came to a solution.

"I have some laudanum. If you take it now you will be floating on a cloud for the next two hours. By that time you'll be on the boat with no way to escape. And then you'll just have to make it through."

I gave him a strong dose and we made our way down for breakfast. I knew that within ten minutes he would be temporarily inhabiting a dream world and was reasonably sure that the joy of being on the ocean on a beautiful morning would help to remove all his fears.

The old sailors were assembled around a table in the breakfast room as I entered.

"Doc," called one of them to me, "can you cook?"

I was not expecting any such question and after recovering my composure, I assured them that I had no such ability whatsoever. I could not recall a single meal in my life that I had cooked for anyone other than myself. I had been provided for by my parents, by school kitchen workers, by the dear ladies at medical school, by the cookies in the army, and most recently, by the blessed Mrs. Hudson. And I was quite certain that Sherlock Holmes's experience was even less than mine.

"We need a cook," stated Captain Trentacost. "One of the local lads was going to do that for us, but he's gone. We'll be out on the water for three days. We have to eat."

In what was either a stroke of fortune or disaster, it so happened that at that moment the young woman, Molly, who had been waiting on us for the past few days, walked into the room to take our breakfast order.

"Miss Molly," said Sir Monroe, "can you cook?"

She gave him quite the look and then replied, "I can cook."

"Have you ever cooked on a boat?" Monroe continued. "Ever worked a galley?"

"I've cooked on a boat," she said.

"Well then," he roared, "will you come and cook for us for

the next three days whilst we sail out to Fastnet and back?"

She laughed spontaneously. "You must be daft. Not if you offered me a hundred pounds would I spend three days on a boat with you old bounders."

"You heard what she said," said Monroe. "For two hundred pounds she'll come and cook for us."

Molly looked stunned. Two hundred pounds was more than she would earn in an entire year. She smiled and replied, "It's too early in the morning for your jokes, sir. How do you want your eggs?"

"We're serious, Molly. Two hundred pounds for three days and we promise to behave."

She looked around and gave a glance to each of us. We all smiled and nodded.

"Very well, but if any one of you gets fresh, I'll put poison in your tea."

"Splendid," said the Captain. "as fair a contract as I've ever heard. Would you mind, my dear, being down at the dock in an hour?"

She put down her notepad and departed. The reverend picked it up and continued to take the breakfast order.

An hour later, in the light of early morning, we were all assembled on the Indefatigable. Our motley crew of five old salts, three young landlubbers, and one wisp of a girl slipped away from the mooring and drifted out into the open waters. Victor was smiling dreamily. We had about two hours to learn what we had to know and master our stations. I looked back at the shore, with the morning sun now causing long shadows to fall to the west of the trees and buildings, and thought, for the last time it turned out, that a sailing adventure was a bit of all right.

As I watched, I noticed three men running from the land out on to the pier. Curious, I pulled out my small set of field glasses to look at them. They were the same three American chaps I had observed the previous evening trying to poach away our local boys. Beside me, Sherlock Holmes was observing the same thing.

"Surprised them didn't we." I said. "They probably thought our yacht would be waylaid after they poached our boys. I think we showed them a thing or two. We London landsmen are made of sterner stuff."

Holmes looked at me in friendly condescension. "As you are known to be a gambling man, my dear doctor, I will lay a fiver that those chaps will be waiting for us in Plymouth and could not care a fig about our local crew."

Something was up. I knew Sherlock Holmes all too well to think he would risk five pounds on a bet to which he did not already know the most assured result. I mumbled a decline of his offer.

The Captain gave a quick introduction to terms and tasks. Our boat was quite large for a cutter, nearly seventy feet long. The crew was spread out all along the deck.

"That is not a rope," he said. "It's a line. And those are not piano wires, they're stays. And that thing at the bow is not a pole-sticking-out, it's a bowsprit." And on he went. Victor seemed to be vaguely familiar with everything, gleaned from years of living with his father. Holmes and I were innocents afloat, but, to my surprise, little Miss Molly was fully familiar with everything already. It appeared that she had been on boats many times before.

"My sister and I came fifth in the junior cat-rigged sloops last year," she said. "My father has worked on boats all his life and he taught me."

Our lessons over, I was assigned to the front of the boat or, having been chastised for calling it that, to the *bow*, and given charge of what the Captain called the *Yankee* sail. The Brits, he explained, used another name, but that was what he learned to call it whilst in America. Holmes was given a post at the staysail, not far from my station.

We practiced our roles through the various points of sail. Close, beam, and broad reaches were covered, and then we tacked several times. Unfortunately, explained the skipper, the first leg of the race, west and down the Solent and through the Needle gap, would require us to tack constantly. A cutter was not as agile in coming about as the sloops, but once out on the open water, he assured us, we would make up for lost time.

Chapter Five
The Race to Fastnet

We were as ready as we would ever be and at 8:30 we sailed past the stern of the signal boat and hailed the officials. "Indefatigable, here!" shouted Senator Tom. "Cleared!" came the reply. I looked out over the water and could see at least one hundred boats of all shapes and sizes, each one jockeying to get itself into the best position for the flying start.

At the ten minute mark the first gun sounded and the Captain sailed away from the start line. At five minutes the second gun was fired and we came about a full one hundred and eighty degrees and sailed close to the wind but under controlled speed. At the one minute mark the final warning gun went off and we turned to catch more wind and began to heel over as we raced toward the line. I watched and held my breath as the line approached, knowing that if we crossed before the gun sounded we would have to turn around and do our start all over again. We could not have been more than twenty-five yards from the line and almost on a beam reach when the starter gun went off. We were flying across the waves and near the head of the pack. Several yachts had jumped the gun and had to turn around and repeat the start, but we had done well.

"Good work, there mates!" shouted the skipper. "Now get ready to hike out when the wind picks up. We're going to do a right proud piece of work here." In truth, he peppered his shouts to us with no end of colorful oaths and curses which are best left to your unholy imaginations. The effect, however, of flying over the waves with the wind streaming across my face was intoxicating. I was keeping close eye on Victor to see how he was managing. The laudanum had worn off and I feared his terror of the sea would take over, but he appeared to be caught up in the moment every bit as much as I was. Holmes was uncharacteristically beaming with a smile and actually laughing every time a spray swept across the boat as we plunged down into the trough of the next wave. All across the water of the Solent, I could see sail after sail of sloop, yawl, cutter, ketch, and the occasional schooner. It was one of the most euphoric moments of my life and I was enjoying it to the hilt.

Our first tack had led us toward the north shore of the waterway and we would soon have to come about and take a starboard tack back across.

"Prepare to come about in five minutes," came the command from the Captain.

"No! No!" came a scream from the door of the cabin. Miss Molly was standing there wagging her head from side to side. "Five will take you too close. There's dirty wind off the point. Three minutes, no more!"

It struck me as highly irregular to have a teenaged cook contradicting a sixty-year-old captain, but there she was. The Captain glared at her for several seconds and then shifted his gaze to the fast approaching shore.

"As I said!" he shouted. "Coming about in two minutes!"

He then beckoned with his index finger to Miss Molly and indicated that she was to sit in the seat adjacent to the helm. She came over and sat down.

It took us at least an hour and a dozen more tacks to work our way down the western side of the Solent and then through the gap and around the gleaming white cliffs that towered over the Needles. From there it was smooth sailing on a close reach all the way across the open water and past Swanage. We gave a wide berth to the Swanage Point and I could see the waves crashing and foaming on the rocks and shoals that extended well out into the water. Sailing into a stiff Westerly, we rounded the Durlston headlands and again into the wide open water of the English Channel. We headed on a bearing of 270 degrees and, unless the wind changed, we would just stay the course, passing the Isle of Portland and on to Star Point.

There was now not much to do. So I found myself a cushion and relaxed, enjoying the splendor of the waves and the passing shore. We were all gathered on the deck and the reverend offered an exceptionally well-informed travelogue on the various towns and natural features on the passing shore. Quite the knowledgeable chap.

In the distance I could see the headlands of the Lizard, the southernmost point of Great Britain, and I remembered from my schooldays that we were passing through what was known as *The Graveyard of Ships*. The waters off England's southwest coast were some of the most treacherous on earth. The rocks and shoals that stretched out from the Lizard had claimed many passing boats and countless lives over the past five hundred or more years. I was not worried, however, as I trusted the Captain to swing out into the open waters to the south and give a very wide berth to the dangerous area near the shore.

As we came closer and closer to the Lizard shoals, I started to think that he was cutting it a bit close. Most assuredly we were in a race and shortening the distance by coming as close as possible to sands bars and rocks was an honored strategy, but I kept thinking that he was going to make it a near run thing.

I glanced over at Miss Molly and could see that she was having the same thoughts as I was. When we were no more than one hundred yards from the waves crashing on the rocks, she finally leaped up and shouted at the helmsman.

"Are you daft, man? Get us out away from the shoals before we smash."

He smiled at her. "They're only dangerous if you don't know your way through them. And I'm sure that they have not moved in the past thirty years."

It was now obvious that he was going to run the boat straight through the rocks. I looked around and could see that Holmes and Victor were now standing up and becoming increasingly uncomfortable. What was odd was that the other four men were sitting quietly, smoking nonchalantly, and ignoring the fast-approaching doom of our craft.

"Prepare to come about!" called the Captain.

The old sailors rose and sauntered to their places.

"Ready when you are," shouted the senator.

We were headed directly toward a gap between two massive outcrops of rock that could not have been more that thirty yards apart. I grabbed on to my jib sheet and held my breath, letting it out only after we had sailed smartly between Scylla and Charybdis as if they did not exist. As soon as they were passed, the order was given and we turned a sharp ninety degrees to the south. That was followed by another tack that sent us around an enormous boulder and then back on to our westward course. Twenty minutes and five course changes later, we were back in the open water of the English Channel and aiming for the northern edge of the Scilly Islands.

By the time we sailed past Lion Rock, the sun was low on the western horizon and the gentle constant evening breeze and the night swells had moved across the water. We would cross the Celtic Sea at night, dead reckoning our way to the southern coast of Ireland. By first light we should be somewhere near the Fastnet Rock.

Miss Molly had prepared us an excellent supper and we

sat around on the deck entranced by the setting sun, the appearance of Venus, followed by the stars of the summer triangle, and the unmatched sensation of the gentle breath of Zephyr ruffling our hair and caressing our faces.

Dinner done, the bottle of rum came out.

Some men, when they start into their cups become jovial. Some become morose. Others still cease to speak and turn, taciturn, into their hidden inner souls. Sadly, there are a few who get nasty and pugnacious. The senator from California was from the last group. What had started out as an evening of utmost serenity soon gave signs of degenerating into a highly unpleasant conversation. To this day I do not know whom I should still be more angry at; the senator for ruining the atmosphere, or Sherlock Holmes for taking the bait, unable to resist the urge to show off his brilliance.

"So, Sherlock Holmes," began the senator. "I've read some things about you. Quite the egghead, they say."

"I am sure I have been called much worse," Holmes replied.

"They say you can tell all sorts of things about a fellow just by looking at him."

"That has been said."

"Well then, young master Holmes, let's see how smart you really are. How much can you tell me about me? Go ahead. Give it your best try."

"Tom," interrupted Dr. Jackson. "That is really not necessary."

"It is necessary," snapped the senator. "As far as I am

concerned this bloke's a charlatan. I'm betting all his so-called brilliance is no more than a few parlor tricks. So, c'mon master Sherlock. Tell me what you know about me. I lay down five pounds that you haven't observed a single thing beyond what you've been told by Victor. Five pounds, master Sherlock. Are you game, or not?"

"Tom," this time said by Reverend John. "That is not a good idea. You're a bit drunk and you know how you get. Let's not do anything you'll regret."

"What?" he shouted back. "Regret losing a fiver? It wouldn't be the first time, but I'm not going to lose. I'm going to win if this Mister Detective has the spine to take me up on my wager."

I was prepared to dig into my pocket and find a five pound note to give to Holmes with the direction that he should just hand it over to the older man, take a loss, and not make a fuss when, to my eternal dismay, Holmes rose, walked over to Senator Tom and laid a note beside his.

"I accept."

Something was telling me that this was not a good idea. Bad things were about to happen.

"Ha!" said the senator, and he tossed back another shot of rum. "A proud young fool about to be parted from his money. I love wagers against fools. So get on with it, young fellow. Tell me my story."

Holmes, in what I can only admit was his insufferable arrogance, leaned back and slowly lit his pipe and gave a long slow puff, before responding.

"You are an imposter."

Chapter Six
The Night Turns Hostile

What had begun as a delightful night on the Celtic Sea immediately changed to one of tension and hostility.

"Am I now?" said the senator. "Those are fighting words, lad, so you better back them up on the double before I come over and punch your lights out."

Holmes took another puff and turned to Victor.

"Victor, tell the senator how old you are."

Victor was at a loss but mumbled, "What? Thirty-two. Why?"

"And how old were you when your father and his friends came back to England from America?"

"Three. But what does that have to do with anything?"

"So that means that all of these chaps have been in England since the year 1852. That is simple arithmetic, is it not?"

No one answered. We were waiting for the other shoe to drop.

"You claim, sir," Holmes said to the senator, "to have served two terms in the state legislature of California. I am sorry to have to inform you that California was not incorporated as a state within the United States of America until 1851. There was no senate prior to that time in which you could have been a senator. Wherever you were doing the years before you came back to England, you were not in Sacramento serving in elected office."

The light had now gone from the sky and all we had to see by was a storm lantern that hung from the boom. But in the faint light I could see an angry cloud covering the face of the senator. Fortunately the reverend intervened.

"Ha! He got you on that one, Tom. You're right, Mister Holmes, Tom was not a true senator. It was more like a councilor in some town along the west coast. But if a man wants a high and mighty title in the classless society of America, then *senator* is as good as it comes. So Tom's our senator, aren't you Tom? C'mon there mate, he got you on that one, so slide over the fiver."

There was a round of claps and ha-ha's directed by the men to the not-quite-senator and he shrugged and handed over his note to the chap next to him so that it could be passed along to Holmes.

Holmes should have stopped there. He did not.

"Thank you, sir," he said to Reverend John. "I would say 'thank you, reverend' except for the fact that you are likewise an imposter and are not nor have ever been a member of the Methodist clergy."

"Really," bellowed Tom, now becoming belligerent. "You're insulting my friend, Holmes. Now you better take back those words and apologize if you know what's good for you."

"What would be good," said Holmes, "is that a Methodist minister would have a least a passing knowledge of the great hymns of his church. On several occasions I have whistled the hymns of Charles Wesley within earshot of our supposed clergyman and there was not the least flash of recognition. You may, sir," he said, now to Mr. John, "have darkened the door of a church from time to time, but you have never been a man of the cloth. And sir, I would wager a fiver on that one."

John Wesley Jefferson leaned back and crossed his arms over his chest and smiled.

"You have me as well, young man. But, I must say, this is getting interesting. Why don't you keep going on the rest of us?"

Holmes took the bait yet again and turned to Dr. Jackson Harrison.

"Sir, you are posing as a learned man, a doctor of philosophy. Yet on Tuesday I raised a toast to you, uttered a well-known Latin phrase, and you responded with a smile and wished me the same."

"I remember so doing."

"What I said to you, sir, might be best translated as 'go to hell' and you were not in the least offended. That would lead me to believe that either you are a most tolerant gentleman with an uncanny knowledge of the coast of southwest England, or that you are someone else entirely and do not know a single word of the classical language."

Without giving the chap a chance to reply, he then turned to Sir Monroe.

"Sir Monroe, when agreeing to come on board this boat I pledged to you the service and loyalty of Suleiman. Anyone who is truly a Knight of Malta knows that Suleiman the Magnificent was not your friend. The Turk was your sworn enemy and almost eliminated your order from the earth during the Great Siege of Malta. And yet you smiled and thanked me."

Finally he turned to the Captain.

"Captain Trentacost, you are the father of my friend and have generously extended your hospitality to me in the past, for which I thank you. I will refrain from any unmasking if you so desire."

"You've come too far, Sherlock," Captain Trentacost replied. "You may as well keep going. The truth will out soon enough after what you have already said. My son is now a full-grown man and it's about time he learned the truth of his father's early life. So proceed."

Holmes turned to Victor with a questioning look. Victor shrugged his shoulders and nodded.

"May as well."

"Very well, then. Victor informed me that your occasionally odd way of pronouncing your words was a result of your living in Brooklyn whilst serving as a captain in America's merchant marine. That, sir, is not likely the case. Your accent and syntax betray a boyhood spent not in England but in Italy; most likely in Sicily. Unlike your friends, you have not adopted a name composed of one borrowed from American presidents or famous clergy. You have kept your own and anglicized it. *Trentacosta* is a common family name in Sicily. *Trentacost* is not an English name at all and there is no family history of that name in any part of Norfolk. You clearly have excellent navigational skills to the point of expert knowledge of the shoals, reefs, and rocks off of England's coast. I suspect strongly that it is there that you acquired your sailing experience and not on the east coast of America."

Holmes now leaned back, looking quite smug and self-satisfied.

"Do you, Captain, or any of you wish to contradict me? No? I rather thought so. And would you like me to continue?"

Nothing was said. His question met with glares of animosity.

"Very well, then. I will take your silence as consent and continue. It is a common practice amongst navy men to put a tattoo of the first ship on which they served on their upper arms. When you removed your shirts and took a swim I could see that those of you in the water had such tattoos. However, on the underside of all your wrists is a smaller tattoo, again of a ship, a schooner. I had glimpses of this ship on all of you and most clearly whilst you were swimming. The ribbon under the ship reads *Glorious*. According to *Jane's*, there has never been a ship of the line, or a supply ship, or a vessel in the English merchant marine by that name.

"On the other hand, there *was* a schooner called Glorious that sailed off the southwest coast of England during the years of 1840 to 1845. The annals of crime record that it carried out numerous highly successful pirate attacks on merchant boats and private yachts for several years. The press called the villains the *gentlemen pirates* because of their practice of never harming the crews or passengers of the boats they apprehended, or doing any damage to the vessels. Possibly that was a result of the pirates all having soft hearts and the crews' claiming to be orphans, but more likely it was good business practice, knowing that if you were able to capture a boat once, you could capture it again the following year, and there are reports of one boat having been taken three times."

"Four," came the sharp comment from Sir Monroe.

"I stand corrected, sir," said Holmes. "Truly, these pirates were astute businessmen. Unfortunately, Lloyds became tired of paying for the losses and demanded that the Royal Navy put an end to this nonsense. Whereupon, the pirates wisely sailed across the Atlantic and began to ply their trade in the waters off New England and all the way south to Virginia. They became increasingly specialized in their craft. They ignored large American vessels that might have armed militia on board and concentrated on the yachts of the rich and shameless, of whom there are many on the east coast of America. Rich bankers, industrialists, and occasional politicians were kidnapped and held for ransom. They were surprisingly easy targets and the amount demanded for their safe return was always within the reach of their bank accounts. It proved to be highly successful venture and some in the press who covered the crimes claimed that in excess of one million dollars was extracted over a five-year period."

"Nonsense!" snapped Sir Monroe. All heads turned and looked at him. He ran his hand across his bald head and grinned. "It was more than two million." His colleagues chuckled and nodded.

"Again, sir, I stand corrected," said Holmes. "Allow me to continue. In the fall of 1851 there was a hurricane off the Atlantic coast and many ships and lives were lost. The wreck of the Glorious washed up on the Chesapeake shore and it was concluded that all on board had perished at sea. There were, although, persistent rumors that the crew had escaped, and sightings of them were reported first in Ocean City and later in Baltimore. And then all trace of them vanished.

"If my memory serves me correctly," Homes went on, "the names of the gentlemen pirates were ..." Here he paused, closed his eyes and joined his hands in front of his chin, with the fingertips pressed together. "Ah, yes. I believe that they were Samuel White, Henry Longbough, Fredrick Yeats, Hyman Whitley, and Victor Emmanuel Trentacosta. Other than the Captain, I do not know which of you is which, but you might wish to introduce yourselves."

He was positively grinning and turned and faced each of the men in the order that they were seated on the deck. For several minutes there was no reply. We sailed on in silence. Finally, Reverend John spoke.

"Young man," he said, "you are too clever by half for your own good. You have unmasked us and uncovered a secret that we have carefully guarded for three decades. In doing so, you have become a threat to the continued enjoyment of our pleasant lives. When you boarded this boat you did so as our friend. I fear you have now become our enemy and we shall have to decide amongst ourselves what to do with you."

From his pocket he withdrew a revolver and pointed it at Holmes. Sir Munroe and Senator Tom also pulled out guns and waved them in Holmes's direction.

Holmes was unflappable. "Permit me, sir to correct you. I may be your best friend in the world at this moment. Your true enemies will be waiting for you on the dock in Plymouth when you complete the race, ready to arrest you, transport you back to America and send you to one of their federal prisons if not the gallows."

He paused, enjoying the dramatic effect his words had had.

"The careful efforts you claim to have made to keep your secret were not sufficient. You have, in fact, been rather careless. So much so that rumors of your pleasant life here in England have continued to float back to America. Three months ago, as I am sure you are aware, Lloyds and The Hartford combined their forces and issued a reward for information leading to your arrest. Bringing you to justice even after so many years will have a deterrent effect on any who have thoughts of repeating your success. You all now have a price on your heads. You do know that, do you not?"

Heads nodded in silence. Holmes carried on.

"And I also assume that you are familiar with the Pinkerton Detective Agency?"

That question brought attention looks of apprehension.

"The three American gentlemen who were staying at the same inn as we are did not once this past week get on a boat. They were busy all week chatting with people. By Saturday they were watching the group of you very closely. On Saturday evening they met with your local crew and I assure you that it was not to hire them as sailors. I strongly suspect that it was to warn them that on Sunday morning they would be arresting you and impounding this boat and that your crew should best not be anywhere nearby or have any further connection to any of you if they knew what was good for them. What those American chaps did not expect was that you would Shanghai the three of us and push off into the water at such an early hour.

"I will wager any one of you," Holmes now announced, "a fiver each, that those Pinkertons will be standing on the pier in Plymouth, accompanied likely by Scotland Yard, and will escort you to your fate as soon as you step off this boat."

Not one of them took up his offer. After several moments of silence, Senator Tom spoke quietly.

"Mr. Holmes, it would be good if you, the doctor, Victor and Miss Molly retreated down into the cabin for an hour or so. My friends and I need to have a meeting and I do not think you should be part of it."

The night under the moon and stars, with the warm sea breeze wafting over me was as close to paradise as can be found anywhere in England, and I did not relish the prospect of spending the next hour or several hours cooped up in a stuffy cabin. I was about to voice my objection when Holmes, to my surprise, rose and descended the stairs. Victor followed him and so did the young cook. I was not in a good humor as I joined the three of them.

Chapter Seven
Confined Below the Deck

"Well, Holmes," I said after the cabin door closed behind us. "This is a fine mess you got us in to. If you hadn't been so eager to show off, we might still be out there and no one the wiser."

Holmes was about to reply to my obvious anger when Victor put his hand on Holmes's arm, indicating his request for Holmes to remain silent.

"John," said Victor, "he did it for me."

"What do you mean?" I demanded.

"I have known for many years that there was some dark secret in my father's past. I would have died of shame and humiliation had he been arrested, tried in court and then hanged for his crimes of decades ago. Now he has an opportunity to escape and disappear. I know it seems like an unnecessary display of Sherlock's brilliance, but I assure you, I am humbly grateful."

He then turned to Holmes and quietly said, "Thank you, my friend."

Holmes first smiled at Victor and then turned to me, "My dear doctor, you and Victor are the only true friends I have. I would have done then same if it meant protecting you."

I appreciated his sentiments but was still thoroughly annoyed at the prospect of now having to spend the next day and a half locked up below deck. I harrumphed and stretched out on one of the bunks. The other three followed my example and did the same.

I must have dozed off for several hours, lulled by the gentle rocking of the yacht on the night swells. I was awakened by the jovial shout of loud voice.

"Avast there, me mates! Rise and shine! All hands on deck," shouted the Captain.

Rubbing the sleep from my eyes, I looked through the small porthole window and could glimpse first light in the morning sky. I staggered to my feet and out of the cabin.

"Fastnet Rock will soon be upon us. To your stations," continued the orders.

In the distance I saw the emerging dark mound of Fastnet with the spire of the lighthouse silhouetted against the slowly lightening sky. When I glimpsed over the surrounding waters, I noticed the sails of a score other boats beating their way along the same bearing as we were. Several were well in front of us, and a mass of them were trailing. It had become a very strange adventure, but I permitted myself the comforting thought, that, all told, we were doing not too badly in this race.

Within twenty minutes, the mass of Fastnet Rock was looming off the starboard bow. Following the Captain's commands, we tacked several times as we approached and then swung around it. Standing on the lookout deck of the lighthouse was a race signalman. He waved his flags at us and the Captain signaled back.

Ten minutes later, we had changed course a full one hundred and eighty degrees and were headed back on a southeast bearing and across the Celtic Deep. I relaxed and determined to enjoy this most unusual adventure on the sea.

That was not to be.

"Thank you, mates. Well done. Now, back into the cabin," said the Captain.

That was just a bit too much.

"Look here," I said. "There is no reason we cannot stay on deck. It is not as if we can run away."

On my right ear I felt something cold. I turned my head and found myself peering down the barrel of a revolver.

"The captain said, get back into the cabin," said Senator Tom. "Was there some part of the command you failed to understand, doctor?"

I became an obedient if unwilling sailor and shuffled my way back down the staircase. The door of the cabin was closed behind us and I heard a clunking sound coming from the far side of it. I spun around and attempted to open the door, only to find that while the handle turned the door was fast in place. It had been barred somehow from the other side. We had become captives, imprisoned below deck.

"So," said Miss Moly. "Would you blokes like some breakfast? If those old blighters up there dare ask for anything, I'm declaring a mutiny."

We laughed and cheered her on and soon were enjoying a hearty English breakfast, making fun of our increasingly hungry captors above us. I imagined that they would soon be opening up and demanding their victuals.

They did no such thing. An hour passed, and then another. There was no change in our direction or speed.

"Where are we?" I asked of anyone who might have had a better idea than I did.

"We're moving quickly, at about eight to ten knots an hour," said Molly. "We're on a beam reach and if the prevailing winds stay constant, we won't have to tack until we round Lands End. They won't need us on deck until this evening."

I resigned myself to spending what would have been a splendid day in the sunshine confined to a stuffy cabin and filled the time by writing the story of this adventure in my mind. The morning, mid-day, and the afternoon all passed. We chatted with each other from time to time but for the most part remained silent.

Somewhere close to six in the evening, Victor spoke up.

"They must not be hungry," he said.

"Nor need to use the head," added Miss Molly. "Or else they're fouling the ocean."

We offered a few forced chuckles and returned to the doldrums.

As the sun was setting, I had expected the breeze to die down. Instead it was stiffening and the yacht was heeled over more than it had been all day. Molly walked over to the starboard porthole and peered out.

"Oh, ****," I don't like the looks of what's coming our way."

I got up off of my bunk and took a look. The sky to the south had darkened and the shadows of rain falling in the distance were scattered across the southern horizon.

"We're in for a walloper," said Molly. "They're going to need us on board."

Another half hour passed and the wind was now howling around the cabin. The Captain must have been in a hurry to get to a port and then make a run for it in order to escape the Pinkertons for, as far as I could tell, he had not let out the mainsail and we were now heeled over at a racing angle.

Miss Molly looked out again from the porthole window.

"They're daft. It all lightning out there and it's coming our way."

She walked over to the door and started banging on it.

"You! Out there! You're in a storm. Don't be daft. Open the door and let us out. We're not going to run away!"

There was no response.

She banged harder and shouted louder, but still received no answer.

"I have not been paying attention," said Holmes, "but I do not recall hearing a sound from up above us for at least the past several hours. Either they are sitting in one place silently or they have abandoned ship."

"Bloody, hell," shouted the girl. "Then break down the door, or this thing's going over and we're going down!"

In turn, Victor, Holmes, and I all tried pounding our shoulders against the door, but the position of the doorway in the cabin made it impossible to take a run at it. Try as we might, it did not budge.

"I fear," said Holmes, "that they have barred it securely on the other side. Equipping it in that manner would come in handy when imprisoning kidnapped victims."

He had no sooner spoken these words that we felt the boat heel over sharply to the port side. For a terrible few seconds I held my breath, certain that we were about to roll over. As we righted ourselves a flash of lightning lit up the porthole and the entire boat shook.

"We must find a way out of here," said Holmes. "Is there any tool we can use to unfasten the door hinges?"

This led to a mad scramble as we looked for anything resembling a screwdriver, but to no avail.

I looked over at the porthole. The window covering it was secured with bolts and butterfly nuts. We might be able to unfasten them but the hole was hardly more than sixteen inches across and there was no way we could squeeze through it.

A quiet voice beside me spoke up. "I can get through there."

"Good heavens, child," I exclaimed. "We're not sending you out there to climb up the side of the cabin in the midst of a storm. You'll be blown away."

"No I won't. I'll tie a line onto me and you can pull me back if you have to. Just loosen the clamps and help me get through."

I looked at the other two men and we shrugged and then nodded. I turned to Molly and was somewhat shocked to see that she had dropped her dress on the floor and was standing in the middle of the cabin in just her corset and underwear, busily fastening a bowline around her slender body.

"You're a doctor, right?" she said, looking at me.

"I am."

"Well then you can put your hand on me arse and hold me in the air whilst I wiggle through."

Holmes had undone the fastenings and removed the window. Quick as a wink, Molly raised her hands above her head and extended them and then her head through the narrow opening. I lifted her lithe body in the air. She could not have weighed more than ninety pounds. With one hand on her spine and the other on her posterior, I lifted and shoved while she wriggled.

We were making good progress when a wave suddenly slammed against the side of the boat. Water rushed past her body and into the cabin. I could hear her choking and sputtering, followed by some rather dreadful curses and oaths that were quite unseemly for a girl of her age. I pushed and she wriggled some more and then I felt her body start to move on its own.

"I've got the edge of the deck!" she shouted.

Soon her legs and feet disappeared through the hole and we moved quickly to fasten the window back in place before another wave poured in.

A minute later we heard metallic sounds against the door of the cabin and it swung open.

"There's no one out here. The dinghy's gone," she yelled. In truth, those were not her exact words. What was actually uttered gave evidence of her having spent far too much of her youth in the company of sailors.

The three of us hastened out of the cabin and up onto the deck. The sky was dark and the wind was screaming like a banshee. Rain was falling sideways but the temperature, thankfully, had not dropped more than a few degrees. Victor immediately let out the main sail and the boat righted itself. Holmes and I did likewise to the Yankee and the foresail. Molly had taken over the helm and once I cleated my line in place I walked back to her."

"Any idea where we are?" I asked.

"Not the foggiest."

We sailed on in the dark for several more minutes and then I felt a small hand clasping on to my arm.

"Doctor John," she whispered. "Can you hear that?"

"What?'

"Listen."

Chapter Eight
Into the Storm

I did and I heard a distinct sound that did not seem to be too far in front of us. I looked at our young helmsman.

"What is it?"

"It's breakers. There's rocks or shoreline or shoals or something directly in front of us."

An extended flash of lightning revealed the disaster we were rushing towards. Molly quickly looked back behind us and to both port and starboard.

"Jesus, Mary and Joseph! We're in the middle of the Lizard shoals." And again she added a few choice words that I have not recorded.

"All of you," she shouted. "Tie a line around your body in case you get washed overboard. We're going over the shoal," she shouted. "And get out on the rail and hike for all you're worth. I'll tip her up on her side and get the keel as far away from the rocks as I can. Haul your sails in hard when I yell."

We instinctively obeyed, found a line, tied one end around our chests and fastened the other end to the base of the mast. Then we hustled to mid-ship, fastened our feet under the hiking strap, and leaned back. The cutter was on a close reach as we headed toward towards the surf breaking over the shoal. I was not sure what Molly was waiting for but suddenly she screamed at us.

"Now! Haul in! Hike!"

As we pulled tight on the lines and hauled the sails in as far as we could, the boat quickly turned so that it was on a beam reach at right angles to the powerful wind. We heeled over, and then heeled some more, and more yet, until I was sure that we were about to turn turtle. I felt a swell lift the boat and carry us into the shoal. On either side of the boat I saw surf emerging as the base of the large wave was breaking up against the rocks below us.

There was a moment when my heart stopped and the boat shuddered. The keel had struck rock and the entire craft was shaking as we touched one, and then another and then another. But we kept moving. It seemed like and eternity but then the bouncing ceased and we were back in open water.

"Right. Let out," came the command from the helm.

We did and the boat came back to a more or less upright position. Again, I clamped my Yankee sail in place and made my way over to Molly at the helm.

"Fine sailing, Captain."

"We're not through yet."

I looked ahead but in the darkness could see nothing. Then another flash of lightning lit up a wall of rock that appeared to extend several hundred feet to starboard.

"There's dark water on the port side," cried Molly. "We have to jibe. Pull in the sails. Hard! Now, and get ready to duck."

I started to run back to my post. Molly swung the boat to the port and the wind caught the back of the mainsail and whipped it around from one side to the other. I ducked but not fast enough or far enough. The boom crashed against the back of my head and sent me sprawling to the deck.

I think that perhaps I was knocked out for a second or two but quickly came to my senses and felt for the back of my head. I could tell that a goose egg would soon be emerging and I forced myself to count to ten backwards and recite the Lord's Prayer. Good. There was no serious damage and I now moved over to join Holmes and Victor on the port rail.

"There's more rocks ahead," our captain shouted. "But there's open sea to the south. Hold on. We're going directly into the waves."

On the ocean, in the dark, it is difficult to estimate the height of a wave as it approaches you. Perhaps experienced sailors have their ways of doing this task but I did not. I assumed that we would simply be rising and falling as if we were on a carriage and galloping through some rolling terrain. The next thing I knew I was struck by a wall of water and doing backward somersaults with water on all sides of me. I felt my ankles strike the rail and then I was upside down falling headfirst into the ocean. I had enough sense to reach for the line I had attached to my chest and start pulling. My first three pulls encountered no resistance. My line was slack. In a second of passing terror, I thought I had broken free of the mast and was adrift. But then it went taut and I began to pull myself hand over hand up toward the surface. A few seconds later I felt a sharp tug on my line and could feel myself being pulled powerfully forward. My head broke the surface of the water and I gasped for air. In the darkness I could see the form of Holmes standing at the edge of the deck and reeling me in.

When I arrived at the side of the boat two sets of hands reached down and grasped my arms and lifted me back on board.

"Really, my dear doctor," said Holmes. "You already went for a swim on Thursday last. Must you do so again?"

Both of us wanted to spare a moment and have a chuckle together but our young captain again shouted at us.

"Back to your posts. We're not done yet."

And true, we were not. For the next ten minutes we slid up one side of a massive wave, crested, and then sped down the other side into the trough. Once we were well away from the rocks and shoals, we swung to the port.

"Any port in a storm. We can sail direct to Coverjack. It's not far," said Captain Molly.

None of us answered her, having no idea whether Coverjack was a good idea or not.

"But it should be clear all the way now to Plymouth," she said. Then paused, and added,

"Are you up for it? Shall we finish the race?"

We gave her a rousing cheer of "Aye, Captain."

"Right then, mates. You can let the sails out. We should be able to run free from here."

We opened the sails and soon we were racing over the great waves with the wind at our back. It was an exhilarating few hours in the middle of the night. And then it stopped. The storm had blown past us and clear skies were coming up from the south along with the first light. The wind dropped and once again we sailed with a light summer breeze.

I looked out over the open water to see if I could see any other yachts. There were none in front of us, but off to the west I noticed a few near the horizon, the morning sun now lighting up their sails.

"I say, Holmes, it looks as if we might be in the lead."

"A pleasant thought, but highly improbable. There were at least a dozen craft ahead of us as we rounded Fastnet."

We set a bearing of fifty-five degrees and cruised towards the finish line some sixty miles in front of us.

We had been on a dead run for about half an hour when I spotted something far out in the water in front of us.

"Molly," I said. "Is that a rock out there? Or is it a marker? That round white object straight ahead."

She strained her eyes and looked intently for a minute.

"It the hull of a boat. Upside down. One of the yachts has flipped over. If there are any sailors in the water we have to go and rescue them. We're the closest boat. It's the law of the sea."

She had us trim the sails and we slowed down. As we got closer we could see several hands waving at us. We were still moving at a good speed and I feared we would run over top of them with no chance to haul them on board.

"We'll have to sail past and come back," said Molly and that is exactly what we attempted to do. There were six men in the water, all clinging to the keel and rudder of their yacht. We exchanged shouts as we neared them and confirmed that all of them were safe and accounted for. Once well past, we came completely about and sailed toward them, close hauled and sailing as close to the wind as our cutter could manage. Once we were almost on top of them, Molly turned the helm quickly and threw us into irons. Holmes, Victor and I had lines in hand ready to heave to the chaps in the water, but the wind was blowing us away from the swamped boat too quickly.

"We'll have to do it again," said Molly. With that, we turned around and sailed away, turned again and sailed back. This time, however, she went about ten yards past the boat, close to its stern, before taking us into irons. Now we drifted backwards toward the overturned vessel. We would have no trouble getting the men out of the water.

"My dear," I whispered to Molly, "I think you might want to run down into the cabin and pull your clothes back on."

She first looked shocked and let loose with one or two more choice words and then laughed and hopped down the staircase.

One by one we lifted in the soaking wet sailors. The waters of the North Atlantic are never warm, even in the middle of summer, and half of the fellows were shivering. But soon we had blankets wrapped around them and they were thanking us profusely. The entire rescue had taken no more than forty-five minutes, but during that time another six yachts passed us on their way to Plymouth. Each of them signaled asking if we needed help. We signaled back that we were fine and they sailed on.

"Gentlemen," said one of the fellows we had rescued, "I am Jeremy Middleton, Marquess of Elderbury, and captain of the formerly wonderful yacht, the *Luck of the Irish*. I reckoned that we were at least half an hour out in first place. We should have trimmed our sails more in the storm but we were a bit too eager for the prize and over we went. We do thank you for your kind assistance."

He then looked more closely at us.

"There's only three of you? That is amazing. Who is the captain?"

"In the cabin," said Holmes. "Up in a minute."

A minute later, Molly emerged from the cabin, fully clothed and with her hair more or less back in place.

"Captain Jeremy," said Holmes. "Allow me to introduce

you to Captain Molly Snow of Cowes. One of the finest ever to sail the seven seas."

Victor and I were trying very hard not to laugh at the look of utter bewilderment on Jeremy Middleton's face. He looked at Molly and then at us but we kept our poker faces and gazed placidly out over the sea.

"I say, Captain Molly," said Holmes. "Will you dead reckon us back to Plymouth? Another three hours, what say?"

"Aye, but back to your stations, sailors. I'm sure that these Irish fellows will give you a hand."

And so they did. We chatted amiably with the members of the other crew. I overheard one of them ask Victor how we had done so well in the race. He shrugged his shoulders and with feigned nonchalance said, "Well, you know, if you sail through the shoals rather than around them you can save a great deal of time."

The other chap looked at him in total disbelief.

"But that's impossible!" he sputtered.

Victor turned his head away ever so slightly and looked up into the clouds. "Oh, not really. Not when you have the captain we have."

I bit my tongue and looked at Holmes. He gave me a smile and a wink.

One of their crew was quite a young lad, no more than twenty by the looks of him. He was tall, athletic, and aristocratically handsome. He managed to find a seat directly behind the helm and was soon chatting to our amazing captain.

Chapter Nine
Return to Safe Harbor

By early afternoon, the lighthouse on the Rame Head, the entrance marker for Plymouth Harbor, had come into sight. We rounded it and headed north to our final destination. As we entered the harbor I saw hundreds of people standing on the piers, all waving ribbons and handkerchiefs and cheering us on. Molly steered us to the mooring buoy, we dropped the sails, and a boat from the harbor staff lashed the Indefatigable securely into place. We descended the rope ladder and were taken over to the pier.

Waiting for us were seven men and not one of them looking at all happy.

"Stop where you are!" commanded the smallest one of them. I recognized him immediately. He was a slight chap with a narrow ferret-like face and beady eyes. He held up a badge.

"Inspector Lestrade, Scotland Yard." Behind him stood three English constables in uniform and behind them the three Pinkertons I had last seen on the dock at Cowes on Sunday morning.

The Inspector turned to the Pinkertons.

"Are these the men you are after?"

"I beg your pardon," said Jeremy Middleton. "Just what do you think is going on here? My crew and I are all men of noble birth and these fine people and this remarkable young lady are the heroes who have not only rescued us but who have successfully completed the Great Fastnet Race."

There is no creature on earth more capable of righteous indignation than a still damp English lord who has recently come close both to victory and drowning. The inspector backed away. The Pinkertons looked us all over carefully.

"Where did the other ones go?" asked one of them.

"What other ones?" snapped Lord Jeremy.

"The four guys who were on this boat when it left Cowes?"

"Oh, those chaps," said Holmes with an air of practiced indifference. "They complained of being sea-sick, or perhaps it was just sick of the sea, so we let them off back a ways."

"Where?"

"Ireland. Yes, I do believe it was Ireland. You might try going there to look for them."

At this point, the inspector recognized Holmes and sputtered his surprise.

"Sherlock Holmes! What in the name of all that is holy were you doing on that boat?"

"Manning the jib sheet."

With that, Holmes sauntered on past them and we followed Jeremy up to the judges' stand.

"Congratulations Indefatigable!" shouted one of the officials.

"Why, thank you sir," said Victor, nodding humbly. "But all we did was what any yacht is expected to do and we came to the rescue of our fellow sailors. There is no need for congratulations. Any other boat would have done the same thing."

"Good heavens, man," said the official. "We're not congratulating you for helping the other boat. We're congratulating you because you won the race."

"That cannot be," said Victor. "At least a dozen boats passed us before we entered the Sound."

"They passed you, sir, because you had stopped to perform a rescue. They are gentlemen, sir, and they have duly reported your act and confirmed that you would easily have won have you not stopped. Not one of them would dream of claiming a prize that rightfully belongs to you. So, well done. Please give the desk the full names of the crew."

For a moment we stood, speechless. Victor, having been raised to be a gentleman, quickly recovered his composure and answered.

"Mr. Sherlock Holmes of London, Doctor John Watson, also of London. I am Victor Emanuel Trentacost of Donnithorpe, and this is Miss Molly Snow of Cowes."

"I assume that Miss Snow was your cook."

"That is correct."

"And which of you chaps is the captain?"

"Miss Snow is our captain"

I will leave it to the reader's imagination to contemplate the next few minutes whilst each of us, backed up by Jeremy and his crew, swore that Miss Molly Snow was indeed both cook and captain of the victorious yacht. The General Manager of Blackfriars then presented us with our cash prizes and bestowed on each of us a case of Plymouth Gin. When handing Molly her case, he somewhat arrogantly inquired if she was old enough to partake of alcoholic spirits. I did not hear what she said in reply but it evinced a look of utter shock on the face of the manager.

We were feted and praised and treated to a fine dinner. Victor graciously stood in for our captain and agreed to address the assembled crowd. Molly had begged off in desperate fear and trembling at the thought of having to give a speech. Throughout the evening, however, I noticed that she continued to attract the attention of the young man from the rescued boat.

The festivities of the evening having finally ended, we were put up in the select Duke of Cornwall Hotel. The staff took our clothes and promised to have them all laundered and pressed by morning. The four members of our intrepid crew, clad in bathrobes, slouched into easy chairs in our suite. Miss

Molly was nearly hidden in the large chair beside me, wrapped in a bathrobe that was clearly many sizes too large for her tiny body.

"You appear, my dear," I said, "to have landed yourself a rather large fish today. Quite a catch, I must say."

She blushed furiously. "Oh, Doctor John. His name is Reginald Barclay and he's asked me to come and visit his family on their estate in Sussex. I'm scared stiff."

"My dear, you will be just fine. Make friends with the butler and the head maid and they'll look after you."

"I'll have to mind my Ps and Qs."

"Molly, if you can just manage to mind your ..." And then I let loose with seven of the most forbidden curse words in the English tongue, none of which are ever uttered in polite society and all of which I had heard slip from her pretty young lips over the past forty-eight hours.

"Oh," she blushed again. "Yes. I must try to do that. Gosh and golly."

The next day we boarded a train to Portsmouth and from there took the ferry back to the inn in Cowes to fetch our belongings. The village, so packed and festive just a few days ago was now nearly empty. The sailboats had all departed and the late afternoon sun shone down on the nearly empty bay.

Holmes and I sat out on the porch enjoying tea, which Miss Molly had graciously brought to us. We exchanged a few pleasantries with her and chatted about our recent adventure.

Victor soon appeared. I looked at him and was

immediately concerned. His eyes were reddened, as if he had been crying. In his hands were several sheets of paper and an envelope.

Chapter Ten
The Past is Prologue

"Here. You may as well read this. I've read it. And you may as well keep it too. I don't think I will ever need to read it again."

He deposited the letter on the table in front of us and walked away. Holmes read it and handed each page to me as soon as he had finished. The postmark was stamped CORK, and it read:

```
My dearest son:
    I have long feared that the day would
come when my son, whom I have loved more
than life, learned about my shameful past
```

and that your ways and mine would have to part. I did not expect it to come so suddenly upon me and I and my partners-in-crime are grudgingly grateful to your friend, Sherlock Holmes, for giving us the warning we needed to escape the gallows.

Lord willing, we will be able to meet again in the not-too-distant future, but perhaps not.

I regret having had to abandon ship but knew that it would be best if you did not know where we launched the dinghy in making our escape. I knew that you, and especially Sherlock Holmes, would realize that there was no one left on deck and be clever enough to send the young cook through the window to open the door and sail to the nearest port.

My motley crew will now escape back to America, or possibly Shanghai, or perhaps Buenos Aires. We planned for this day and have deposits in many banks around the world. You need not be concerned for our material well-being.

You are also well provided for. The title to my property in Norfolk is in your name. The rents will provide a comfortable enough income for a gentleman.

There is something else I must confess to you, Victor.

I am not your father.

I took over the responsibility of caring for you and raising you on what was the worst day of my life. As you now know from your friend, Sherlock, we pirated up and down the east coast of America, boarding yachts and kidnapping wealthy members of the sailing crowd, taking care not to harm them, and quickly collecting the ransom. It all went well until one day when a brave but foolish man fired his revolver directly at us. Instinctively, I fired two shots back in his direction to warm him to stop and surrender. As terrible fate would have it, one of the shots struck him and the other your mother. Both died on the deck in front of their two-year-old son.

I did the only thing I could do before God and my conscience, and took you from the boat and adopted you as my son. We then sunk your family's yacht, a sight you also observed and remembered only in your nightmares. Before doing so, I removed all documents that pertained to your family and the boat. As soon as we returned to Boston, and before your family had been declared missing, I went immediately to your home and robbed it. I took no valuables, only all the documents I could find that identified you. These are all locked away in the safe in my office. The key is taped to the bottom of the center drawer.

Seven years after your family disappeared, you were all declared dead and the ownership of your father's estate and his extensive assets passed to your uncle. He is a very wealthy man but entirely honorable. If you present yourself to him, I am sure that he will not only transfer your inheritance to you but will be joyful beyond words to know that you are alive. Your physical resemblance to your father, his older brother, is exceptional.

I understand and accept that you may wish to vanquish me from your life, knowing what you now know. My prayers will be with you until I die.

Your name is not Victor Emanuel Trentacost. It is Charles Cabot Gardner III.

May God bless you, my son.

[This letter has been kept in the files of Sherlock Holmes, undisturbed for the past thirty years. He retrieved it for me so that it could be included completely and accurately in this account. J.H.W.]

Epilogue

17 April 1912. Ten o'clock in the morning.

Having completed our reminiscences, Holmes, Mary, and I raised a cup of tea to the memory of a thoroughly decent and admirable man, Victor Emmanuel Trentacost, and then retired to the porch and enjoyed what had become a lovely April morning, a sad but, in a way, a *glorious* morning.

"You did," I said, "keep in contact with Victor regularly, did you not?"

"I did," said Holmes.

"Did he ever say anything about our time at sea and the Captain who raised him as a son?"

"Yes, he did, and I have honored his request for secrecy. He kept the name he had grown up with and five years after our race to Fastnet, his father contacted him and they re-established some sort of friendship. He forgave his father and they kept exchanging letters and meeting every few years after that, until the old captain passed away."

"Where did they all go after Fastnet?"

"To New York, where they resumed being pirates."

"I beg your pardon!"

"Legally, of course, which is to say they became bankers. They pooled their funds and opened a private bank. And then they took out large and expensive policies with the insurance companies who had been hunting them down and signed up scores of their wealthy clients for life insurance with those same companies. As you might expect, having become far more valuable alive than dead, the bounty on their heads quietly disappeared."

"Holmes," I said. "At times you can be awfully cynical. There is, however, one more question I simply have to ask."

"Then ask."

"Whatever happened to Molly Snow? Is she running an inn in Cowes and tossing beer all over unruly sailors?"

Holmes smiled. "I believe the person you are referring to is now known as Lady Reginald Barclay and the first woman to serve as a governor of the Royal Thames Yacht Club. She is quite the famous regatta captain, and rather well-known for her scandalous language after several rounds of Plymouth Gin."

Did you enjoy this story? Are there ways it could have been better? Please help the author and future readers by posting a constructive review on the site where you bought your book. Thank you.

Historical and Other Notes

According to The Canon, as recorded in *His Last Bow*, Sherlock Holmes spent considerable time from 1912 through early 1914 in Chicago and Buffalo, infiltrating a network of German spies. He returned to England prior to the outbreak of The Great War so that he could bring down the espionage efforts of Baron Von Bork.

From 1882 to 1890, Arthur Conan Doyle lived at 1 Bush Villa, Elm Grove, Southsea, Portsmouth, and established his first independent medical practice. It was while living there that Doyle created the character of Sherlock Holmes and wrote the first two stories about our beloved detective. Since, in this story, Holmes and Watson have to travel to Portsmouth, it seemed fitting that they should stay in the same place.

The Sailors' Home described in this story was opened around 1850 and in 1855 received a Royal Charter. It has continued from that time until the present as the Royal Maritime Club. It is now a lovely historical hotel and no longer reserved for sailors.

The Cowes Week regattas date back to 1826 and, except for years during the wars, they have continued to be held annually. To this day, they attract hundreds of boats and thousands of participants and spectators. It is one of the great events of the yachting world.

The Fastnet Race did not actually start until 1925. The

course is as described in the story and it is famous for being one of the most demanding and dangerous of the world's great sailing races. The race in this story is a fictional proto-type of the Fastnet.

The south coast of Cornwall is well know as "the graveyard of ships" and the shoals, reefs, sandbars, and currents have claimed many ships and lives over the past eight hundred years.

A "cutter" was a popular design of sailboat in the past and a few are still sailed today. It has a large mainsail and two forward sails, with the "Yankee" sail affixed to a bowsprit, whereas a sloop has only one forward sail or jib. Edits from those readers who know more about sailing than I do are welcomed.

The story is a tribute to *The Gloria Scott*, with a nod to *The Pirates of Penzance*.

A Most Grave Ritual

A New Sherlock Holmes Mystery

Chapter One
What the Dickens?

Charles Dickens is, in my humble opinion as I am no scholar, the finest novelist of our age. As a school boy, I daydreamed away the lazy, vacant hours of summer looking out over the North Sea with one of Mr. Dickens's books in my lap. My mind disappeared into the endless stories of crimes, passions, adventures, tragedies, courage, revenge, retribution, and, of course, the thousand or more uniquely individual characters. When he died in 1870, while I was taking my medical studies, I felt as if I had lost a friend.

In the years since his passing, I read and re-read his stories in the barracks of the Afghan campaign, where my comrades-in-arms would pass around dog-eared copies of *Nicholas*, or *Martin*, or *Bleak House*. More than once I saw tears streaming down the face of a battle-hardened foot-soldier of the BEF who one would have thought had a heart of stone. He would be holding *The Old Curiosity Shop* in his hand, and I knew that Little Nell had just died.

Now, more than a decade later, I keep my collection of Dickens on my bookshelves along with my other favorite authors. The books are not as neatly lined up or ordered as perhaps they should be, given that I am a medical man. But it matters not. They are my old friends, and I know where they all are resting. If one should, perchance, wander away, he cannot go far before being found again.

You may wonder why I bring Charles Dickens to your attention. I have no choice. He played a leading role in this case—a case filled with murder, greed, fraud, deception, foolishness and a cast of unusual characters—and had it not been for Mr. Dickens, the villains might have triumphed.

Sherlock Holmes and I, as my readers know, are in many ways no more alike than chalk and cheese. Although my books and papers are kept decently and in order, our rooms in Baker Street are strewn with Holmes's chaotic piles of papers, files, reports, and oversize envelopes. On the floor beside his bedside table is a two-foot tower of police reports. On the mantel, immediately above the Persian slipper than holds his tobacco, are files of past cases. Beside his chair by the hearth is where *The Times* is filed, and London's less reputable newspapers, of which there is a multitude, find their way to the floor of the WC, leading me to contemplate the obvious alternative use to which they should be put. Such was the detritus of Holmes's reading habits, and I was quite certain that a respected novel had not crossed his path since his school days.

These cluttered surroundings are where we found ourselves on a cold, dark evening in late November of 1885. It was that time of year when the sun sets before four o'clock in the afternoon and by five the street lamps had been lit. We had finished our supper, and I was enjoying the last few pages of *Oliver Twist* whilst Holmes was reading a police file on the latest murder of yet another school teacher.

I laid *Oliver* down and sat in silence for several minutes before engaging my friend in conversation.

"A penny for your thoughts, Holmes."

He glanced ever so slightly in my direction. "If you were Scotland Yard, the fee would be a pound. But as you are my friend, then a penny will have to do. Your glancing around the room, eyeing my collected references and sources with a clear mark of disapproval, reminds me that perhaps it is time I re-organized my files. I try to do so on average at least once a year."

"We have been sharing rooms, Holmes, now for four years. To date, you have engaged in such a virtuous act precisely once. If you were to do so again, now, then the best average you could claim would be once every *two* years."

Holmes shrugged and casually lit a cigarette. "Very well, since it is a lost cause, I shan't bother until the mean reaches once every three years. So, my friend, kindly remind me again in two years' time."

He smiled back at me, and I shook my head in playful defeat.

"But do tell, Watson, since it is my turn to ask, what profitable thoughts were you having after yet another re-reading of your dear *Oliver Twist*?"

He looked as if he were sincerely asking the question, and so I offered my considered reply.

"I was wondering about what indications a man, or a woman for that matter but it usually a man, gives to another man that leads that man to believe that the fellow can or cannot be trusted."

Holmes gave me a look of mild condescension.

"My dear, Watson, that is not a question that should arise from reading Dickens."

"And why not?"

"Because the answers are all found in Dickens."

I was befuddled. "You have me in a fog on that one."

"Please, my friend, stop and think about all those characters in Dickens whom you knew, within a paragraph or two of encountering them, to be trustworthy men of good character. Think of Mr. Brownlow, Bob Cratchit, Sydney Carton, Nicholas Nickleby, the Cheeryble brothers, Mr. Micawber ... there is a score of them who leap to mind. Every one of them is immediately described in such a way—their mannerisms, their speech, their attire, their offhand small actions, the way they treat drivers and the help, the furnishings of their homes, the way they look at another person, the way they conduct themselves in the presence of a woman ... need I go on?—that the reader knows immediately whether or not they are to be trusted.

"Now, consider the villains. Bring to mind Fagin, Mr. Bumble, or Bill Sykes, of whom you have just been reading, or Mr. Gradgrind, Madame Defarge, Mr. Vholes the lawyer, Daniel Quilp, Mr. Smallweed and his lawyer Josiah Tulkinghorn. For that matter, almost any lawyer. Now bring to mind all the ways in which villains are described by Dickens. Their multitude of actions gives them away. You do not need to be told that they are not to be trusted. Dickens lets you know that.

"Wait a moment," Holmes continued, and he walked over to my well-tended bookcase and pulled down *David Copperfield*. He thumbed through the pages quickly until he found his spot. "If I remember correctly ... ah ha! Here it is. Listen to this: this has to be one of his best. The man our young hero has just met is ...

"a red-haired person—a youth of fifteen, as I take it now, but looking much older—whose hair was cropped as close as the closest stubble; who had hardly any eyebrows, and no eyelashes, and eyes of a red-brown, so unsheltered and unshaded, that I remember wondering how he went to sleep. He was high-shouldered and bony; dressed in decent black, with a white wisp of a neck cloth; buttoned up to the throat; and had a long, lank, skeleton hand, which particularly attracted my attention, as he stood at the pony's head, rubbing his chin with it, and looking up at us in the chaise. He had a way of writhing when he wanted to express enthusiasm, which was very ugly."

And down went *David Copperfield* unceremoniously upon the coffee table in front of me.

"Could anyone possibly trust Uriah Heep after such a description? Of course not. What Dickens does with his characters is precisely the same as I do every time I meet a man. I observe his smallest details, and they always give me the answer, immediately, as to whether or not a man can be trusted. And I freely confess my debt to Charles Dickens, from whom I learned so much.

"So, there, my friend, you see why the question you asked, having read Dickens, is nonsense. The answer to it is contained a hundred times in his pages."

He gave me a forced, triumphal grin, lit another cigarette, and picked up the file he had been reading. But a moment later, he turned back to me, this time with an unfeigned smile.

"I fear I was inconsiderate in the way I responded to you, my dear doctor. Everything I said you already know, but you know it all implicitly from your reading and your extensive experience dealing with men in the forces and in your medical practice. The only difference is that I know these things explicitly and have consciously incorporated them into my science of deduction.

"And, my friend, within the half hour, both of us are going to be called upon to make use of what we have learned from Mr. Dickens and judge two men who will be coming to see me. I have met neither, although I some background knowledge of one of them. Your assessment of their character would be most welcome."

My feelings, which had been smarting from the earlier rebuke, were somewhat mollified and I smiled back.

"Happy to assist in whatever way I can, if you truly believe that I am capable of it."

I admit that I was fishing for a kind word and Holmes did not disappoint.

"Excellent, my good doctor. Your insights would be helpful, and I am depending on you."

"Very well, Holmes. Then you should start by telling me what you know about them."

Chapter Two
Enter the Royal Ghost

I poured out a couple of brandies for us while Holmes lit yet another cigarette.

"Do you recall," he began, "that two yeas ago I recounted to you one of my earliest cases? I took it on shortly after leaving my studies and whilst I was living over on Montague Street by the Museum. It was the case related to the Musgrave family in Sussex."

"Ah yes," I replied, "I remember your account of it. It was immediately after you took your pistol to our wall, was it not? The case involved the solving of an ancient riddle. Some sort of 'one if by land, two if by sea; what walk on four legs in the morning; and wait until the sun is over the yardarm.' Something like that?"

Holmes smiled at my feeble attempt at wit and nodded. "Yes. Something like that, precisely. It appears that the chickens have come home to roost, for now the much wealthier side of that ancient family is facing difficulties and have been sent, on the recommendation of Reginald Musgrave, to seek my services. Do you know anything, Watson, about the family? And no need to be clever."

"I know that they are reputed to have more money than the Almighty Himself; to have a vast estate in East Hastings and large interests in firms in Great Britain, America, Europe, and the colonies. Beyond that, not much. Oh yes, I read somewhere that their old ancestral home is haunted by the headless ghost of Charles the First."

Holmes chuckled, "Right on all counts. They trace their lineage back to William the Conqueror. The family name back then was Monsgrieu which, over the years has been corrupted to its present form. One of their forefathers did well enough to build a castle at Herstmonsgrieu, as it was then. Now, of course, we know it as Herstmonceux. They were fiercely loyal royalists, supporting King Charles until his demise and paying heavily for their allegiance once Cromwell came to power. Several of them spent time in prison, but with the Restoration they were not only restored but rewarded and have not looked back. As to the ghost of the king, that story is the stuff of legend. You may recall from your school classes in history that in 1648 Charles was imprisoned in Hampton Court. He escaped and made a mad dash to Southampton, hoping to flee to Europe. That much is historical. The apocryphal part of the story claims that he took a very large portion of the Royal Treasury with him and stopped at Herstmonceux, where he believed he could trust whatever aristocrat was stationed there. Together they hid the gold and jewels and then the king went on to Southampton.

"Of course, the poor fellow never made it to Europe. His trusted friend in Southampton locked him up and then returned him to London and the rest, of course, we all know."

"What then," I asked, "happened to the treasure?"

"That is what no one knows. Legend says that it is still hidden somewhere on the property and that the ghost of the king may be seen riding around, *sans* his head, looking for his money. But since the family has more money than they will ever need, they treat the story as entertainment. However, it has come back, you might say, to haunt them. Did you read the account in the press about the recent death of William Musgrave?"

"I did. Very strange, it was. Said that he and his son were in the family graveyard when, according to the son, he suddenly died whilst the lad was searching a crypt. And the word going around was that the boy killed his father."

"Exactly, Watson. And it is that boy who is on his way to meet me, seeking my help to exonerate him."

"Is he coming alone?"

"No, his uncle, of whom I know nothing, will be with him. They should arrive any minute now and whilst I converse with them I hope that you might apply your insights from Mr. Dickens and take their measure."

He picked up the file, sat in his chair beside our bay window, and resumed reading. I retrieved my recently abused copy of *David Copperfield* and searched for the passages that introduced Barkis, Murdstone, Steerforth, the Peggottys, Mr. Micawber and Uriah Heep.

A half hour passed before the bell from Baker Street sounded, and subsequently Mrs. Hudson entered the room.

"A Mr. Rochester Musgrave and a Mr. Shaw Musgrave to see you, Mr. Holmes. Shall I show them in?"

"Yes," said Holmes, "kindly do so, Mrs. Hudson."

The footsteps I heard climbing the stairs were quick and energetic. The first man to enter our sitting room was about my height and weight, but I would say perhaps a decade or more older, possibly in his early fifties. He was fashionably dressed and, upon entering, casually removed his hat and placed it along with his gloves on our side table beside the door. His face, now clearly visible was handsome, bearing a trim gray-flecked mustache and framed by a full head of silver-on-its-way-to-white hair. He took a quick look over the room and strode immediately to Holmes. Upon reaching him, he extended his hand and bowed his head slightly.

"Ah, Mr. Sherlock Holmes," he said, "so very kind of you to see us on short notice and such a miserable, winter evening. And you, sir," he said turning to me, "must be Dr. John Watson. I have read several of your stories, and I must say, sir, you have a gift for entrapment of a reader's imagination. Do keep them coming, doctor."

He had turned and approached me, again giving something between a bow and a nod and extending his hand in greeting.

"Permit me to introduce, myself," he continued. His baritone voice was quiet, but his enunciation of each and every syllable was clear and distinct. "I am Rochester Musgrave, and this is my nephew, Shaw Musgrave."

My attention now turned to the young man who had stopped just inside our door. He was as tall as Holmes and as thin. My first instinct was to walk over, grab him by the hand and lead him to a chair for he looked dreadfully ill at ease. His young, flushed face was attractive, and he was required to shave it, I would guess, no more than once a week. He had neither hat nor gloves and had already shifted his hands from his pockets, to clasped in front of him, to behind him, and back to his pockets. He did not walk over to greet either Holmes or me but simply uttered, "Hello," and walked over to the sofa and sat down. His eyes glanced quickly at Holmes and then at me, and then at another dozen objects in the room. I took it upon myself to try to help the poor fellow relax and walked over to him, extending my hand and smiling.

"Good evening, young man," I said. "Welcome to our home. I can see that you are under a good deal of stress, and I can assure you that you have come to the right place to assuage it."

He took my hand briefly, giving what in the armed forces we used to call a 'dead fish handshake.' He quickly withdrew his hand and did not look up at me.

I returned to my chair and Holmes, as was his habit, took charge of the conversation.

"Gentlemen, I know only what I have read in the press regarding your situation. So I must ask you to fully introduce yourselves to my colleague and me and to state your case. If I can be of assistance, I will inform you. If not, then I will not waste your time. Pray proceed, and Mr. Rochester Musgrave, perhaps you could start since my data concerning you are nil. So, please sir. The floor is yours."

He gestured to the older gentleman, who in return nodded graciously and cleared his throat.

"Yes, well, of course, I can do that, Mr. Holmes. Now then, where should I begin?"

"With who you are and your relationship to Mr. Shaw Musgrave. Are you his uncle? The brother of his father?"

"Yes, yes. Well, no. In point of fact, our connection is somewhat more distant. My grandfather and Master Shaw's great-grandfather were brothers. So I think that makes us third cousins, or is it fourth? It matters not. The family is not large or spread out. Each generation had only a few children, which was to be expected since we are of the Church of England and not Catholics. But we have remained close and since childhood, Master Shaw's father, William, or Billy as he preferred to be called, and I were very close. Like brothers to each other, yes, I suppose you could say that, since neither of us had any other brother we became like brothers, yes. That is how I have come to see Master Shaw as my nephew and he to know me as Uncle Rochester, or Uncle Rock, as it has come to be."

"And when," asked Holmes, "did that come to be? Did you live in close proximity to him as he was growing up? Did you live on the estate?"

"Yes, yes. Well, no, actually. I confess that the life on a country estate was not to my taste, nor was too much school for that matter. So whilst still a young man I decided to make my own way in the world and became the wayward black sheep of the family and joined the theater. That has been my calling for these past thirty-five yeas, but I kept coming back to Sussex and have always regarded it as my home. So, yes, I did live on the estate at times but, no, not all the time."

"I see. Please continue."

"I assume, Mr. Holmes, that you are aware of the difficulties the family went through with regards to Mrs. Melody Musgrave, my nephew's mother. It is a rather delicate and painful subject, and I do not wish to dwell on it at any length. My nephew is already under more than sufficient stress and grief, and I do not wish to add to it by dragging out that unfortunate incident in his past."

"You are referring," said Holmes, "to Mrs. Musgrave's flagrant and shameful affair with another man, the abandoning of her husband and family, and her subsequent divorce and re-marriage, I assume."

Holmes at times was utterly tactless, and I cringed at his blunt comment. I saw a flash of anger as well cross the face of young Shaw Musgrave as Holmes spoke. Rochester Musgrave simply nodded placidly and responded.

"Yes, yes. That was it. And no, that is not entirely correct. Melody Musgrave did not abandon both of her children, only one, my nephew here, Shaw. She took his brother with her, and they have had no communication between them for nearly ten years. It has been a source of constant pain to the heart of my nephew. And, I must add, to his father, my cousin, William Musgrave. May his soul rest in peace, as I hope it will now that he no longer has to endure the memories of that humiliating and tragic event."

"As he is now dead," said Holmes, "that hope would appear to be achieved. Please continue and kindly tell me what you know about his death."

Here the fellow stopped for several seconds and drew a deep breath and let it out slowly.

"Forgive me, Mr. Holmes. As a detective, you are faced with terrible tragedies all the time. My nephew and I are not. He has been dealing with overwhelming grief from the loss of his father, to whom he was very close, and added to that the horrible rumors, questions, and accusations that are being bandied about. He is doing his best to bear up, brave young man that he is. It has affected me in much the same way, but, as you can see, I am far from a callow young lad and the scars of years gone by have given me a bit tougher hide. I trust you can understand, sir."

"Indeed we can. Now, what can you tell me about William Musgrave and his death?"

"Yes, yes, of course. Very well, sir. My cousin, Billy, as he was to me and his friends, never fully recovered from the dissolution of his marriage and the tearing apart of his family. He was still as sharp as a tack in his business dealings and he continued to prosper in that way, but his mind, his soul perhaps I should say, was crushed. He was in so many ways a broken man. He filled his life with all sorts of short-lived pursuits, anything to take his attention away for a while. If it was not pheasant shooting it was fly fishing; if not that then sailing. He joined the Theosophists and after finding them too other-worldly, he helped found the Fabians."

Here I involuntarily interrupted. "The Fabians! But they're a troop of socialists. He was one of the wealthiest men in England. How could he possibly be a socialist?"

Holmes smiled in his condescending way and responded quietly. "Elementary, my dear Watson. All the leading socialists are men of considerable wealth. If they did not have income from their rents and dividends how could they possibly afford to spend every working day romping around the country demanding that the poor be provided for out of the public purse?

"Pray continue, Mr. Musgrave," he then said.

"Yes, yes. Not sure what else I can say. This is difficult for me as well, sir. Billy Musgrave was, like I said, sir, a brother to me, and I still cannot believe that he is gone." He stopped speaking and took out his handkerchief and held it briefly to his eyes.

"You have," said Holmes, "already covered your relationship to the deceased. Please explain what you know of his death. Were you present at the time?"

"Yes, yes. Well, actually no, not really present. I was in the manor house, in the library. It was late in the afternoon. The sun had already set as it does this time of year. I had the lamps lit and was reading. And then Master Shaw comes charging in all terribly upset and shouting that his father is lying dead outside. I rushed immediately to the site where Billy was lying."

"You went immediately? How did you know where to go?"

"Yes, well not actually immediately. Master Shaw was in a terrible state, and I had to settle him down first, then I took his arm, and he led me to the place. That is what happened, sir. It was a very trying time for me as well, Mr. Holmes. I hope you appreciate that. Recalling it is troubling and I may be getting some of the details mixed up."

"You are doing quite well, Mr. Musgrave. Permit me now to ask your nephew some questions concerning his account. Master Shaw, could you please tell me what happened and, if I am to assist you in proving your innocence, you will have to be entirely candid and forthcoming regardless of how difficult it may be."

The young man gave Holmes a dark and hostile look. His voice had a taint of a snarl as he responded.

"I find it offensive, Mr. Holmes, that you would think I would be anything other than candid."

"If I am to take your case on, young man, you will most likely be offended several more times before I conclude my investigations. Now, kindly get on with your account."

Shaw Musgrave glowered back at Holmes, and then looked toward the window and drew a deep breath.

"I ... I am a devoted scholar and reader. My home has a very large and reputable library, one of the finest in the south of the country. I spend a great deal of my time there reading and studying."

Here he stopped and clenched his fists. Then he placed his elbows on his knees and dropped his head into his hands.

"My nephew...," said Rochester Shaw, but Holmes cut him off.

"Your nephew, sir, is perfectly capable of giving his own account. Now then, young man, what has your attraction to old books to do with the death of your father?"

Shaw Musgrave raised his head. His eyes were tinged with red. He took another deep breath and continued.

"This fall, I have been working my way through a section of the library. I was perusing the shelf numbered one hundred and two when I chanced to come across a very old book. I looked at it and opened it. Inside, on the fly leaf, was a message. It revealed the secret of the hiding place of the treasure of King Charles I."

Rochester Musgrave interrupted. "Allow me to explain ..."

"That will not be necessary," said Holmes, cutting him off. "I am familiar with the legend. Go on, Master Shaw."

"I thought it nonsense, but the message was signed by some ancestor of mine and underneath the name were the words 'written in my blood before they break down the doors and take me away to be hung.' Well, Mr. Holmes, I suppose that even a private detective like you who is bereft of any interest in scholarship would know to take such a note seriously, so I read the message. It gave quite clear directions to a location in the family graveyard. There was not much daylight left, and I now loathe myself for not waiting until morning, but my curiosity was burning within me. So, I took a torch and followed the path. It led to a mausoleum. There are several of them in the cemetery. The final line of the message told me to 'look under old Dacre.' The oldest name in the edifice was one of the Barons of Dacre, and it was carved into a stone that lay in the corner of the room. I pushed the stone away and discovered a staircase leading to an underground chamber. Again, my scholarly curiosity took the better of me, and I entered. In the room, I could see at least a score of large wooden chests, and I was overcome with the thought that I had discovered the treasure of the King, hidden for over three centuries. I dashed back up the staircase eager to alert my father but alas, as I was running out of the crypt, I tripped over something..."

Here he suddenly stopped speaking and again dropped his head into his hands. When he lifted it, his eyes had reddened further, and his fists were clenched until his fingers were white. His voice disappeared to a halting whisper.

"It was the body of my father."

He closed his eyes and said nothing more for a full minute. I started to stand up out of my chair to get him a glass of water or brandy, but Holmes held up his hand in silence to bid me halt. I did so and another full minute passed before the lad opened his eyes and began to speak again.

"I had dropped the torch when I tripped, and it was now nearly extinguished, but I could tell that it was he. His face was contorted in frightful terror. The body was still warm, but his breathing and his heart had stopped. For some time I shouted at him and slapped his face, desperate to bring him back. Then I held his head to my chest and sobbed. I was beside myself. I cannot say how long I stayed in that position, but I finally stood up and returned to the house, where I came upon Uncle Rochester and told him what had happened. We took two more torches and returned to the graveyard. That was when I saw the message that my father had carved into the dirt beside him. It was not terribly legible, but it clearly read, 'the ghost.' Uncle Rochester can vouch for what I have said as he saw it as well."

"Yes, yes. That I did," said the Uncle.

"Where," demanded Holmes, "is this book?"

The young man said nothing but opened his satchel and extracted a small leather-bound volume. He held it out in his hand but not did not rise from his chair. Holmes did not stand up to walk over and fetch it and the lad, with a brief sneer and a shrug, tossed it across the room. Holmes caught it and handed it over to me. It was a slim volume bearing the title *Bellamira, or The Mistress,* by Charles Sedley. I remembered it from my school days as one of the earliest of the Restoration Comedies, howbeit one we were not, as schoolboys, permitted to read owing to its infamous and licentious contents.

"Who then," asked Holmes, "called the police or a doctor?"

"Yes, I looked after that," said Rochester Musgrave. "Poor young Shaw was beside himself, and I summoned Sinden, the butler, and a groom and had them harness one of the faster horses to a dogcart and run off into the village. The estate is a ways out of the village, and it took just over an hour for them to return. Both a doctor and the local constable came."

"And what did they accomplish?"

"Yes, yes. Well, the doctor pronounced Mr. William Musgrave dead, as you might expect, Mr. Holmes."

"What cause was recorded?"

"He put it down to heart failure. He said it was common in men of his age who had a habit of eating too much rich food and never getting adequate exercise. So, heart failure it was, sir."

"And the constable, what did he report?"

"Yes, the constable. Well, you see, Mr. Holmes, not much exciting ever happens in a small village and having the richest man in the county dropping dead and scrawling a message about a ghost, well, sir, you can imagine that our village constable was quite exercised by what he had observed. So he gave an order that no one was to leave the premises and that he was going to call in Scotland Yard. So he must have done that, yes, since a chap from London appeared the next morning."

"Who?"

"An Inspector Lestrade."

"And what did he say?"

"I assume you know the man sir, and even if he might be a friend of yours, I must say that he was most disagreeable."

"Why do you say that?"

"It was plain to all that my nephew was beside himself with grief. He did not sleep the entire night and in the morning he was not capable of enduring questions from a police inspector. But that did not stop that Lestrade chap, no sir. He made it right clear that he suspected that Shaw had murdered his father. He accused him of killing him so that he could gain the inheritance immediately. He is the sole heir according to the will and the inspector said, terribly unfairly I must say, that my nephew could not wait another twenty or thirty years to get his money and wanted it all now."

"Has he been charged?" asked Holmes.

"No, no. Not officially. But he may as well have been. Inspector Lestrade must have slipped a note to the press and by the next day a dozen of those miserable louts from Fleet Street were crawling all over the property, knocking on every door, and peering in every window. I had to threaten to let the dogs out if they would not withdraw beyond the gate. But by the following day, you must have seen it, Mr. Holmes, the story was in all the papers with all fingers being pointed at my nephew and scorn heaped upon the final message of Billy Musgrave regarding the ghost. Poor Shaw was accused of having written that himself. And Mr. William Musgrave suddenly became a great hero of the common man, seeing as how he was an ardent socialist, and the papers were stating, as if it were holy writ, that he had intended to give away his fortune to the poor and the Fabian cause and that his son had must have murdered him to make sure that could never happen."

"And had that," asked Holmes, "been William Musgrave's intent?"

"The answer to that question depends on who you ask, Mr. Holmes. There are some local socialists who claim that Billy showed them his new will with those instructions included in it, but no one else has seen such a document. None of his staff or family could locate it, and a search of his records showed no sign."

"And why are you seeking my assistance?"

"Yes, yes, well, Mr. Holmes. Two parties recommended that to us. You did some work a few years back for another member of the family, Reginald Musgrave of Hurlstone. He lives about thirty miles from us and, as news travels quickly, he was there by the next day giving his consolations and his advice, and the first and foremost piece of his advice was that we needed to contact Mr. Sherlock Holmes straight away. He spoke most highly of you and gave us your address, Mr. Holmes, and so here we are."

"Who was the second?"

"Inspector Lestrade. It came second hand from the constable. He said that Lestrade said that this case was passing strange, what with ghosts and mysterious secret books and crypts and all that, so he would just as soon as have you go prowling amongst the tombs as he. So he said we were to call on you."

Holmes could not resist a smug smile. "Of course, if you engage my services and not the Yard, then he knows to whom I must send my bill."

Holmes sat up straight and placed his hands on his knees

as one does when about to stand up, but he stopped before doing so.

"Oh, one item I forget to ask about. Young man, if I may call you that, what were you doing during the three hours prior to coming to my door?"

The lad looked taken aback but quickly responded, "We were on the train to Victoria Station and then on our way here."

"Do not lie to me, young man," snapped Holmes. "You have an LBSC train ticket in your pocket, and I can see from here that you took the one o'clock train out of Eastbourne. It arrives at Victoria at a quarter past four. You knocked on my door at seven o'clock. Now, where were you? If you cannot tell me the truth, then kindly leave this room and do not return."

Holmes's rebuke was followed by an awkward moment of silence, but then Rochester Musgrave let out a sigh and took on a smile of chagrin. "I can answer that, Mr. Holmes, as it is embarrassing for my nephew. I felt that an hour or two of, shall we say, 'comfort measures' would be in order to help remove some of his stress and we spent some time and some money at the Princess of Prussia over in the East End. I assume that I do not have to say any more, sir, and I know that our confession will not leave this room."

Holmes gave both of them a hard look and then said, "It will not, and I will take on your case. Three days from now I will visit your estate in Sussex and shall arrive at noon. Please be waiting for me."

On that note, we all rose and the latest clients of Sherlock Holmes departed from 221B Baker Street.

"Very well, Watson," said Holmes after they were gone. "Your Dickensian deductions, please."

I had expected as much and not wanting to be the victim of his disdain, I collected my thoughts.

"The older chap seems a decent sort. Nothing to raise any suspicions. Not afraid to look you in the eye. Quite comfortable and self-assured but not putting on airs. Seems like a decent Englishman."

"At first blush, I would agree," said Holmes. "Now, the nephew. What of him?"

"Hard to decide if he is arrogant, angry, fearful, or just plain nasty. Bit of a weasel, if you ask me. And very high strung. Dickens might say he was as nervous as a drunkard desperate for his glass of wine."

"Yes, he might say that," agreed Holmes. "Or, if I were to borrow a line from the American writer, Mr. Twain, he was as nervous as a long-tailed cat in a room full of rocking chairs."

I laughed at the image and agreed that it was rather fitting.

"Being ill at ease," Holmes continued, "does not necessarily equate with not to be trusted. But do you think, Watson, that I was too quick in agreeing to take the case?"

"Oh, come, come, Holmes. What with vast fortunes, inheritances at risk, affairs of the heart and bitter divorces in the past, ancient secrets in mysterious books, dead bodies at the entrance to a crypt, and murderous ghosts of decapitated kings, you know perfectly well you could not resist it."

This time, he laughed. "My dear doctor, I fear you have come to know me all too well. Then let us have another glass of brandy to welcome this most promising case."

I poured us each a nightcap. He sipped at his whilst poring over the old book that our client had left behind. I watched him as his eyes slowly widened and his face took on an intense glare. He quickly reached inside his jacket for his magnifying glass and began to scrutinize the front matter pages. Suddenly he stood up from his chair and walked to the back section of our main room where he kept his chemicals. Inwardly I groaned, fully expecting that my nose and lungs were once more to be assaulted by noxious fumes and my eyes made to water.

"Kindly relax, my friend," he said, once again reading my mind. "There will be no odors or vapors."

"Then what, Holmes, are you going to do?"

"Your medical bag is beside you on the floor. Might I bother you for the use of your surgical scissors? I am certain I have another pair somewhere, but yours are the closest at hand."

I did as requested and brought them, remaining behind him in order to observe what he could possibly be doing. He took the shears and rapidly cut out a portion of the front flyleaf page.

"Good heavens, Holmes," I gasped. "That is an ancient book from a private collection. You cannot just go destroying it like that?"

"Is that what it is, Watson? I would not have known. And would you mind terribly handing me the glass-stopped bottle the fourth from the left on the counter? Yes, that's the one. Thank you, my friend."

"Holmes, what are you doing?"

"The very same thing I was doing the day you first met me, my friend. You will recall how excited I was to have finally, by painstaking trial and error, discovered a test for confirming the presence of blood at a crime scene."

"I do."

"Well then, I am about to test my reagent on this message which purports to have been written in blood. A drop on the sample followed by warming it over the alcohol lamp should tell me in a few seconds."

He proceeded to carefully place a drop from the bottle on the sample cut from the page and spread it out over a section of the writing. Then, holding it gently in a pair of tongs, he waved it slowly over the flame. I watched, spellbound, as the clear-colored liquid turned distinctly red.

"Ah ha!" he exulted. "Yes. It proves that this message telling the reader where to find the treasure was indeed written in blood."

"So the book is authentic," I said. "Well done, Holmes."

"No, my dear doctor. It is not authentic at all. It is utterly fraudulent."

This I found highly confusing.

"Holmes, you have just proved that the message that claims to have been written in blood was done so. How can you say it was fraudulent?"

"Elementary chemistry, my good man. This test will detect the presence of blood freshly left at the scene of a crime, or on the clothes of a criminal. It is valid with fresh blood, for blood discovered a day or two later, and reasonably reliable for up to a fortnight. Some traces may still be evident for even a month. But nothing, nothing whatsoever will be evident after two hundred years. Two hundred years, Watson. Utterly impossible, but here it is."

"So this note," said I, "was written recently. Is that it?"

"Within the past two weeks, three at the most. Now then, use the glass and look carefully at the page after the title page, where our publishers today place their copyright notice. What do you see?"

I looked.

"There is no notice of copyright page."

"Correct. Such pages were not used during the 1600s and so would not be present in a much older volume. Now look carefully at the very inside edge of the pages. What do you observe?"

Using the glass, I carefully examined the line where the page of the title page joined the spine.

"There is just the trace of a page of paper, as if it has been cut very closely with a fine razor."

"Thank you, doctor. This book is no more than fifty years old. Some water damage has been inflicted on it and them most likely it was set to dry out in an oven so that the pages would be uneven and mottled. But I would wager that it was purchased from an antiquarian book dealer on Cecil Street within the past month, adulterated as required and placed on the shelf in the Musgrave library exactly where our client was bound to find it."

"Your case," I observed, "is becoming curiouser and curiouser."

He had begun to rub his hands together in eager anticipation.

"It has indeed. And so, my friend, tomorrow and Wednesday, whilst you are at your medical practice, I shall gather such data as I can and then on Wednesday afternoon I shall make my way down to Sussex. I do hope you will be able to accompany me."

"Headless ghosts could not keep me back."

"Splendid, and kindly bring your service revolver with you."

Chapter Three
The Data of the Case

At three o'clock on the Wednesday afternoon, I met Holmes on the platform of Victoria Station. The ride down to Sussex was a pleasant one, through small farms, grand estates, and the stretch of forest south of Crawley. Holmes was carrying a valise that I assumed was stuffed with his 'data' and I brought along a copy of Dickens's collected ghost stories, which I considered quite condign for this adventure.

For the first hour, while daylight permitted, both of us read in silence. It being the final days of November, the sun set early and soon we were compelled to lay down our reading materials. I took advantage of the situation to engage my friend in conversation.

"Very well, Holmes. Yet another penny for your thoughts. What were you able to discover?"

He offered a quick, forced smiled and leaned back in his chair.

"I made quite successful visits to both Scotland Yard and *The Times* to inspect their files, to the Doctors' Commons to review past wills of the Musgrave family, and to the West End theater district."

The first three made sense; the last one not at all.

"The theaters?" I asked. "What was their possible connection?"

"You may recall, my friend, that in the first story you wrote concerning my investigations, the long and overly dramatic one you called *A Study in Scarlet,* that in your generous but exaggerated way you told your readers that the stage lost a fine actor when I became a specialist in crime."

"I do indeed recall that."

"That was very kind of you even if well beyond the bounds of accuracy but there was a short period of time when, as a young man, I turned my mind to strutting and fretting my hour upon the stage. Doing so bequeathed to me a very valuable knowledge of theatrical makeup and disguises as well as a few friendly acquaintances with whom I keep in contact from time to time. Like all actors, these chaps are excessively dramatic in their behavior and interests both on and off the stage and are quite thrilled when I ask them to assist in what appears to be a nefarious and juicy criminal case, as our present one most certainly is. They are all the more eager when I swear them to secrecy, knowing full well that they will not allow an hour to pass after our conversation before rushing to discuss the matter, in strictest confidence, of course, with the first colleague they encounter. And so, since our Uncle Rochester claimed to have spent the past three decades working in the theater, I sought to verify his account and get that item off my list of matters to be confirmed."

"Really, Holmes. I would have thought you considered him rather trustworthy, given our Dickensian tests for proof of character."

"He did indeed, but I have learned to follow the advice given recently by an American chap in Chicago who succinctly reminded us to "Trust, but cut the cards." And so I asked my acquaintances if they knew of this fellow and if his account was factual."

"Yes, and what did they say?"

"They confirmed that his claims were entirely truthful. He never made it as far as the leading theaters of the West End, but played many roles in some of the better theaters in the Midlands and the North."

I was tempted to remind Holmes that he would, under usual circumstances, deem the phrase 'better theatres in the Midlands and the North' to be a contradiction of terms given that he was convinced that all evidence of intelligent life vanished once an Englishman travelled north of Cambridge; however I held my tongue and continued to listen.

"Mr. Rochester Musgrave has played many leading and principal roles of characters young and old, rich and poor, hero and villain in Shakespeare, Marlowe, the rare Ben Jonson, Congreve, Sheridan, adaptations of your friend

Charles Dickens, and most recently that Bulwer-Lytton chap whose stories are even more sensational than yours, if that were possible."

I ignored the barb and let Holmes carry on.

"They made some passing comments about the way he lived. He had rich tastes, as they say, and always treated himself to excellent food and wine, a good night's sleep in a select hotel or at least what passes for select in the Midlands and the North. His attire was always stylish and of good quality, as were his shoes. He never boarded a train without booking a first-class cabin. His personal expenses always exceeded his modest income from the theater, but he appeared to have other sources of money from rather high-risk investments in tea gardens in the colonies."

"And his connection to your client?" I asked.

"As claimed. He is the scion of another line of the family, descending from his grandfather, who was the younger brother of the eldest son. Comfortably provided for, but the bulk of the Musgrave fortune came down through the older brother who was older by a matter of mere seconds."

"Ah, they were twins?"

"Precisely, Watson. And like Jacob and Esau of old, the second emerged grasping the heel of the first, or the metaphorical equivalent."

"And is the fortune as vast as reputed?"

"As much as or more so. Upon the death of his father, young Shaw Musgrave became one of the dozen or so wealthiest men in England. It is not without reason that

Scotland Yard is highly suspicious and that the press have accused him without a shred of evidence; not that such a problem has ever impeded either of those two parties."

"And the father? Billy the rich socialist? What do we know of him?"

"He had been a stalwart land-owner, father of two young boys, a respected Tory, and minor lord. That ended seven years ago when his wife up and left him claiming that one cannot help whom one falls in love with and that she had fallen for another man. The divorce was acrimonious, and she took the younger of the two boys with her, and there has been no communication at all between them since that time other than through their barristers and solicitors. I did not bother to secure any more information about her since she appears to have been totally removed from the family, the estate, and all for Sussex for that matter, since then."

"And what of his death? What did the police reports have to say?"

"Officially the cause was given as heart failure. Lord Billy had neglected his health for several years, had added considerably to his weight, placed no tax at all on his legs, arms, heart or lungs, and consumed copious amounts of gin. That he could have fallen over dead at any place and at any time was considered a distinct possibility."

"Did you speak to Lestrade?"

"No, but I suspect he is feeling quite smug having tossed me a bone, that being a very rich client who needs to have his name cleared by a thorough investigation, which Lestrade is either too lazy, or too busy to do himself."

"And where do we start?"

"Tomorrow we visit the estate and do a full inspection of the premises, including the library, the graveyard, and the crypt. I expect that it will be quite fascinating."

We descended the train at Polegate, just north of Eastbourne, and hired a driver to take us to the village of Herstmonceux. He let us off an hour later just east of the village at the Horseshoe Inn, a small local inn, attempting a Tudor atmosphere, with a reputation for excellent breast of duck. As it was well into the evening by the time we arrived, we enjoyed our supper, chatted more about the case and all the questions Holmes needed to ask our clients, and then went off to sleep.

The next morning we reassembled in the dining room and waited for the arrival of our full English breakfast. The large plates loaded with 'fry-up' had just been placed in front of us when Holmes glanced toward the doorway of the dining room.

"Uh oh, what have we here?" he said.

I turned and saw, entering the room, the familiar weak-chinned face of Inspector Lestrade, accompanied by a local constable. Lesstrade's eyes darted around the room and settled on Sherlock Holmes. As he made his way toward our table, I stuffed as much of my breakfast into my mouth as possible, fearing that it was likely all that I might get to eat of it.

"Well, well, well," said Lestrade as he arrived at our table. "If it isn't our beloved detective-for-hire, Mr. Sherlock Holmes. I trust you are grateful, Holmes, for my sending you such a rich client. Wouldn't want an amateur detective to go hungry, would we? Now, being a professional detective, I could guess why I am finding you in this forgotten corner of Sussex on a Thursday morning in November, but why don't you spare me the mental effort and tell me."

He sat down as he spoke and indicated to the constable to do likewise.

"Of course, Inspector Lestrade," said Holmes with a forced smile, and then he proceeded to slowly load up his fork with a mixture of black pudding and egg and lift it to his mouth. He chewed it thoroughly before swallowing and followed it up with a sip of coffee.

"I am visiting my client," he said and turned his attention back to his plate. Before ingesting another forkful, he smiled again at Lestrade and returned the question.

"And for what reason, my dear Inspector, do I find you here, given that you had elected not to investigate this case yourself but had directed Master Shaw Musgrave to seek my services instead?"

"I am here on account of one of my staff having come hammering on the door of my house at four o'clock this morning and telling me I had to get down to Sussex. Yet another strange death has taken place in the graveyard of Herstmonceux. That's what brings me here, Mr. Holmes."

Holmes swallowed quickly and laid down his fork. "And who, might I bother you to ask, had died?"

"Some young lad named Master Shaw Musgrave. I believe that was the name of your client, was it not, Holmes? So terribly sorry that your fee now appears to be uncollectible.

Seeing as I get paid by Her Majesty no matter what, I will not think any the less of you if you take the next train back to London and wait for a better case to show up at your door."

Holmes retained his cool demeanor, but I could tell just looking at him that he was inwardly in turmoil. Nevertheless, he politely posed a question to Lestrade.

"Would you mind telling me what happened?"

"Not at all, seeing as how I do not know very much yet. Haven't been over to look at him. Just got in here off the train myself, found the constable and came looking for breakfast and a place to stay the night. So, very well, Holmes, all games between us aside, this looks very suspicious, and I would invite your participation as you do seem to have a bent for these types of cases."

He pulled his chair into the table and again motioned for the constable to do likewise and then he called over to the serving staff for two breakfasts. Relieved, I relaxed my pace and began to enjoy my bacon and fried bread.

"What little I know," Lestrade went on, "is that he was seen in the early hours of the morning, hanging by a rope from a limb of an oak tree in the cemetery. One of the grounds staff, on his way home from the pub, spotted him and came running for Constable Duncan here. Now it's a mile from the estate back into the village, and the chap is no great runner but he finds the constable, and they hitch up a dogcart and return. The constable takes a look and sets the groundskeeper as a watchman and hurries back to the village and sends a wire off to Scotland Yard. Then he returns to the place and looks around, careful not to disturb anything. On the ground,

263

held down by a stone, just underneath the swaying feet is a note. What we all call a 'suicide note' of course. And here it is."

He handed over a dirty piece of paper to Holmes, who read it and handed it on to me. It was written in a masculine hand and ran:

"My beloved father is gone. My fiancée has thrown me over. I am falsely accused of murder. My name will be shamed for the rest of my life. Death is my only choice."

It was signed by Shavington Wentworth Brewster Musgrave.

"Eat up," commanded Lestrade. "We will get down to the estate before the crowd of onlookers grows too large."

Chapter Four
A Body of Evidence

Lestrade spoke too soon. By the time we reached the small graveyard at All Saints Church, adjacent to the manor house, there must have been sixty people standing along the low stone wall. Several of the estate staff, on instructions from Constable Duncan, had kept the crowd back and tried to preserve the site as untrammeled as possible. As we entered the gate, Holmes asked if we would wait for several minutes whilst he did an inspection of the grounds.

"All right, Holmes, but be quick about it," said Lestrade. "We need to get him down and out of here before we have the whole village looking on."

Holmes moved much more quickly than he usually did and looked over the ground in the immediate vicinity of the oak tree. Ten minutes later he gestured to us to join him.

"You may undo the rope and let him down. Perhaps we can take him into the church hall if the rector does not object."

"If we give him a choice," said Lestrade, "between his sanctuary and his hall, I am sure he will not object to the hall."

The rope with which Shaw Musgrave had hung himself had been tied by one end to the trunk of the large, old tree. A small ladder was leaning against the trunk, permitting him to climb onto one of the lower, spreading branches and, carrying the rope, walk out until he was several yards away from the trunk and a good twenty feet above the ground. From there it was merely a matter of slipping the rope around his neck and stepping off. The fall and the immediate snap would likely have broken the neck and made the death relatively quick and painless.

The constable and a groundskeeper carefully untied the rope from the tree and, letting it out, lowered the body to the ground. Two more of the staff, who had apparently been organized by the diligent constable, brought out a stretcher and a sheet, lifted the body, covered it, and bore it to the door of the church hall. We followed and the crowd, seeing as they had witnessed as much as they were going to, began to disperse, chatting amongst themselves as they did so. As the only medical man present, it fell to me to examine the body and determine, for official purposes, the cause of death.

During my service in the Afghan Campaign, I had

examined countless bodies of young men. I was used to it, but it did not make the tragedy any the less when called upon to discern what events had been the immediate cause of the ending of a young life. Shaw Musgrave had only recently turned twenty years of age. Three days ago he had sat in front of me, arrogant and under duress perhaps, but with an entire life ahead of him without a single worry for money or life's necessities. Now, as the sheet was removed from his body, I was again looking at him but this time with a contorted and discolored face and a body that had soiled itself whilst hanging for several hours.

Over the next twenty minutes, I examined the deceased and scribbled in my notebook whilst doing so. When I had completed the sad task, I handed my notes to Sherlock Holmes. He read them over quickly and turned to Inspector Lestrade.

"Inspector," he said, "this man was murdered."

Lestrade slowly folded his arms across his chest and sighed. "I was afraid that is what you would say, Holmes. Very well, then, present your argument."

"It is rather elementary, Inspector. I shall begin with the scene of the death and ask that my colleague convey the evidence from the body. The hanging was staged for dramatic effect. Now, there are from time to time suicides who have a flair for the dramatic, but not many. The deceased lived in a country manor house in which there are, no doubt, numerous hunting rifles and pistols. Blowing his brains out would have been infinitely easier. On the path leading to the oak tree, I could readily discern the footprints of Constable Duncan's standard policeman's boots and well as the softer soles of the grounds keeper who first found Master Shaw. There was another set of prints that led from the gate of the cemetery to the tree, except that they were facing the gate and sharply indented at the back of the heel. On either side of those prints were two small furrows about shoulder width apart. The story they told was of one man walking backward whilst dragging another man. Although the ground around the base of the tree was bare and soft, the steps of the ladder were spotless, not a trace of dirt, as you would expect had a maid wiped it down and put it back in the closet after its last use. The rope was half an inch thick, and a fully constructed hangman's noose was fashioned at the end of it. Now, knowing how to tie a hangman's noose it no secret, but neither is it common knowledge, and it is not taught in the public schools to sons of wealthy landowners. I will now yield the floor to my colleague, Dr. Watson."

While Holmes was capable of speaking extempore, I was more comfortable relying on my notes and did so, reading from them.

"The first indication of foul play could be seen in the marks around the neck. The bruising indicated that the ligature used was of a thin to medium diameter, no more than a quarter of an inch. The rope found around the neck was of twice that diameter. As my colleague, Mr. Holmes, demonstrated several years back, bodies cease to show bruising not long after death. There were no bruises corresponding to the thicker rope. The rope had caused significant lacerations and abrasions to the skin, but there was no sign of any bleeding. Furthermore, the use of the heavy, knotted noose and the drop of over twenty feet corresponds to current practices in capital punishment where the force of the drop and the knot combine to snap a prisoner's neck so that he dies immediately and the gruesome spectacle of him kicking and twitching for several minutes, so beloved by the populace in previous centuries, is obviated. The deceased's neck, however, had not been broken. In addition, there are numerous deep scratches on the neck to each side of the Adam's apple, most likely made by the victim's fingernails as he struggled to pull the ligature away from his throat. From a medical point of view, Inspector, this man was dead, strangled, well before he was pulled up and hung from the tree."

The inspector nodded and turned to the constable.

"Constable Duncan," he said, "kindly note that Scotland Yard has concluded, with the support of noted pathologist Dr. John Watson and the consulting detective, Mr. Sherlock Holmes, that Mr. Shaw Musgrave, sadly and tragically, took his own life, and we extend our condolences to the family. You may release the suicide note to the press. I am sure they will be eager to print it."

I gasped in disbelief. In outrage, not pausing to care a fig how it would be received, I shouted, "Are you a complete imbecile, Lestrade? That would be a blatant falsehood and utterly irresponsible!"

My fists were clenched in anger and my muscles had tensed up like a coiled spring.

I expected a sharp reply from Lestrade, but instead he slowly turned to face me and gave me a forced, sweet smile.

"Perfect, Dr. Watson. Well done," he gloated. "But allow me to suggest that telling the public that we have concluded that the suicide was staged to cover up a murder might not be in our interests. If I were to make that statement, then just how far away do you think our murderer would be by morning? Calais? Amsterdam? Or within a fortnight? Moscow? Or maybe the other direction and all the way to Saskatchewan. Ah, no. Winter is coming, so perhaps Burma. What is your guess?

"*That* would truly be imbecilic," he continued. "So we shall allow our villain to think that he has fooled us and in doing so, he is most likely to remain right here under our noses. All we have to do is find him. I suspect that Mr. Sherlock Holmes would approve of my decision."

He looked directly at Holmes, who gave a quick, forced smile in return.

"Full marks on that one, Inspector. I agree."

"Thank you, Holmes," said Lestrade. "Now then, gentlemen, your consulting fee has vanished but, knowing you, I expect that you will want to continue your investigation all the same, and you have Scotland Yard's permission to do so. You have your methods; we have ours; the only difference is that ours are approved by Westminster and yours -- well, who knows what you will come up with next? My only demand is that you keep me informed. Will you agree to those terms, Holmes?"

Holmes nodded his agreement, and the inspector continued.

"Right. The other immediate problem is that with father

and son now both dead I shall have to find a magistrate to appoint a trustee to supervise the estate unless there are any immediate relatives that we can turn to."

The local constable spoke up. "There is a cousin, a Mr. Reginald Musgrave, who lives at Hurlstone. It is about thirty miles away, on the way to Brighton."

"I know this man," said Holmes. "He is a former classmate and a client of mine, and I can vouch for the probity of his character."

"What about," I said, "that uncle fellow, Rochester Musgrave? Isn't he living right here on the estate."

"He is, doctor," said Constable Duncan. "But I asked about him and the staff said that he had not been around since Tuesday. Gone to see some friends in Eastbourne. I've sent word through the police office there to tell him of what has happened and to come back here straight away. However, sir, he is a more distant relative than the chap in Hurlstone, so best we go with that one."

"Agreed," announced Lestrade. "That's what we will do. And Duncan, could you call the local funeral service and have them come for the body?"

"Their wagon is already waiting by the road," said the constable. "It's a small village, Inspector, and news travels quickly. Looking after the funeral of the richest lad in the county is a good piece of business. I'll let them know that they can come in now."

Chapter Five
Going By the Book

We rose and parted. Once we were back outside, I came up close to Holmes.

"Not surprised that you did not want to drop the case, Holmes. But, pray tell, what happens next?"

"We are already in the cemetery, I suggest that we look into the mysterious crypt."

"Do we know how to find it?"

"No, but I have the book with me, and I am fairly certain that if Master Shaw Musgrave could follow its instructions, so can we."

He pulled the copy of Sedley's *Bellamira* from his shoulder bag and opened the front cover.

"The first instruction," he said, "tells us to begin at the gate and walk uphill one hundred and fifty-three paces. That is easy enough."

We went to the gate of the graveyard and paced off along the central pathway. Those steps took us to the crest of the hill on which the cemetery had been set.

"Excellent," said Holmes. "Now, right for sixty-six."

That sent us along a row of stones and monuments that had been placed at the top of the hill. These were among the oldest of the markers in the graveyard. Some had broken off and been restored and, in passing I could see dates inscribed on them from the late seventeenth century.

"And now," Holmes, said, "walk around the old tree stump and then another twelve." He moved on as he spoke.

"And finally, ten to the left and three right."

We were standing dead in front of one of the several mausoleums, more like a small stone building. It was weathered, but the name of Dacre was clearly readable across the lintel.

"That was rather easy," I said.

"Yes, said Holmes. "Absurdly easy. Whoever wrote these directions did not want the reader to have any chance of not understanding them. I suspect that inside this edifice there is a grave marker to Baron Dacre, and if we lift the stone we shall find steps leading to a crypt. Shall we go?"

"It is," I observed with a smile, "broad daylight, so no ghosts are about. Lead on."

We entered the mausoleum and in the corner, as expected, was a flat stone marker bearing the inscription, *Thomas Lennard, Baron Dacre and Earl of Sussex. 13 May 1654 – 30 October 1715.*

"This is it," said Holmes. "And it appears to have been moved recently. Come, Watson, take the far end, and we can see what lies underneath."

The slab of granite measured about four feet by two feet and, while heavy, was not difficult to lift a few inches and then push to the side. Below was an open space and a steep set of stairs cut out of limestone.

"We'll need a torch," I said.

"Perhaps," said Holmes. "But the light from the morning sun is strong, and we can take a look around. We can return with a torch if necessary."

First, he descended the stairs and I followed. The room, if you could call it that, was cramped, not more than five feet in height and about ten feet square. Once my eyes had become accustomed to the darkness, I could see enough to make out about a dozen large wood and metal cases, each roughly the size of a steamer trunk, stacked up one on top of the other against the walls. Holmes hunched over and walked to the closest pile. He placed his hands on the nearest corners and gave a bit of a lift.

"This is not overly heavy, Watson. Come, give me a hand and we can lift it up the stairs and out."

It was awkward to move it in the cramped space, but it was not, as Holmes had noted, particularly heavy. Without too much effort we were able to lift and push it up the stairs and then carry it out into the open sunlight. Holmes bent over and examined it. He took out his handkerchief and dusted off the top. Though faded, the coat of arms of the King of England could be seen. The lion on the left, the unicorn on the right, and the lion perched on top of the crown were all easily discerned. Around the shield were the famous words, first uttered by King Edward III:

HONI SOIT QUI MAL Y PENSE

and on the scroll beneath the shield, the familiar

DIEU ET MON DROIT.

"This once belonged to the King," observed Holmes. "And, if I am not mistaken, it has been opened quite recently. So, let us see what the King left behind."

With little effort, he pulled back the latch and opened the top of the case.

It was completely empty.

"Ah, Watson, we did not discover a buried treasure. So, shall we try again? It was not too great a task to get that one out. What say, are you game to hoist the rest of them?"

I muttered my agreement and for the next hour we shuffled and pushed and hoisted until all of the cases were out of the crypt and sitting on the grass in the sunlight. Then, one by one, we opened them. Every last one of them was empty.

With the interiors being lit up by the mid-day sun, Holmes looked them over thoroughly.

"These have been empty for eons," he said. "The dust on the bottom has not been disturbed. Not a single diamond, or a sovereign. Not even a farthing. But what is this?"

He was looking closely at the inside of the top of one of the cases. I bent over behind him and read the words, scratched into the wood:

lector, si fortunae requires circumspice

"These words," I said, "are vaguely familiar. Where have I seen them before?"

"Good heavens, Watson, of course they are familiar. Except for one word they are the famous tribute to Christopher Wren in St. Paul's."

"Ah yes, 'Reader, if you seek his monument, look around.' Yes, of course. Except that 'monument' has been replaced by 'fortune' and it is in the genitive case. So it would be 'Reader, if you seek my fortune, look around.' Something like that, right, Holmes?"

"Exactly like that, Watson."

Holmes stood up and slowly looked around at the hills and forests, the old castle, and the great manor house that could all be seen from the top of the cemetery hill. A smile slowly formed on his face.

"So where," I asked, "is the King's fortune? What happened to it?"

"It is yet another piece of data," he said, "for which I have yet to formulate a comprehensive theory. That will just have to wait. So, come, Watson. Let us place these crates back in the building so that they are protected from the elements. Under some sort of law or regulation, such historical artifacts must be turned over to the Crown by way of a museum. So, no need to return them to the crypt. And then we shall look into the library."

The cases were moved back, and we next found ourselves in a large and very impressive library. The walls, every one of them lined with bookshelves, were at least twenty feet in height, and along them were leaned several ladders, each attached to a rail at the top and with a set of locking casters on the base.

"My word," I said. "There must be ten thousand books in here. What are you looking for, Holmes?"

"Bear with me, my friend, for a few minutes. This might not be as daunting a task as it looks."

He then walked around the room, stopping numerous times to pull a volume off a shelf and quickly looking inside it before replacing it. He worked his way around the room doing so and returned to me with a smile on his face.

"As I suspected. The only logical way to organize a library that has been collected over two centuries is chronologically. Each owner of the house, beginning with the First Earl of Sussex, added his books. He was followed by the next owner and the next. The earliest books are immediately to the right of the doorway, the latest to the left. The shelves are numbered accordingly. Do you recall at what shelf Master Shaw said he was reading when he came upon the book with the directions to the crypt?"

"The hundred and second."

"Yes, that was it. Thank you, Watson. That would indicate that our man was interested in more recent additions, those added during our current Queen's reign, perhaps. And therein is another reason to conclude that the volume of Restoration Comedies that he came upon was planted there with the intent that he find it. We, on the other hand, are looking for a volume left behind by a much earlier resident. And, as he was also the one to have built this house it is to be expected that it is among the earliest books placed on the shelves."

He turned to his right and began systematically to remove each book from its place on those shelves where the oldest volumes were held. He took a full minute with each book, turning the front and back sections over carefully before returning it to its place. I sensed that this search could go on for a long time and consequently turned left and looked for something more recently published with which to amuse myself. I was delighted to find the latest from Rider Haggard, *She*. I settled into a chair and was soon engrossed in the quest to find She-Who-Must-Be-Obeyed. Just as my characters were shipwrecked and in peril for their lives off the coast of Africa, I was rudely interrupted.

"Ah ha!" Holmes cried out. "Here it is."

"Here is what?"

"The volume in which the original instructions to the crypt are to be found."

He walked quickly over to where I was sitting and inconsiderately grabbed *She* from out my hands and replaced it with another book, this one much older—*The Pilgrim's Progress*.

"Our dear departed earl," said Holmes, "had a touch of irony. *The Pilgrim's Progress*, indeed. Now look on the front flyleaf of this book."

I did, written in an unsteady hand and in lettering that was of many years ago, I read the following:

> Dear Pilgrim, written in my blood, are the steps to the celestial city. Follow them faithfully to find your eternal fortune.
>
> Enter the Temple at Beautiful and to Zion go a step for each of the Miraculous Fishes caught upon the other side. Turn to the Sheep and Measure a step for each of the Books in the Bible. Here you will encounter Knowledge of Good and Evil. To the Sheep again by the Churches of Asia Minor; to the Goats by the Times around Jericho; Again to the Goats by the Years of the Tribulation, and Life shall be Behind you. Now move Forward by the Tribes and then to the Goats by the Cubits within the Sanctus Sanctorum in the Temple. Advance by the Trinity and Harrow Hell.

"Good heavens, Holmes," I exclaimed. "This is utterly obscure. I would have to find a biblical scholar to decipher it."

"Or," said he, "you could look in the first book that master Musgrave gave to us and find that someone had already deciphered it. And, in truth, Watson, it is not all that difficult if you will simply recall your Sunday School lessons. I assume you attended as a child."

"Of course, I did. But I have forgotten almost all of what I learned, haven't you?"

"Frankly, no, my dear doctor. Shall I decipher the code for you? It will not take more than a few minutes."

"Go ahead."

"Beautiful is a name given to one of the gates of the Temple, therefore start at the cemetery gate. Zion is the holy mount to which the children of Israel ascended in worship; therefore climb the hill. The miraculous draught of fishes brought in one hundred and fifty-three, the number of steps we took from the gate to the top of the hill. The sheep in Scripture are placed on the Lord's right, the goats on the left. Therefore turn right and walk sixty-six steps, one for each of the books in the Protestant Bible. There is a tree in the way, here referred to as the one of the Knowledge of Good and Evil and you are instructed to walk around it and return to your path. Seven to the right for the churches in Asia Minor as recorded in the Apocalypse, seven to the right for the number of days Joshua led the Children of Israel around the walls of Jericho, and seven again to the right for the years of the Great Tribulation. The Holiest of Holies is not, as you have placed it in your writings, in Westminster but in the Temple and it measured twenty cubits by twenty cubits. Are you following me?"

"Right. What's a cubit?"

"The distance of an average man's forearm, roughly a foot and a half. So two cubits is equivalent to about one yard.

And I trust you do not need any explanation of the Harrowing of Hell?"

"That would be the stairs down into the crypt."

"Precisely."

"Splendid, Holmes. And how does this help us find a murderer?"

"It gives us me more data."

"That's all?"

"For now, yes. The day, however, is over, and I suggest we return to the inn before the sun sets and have our tea and then our supper. Shall we go?"

One of the staff was requested to drive us back and, subject to being given a few shillings for his time, obliged. As we entered the Horseshoe Inn, the innkeeper caught us just beyond the door.

"Mr. Holmes and Dr. Watson. There is a gentleman waiting to see you. I will have our staff serve you your tea in the parlor if you wish me to."

"Please, do that," said Holmes. We entered the front sitting room where a fellow, whose family resemblance was unmistakable, was sitting. He rose and smiled at Holmes.

"Reginald!" said Holmes quite enthusiastically. "So good to see you again."

He strode over to the fellow, who I now was quite sure must be Reginald Musgrave from Hurlstone, Holmes's college classmate from two decades back. They shook hands happily, Holmes introduced me, and we sat down together.

"I would," said Holmes, "that we were meeting under less unhappy circumstances but nonetheless, it is nice to see you. It has been nearly a decade since that dreadful business with Brunton and the Welsh maid. Did you ever track her down?"

"We had some reports that she had run off to America, but with the Welsh, you can never be sure. She might be running a bookshop in Hay-on-Wye for all we know. And you Holmes, you are continuing to live by your wits and doing rather well, if I can judge by the stories I read about you."

"Indeed," said Holmes. "We have much to catch up on, but I fear that shall have to wait until a future date. At the moment I trust you will forgive me if I press you for anything you can tell me about these deaths, two now, in your family. And please accept my sincere condolences."

"Thank you, Sherlock. But truth be told, we had not been that close. It is only thirty miles, but we may as well have been the Smiths and the Johnsons. The main branch of the family, by which I mean those with the greatest part of the wealth by far, was here in Herstmonceux. We were even more estranged since Billy's divorce. He pursued his own life and business after that time and had very little to do with us."

"Did you," asked Holmes, "get to know his son very well?"

"Which one? He had two. They were both just schoolboys when he and Melody separated. She took Trevor, the second boy, off to London and Shaw stayed with his father. I did not see much of either of the lads after that."

"Did you speak with Shaw," asked Holmes, "following the death of his father?"

"Oh yes, I came up for the funeral and such. Shaw was quite composed but determined that he was going to find out who had killed his father. He had nothing but contempt for the silly superstitions about headless kings. I suggested that he contact you, Holmes. I assume that's what brought you here."

"Indeed it did. You say he was convinced his father had been murdered. What did he make of the accusations and suspicions that were directed toward him?"

Reginald Musgrave gave a shrug. "Not much. He generally despised the press, much as Billy did. He knew that all he had to do was offer a prize for the best story of the season on the local hunt, and he would be their darling once again. He learned that from his father, who said he learned it from his fine socialist friends. Always giving prizes to the press, those chaps are. So no, Shaw did not strike me as being upset at all by that."

"What about his fiancée?" asked Holmes.

"Fiancée? Did not have one. Not so far as I know. He had just turned twenty and could have had the pick of the crop of any well-bred daughter in London, given all the money he had. In another year all the mothers in the land, Socialist and Tory alike, would be sending him invitations to come up for the season."

"He was the sole heir? You know the law, Reginald, being a member of parliament as you are. What happens now to the estate?"

"Well, I saw Billy's will. He had no wife, and he expressly said that the estate and all its trappings were to go to his son, Shaw, and no one else. Shaw was not married, so everything will go to probate and the lawyers will kick it around for a few months and then disperse the money and property. The brother will have a strong claim. I will put in a claim. This other cousin, Rochester Musgrave, will lay a claim. And to make matters worse, we have not been able to locate the certificate of divorce. But eventually it will all get sorted out, and life will go on. The courts are not really as bleak and deadly as Dickens would have us to believe."

"How then, my old friend, do you explain his suicide note?"

"Most ridiculous thing I ever heard. Unless he had a crushing bout of brain fever last week, I do not believe he wrote that. I suspect that a murderer is on the loose, and I am glad you have to look after that department, Holmes and not me." He chuckled as he spoke and Holmes responded with a smile.

"That is, as you say, my department and I am inclined to agree with your conclusion. There is something, however, for which I have had no one offer an explanation."

"And what might that be?"

"What was William Musgrave doing wandering around the graveyard in the first place? I was told why young Shaw was out there, but no one has an explanation as to why the father followed him."

"Oh," said Reginald, "I can probably help you on that one. I asked the same question of Sinden, the butler. He had been with Billy when they both heard a child crying for help. It had just gone dark in the late afternoon, and they were in the hallway of the house and heard a voice coming from the cemetery. So Billy went immediately to see what was the matter."

"And was any child ever found?" asked Holmes.

"No. So the staff have all reached the only possible conclusion."

"And that would be?"

"The ghost was on the loose again. King Charlie was out and about and crying for his mommy after losing his head."

"Thank you, Reginald. I am so glad you cleared up that mystery for me."

He and Reginald both laughed and Holmes continued.

"But let us put that aside for now and may I enjoin you to eat some supper with us?"

"I would dearly love to, Holmes. But I must now get down to the great manor house since I am informed that the magistrate has named me as the trustee and goodness only knows what I'll find there. It may be bankrupt, or there may be a million pounds hidden away. You have heard the old legend, haven't you?"

"We have," said Holmes, "and I can assure you that the treasure is long gone."

"You don't say. And what happened to it?"

"It was last seen being carted off by a headless king."

Reginald roared with laughter, rose from his chair, gave Holmes friendly clap on the shoulder and departed. The two of us then sat down for dinner and a review of the events of the day.

As the staff were clearing away our dessert plates, the innkeeper came over to our table.

"Gentlemen, I am terribly sorry, but there is a young woman waiting in the parlor who insists on speaking to you. She's one of the local girls, and I have told her to be on her way, or I will call the constable. She says that she has already seen the constable and an inspector from Scotland Yard, and they sent her over here to see you. Would you mind terribly chatting with her for a minute and then I can show her the door?"

"Not at all. Come, Watson, more data from even the most unlikely sources can never hurt."

Chapter Six
Cherchez la Femme

In the inn's front parlor we were greeted by a young woman or, more precisely, a girl who could not have been out of her teen years. She jumped to her feet when we entered, clasped her hands under her chin and closed her eyes briefly as if sending a prayer of thanksgiving to the heavens. She struck me as a normal English working girl, raised most likely on a farm nearby. Her face was round, as was the rest of her body. She did not appear to be in the least obese, but her arms, shoulders, neck, and torso gave evidence of having done demanding physical work since she was a child. She forced a smile on us, which made her appear quite attractive even if her teeth were not entirely straight.

As is our custom when first meeting women of any age, I stepped forward, and Holmes waited behind me.

"Good evening, miss. I am Dr. John Watson, and this is my friend and colleague, Mr. Sherlock Holmes. We are told that you wished to speak to us. Is that correct, miss?"

"Yes, sir. Yes, doctor. Yes, Mr. Holmes. Thank you. Thank you." She nodded as if not sure if she was supposed to bow.

"Please, miss, do be seated and introduce yourself and let us know how we may be of assistance to you?"

We sat down, and she placed her hands in her lap and raised her head to look straight at us.

"I spoke a few minutes ago…"

"Young lady," said Holmes, interrupting her, "you were told to introduce yourself. Please do so."

She was quite unsettled by Holmes's rebuke, but she again closed her eyes briefly and then started again.

"My name is Edith, and my parents are Florence and Edward Tucknott. We have a farm—landowners, not renters—just off the Hailsham Road. The innkeeper here can tell you that what I am telling you is true. I came here because the man from Scotland Yard—I spoke to him at the constable's office—sent me here and told me I must go and tell my story to Sherlock Holmes. I do not know why he told me that, but I came here to tell you my story."

I had a good idea why Lestrade would pawn off one of the locals on Sherlock Holmes, and I was sure that Holmes had the same idea. I smiled and nodded and indicated to her to continue. Holmes, however, interrupted again.

"How old are you?"

Again she paused but took a breath, looked Holmes in the eye and responded.

"I am sixteen years old, sir. I turned sixteen this past August. August the fifteenth, sir."

"Thank you," said Holmes. "Go on."

"I have some information about Shaw Musgrave. I tried to tell it to the inspector, but he wouldn't listen and sent me over to see you."

This appeared to catch Holmes's interest.

"Young lady, I am listening. Please state what you know about Shaw Musgrave."

"I know, sir, that the story that is going around about how he committed suicide and all is a horrible lie. I knew Shaw, sir. I knew him well, and he would never have taken his own life, sir. I know that for a fact, sir."

"Do you, now," said Holmes. "Please, keep going."

"Shaw was terribly saddened by the death of his father, but he was a very happy man. He was usually that way when he was not feeling sad about his father. Or sometimes he was angry at the police and the press over the things they said about him, but he was not unhappy, sir. He had his plans set to go to school first thing in the new year, sir. He was going to go to Paris. He had been accepted at the Sorbonne, and we were very happy about it."

"We?" queried Holmes. "Just what was your relationship

to Shaw Musgrave, Miss Edith? Allow me to be blunt. Were you lovers?"

"No, sir. We were more than that. He was my husband, and I was his wife."

She blushed a deep red as she spoke these words and I confess that the first thought that raced through my mind was that we had an opportunistic young gold digger sitting in front of us. Inwardly I sighed, thinking that more of her ilk would likely emerge, every one of them eager to claim a piece of the vast estate.

"And when were you married?" asked Holmes, as if the last piece of news was not in fact beyond belief.

"On August the sixteenth, sir. The day right after my birthday. That was the day when it all became legal, and we could be married without our parents' permission, sir. We had been sweethearts for over two years and were mad in love, sir. And in August that preacher, Reverend Hugh Hughes, sir, was holding revival meetings in Bexhill, and we went, and he said that anyone who needed guidance for the Lord should come and speak to him after the meeting. So we went, and he told us, real firm he told us, sir, that it was better to marry than burn with lust. That was his word to us from St. Paul. It's in the Bible somewhere, sir. So the next morning we came back to see him and said we wanted to be married, and so he fetched his wife and one of the lads who played in his gospel band and they were witnesses, and we were married that day. And we were as happy as can be imagined, sir. And we had plans to go to Paris after Christmas, and we talked about it up as recent as three days ago. So that's how I know Shaw

Musgrave ... how I know that my husband could not have taken his own life, sir."

At this point, her composure failed her, and tears started streaming down her round face. I handed her my handkerchief whilst Holmes sat and patiently waited. I noticed Lestrade and the constable passing the door of the parlor. Lestrade stopped briefly, looked at us, and gave a self-satisfied smirk.

"Miss Edith," he said a full minute later, "pray continue. I have no doubt that every young woman in this parish has fancied running off to Paris with a handsome, wealthy young man. Can you provide any additional evidence that Master Shaw Musgrave was not of the mind to take his own life?"

Her face, already marked by tears showed the pain of Holmes's rebuke, but she soldiered on.

"A fortnight ago, sir, his brother paid him a visit. They had not seen each other for seven years, and he was overjoyed. They had been very close, and the divorce of their parents had hurt them both deeply. But with their father dead it opened the door, so to speak, for the brothers to become close again, sir. He introduced me to Trevor, and we planned, in secret of course, that he would come and visit us in Paris. You may go and speak to Trevor if you wish to have his word on that."

"I may do that. Now tell me, Miss Edith, why you kept all this a secret? Your doing so does not reflect well on you, given the events of the recent past."

Now her face took on a look of disbelief.

"Mr. Holmes, we live in a village. Have you never lived in a village, sir? Everyone knows everyone and everything there is to know about everyone. As soon as the word was let out, they would all know within a few hours. And it would give them all something to talk about, sir. They would all be saying that Shaw, my husband, was no more than a young billy goat who could not wait to lose his trousers, and as I am a farm girl, they would be cruel and nasty and say that I was a greedy gold digger. We were going to go to Paris and by the time we came back in four years, my husband would be of age to take over the business of the estate, and I would be a proper lady and learned how to *parlez vous* and how to make a sooflay and all and they would have to respect us as a young gentleman and his lady."

"Indeed they would," said Holmes. "However, Miss Edith, I do not have to tell you that now that your husband is dead there will be many who will challenge your story. What proof have you to offer that everything you are telling me is the truth?"

She nodded again and reached into her bosom and extracted a small leather case. From it, she took out a piece of paper and unfolded it carefully.

"This is our certificate of marriage, sir. Reverend Hughes was empowered by Her Majesty to perform marriages, and we registered it with the town clerk in Bexhill. He was a Methodist like Rev. Hughes, and we felt we could trust him not to be a gossip monger. And people can say what they like and say the marriage has to be annulled, but they can only do that if it was not consummated."

Here she lowered her face and looked down and spoke quietly.

"I can assure you, sir, that it was indeed consummated many times over, and it is possible that I am now with child."

Again tears came to her face, and again she took a deep breath and carried on.

"And if there are any who are so cruel as to say that I was only after my husband's money then you can tell them that they can take the money and give it to the missionaries or to all those poor people in Montreal who died of the pox and then were flooded out of their homes. I have never had any money, sir, and I never expected any. I married my husband because I loved him."

Holmes's voice became markedly more sympathetic, and he leaned forward and smiled at her.

"I have no doubt you did, miss. Now, tell me, Edith, did you tell all this to Inspector Lestrade, the man from Scotland Yard?"

"I went first, sir, around noontime, to the office of Mr. Nuttles. He's the solicitor in the village, and he did the legal work for my mum and dad when they bought their farm, and he was the only person I knew who was a solicitor so I went to him. My dad always said that when having to deal with legal matters you had to find a good lawyer if you possibly could and then you had to let him fight your battles for you. My dad used to say that it was not very smart to buy a dog and then do your own barking. So I went straight away to Mr. Nuttles and told him about our marriage and showed him the certificate, but when I told him that I was certain that Shaw had not committed suicide and had been murdered, he stopped me from saying any more and told me I had to speak to the constable and the chap from Scotland Yard. So I went to them and tried to tell them what I knew, but I hardly got started, sir. When I got to saying that I was married to Shaw Musgrave, he laughed. He laughed in scorn, sir. That's when he told me to go and tell my story to Sherlock Holmes, sir."

You have been a brave young lass in doing so," said Holmes. "I will take what you have told me and will give it my full attention."

"You will try to find what happened to him, won't you Mr. Holmes? You will try, won't you?"

"Most certainly, miss. But let me ask you a question on that matter. Who do you think might have had reason to kill your husband?"

"Oh my goodness, sir. When there is as much money at stake as there is in the Musgrave family, any number of people might have wanted my husband out of the way and not to be able to claim it all. And, of course, you cannot forget about the ghost, sir. He comes around real regular, and many of the people in the village have seen him, sir, in the past year even, sir. So, you cannot forget about him, sir."

"No," said Holmes, "it appears that I shall not be allowed to forget about the ghost. And now I have to give you an even more difficult task than you have already accomplished."

"Oh, sir. What is that?"

"You really must go back to your home and tell everything to your mother and father. They may be very upset, but you are still their daughter, and they will love and support your and your child. You do have to do that and now is as good a time as any."

The poor girl nodded and prepared to depart when Holmes spoke to her one last time, as if suddenly remembering an item that had piqued his interest.

"Miss Edith, before you go, two more questions, if I may. You did not say anything about your husband's visit to me in London on Monday. Did he not tell you he was going up to the city with his Uncle Rochester?"

The girl looked very perplexed. "No, sir. He said nothing about going up to London, sir."

"No? Very well, then, my final question: you spoke briefly of Shaw's brother Trevor. What did you think of him?"

"I liked him, sir. He was a nice man and was respectful to me. He was very much like my husband, sir. Very much like him."

"In what way?"

"Well, to begin with, sir, they were twins. Even I could hardly tell them apart."

Chapter Seven
A Beating Given in Return

Miss Edith pulled on her coat and departed into the cold, dark November evening. She was no sooner out the door than Holmes turned to me.

"It's a brisk winter evening, Watson. Fancy a bracing walk for a mile or two?"

"Can't say as I do, Holmes. What in the world for?"

"To follow our young Mrs. Musgrave and see where she goes. If she walks directly to her family's farm, then we shall turn around and come home. If elsewhere, then we will have some more sleuthing to do."

"Oh, come, Holmes. Do you honestly believe that the poor girl was lying to you?"

"Of course not. She clearly believed every word she told us, but that does not mean it was the truth. It is not uncommon, Watson, for a young woman, or a woman of any age for that matter, to dream a story, convince herself that it truly happened, and then to go on believing that it actually took place. I am sure you have encountered that behavior before. Come, grab your coat and let us enjoy the night air."

I was about to counter by saying that such behavior was every bit as true for men as for women, but Holmes was already pulling on his coat and moving toward the door. I checked the pocket of my coat to make sure that I had my service revolver with me. One never knows what uncouth characters or wild beasts one might encounter on a dark country road in late November.

There was a half moon shining, and it gave us enough light to see the form of Miss Edith on the road a half a block in front of us. She had started walking west toward the center of the village, the direction of the Hailsham Road. Then, only a block past the inn, another figure appeared, walking between us and Miss Edith. It was clearly a man and he was walking quickly as if attempting to catch up with the girl. Holmes and I looked at each other and quickened our pace.

Another fifty yards down the road the man began running, caught up with Edith and violently pulled her off into the verge and bushes. We ran toward her, and I could hear her screaming in pain. From a few yards away I heard a man's voice shouting.

"No more about Shaw Musgrave, you hear me? No more. Another word about him to anybody and I'll cut your pretty face all to ribbons."

The man had Edith on the ground, flat on her back and was sitting on top of her and raining down blows to her face with his fists. She was screaming and trying to shield her face with her hands. I ran up behind him with my revolver drawn and, using a maneuver that had proven useful in the army and not wanting to have to treat a bullet wound, I held the gun an inch from his ear and fired a shot into the ground beside him.

He immediately lurched back and in obvious shock and pain, covered his ear with his hands, and fell to the ground beside the girl. I dropped my knee onto his chest and held the gun to his face. He responded with a string of curses and shouted at us.

"Be off, whoever you are and mind your own business. This is my wife, and I have to teach her a lesson."

Miss Edith had recovered enough to blubber through her gasps and tears.

"He is Wilf Pike. He's the town's worst man. Ask any woman. He's a brute and a monster."

I was quite sure that Holmes was about to do something painful to the fellow when another voice broke through from the bushes.

"HALT! All of you. Scotland Yard here. Stand aside all of you. What's going on here?"

Inspector Lestrade must have heard my gunshot and had come running.

"About time you took an appropriate interest in this young woman, Inspector," said Holmes, his voice tinged with sarcasm. "As there was no policeman available we took it upon ourselves to save this young lady from a man who was beating her."

Another voice came from the bushes. "Well, there is a policeman here now, Mr. Holmes."

Constable Duncan had followed Lestrade down the road and entered the small clearing with a nightstick in hand.

"Get up, Pike," he commanded the man who was still on the ground with his nose less than an inch from the muzzle of my revolver. I stood up and let the fellow rise to his feet.

"Mind telling me what this was about, Pike?" said the Constable. "You have no business with the Tucknott girl or her family."

Pike, cursed the Constable and said, "It was a lover's quarrel, that's all."

Constable Duncan spoke to Holmes and me and said, "I would appreciate it, gentlemen, if you would see Miss Tucknott home to her family. They're not far down the road. And if you will drop by the police station on the way back I expect that Mr. Pike will provide whatever information you need."

I offered my arm to the girl, and she took it and walked smartly down the road. After a twenty minute hike, we reached the drive leading to her family's farmhouse. There, she turned to us.

"Thank you. I am very grateful for your help. I will

continue on my own from here. And please, sirs, find out what happened to my husband. That is all I ask. Good night, sirs."

Holmes and I walked in silence back to the village and to the local police station. We entered and found Inspector Lestrade sitting at a desk in the front of the office, leaning back in a chair and reading a newspaper.

"Constable Duncan is in the back with that Pike fellow. He's ready to talk to you." He motioned with his head to a door on the back wall, and we entered through it.

I stopped in my tracks and gasped. In front of us was a small cell behind a wall of prison bars. Manacled to the back wall with his arms outstretched above his head and chained to rings above him was a man, facing the wall and stark naked. His entire backside was a canvas of screaming red welts. Sitting on a chair inside the cell was Constable Duncan, reading a book. He looked up at us as we entered.

"Mr. Pike needed a bit of coaxing to talk, but now he's ready."

"Good Lord," I said, "Did you have to do all that to him to make him talk?"

"Not exactly, doctor. It only took a few whacks with a cane before he agreed to tell me what he was doing beating up on the Tucknott girl. The rest was his punishment."

"Constable," I said sternly, "torturing a prisoner like that is against the law. You must know that."

"Must I, doctor? Well let me tell you what I know, doctor. I know that a village constable must take an oath before Almighty God to protect the folks in his village. I also know that when a man gives a beating to a woman, the woman most likely will never breathe a word about it or if she does and comes and tells us, and we take it to a magistrate then it is his word against hers. He will have found a couple of his pals to testify that he was with them playing cards or some such lie, and he will walk away and then go and do it again. So doctor, some of us constables, something of a brotherhood we are, decided a decade ago that the despicable beating of the women in our towns had to stop, and a thorough flogging is about the best way we know to stop it. Pike will recover in a fortnight, but he'll remember for long after that. And if he ever comes in here again for the same reason then he will be facing me whilst I give him a flogging, and I don't think he will like that at all. Will you, Mr. Pike?"

The body chained to the wall made no sound but shook his head in silence.

"Good there, Pike. Glad we have an understanding on that matter. Now how about you tell Mr. Holmes here what was behind your actions? But hold on a minute, let me fetch the inspector. He'll want to hear as well."

He walked over to the door and called for Lestrade to come and join us. He did and gave a glance to the thrashed body before sitting down.

"Oh, dear. That poor fellow must have run into a thorn bush on his way to jail. Pity. So, good evening there, Holmes. What do you wish to know? I am sure that this Pike chap will be most willing to answer whatever you ask."

Holmes gave Lestrade a sideward look and walked over to the prisoner.

"Who put you up to this, Mr. Pike?"

"Like I said, it was just a lovers' quarrel."

"Very well. Constable, would you mind?"

"All right, all right," the prisoner muttered along with several choice profanities. "Three weeks back this woman comes into the pub asking for me. Says that she has been told that I will deliver unsavory services for hire."

"What was her name?"

"She didn't say, and I didn't ask. That's the way blokes like me do their business."

"Where was she from?"

"She didn't say, and I didn't ask, but I would guess from somewhere in London by the sounds of her."

"And what," continued Holmes, "did she ask you to do for her?"

"She said that I was to go and scare the bejesus out of the Tucknott girl seeing as she was getting too friendly with Lord Billy's boy. I was to let her know that she was to have nothing to do with him ever again, or she would be beat up and cut up. That was all she wanted."

Holmes glanced over to the three of us with a very perplexed on his face.

"Shaw Musgrave was dead. He died last night. Did you not know that?"

"Of course, I knew it. Went and saw him hanging there myself. Everyone knew he was dead."

"Then how, in heaven's name, does it make sense to go

and terrify the girl if the one who she is to keep away from is already dead?" asked Holmes.

"I had taken the lady's money. She paid me five pounds to do the job, and I hadn't done it. In my business, word goes around if a bloke takes on a bit of service, takes the customer's money and then does not deliver the service promised. That's how you lose your business. You got to be honest to stay in the business. Your reputation is all a man has."

Holmes looked at us again, this time with a shrug and a smile.

"I believe you are quite right on that point, sir. And I thank you for reminding that there is honor among thieves."

"Now look here, mister. I am no thief. You get that straight. Never taken a farthing I did not earn."

"Of course, not, Mr. Pike. But do tell me then, what possible reason did this lady have for wanting Miss Tucknott to have no further intercourse with Shaw Musgrave? Did she give you any reason?"

"Oh, yes, she did. Now, I can't say if she was telling the truth or not, and I suspect not. Those of us in this line of service have to be honest in our dealing with our customers, but they are more often than not dishonest with us, but they have the money, and we need it so there's is nothing to be done about it. What she said was that she was young Shaw's sister, and she didn't want the estate going to some young trollop who had heated up the blood of her older brother. That's what she said, mister. Course, that was news to me seeing as no one around here ever knew Shaw had a sister.

So, like I say, maybe she was lying and maybe not. You'll have to sort that one out. And, God's truth, that's all I know."

Holmes stood silent for several seconds and then turned and came and sat down beside me, giving a word to the constable as he passed.

"You may as well release him and send him home, Constable. I do not believe that there is any more he can tell us."

Constable Duncan nodded and unshackled Wilf Pike and handed him his clothes.

"Go on home, Pike," said the constable. "Your backside will heal, and the pain will soon be gone. But if I ever even suspect you of bringing harm and fear to a young girl of this village again you will be crawling back home and clutching the crown jewels for a month. You follow me, don't you Pike?"

The brute growled something and sullenly pulled his clothes on and departed. We bade good evening to Lestrade and the constable and Holmes and I returned to the inn.

Chapter Eight
What the Innkeeper Knew

"My dear, doctor. This case becomes increasingly complex, and thus steadily more interesting. There is one chap, however, that I believe we need to speak to, and fortunately, he is close at hand."

"And who might that be?"

"Our innkeeper. He also serves as the village postmaster. I suspect that he will be a font of knowledge on the past lives of the dear people we are dealing with."

The innkeeper, a friendly chap named John Previtt, was happy to oblige and, upon our ordering another round of brandies including one for him, sat down with us and responded to Holmes's questions about the Musgrave family.

"Well now, Mr. Holmes. There was a lot of speculation, as you might imagine, when the Lord and his Lady, Billy and

Melody as we all called them, separated and divorced. Something powerful nasty must have taken place for a very wealthy woman to walk away, with just her clothes, leaving one of her sons and a fortune behind. Some of the folks in town, mostly the women, saluted her, saying that Billy must have been something of a monster for her to run away like that. Of course, most of the men in the village sided with him, seeing as it became known that she had a lover in London and went straight away and lived with him; lived in sin they did until the divorce came through and then, we heard that they got properly married. But even that is not known for sure."

"I have been told recently," said Holmes, "that the two boys were twins. Is that so?"

"Aye, so much so that we could never tell who was who. And they seemed to like it that way. Boys will be boys, of course, and they thought it quite fun to wear the same clothes and comb their hair the same way, and they always seemed to get along. Never saw the one without the other."

"I have also just been told that they had a sister. Is that so, Mr. Previtt?"

"A sister? No. Never heard tell of any sister. There was just the two boys, that was all."

Here he stopped and gave his chin a rub.

"Mind you, I suppose that there is a possibility, not much of one but a possibility all the same, that Melody was expecting child when she departed. It had been twelve yeas since she had given birth to the boys, and she and Billy weren't getting along very well, so, like I say, it is highly unlikely, but always possible."

"Where is the mother now? Did she come to visit ever? Did she keep in contact with her other son?"

"No, Mr. Holmes, she never came back here. As postmaster, I saw letters from her come once a week addressed to Shaw. But then one day, the butler, Mr. Sinden, comes and hands me a stack of letters all unopened and says they are to be returned to the sender. They were all the letters the mother had sent to her son. I assumed that Billy had them held by the staff and never let the lad see them. Then the letters stopped. I hear most of what goes on in the village, sir, but I never heard of any visit by Melody back to Herstmonceux, nor of Master Shaw making a trip to London to see his mum."

"I also heard," said Holmes, "that the brother from London came here recently and visited. Do you know anything about that?"

"Funny you should mention that. Yes, back in the fall a couple of folks said they saw Shaw Musgrave with a man that was identical to him, walking along some of the lanes of the estate, and they said that the Tucknott girl was with them. Now it so happened that the folks who claimed to have seen them were the same local folks who are always reporting sighting of King Charles riding around in the moonlight with his head tucked underneath his arm. So no one gave much credence to what they said. But yes, sir, now that you mention it, yes, I did hear that."

"And what of the mother, this Melody woman, what became of her?"

"I'm sorry I cannot be more helpful on that one, Mr.

Holmes. When the letters came for Shaw I remember that some of them bore the return address of a school where I am guessing that she might have been a teacher. She had a very fine education herself so she would have no trouble finding work as a teacher."

"Do you remember the name of the school?"

The innkeeper sat for a moment looking into his snifter of brandy, then he looked up at Holmes.

"The Queen's Gate. Yes, that was it. I remember thinking that it was an easy one to remember since the address was Queen's Gate and the name of the school was the same. I think it's in Kensington, but you would know that better than I would, Mr. Holmes."

"Your memory, sir, is excellent. Queen's Gate is indeed in Kensington and the school by the same name is exactly where you recalled. And another question to tax your memory: have you ever seen a ghost of a headless king riding around and frightening people half to death?"

The innkeeper gave a hearty laugh.

"No, sir. Cannot help you with that one at all. Mind you, as I said, there are other folks who have seen the old boy more than once. I must not have enough blue blood in me to be worth his bother. But I will warn you, sir, you could put yourself in far greater mortal danger by walking into the pub and saying that the king's ghost is a silly fairy tale than you would if you ran into the fellow himself." He laughed again, and we joined it.

Holmes asked the gregarious chap several more questions, but no more pertinent information was forthcoming. We thanked him for his assistance and with two generous brandies already having been consumed, we settled for a late evening cup of tea by the fire.

I asked him my usual question.

"What next, Holmes? With every passing day, your list of people who might have strung up young Master Shaw grows longer. For all I know, you have already added this poor farm girl and the sister."

Holmes smiled back at me. "Of course, they have been added. When millions of pounds are at stake, every person who can put his, or her, finger in the pie becomes a suspect. However, in response to your question, tomorrow we shall return to the estate and see if we can find any data regarding mother, brother, and sister. And, assuming we are successful, we shall return to London and pay them a friendly visit. And I shall see you for breakfast, my friend."

At just after nine o'clock the following day we returned to the manor house and were greeted by Sinden, the butler.

"Good morning, gentlemen," he said, maintaining the stone face that is ascribed to every English butler. "Is it Mr. Reginald Musgrave you wish to see, or Mr. Rochester Musgrave?"

Holmes confirmed that we wished to speak with Reginald Musgrave, and we were led through the house and to the study in the back corner of the north wing. I could not help but take notice of the furnishings and artwork as we walked along the hallway. None were labeled, and I am no connoisseur of English painters, but I was sure that some looked remarkably like paintings by Stubbs or Gainsborough, and even one, all yellow and gold, that could only have been by Turner. Any one of them after auctioned by Sotheby's would bring enough wealth to support a man for the rest of his life.

There were several more hanging on the walls of the study in addition to the obligatory knight in full armor standing just behind Reginald Musgrave, who was seated at the desk in front of the window.

"Good morning," he said cheerfully as he rose to greet us. "Such a welcome and pleasant surprise. Nothing like a friendly face to chase away the gloom and doom that hangs over this place. Some coffee, gentlemen?"

We assured him that we had been well fortified by the inn and asked after his health and the well-being of the staff.

"The staff are just fine, as you might expect. Lords of the manor come and go in these old houses, but the help stay for a lifetime. Sinden is in charge and has been for several years. Billy treated them well and paid them all a wage that was well above the local market. He even allowed Sinden to organize them into a union of sorts so they could all live merrily under the illusion that they had a modicum of power, so no problems there at all. They don't much miss Billy, but they were quite fond of young Shaw."

"I can imagine they were," agreed Holmes. "Most of them would have watched him grow up here from his infancy. Will they be able to keep their positions, or will financial pressure force you to let some of them go, union or not?"

"Oh, no. No problem on that front at all, Holmes. I have

spent the past day poring over the books and records. Oodles of money being received every month from the rents. No debts that I can see. All the properties are free and clear. There is no end of outstanding letters and files and issues to be dealt with. Billy was somewhat lax over the past year in keeping up with standard business transactions, but nothing that is at all untoward. I shall have to hire a manager posthaste since I have to return to Westminster in January when the House comes back into session, but otherwise, everything appears to be above board."

"And the estate, has there been any action there? Claims being made and such?"

"You will have to ask my cousin Rochester about that. He came back here yesterday afternoon, and we sat and had a nice chat. Prince of a fellow, but terribly upset by the death of Shaw. He and I decided to divide and conquer as they say. I have taken on the management of the estate, and he has kindly agreed to oversee the lawyers and the probating. I'm afraid it is going to be complicated, but it will, as I mentioned the other day, sort itself out in time."

"Was not the will clear as to William Musgrave's intentions and his bequests?"

"Entirely, he left everything to his son, Shaw, but that does not stop every Tom, Dick, and Harry from registering his interest or claiming that Billy had promised him something. That stack of letters on the credenza had all arrived even before the death of Shaw, and this one has come in just this morning. Billy seems to have promised something to everyone he ever had anything to do with. The local hunt club is expecting a new hall. The rector let me know that he had agreed to pay for the new roof, and the local league of socialists has asserted that he was giving them a thousand pounds a month, and they expected that I would continue to do so."

"And was he?"

"According to the ledger, yes. But that doesn't mean that I have any obligation to continue to do so. I do, after all, hold the riding next door for the Conservative Party and I would be dismissed to the back row if they got wind of my sending money off to Keir Hardie and his ilk."

"And what about other family members?"

"Interesting you should ask, Holmes. We are coming out of the woodwork. As you know, both my cousin Rochester and I have some standing. The second brother, Trevor, would usually be the first in line. But I just received a note from Melody's solicitor claiming that she was never legally divorced by Billy. And then finally, if you can believe it, there is a local farm girl who says she was married to Shaw."

Holmes gave a forced chuckle but did not respond one way or the other to the question.

"Would you mind," he asked, "if I spent some time going through some of the family records? I assume you are aware that Scotland Yard has requested that I do some investigating since they considered both of the deaths to have some questions attached to them?"

"No. Not at all. If you need to borrow anything, just leave me a note. And if you want to know any more about all the eager relatives you can speak with Rochester. He's in the library. I have to leave now and return to Hurlstone briefly, but you know how to find me if you need me.""

Over the next hour, Holmes poked through the personal files of Billy Musgrave. He made a small stack of selected documents and, when finished, placed them in his case.

"Anything interesting or untoward?" I asked.

"Not really. Lord Billy was quite an organized chap, and all seems to be in good order in what has become a very large and complex web of properties and holdings. His will is not here, but I suspect that Rochester has it. The other item that is missing from his personal file is the certificate of divorce from Mrs. Melody Musgrave. Perhaps Rochester has that as well. Time to go and pay him a visit."

Rochester Musgrave was in the great library, sitting back in the far corner and ensconced in a large, comfortable chair. He had a book in his hands and appeared to be engrossed in it, so much so that he did not notice our entry and we are only a few feet away from him when he suddenly startled and looked up at us. He leaped to his feet and put the book down hastily.

"Ah, Mr. Holmes and Dr. Watson, I see you are still with us in Sussex. How might I be of assistance to you?"

Holmes did not reply immediately but quickly cast his glance to the book that had been put down so quickly, as if we had come upon a school boy leering over the latest edition of *The Pearl*.

"Yes, yes, Mr. Holmes," said Rochester. "I am once again reading Charles Dickens. All men, as I am sure you will agree, have ways of fortifying our souls when we meet with times of bereavement and grief. Some men turn to pharmaceuticals, some to wine and spirits, some to the comforts of the flesh. I confess that my particular crutch has been the great stories of literature. When I enter into a play or novel, my mind is taken away from the immediate events of life and for a time, at least, the pain is numbed. I recollect, Mr. Holmes, reading in one of Dr. Watson's stories about your adventures that you made occasional use of a seven percent solution, did you not? Very well, sir, Dickens is my solution. I am sure you understand."

He smiled warmly if somewhat sheepishly, and I knew, and I was sure Holmes knew, exactly what he meant. I could see that he had set up a small bookcase behind his chair on which some twenty books had been placed.

"However, gentlemen, I am also sure that you did not here to discuss my dear friends, the great books. How may I be of assistance to you?"

"You were kind enough," said Holmes, "to bring your nephew to see me and to engage my services. You may not be aware that following his tragic death, Scotland Yard has requested that I continue with my investigation."

Rochester Musgrave's eye widened on this news. "Why no, I had not heard that, but I must say that I am very grateful, very grateful indeed, Mr. Holmes to know that you are assisting the inspector..."

Here he stopped speaking, and his voice faltered. He struggled to take control over his feeling and continued.

"I am sorry, sir," he said, in a whisper. "Please bear with

me. I confess that I am having great difficulty in coming to terms with what has taken place. I was terribly fond of and close to both my cousin and my nephew and their tragic loss has been very grievous. I do hold myself responsible in part for the loss of my nephew. My journey down to Eastbourne was of no great importance, merely an opportunity to visit with an old acquaintance from my days in the theater who is performing a role in a local production of *Pinafore*. But it is scheduled to play for several weeks. I could have gone at any time, and I should have known … I should have seen …"

Here he faltered yet again and took out his handkerchief to dab his eyes.

"I should have known how fragile his spirit was. Had I been here I am sure that Shaw would be alive today. But I was not and …"

At this point, he lost control and collapsed back into his chair, dropped his head and shoulders and covered his face with his handkerchief.

Holmes pulled up a hard-backed chair and sat down, motioning to me to do likewise.

Rochester Musgrave looked up at us again, and again the poor fellow muttered an apology, but he appeared to have overcome his emotional state and looked directly and Holmes. His voice was now more confident.

"Forgive me, Mr. Holmes. I was asking how I might be of assistance to you."

"There is," said Holmes, "an old adage that tells us that where there is a will, there is not only a way, but there are also eager relatives."

"How true, how true."

"And I understand from Mr. Reginald Musgrave that you have taken on the onerous duty of engaging with the powers that be and guiding the estate through probate. Is that correct, sir?"

"It is. It seemed the least I could offer to do. Having some sort of work distracts the mind almost as effectively as reading a tragic story. So yes, that lot has fallen to me."

"And is it truly all that complicated?" asked Holmes. "I am not a lawyer, but it is my understanding that when the beneficiary named in the will dies intestate himself, then the law applies the rules of intestacy and determines and awards portions of the estate. I am informed that the younger brother, a Mr. Trevor Musgrave, of London, is the closest relative and next of kin. Am I mistaken, Mr. Musgrave?"

"Yes, yes. Well, no, to be more exact. The issue is not Billy's will but Shaw's will, or in this case, the lack of it and our inability to locate the certificate of divorce from Mrs. Melody Musgrave. It was complicated enough before the latest turn of events. I assume that Reggie told you about the local farm girl."

"He did."

"No one knew anything about her, and we have all concluded that her documents are forgeries, but it may take some time to prove all of that."

"Have you any idea," asked Holmes, "where the former wife is to be found?"

"Haven't the foggiest, sir. I suppose she could be tracked

down, and perhaps you could do that for us, sir. I am not being serious in suggesting that, Mr. Holmes. It is the responsibility of the estate to look after those matters, and as you are now working on your own shilling, we certainly would not expect that of you.

"Is there any other matter with which I can help you, Mr. Holmes? I fear that your visit has reminded me of all the many tasks on my plate and I must, with regret, leave Pip and Estella for the present and get to them."

He rose from his chair and in a most gracious manner let it be known that we should be on our way if we had no further purpose to our visit. We acknowledged his assistance and departed.

Chapter Nine
A School Not for Scandal

On the train back to London, Holmes opened his case and began to review the documents taken from the files of Billy Musgrave.

"My dear doctor," he said, "is it correct that the occurrence of twins is an inherited trait? Why do they seem to be common in some families and unknown in others?"

"The *why*," I replied, "we do not know. But yes, it is a fact that some families may, over many generations, have quite a few sets of twins whilst others have none. But there is no systematic Mendelian ratio or anything approaching it. You might say it is predictably irregular."

"Ah, yes. An excellent way to describe it. I found a

number of documents pertaining to Lord Billy's ancestors, and it appears that there were at least seven set of twins over the past century. That many would be unusual, would it not."

"Unusual for an average family," I said, "but normal for a family that was prone to giving birth to twins. We medical men are, on balance, happy to deliver twins. Although the birth itself is more dangerous for the mother, it tends to make for happier English families. The children always have a playmate, and they tend to care for each other long after they become adults. Some until they become aged and pass away."

"Yes," agreed Holmes, "a good thing from the perspective of the medical profession. And an even better thing for the lawyers when they appear in wealthy families. It gives them all sorts of lucrative work to do as siblings battle out issues of inheritance. Unless families are very careful, which they tend not to be in the intensity of childbirth, it is easy to confuse which twin was which when they entered the world. *Primogeniture* may at times be only a matter of seconds. And *that* appears to be what has happened in the family tree of the Musgrave-Dacre dynasty. There are several accounts of a battle royal being fought. Quite fascinating."

"Are we going now to speak to Master Shaw's twin brother?"

"We will," said Holmes, "if we can locate the fellow. Our only reference at the moment is his mother's last known place of employment."

"The school in Kensington?"

"Precisely."

The Queen's Gate School for Girls has a well-earned

reputation for giving young women from some of our better-off families the finest not only in intellectual training but in all-round preparation in manners, culture, and household management that are required by a young woman as we approach the dawn of a new century. It recently relocated to a new location on one of London's more select residential streets and from the outside was indistinguishable from the neighboring row houses.

Upon ringing at the front door, we were met by a young woman, one of their senior students I assumed, who gave a shallow curtsy and a friendly smile. She was not, even by English standards, overly attractive, but possessed an obvious charm and self-confidence.

"Good morning, gentlemen, and welcome to Queen's Gate. My name is Camilla, and I have door duty for this morning. How may I assist you?"

"We would," I said, "appreciate an opportunity to speak to your headmistress, Miss Kamrose."

"Oh, I am so sorry, gentlemen, but she is currently teaching a class and has classes all morning. However, our administrator, Mr. Cushway, is available. Shall I let him know that you wish to speak to him or would you prefer to return this afternoon?"

"Your administrator would be just fine, Miss," I said.

"And whom may I say is calling on him?"

"My name is Dr. John Watson, and this is my colleague, Mr. Sherlock Holmes?"

The young lady's eyes widened for just a second and then she smiled again.

"Please, gentlemen, this way. Shall I have one of the staff bring you some tea?"

"No miss," I said. "Thank you for asking, but that will not be necessary."

She led us to an office door and bid us be seated on the bench outside of it as she entered to announce us. Whilst sitting there for several minutes, like errant school children, Holmes squinted his eyes and read the notices on the wall across from us. I was content to reflect on the well-mannered young lady we had just met.

"Quite the confident young lass," I noted. "I am sure she will marry well."

"I have no doubt," said Holmes, "that she will, perhaps more than once."

He could be terribly cynical at times.

Miss Camilla returned and graciously informed us that our man was terribly busy but would, of course, be happy to interrupt whatever he was doing and speak to us briefly.

"Ah, well, this is a pleasant surprise," said the tall and well-groomed gentleman who stood to greet us. "Of late Mr. Sherlock Holmes and Dr. Watson have caused all sorts of havoc here at Queen's Gate. Our senior girls are quite enlivened by reading the stories of your exploits in *The Strand*. They will be very excited to learn that you have visited us. By tomorrow they will have made up all sorts of imagined mystery stories as to what must have happened up in the attic."

He gave a soft laugh and continued. "No doubt our headmistress will be hearing reports of bodies, ghosts, and murderous mistresses for weeks to come."

Again, he laughed at his pleasantry, and I joined him in doing so.

"I fear," I said, "that our visit has no such fascination attached to it. We need to make contact with one of your staff. Perhaps she is no longer employed here, but you might have an address on file. It is an urgent family matter."

"More than happy to help, if I can. Who might you be trying to locate?"

"A Mrs. Melody Musgrave," I replied. "Is she now or has she recently been a member of your staff?"

The man sucked in his lips ever so slightly and, after holding that pose for several seconds, shook his head.

"I am terribly sorry, gentlemen. But I cannot help you with that one. There is no one here by that name now, and if she taught here in the past, it must have been more than five years ago. That has been the duration of my tenure and no one by that name has served here in my time. As I said, I am terribly sorry, gentlemen. I can ask our Headmistress on your behalf when she has finished her classes. Or, have you considered trying the Post Office? They sometimes keep addresses on file. Our local one is just around the corner on Cromwell, right across from the *V and A*. One of our senior students could take you there if you require directions. Shall I ask for one of them?"

"That," I assured him, "will not be necessary."

Once back out on the street, I turned to Holmes.

"That was not particularly productive. Mind you, if I were the father of daughters I might wish to send them here. What now, Holmes. Back to Baker Street?"

"Until the end of the school day and then we shall pay a call on the former Mrs. Melody Musgrave."

I gave him a raised eyebrow. "And just where are we going to do that, Holmes?"

"She lives on Elm Park Road. It's in Chelsea, not far from here. We can give her a call once the school day is over. Around 4:30 this afternoon should do quite well. Come, Watson, let us find a cab back to Baker Street."

It was not the first nor would it be the last time I was struck dumb by something Holmes had said. Once in the cab, I recovered my voice enough to demand an explanation.

"My dear, doctor," he replied. "Will you never remember to look around you whilst you are engaging in an investigation? To begin with, on the roster of teachers' names on the notice board was one that read 'Mrs. Melody Cushway.' The name Melody is not rare, but neither is it all that common. That was the first clue that not only was our lady here at the school, but that she was also the wife of the school administrator. Upon entering his office his office I could see the scribbled notes on the paper in front of him that included the words 'Strand, murder, attic, and seniors,' all of which he used in his immediate greeting with us. There was nothing nonchalant in his conversation; it was entirely rehearsed in his mind just before we entered. He wanted to appear offhand, but I rather suspect that he knew perfectly well why we were making our visit. He had an envelope on his desk that had been sent to his personal residence, bearing an address on Elm Park Road. Therefore, that shall be our next stop this afternoon. Now, if we make haste, we may be able to persuade our dear Mrs. Hudson to prepare some lunch even if we most inconsiderately arrive without warning her."

Over lunch and for two hours following, Holmes said nothing. He had retreated into his exceptional mind and was clearly attempting to put some order to the multitude of facts and suspicions that were emerging in this case. At four o'clock we hailed another cab and drove to Chelsea and knocked on the door of a nondescript brick row house. It was opened by a woman of a certain age whose face immediately conveyed her recognition of Holmes and me. Before she could say a word, Holmes immediately spoke sharply to her.

"Mrs. Cushway, I wish to speak to you because I have evidence that your son, Shaw Musgrave, was murdered and did not take his own life. Are you willing to listen to me?"

The poor soul immediately lost the color from her face and gasped. In a voiceless whisper, she responded, "Go away."

Regaining control over her emotional state, she raised her voice, "Go away!"

As we made no move to comply, she then screamed at us. "GO AWAY!"

This response brought her husband, who most likely had heard what Holmes had said, running down the stairs. He looked at us, and the anger spread across his face.

"Get out of here," he ordered. From the hallway, he

picked up a cane of the sort used on the backside of misbehaving schoolboys and raised it above his head.

"I said, be gone." He then apparently thought better than to assault us with a weapon and slammed the door.

"Perhaps," said Holmes, "we should make a strategic retreat, but I do not suggest that we leave the battlefield."

He walked back from the door and a few steps along the pavement. We waited for several minutes until the door re-opened and Mr. Cushway emerged.

"Holmes, Watson, come here!"

We did as bid.

"What you just did was vile, inhuman and despicable. However, my wife wishes to know what you believe happened to her son. You may enter and explain."

We stood just inside the entry and the lady, Mrs. Melody Cushway, returned and stood beside her husband.

"Mr. Holmes," she said, her voice trembling, "yesterday I was informed by the police that my son, Shaw Musgrave, had taken his own life and that he had left a note saying that his doing so was a result of his being falsely accused of the murder of his father. Even though I have had limited contact with him in the past few years, he was still my son, and that news was very difficult to bear. I know who you are, and I have to assume that you have reasonable evidence to support what you said. Please, tell me why you believe he was murdered and who could possibly have done that to him."

Tears were running down her face as she spoke. Her arm, which had been supported by her husband, was now taken back to her side, and she stood resolutely in front of Holmes, looking straight at him.

Holmes patiently and methodically explained the evidence that we had observed at the graveyard and on the body of Shaw Musgrave, leading to the inevitable conclusion that her son had been the victim of foul play.

"As to your question, madam, of who might have done this, I have, at the present, no answer. I am, however, determined to find whoever was responsible and bring that individual to justice. I am attempting to gather as many insights into what has taken place as possible. To that end, I would also like to speak to your son, Trevor. Does he reside with you?"

"No," said Mr. Cushway. "Master Trevor is of age and has acquired his own residence."

"And where might that be?" asked Holmes.

"That is none of your concern," said Cushway. "We shall meet with him and inform him of the news you imparted. We have no wish for you to assault him in your tactless manner. And now, Mr. Holmes, unless you have more to say, we bid you good day."

"I do have one more thing to say. I am also of the opinion, although with less evidence to support it, that your former husband, Mr. William Musgrave, may also have been murdered and not merely suffered a heart failure."

At this news the lady again became distraught, and she turned and walked back into the house. Without saying anything more, her husband opened the door and gestured to us to leave.

"Do you," I asked Holmes, "now wish to find the brother?"

"Oh, we have already done that," said Holmes. "Once again, they did not think to cover the addresses on the unopened mail on the hall side table. A letter to Mr. Trevor Cushway was sitting there with his forward address written on it. It appeared to be from a hotel in Paris."

"Are we now to pay a surprise visit on him?"

"Allow me, my friend to ponder that one for the time being."

And ponder he did. I resigned myself to another supper during which any conversation would be absent. Holmes picked away at his food and, leaving most of his dinner on his plate, returned to his chair and lit his pipe. I had lit a cheery, small fire in the hearth, and Holmes turned his chair so that he could look directly at the flames, and for an entire hour that was all that he did.

I picked up yet another of Dickens's novels—this time *Great Expectations*—and caught up with Magwitch, Pip, Mrs. Havisham and the beloved lot of them. My enjoyment was suddenly interrupted by Holmes leaping to his feet.

"Oh, Watson," he shouted, "How could I have missed it? It is utterly elementary, Watson."

"Merciful heavens, Holmes. What is?"

"The inscription. It explains it."

"Holmes, what *are* you talking about?"

"The inscription, Watson. The inscription: *lector, si fortunae requires circumspice*."

327

"What about it?"

"Look around. *Look around.* And what did we see as we looked around? Standing on the top of the hill, what did we see?"

"A lovely view. Acres of field and forest and sheep and crops. What were we supposed to see?"

"The fortune, Watson, the fortune. He *spent* it."

I had to think about that for a moment. "Ahhh, yes," I said. The light was dawning on me as well. The current Musgrave estate in Sussex held over seven thousand acres. There were a dozen or more other properties in other parts of England and Scotland and several on the Continent. The royal fortune had all been spent on property.

"The father," said Holmes, "who was loyal to King Charles, kept the fortune safe, but his son took it and spent it. No wonder the First Earl of Sussex became so wealthy so quickly. And so much for loyalty to the Crown."

"But how does that put us any closer to the murderer?" I asked.

Holmes did not answer. He gave a small shrug and returned to his pipe and his chair but turned it around so that now he was facing me.

"Watson, we were not the first to discover the crypt."

"No, young Shaw had been there before us. We know that from what he told us."

"Yes, he did. But he was led there. Someone had previously discovered the old book, deciphered the clues, found the crypt, and opened the cases. He must have understood that the treasure now consisted of the vast Musgrave estate. The same person created the fraudulent book with the simple clues and placed it where Shaw would find it. And somehow by murdering both father and son, the estate, or at least a portion of it, would come his way."

"But who? And how?"

"Ask me that later."

He brought his feet up under his body, closed his eyes and sat like a swami with his hands together and his fingertips pressed against each other. I could see that the conversation had ended and returned to Dickens. From time to time I glanced up as I turned the pages and twice caught Holmes looking at me. However, I said nothing as I was quite engrossed with the story.

Suddenly he leaped to his feet.

"Ah ha. Ah Ha! AH HAA!!" he bounded across the room and leaned down toward me, clapping both my shoulders with his hands and then doing it again.

"Oh, my dear, dear chap, Watson. How splendid of you. You have given it to me."

He was leaning his face very close to mine.

"Oh, my dear, friend," he was shouting. "Oh, if I were French I would kiss you on both cheeks. Since we are English, you will just to imagine that sensation. How good you are to me."

He quickly stood up and rushed off into the bedroom. I sat in total bewilderment until he came charging back a few minutes later bearing his small overnight valise.

"My dear doctor. I have some things I must do at once. Do arrange to meet me the day after tomorrow in the village. Noon at the Horseshoe Inn would do perfectly. Could you do that?"

"Of course, I can, but what is going on? You must tell me."

"Havisham," he shouted as he departed the room. "We have been tricked by Miss Havisham." These last words faded as he ran down the stairs and out the door. A second later the door re-opened.

"And bring your service revolver."

Chapter Ten
In the Library with a Revolver

It was difficult the following day to give my full attention to my patients, and I was relieved when the day had ended and I had not inadvertently poisoned anyone. I slept only a few hours and rose early. I was out of the house well before first light and assumed that if I were going to wait I may as well do so whilst looking out over the rolling hills and old castle of Herstmonceux as the interior of our rooms on Baker Street.

I got off, as before, at the Polegate station, just ten minutes in advance of Eastbourne and the ocean. I arrived at the inn just before eleven o'clock and took a chair outside along with a hot cup of tea. The first of December had come and passed, but I was only a few miles from the south coast, and the weather was mild and sunny. At eleven thirty a police carriage pulled up and out of it climbed Inspector Lestrade and Constable Duncan. Lestrade acknowledged me and walked over.

"Good morning, doctor. I assume that you have no more idea than I do as to why Sherlock Holmes has summoned us here."

"Quite correct, Inspector. I am as blind as a mole on this one, I'm afraid. However, the tea is excellent, and the view is pleasant."

He grunted and waited inside.

At noon a dog-cart came up the road from the estate manor house and stopped at the inn. Holmes got out. I recognized the look on his face. It was a smug smile of triumph I had seen so many times in the past when he was about to pounce on his prey.

"Ah, so good to see you all," he said. "We must make haste back to the house and be sure we cannot be seen. If that were to happen the game would be up. So please, come with me."

We clambered into the police carriage and were delivered to the stately old house. Once there we were met at the door by Sinden, the butler, and led into the library.

"Holmes," whispered Lestrade. "Have you conscripted the butler into your venture? Surely not."

"Yes. He is quite reliable and was eager to help."

"Holmes, he's a raving unionist. He's right on the top of my list of suspects."

"Then, my dear inspector, you will have to adjust your list. Please follow me."

We followed him into an alcove off of the great library. Holmes sat down on the floor, and we did likewise and ceased making a sound. He motioned for Lestrade to sit in a place that offered an opportunity to look into the main room. We all curled up our legs and sat and waited.

At just before one o'clock we heard the door of the room open and one man's footsteps walk toward the desk in the back corner. Then, for another ten minutes, there was nothing and we continued to hold our positions in uncomfortable silence. At about ten minutes past the hour I heard voices chattering and the door open again. This time, several people were entering the room and walking across it. Lestrade held up his hand, his thumb curled in and four fingers extended.

"Good afternoon," said the voice from behind the desk. "I trust you had a pleasant journey."

I recognized the mellifluous baritone of Rochester Musgrave.

"There is nothing good about it," came the sharp reply, "and this is not a pleasant journey."

Although I could not see the speaker, I remembered hearing that voice recently. It was the school administrator, Mr. Cushway.

"Then I am sure," said Rochester Musgrave, "that a candid conversation amongst us will clear up any concerns and keep us all on track. Now please, all of you, have a seat and let us sort things out."

I could hear chairs being moved and assumed that the group of them had gathered together and seated themselves.

"You say that you have some concerns," said Mr. Cushway. "So do we. You had promised us that all we had to do after Billy's death was to claim that the divorce had never been completed and that the bulk of the estate would then come to us."

"It was," replied Rochester, "a splendid opportunity that we all agreed to take advantage of. I could not have known that a copy of the certificate would be on file at the village clerk's office."

"And then," continued Mr. Cushway, his voice now quite a bit louder, "you told Trevor that all he had to do was reconcile with his brother, and he would have his share of the estate. But you somehow failed to know that Shaw had got himself a wife. How stupid could you have been?"

"Nobody knew that! They kept it a secret!" Cushway snapped back.

"Yes, and you said that she was nothing but a stupid farm girl." These words came from a young woman whose voice I did not recognize. "So you had me pay the local brute to intimidate her, but instead she ends up talking to a lawyer and that detective."

"And now," shouted Mr. Cushway, "that detective, Sherlock Holmes, arrives on our doorstep all full of questions and accusations."

"Did you...," said an older woman's voice, "did you murder my son?"

"Oh, my dear Mrs. Cushway, I know it is hard to bear, but your son and my nephew, of whom I too was terribly fond, took his own life."

"That is not what that detective said," said Mrs. Cushway. "Sherlock Holmes has informed us that regardless of what the press reported, the police know that Shaw Musgrave was murdered."

"Did you kill my brother!?" came a shout from another man's voice. "You did, didn't you?"

"And you murdered Billy!" shouted Mrs. Cushway.

"You used us," said Mr. Cushway. "You used us to commit fraud and be part of your murderous scheme so that you could get part of the estate that never came to you. You used us, and you are a murderer!"

Several voices were now shouting. The shrillest of them all was Mrs. Cushway, who kept screaming "Murderer! Murderer!" at Rochester Musgrave.

"Bloody hell," he screamed back. "So what if I am? You fools can send me to the gallows if you want and then you will all spend years in prison as accomplices to murder and fraud, or you can keep you bloody mouths shut, live in peace and have millions!"

For several seconds no one spoke.

"Is that," said Mr. Cushway, "why you demanded that we come here? So you could force our silence?"

"Do not be foolish. I did not demand that you come here. You told me you were coming and demanded that I be here. That bloody detective must have terrified you."

"We did no such thing. You sent us a telegram saying that some great problem had come up and that we all had to come here immediately, at precisely this time."

"Are you insane? I did no such thing. You demanded this meeting. I have your telegram right here and ..."

He suddenly stopped speaking. Holmes looked at the rest of us and smiled. In truth, he grinned.

"I believe," he said out loud, "that this is the place in the script where the instructions say *Enter Sherlock Holmes, Stage Left.*"

He jumped to his feet and strode into the room.

"And I really must thank you all for responding to my summons. So very courteous of you."

Lestrade and Constable Duncan immediately followed him. I brought up the rear guard. The combination of shock, anger, and fear on the faces of the five people we were approaching was somewhat amusing.

Holmes marched up first to the young man.

"Mr. Trevor Musgrave, I assume. So nice to see you again. I believe the last time we met was…oh, let me see…ah, yes, in my office on Baker Street. You are not a very good actor. I suggest that you consider another line of employment…after you get out of prison."

He next turned to the young woman.

"Forgive me, miss, as we have not been introduced. My name is Sherlock Holmes. Your family name is Cushway, of course, as is your father's and your step-mother's. Did no one tell you that it is a serious criminal offense to hire someone to assault a young woman? No? Pity. Someone should have.

"And Mr. and Mrs. Cushway, how do you do? You both had quite a comfortable life at the school and a pleasant home in Chelsea. Such a shame that you gave in to greed and fell for a promise of instant riches. I am quite certain that you teach your students the exact opposite and hope they remember to apply their lessons to their lives. Unfortunately, you appear to have failed that class."

He now turned and addressed Rochester Musgrave, who sat glaring at him, unable to keep the apoplectic anger from his face.

"Your branch of the family, by an instant of cruel fate during your grandfather's birth, was cut out of the vast fortune of the estate. When your foolish investment in Ceylon came a cropper you had no choice but to come cap-in-hand to your wealthy cousin, William, and ingratiate yourself to him. With nothing else to do, you discovered the old copy of *Pilgrim's Progress*, deciphered the clues, found the treasure and realized that all the wealth had been transferred to expanding the estate. The only way you could ever have a portion of it was if William were to die and if you were to arrange that the inheritance go to his former wife and second son. How much did you demand as your share for doing so? A third? A half? Two-thirds?"

Rochester said nothing in response to Holmes's taunt.

"He wanted a half," said Mr. Cushway.

"A reasonable request," said Holmes. "First, you planted the false book in the section of the library that you knew Shaw Musgrave would soon discover. When you saw him follow the much-too-simple clues to the crypt you lured Billy into the graveyard by calling as if you were a child in danger."

"Idiotic nonsense!" snapped Rochester. "That is nothing but your groundless conjecture."

"Conjecture, you say? I prefer to call it deduction, sir. And it is supported by your colleagues in the theater who can give endless accounts of your ability to mimic voices of all ages. And having lured your cousin to the door of the crypt you assaulted him, silently, most likely with chloroform to render him unconscious and likely kept him smothered with chloroform until his heart gave out. And how silly of you to attribute it to the ghost. Really, sir, Hamlet's father and Banquo might work wonderfully well in the theater but to a detective and even to the police, they do not exist. But then you purloined the certificate of divorce from cousin Billy's private files and then you convinced these foolish people that if they would go along with you they could have half the estate."

"But your plan fell apart when another copy of the divorce papers showed up, and your determined plan became even more diabolical. You convinced Trevor that he could pretend to be his brother and act as if he were severely distressed and on the verge of taking his own life. You told him the words and actions he would need to be convincing and then you brought him to no less a witness than me so that I would acknowledge to the police how distraught he had been.

"Now you only had to get rid of the elder son and the estate would fall to the second son. So you strangled your nephew, Shaw Musgrave, and then hung him from the oak trees and tried to make it look like a suicide. Perhaps it might have been convincing on a stage in Liverpool, but it was so clumsy that even Scotland Yard was not taken in."

"That is a lie!" shouted Rochester. "I was nowhere near here when that happened. I was miles away. You have no basis whatsoever for that accusation!"

"Ah, do I not? You did indeed make a visit to Eastbourne to see a play and spend time with an old colleague, who says, by the way, that he was surprised to see you as you had really not been at all close friends and you had never come to see him perform in the past. But then there is the livery man who will testify that he picked up a gentleman who was of the same height and weight as you at the late train at Polegate and delivered him to the Musgrave Manor House around eleven o'clock in the evening and following instructions, waited for him all night and returned him to Polegate in time for the first morning train back to Eastbourne. Of course, he will also testify that the man he drove back and forth did not look at all like you, and as you had used your skill in theatrical make-up to disguise yourself, that made it impossible for us to deny your alibi. Unfortunately, even for a very short journey by train, you would not give up your habit of traveling in the first-class carriage, which requires a reserved ticket, which you made in your name at the Eastbourne station. The station master is prepared to identify you as the one who purchased the ticket.

"Again, everything was now within your grasp with Shaw Musgrave dead and gone, every farthing would go to his brother, Trevor. But Shaw had not let you in on the secret that he had gone and gotten married. You knew you would have to threaten and chase away the poor young farm girl who was now his wife. You could not do that yourself since you did not even know who she was or how to find her. So you hired the local brute, Wilf Pike, to do your work for you. But again you could not do that directly as he knew who you were and could easily identify you if he were caught. So you brought the only remaining member of the family into your scheme, Mr. Cushway's daughter by his first wife. She came and hired Pike and paid him to give a beating to Edith Tucknott. But you did not count on his tardiness in doing the job he was paid to do, nor in the cleverness and determination of the girl. By your evil actions, you have destroyed this family and rendered Miss Edith the sole heir to the great Musgrave fortune."

Here Holmes stopped. Neither Rochester Musgrave nor any of the Cushway family spoke.

"Have you anything," asked Lestrade of Rochester, "to say for yourself, sir?"

Rochester said nothing, crossed his arms on his chest, and defiantly shook his head.

"Then," continued Lestrade, "allow me to suggest that you find yourself a good lawyer. Now, all of you, come with me."

Lestrade gestured to the five of them to follow Constable Duncan out of the library. They stood in silence, and did as they were told.

.

Chapter Eleven
Good Night, Miss Havisham, Wherever You Are

By supper time Lestrade had returned to the Horseshoe Inn and joined Holmes and me for an excellent dinner of lamb chops enhanced with generous mounds of mint jelly.

"Well done, Holmes," said Lestrade. "That Rochester chap had me completely fooled. He seemed so completely trustworthy."

"I confess," said Holmes, "that he had me the same way. He is a very experienced actor who has played every role on the stage, and he knew exactly how to act in order to be completely convincing. Were it not for our good doctor's reading habits I might not have seen through him."

"Holmes," I said, "you really must explain that one. And

what, in heaven's name, did Havisham have to do with it?"

"You were reading Dickens," said Holmes. "Do you recall that I had said that he was the master of giving his characters all those actions, words, ways of dressing and moving, and all those odd small quirks of behavior that led the reader to know, most assuredly, if the character was to be trusted or not?"

"I do recall that."

"I sat across from you as you read one more time about Pip and Miss Havisham. The poor lad was deceived by her into believing that she was his benefactor. She was the master at acting and speaking in such a way as to deceive him. She kept it up for years, did she not? Rochester had taken on his own Miss Havisham. He knew exactly what to do and what to say consistently so that all of us would trust him completely. When I sat looking at you, it suddenly came to me and so I thank you, my friend. Had it not been for you I would still be in his thrall."

"You really must thank Dickens, not me."

"You can thank him," said Lestrade, "all you want, but he's dead and gone and cannot respond. And so, Holmes, is your client. A shame you will have yet another case paid for by your own shilling."

Homes sat back and lit his pipe.

"I rather suspect, Inspector, that in a year from now, when Mrs. Edith Musgrave finds herself to be one of the wealthiest young women in the realm, that she might be willing to pay my fee if I submit it to her. Do you think she will do that, Inspector?"

Lestrade laughed. "Oh, I am sure she will. She will be in your debt, as long as she does not have to wait a decade to see her money."

"Ah, Inspector. You have given me the solution to that one."

Lestrade gave Holmes a raised eyebrow.

"I will," said Holmes, "wait here in the village for two more days and then shall offer to accompany Mrs. Edith into London. There I will give her advice directly from the lips of Inspector Lestrade of Scotland Yard."

"And what, Holmes," Lestrade asked, "might that be?"

"I will say to her, 'My dear young lady, get yourself a good lawyer.' "

Historical and Other Notes

The years from 1640 to 1660 were tumultuous ones for England. The Civil Wars of the first decade divided the country and culminated with the beheading of King Charles I and the installation of the Commonwealth under Oliver Cromwell. In 1660 the Glorious Revolution brought back the monarch, Charles II, and ushered in the Restoration Period and the flowering of literature, theaters, and the arts. The historical references in the story are more or less accurate.

King Charles I did in fact try to escape from the palace where he had been imprisoned and make his way to Europe via Southampton. The attempt failed and he was returned to London to face trial and execution. The detour through East Sussex is fictional as is the idea that he took a portion of the royal treasury with him. His ghost, with his head tucked underneath his arm, has been seen in many places throughout England but Herstmonceux has not been favored to be one of them.

The castle at Herstmonceux was built in the 1440s by Sir Roger Fiennes, the Treasurer of the Household of King Henry VI. It was a significant residence for two centuries until it was allowed to become derelict in the late 1700s and it was still in that state at the time of this story. Beginning in 1913, restoration began on it and for several decades it was used by the Admiralty and the Royal Greenwich Observatory. In 1992 it was purchased by Alfred Bader, a wealthy Canadian industrialist, fully refurbished as a state-of-the-art learning center and donated to Bader's alma mater, Queen's University of Kingston, Ontario, Canada so that it could serve as their International Study Centre.

I have visited the Centre and two of my daughters and my son-in-law spent a term at 'The Castle.' It provided them with an exceptional educational experience, even if most of the stories that I heard about their time there somehow had more to do with field trips to London and the Continent and pub crawls.

There is an All Saints Church adjacent to the castle, but there is no great manor house.

Although I write these stories as a Sherlockian and devotee of Conan Doyle, I must agree with Dr. Watson that Charles Dickens was the greatest novelist of the Victorian age.

Corrections and suggestions for improvement to the historical elements of this and all New Sherlock Holmes Mysteries are always welcomed and appreciated.

Did you enjoy this story? Are there ways it could have been better? Please help the author and future readers by posting a constructive review on the site where you bought your book. Thank you.

The Spy Gate Liars

A New Sherlock Holmes Mystery

Chapter One
Rushing to Nancy

Crossing the Channel on a fine morning in the early spring of '87, with the sun shining over a calm sea, the breeze in my face, and the white cliffs of Dover fading behind me should have been an uplifting experience to my soul.

But I was worried sick.

I had not slept a wink the night before. At six o'clock that morning, I had rushed out of our rooms on Baker Street, shouted at the cab driver to hurry to Victoria Station, and then stood and paced up and down the railway platform waiting for the first train to Dover.

Now I was pacing fore and aft on the deck of the Dover to Calais ferry, knowing full well that my doing so would not speed the boat up in the least.

The reason for my distress was in my pocket; a telegram that had arrived in the late afternoon of the previous day. It ran:

```
Cher Docteur Watson:

Votre ami, M. Sherlock Holmes est très
malade. Il est à l'article de la morte.
Veuillez vous rendre à Nancy dans les
plus brefs délais.

Dr. Alphonse Stoskopff
Médicin du garde
Hotel Grand Dulong
Place Stanislas, Nancy
```

I had immediately sent a return telegram to the house doctor demanding more information but had received no reply, which was not at all surprising as French doctors seldom work past five o'clock, even if they do not get back to their wives before seven.

Holmes never took sick. His constitution was made of iron and I had, in utter amazement, observed him over the past few years as he went without sleep for days on end, kept alive only by tobacco and coffee, when in hot, intense pursuit of a case.

During the past several months he had worked non-stop all over Europe identifying one criminal after another who was part of the notorious *Trapani Mandamento,* and seeing them off to prison or the gallows. As he had begun to pull on one strand of their web of underworld enterprises, he continued to discover yet another dastardly activity. Arms and armaments were being illegally sold across borders for the equipping of any anarchist group who placed an order for them. Young women and even some young men had been smuggled in from India for immoral purposes. Bank vaults had been broken into without the bankers' noticing until the money was long gone. Holmes methodically unwound each of the intricate plots and solved the mysteries.

Far from wearing him down, it invigorated him. He sent brief notes affirming that he was beside himself with zealous satisfaction, hardly able to contain his sheer joy, and grudgingly taking only an hour or two of sleep when sitting in a train cabin. He was utterly and completely alive.

For Sherlock Holmes to be near death was unheard of, and I feared that he had been poisoned by some fiend. I had packed my medical bag full of every known antidote for every deadly concoction that could have been administered to him unawares, and I hoped and prayed that he had not succumbed already.

Long before the ferry alarm sounded announcing our pending arrival at the port of Calais, I was standing in the front of the line at the exit, ready to rush off and run across the center of the town to the railway station. As soon as the stevedores lowered the wide gangplank, I was on my way. Calais is, like the rest of France, supremely unorganized and the docks greeted me with a cacophony of peddlers, swindlers, touts, illicit appeals, and cab drivers who I was sure would take over an hour to deliver me to the train station. I was having none of it. I trusted my shoe leather and walked smartly through the streets, past the great lighthouse, and on to the train station a few blocks to the south. By the time I arrived on the platform, I was breathing heavily and sweating, but I was in time for the 12:45 train to Paris, Gare du Nord. I purchased a ticket and found my seat with just a few minutes to spare and permitted myself a brief interval of reflection. In my mind, I reviewed all the most common poisons I knew of and their treatment. My medical case was opened and closed thrice as I checked yet again to make sure that I had packed the appropriate medications.

Twelve forty-five came and went. So also did one o'clock and the train did not move. I had not traveled much on the Continent, but Holmes had advised me on numerous occasions that trains in England at least make an effort to be on time. Those in Germany always arrive and depart on the exact minute. French trains, however, leave at random when the conductor has finished his lunch. The French were, to their credit, more reliable than the Spanish or Italians whose trains might or might not adhere to the day let alone to the hour on the schedule.

The train did eventually depart from the station and rolled along over the hills and fields of Picardie. I chatted on and off with my seatmate, who seemed just a bit too inquisitive for my taste. Holmes had warned me that all Frenchmen were either spies or wished they were, and I was undecided whether or not this chap was being friendly or an agent of Holmes's enemies.

I was relieved when we finally pulled into the Gare du Nord. Baedecker had recommended a small *pension* conveniently located halfway between the Gare du Nord and the Gare de l'Est, where I would depart from the next morning. I gave my name to the desk, not thinking for a moment that doing so might not be the best idea. The fellow behind the desk immediately looked up at me and broke into a broad grin.

"*Mon dieu. Vraiment*, le Docteur Watson? The writer? The writer of the stories of the Sherlock Holmes? *Merveilleux.*"

He turned and retreated into his inner office and came back bearing a copy of *Les Aventures de M. Sherlock Holmes*. I was not aware that my publisher had arranged for a French translation of my stories and, for a brief, fleeting moment thought that I might soon see another strand of royalties coming from the Continent when it occurred to me that what I was looking at was no doubt a pirated copy. I was fit to be tied and was tempted to rip the chap's book into pieces, but he was not the culprit and had likely purchased the book in good faith. So I signed his copy and smiled back at him.

The following morning, I departed early and walked the block to the great Gare de l'Est and boarded my train to Nancy. I tried to force myself to relax but my mind was racing, and I could not stop worrying about Holmes. I found myself condemning my ignoring his earlier letters and telegrams. Surely I should have seen in them hints that he could be in danger. He had no close friends in the world other than me, and I felt a deep responsibility to care for his physical well-being. I feared that I had let him down.

These unpleasant thoughts were only banished from my mind when I descended from the train in Nancy, an ancient town in the far east of France. Before the war between France and Prussia, it was still some fifty miles from the border with the German states, but with the German annexing of Alsace, Nancy was now the closest French town to the frontier. I knew little about it other than what I had read in Baedeker.

The Grand Hotel Dulong occupied the far corner of the central square and, with its ornate façade and rows of large windows, appeared to be the best accommodation in the town. If Holmes was going to die, he at least had picked an elegant hotel in which to do so.

"Good morning," I said to the man behind the hotel desk. My French is weak, and I am of the firm belief, proven during my years under the Raj, that anyone in the world can understand plain English as long as it is spoken loudly and enunciated clearly. "I am here to see one of your guests, a Monsieur Sherlock Holmes."

The fellow was visibly startled and without saying a word, turned and retreated to the hotel offices. Two minutes later he reappeared, followed by a nattily dressed man of about the same age as me.

"Ah, Docteur Watson. Vous êtes arrivés. Dieu merci. Venez avec moi tout de suite."

I assumed that this must be the house doctor and I followed him up the staircase to the third floor. He used a pass key and ushered me into a spacious a room that would have been filled with sunlight passing through the large windows had they not been entirely covered with dark curtains. On the far wall was a double bed and under some blankets was a hump that I concluded must be the semi-comatose body of Sherlock Holmes. The doctor opened one set of drapes and allowed the light to enter. Then he went to the bedside and gently rocked Holmes's right shoulder.

"M'sieur Holmes. M'sieur Holmes. Réveillez-vous. Votre ami, Docteur Watson, est ici pour vous. Réveillez-vous."

Holmes moved very slowly and struggled to raise his upper body to a sitting position.

Good heavens, I thought to myself. He looked utterly ghastly. His face was inflamed, and there were horrible dark circles under his sunken eyes. His lips were gray. He was blinking his eyes as if he could not clear his vision. As he raised his hand and pointed his finger at me, I could see him grimacing in pain. Mentally, I was making note of his symptoms and trying to assign them to the effects of one poison or other, but he seemed to have been afflicted by more than one horrible potion and I could not decide which of them to try to treat first.

"Waaaatson," his feeble voice said. "Is…that…you?"

"Yes, Holmes. It is me."

"Ohhh…how good of you…to come. You may tell…the hotel doctor…to go…and do thank him." After uttering the final word, I heard a terrible long wheeze and assumed that his respiratory system had also been attacked.

I turned to Doctor Alphonse.

"Merci, very much, my ami. You may departez now. I will look after Monsieur Holmes."

The doctor took a few steps back from the bed but did not turn to leave the room. Holmes raised his trembling hand and waved feebly to him.

"Thank you…doctor…you have been very kind…please let my own doctor attend to me." This utterance was followed by another extended wheeze.

"Waaaatson… in the loo…there are towels…please soak one in cold water…and bring it to me…I am burning up."

I went immediately into the adjoining lavatory and ran cold water over a small towel and brought it back to Holmes. The hotel doctor was still in the room.

I placed the wet towel in Holmes's shaking hand and turned to the hotel doctor, thanking him again. In a friendly manner, I took his elbow and directed him to the door. He was obviously reluctant to leave the room, and so I was forced to deliver instructions in English.

"Mr. Holmes wishes to be left alone with me. We thank you for your kind attention. I will look after the bill for your services when I pay for my room. Thank you, sir."

I walked beside him until he had departed and the door was closed. On turning to Holmes, I saw him dabbing his face with the towel.

"Haaaas he…gone?" The voice was muffled by the towel that was now covering his face.

"Yes. It is just you and me in the room now."

"Pleeeeease…lock the door."

This seemed a strange request as we did not appear to be in any danger, but I did as he had asked.

"The door has been secured, Holmes. Now put the towel down and let me have a look at you."

The towel was immediately placed on the bed, and I was horrified by the discolored blotches that had stained it. On looking up from it, I stared into the beaming, healthy, smiling face of Sherlock Holmes. He immediately swung his legs over the side of the bed and stepped toward me. Both his hands clasped my shoulders.

"Watson, Watson. My dear, dear chap. I am so sorry to have given you such distress and brought you all the way across France. I had no idea that a French doctor would think to call in an English one. But it was so good of you to come, my friend."

"Good heavens, Holmes!" I exploded. "What in the world are you trying to do? You had me convinced that you were at death's door. What is the meaning of this nonsense?"

He smiled warmly and tenderly at me, and I knew I could not remain angry with him for long.

"Ah, my friend," he said. "These borderlands between France and Germany are a hotbed of spies and counterspies. The French have spies everywhere and so do the Germans. Like the Cretans, all Alsatians are liars and are either spies or are pretending they are. They have been on me like a plague of fleas for several weeks. The only way I have been able to gather any data or do any investigating is to feign sickness all day long and slip out through the service entrance after five o'clock. But do sit down and have a brandy and let me explain."

I was still shaking my head in amazement. Holmes had tricked me more than once in the past with his disguises, but never had I been so thoroughly taken in as I had been on walking into a hotel room in the eastern frontier of France.

"The French," he began, "do make an excellent brandy. Allow me to pour one for each of us. You deserve one for all your troubles on my behalf."

We took our seats in two comfortable chairs. I loosened my collar and tie and Holmes, still in his housecoat, lit his pipe.

"I have been doing a bit of work for the French *Ministre des Affaires étrangères*. It was not covered by the press in London, so you are not likely aware that so far this year five former German army officers have been murdered."

That was serious, but it made no sense to me.

"You said," I said, "that you were hired by the *French*. Why would they care if the Germans lost an officer or two? I would have thought they would be rather pleased. There does not appear to be any love lost between the two countries after their war."

"Excellent observation," said Holmes. "But the chaps in Berlin, right up to Otto what's-his-name, are placing the blame on the French. You know how they are about honor and seeking revenge and all that. The Germans are threatening, quietly so far, that they might go to war again if the Frenchies do not stop killing off their men. The chaps at the Quay d'Orsay really do not want another war, regardless of their posing in the name of French honor. They lost the last one rather badly, a *folie de grandeur* I believe it what they called it. They had to give up the entire province of Alsace and were generally humiliated.

"Those French chaps are insisting that they are not behind it, but who else could it be? So they have hired me to find out who is doing it and make them stop. It has all been quite fascinating, but I am not even close to solving the crime, and every time I turn around I find some spy—French, German, Alsatian—on my tail. I detest having my every move recorded and reported on and so the ruse of feigning ill. I am terribly sorry, my friend, for having disrupted your medical practice but I must say that I am thrilled to have you here. Your assistance will be invaluable."

"And what," I asked, "do you expect me to do? I came prepared to attend to your physical ailments, not to go gallivanting around the far regions of France after dark."

Holmes smiled and was on the verge of laughing at me.

"Of course you did, but you and I know full well that you become bored quickly with your patients and cannot resist the adventure. And I am quite certain that at the bottom of your medical bag lies your service revolver that you packed just in case. Am I right?"

Of course, he was right. He invariably was. And I must admit that I involuntarily smiled back at him.

Chapter Two
The Cat Burglar

"When do we start?" I asked.

"It would be very helpful if you could begin straight away. Your presence here is a godsend and allows me to banish the overly attentive house doctor from this room, demanding that I only be seen by you. Might I suggest that you go now into the village market and procure several days supply of fresh fruit and vegetables and then announce to the hotel desk that you have diagnosed me with some horribly deadly and contagious disease that might be overcome by healthy eating, but other than seeing you I must be quarantined for the sake of the health of the village children. You can make up something like that, I am sure."

"There is no known contagious disease that is cured by fresh fruit and vegetables," I objected.

"Then make one up. How about ... oh ... *Llasa Double Pulmonary Fever*? That should do it. Terribly contagious. The virulent Tibetan strain, not the African one. I contracted it years ago whilst in Tibet, and it recurs every so often, much like malaria only potentially fatal."

"But how then," I asked, "am I to be spared contracting it from you?"

"Good heavens, Watson. Use your imagination. Say that you were also stricken with it whilst you were in Tibet but recovered fully and are now immune."

"But I have never been in Tibet," I said.

"My dear chap, we are making this up. It is quite acceptable to imagine Tibet if you are going to imagine the disease itself out of whole cloth."

"Oh ... yes. I see your point. I suppose I could do that. And then what happens?"

"We will wait until after five o'clock. At that time all of the spies, as required by their unions, leave their posts, visit their mistresses, and then go home to their wives and children. We will be able to exit through the back of the hotel, find our dinner in one of the many pleasant cafés, and then attempt to break into one of the finer homes in this town. Now please, on your way. The market is a block to the south of the square. And kindly refrain from the appalling French practice of holding baguettes in your armpit."

I did as requested and returned to the hotel with several

sacks of perfectly formed fresh fruits and vegetables. At the hotel desk, I explained the circumstances of Holmes's quarantine to the staff, for good measure adding that one of the consequences of the horrid disease was what the French referred to as *couper le pin*, a non-medical term that I was sure our inquisitive house doctor would take note of, assuming that he did not wish to be impotent for the remainder of his days.

Over a brief repast of *foie gras*, brandy, and baguettes, Holmes provided a few more details of our mission.

"Five men, all former officers in the Prussian army, have been killed. The most recent were two men who had been living here in Nancy. Two weeks ago, the chaps at the Quay d'Orsay requested my assistance. My sleuthing to date has confirmed that all five of them served in the war and were part of the same battalion. Since arriving here in Nancy, I have discovered the location of the houses in which the murders took place. Each house was the abode of the deceased, and this evening you are I are going to pay a visit to them. We are too late to do an examination of the body and the site of the crime, but we need to learn how it was that the killer entered the house, committed the crime, and then escaped."

"Are you saying," I asked, "that they were murdered in their own homes?"

"Precisely. Not in a tavern or a brothel as is customary when the French are disposing of unwelcome Germans, but in their homes, in their bedrooms, and late at night after the household staff had gone to bed. There were no reports of a struggle, no cries of pain, no doors slammed."

"That is most peculiar," I said.

"And that is why it makes for a most fascinating case. But come now, we must don our disguises so that we will not be recognized as Englishmen as we wander the dark streets of Nancy."

From his valise, he procured a black tam, a cravat, and a thin theatrical mustache.

I put them on and regarded myself in the mirror.

"Would you not agree," said Holmes, "that you now look like a highly typical mid-level functionary of the French municipal administration?"

"I would say I looked more like a comic buffoon *poseur* seen on stage in the West End," I replied.

"Correct, and a redundancy," said Holmes.

It was dark by the time we had departed from the hotel and found a delightful dinner in a local café. Holmes led me along several tree-lined streets until we were in an obviously better-off neighborhood. He stopped at a perimeter fence of a large three-story house. The fence was made of steel stakes, all painted black, and topped with gold-colored sharp spear tips.

"Somehow," said Holmes, "the killer must have been able to scale this fence, enter the house late at night, find his way to the third floor, and murder the victim as he lay in his bed."

"How did he kill him? You said that no shots were heard."

"Every one of them was stabbed in the eye with a dagger."

"That is again most peculiar," I said.

"Precisely. What is inexplicable is that in all reports from the coroner it notes that there was also a small wound above the eye and the larger penetration directly into the eye socket."

"Hmm, very peculiar," I said, repeating myself. "I suppose it is possible that the first attempt might have failed and the second succeeded."

"Come, come, my dear Watson. Once perhaps. But four times? Impossible."

Holmes now turned and grasped a fence stake in each hand, glanced up and down the structure and then turned to me.

"Let us see if we can repeat his moves. This may require some gymnastics on our part, but if you will drop to one knee and allow me to step from your leg to your shoulder and then stand up, I should be able to straddle this fearsome fence without impaling myself."

I did as requested and soon was on my feet with Holmes standing on my shoulder with one foot and swinging his leg, unimpeded, over the top of the fence.

"Now," he said, "press your body up against the fence, and I will be able to use your shoulders again as a ladder on my way back down."

I pushed myself flat against the stakes and felt the toe of his boot slip through the gap and settle on my shoulder. The other foot followed, and then he gave a jump and landed on the ground on the other side.

"That was," I said, "all well and good, but what am I now supposed to do? I do not believe that we can do the same maneuver with you on that side and me on this."

"An excellent observation, Watson. So I suggest that you walk around to the main gate and I will unlock it and let you in. There is no sentry on duty after seven o'clock."

A few minutes later both of us were standing against the back wall of the large house trying to discern how a killer could possibly have broken in without making a disturbance. The windows on the ground floor were all locked and protected by rows of metal bars. The back door was secured by a lock that Holmes himself admitted would be difficult to pick. The only access to the second floor would have required an individual who was more ape than man and able to climb drainpipes and cling to protruding bricks with only his fingertips.

"The killer," concluded Holmes, "appears to have the skills of a cat burglar. He had to both ascend the wall and then open the window whilst hanging on with one hand. Quite the exceptional adversary we are up against."

For the next fifteen minutes. Holmes paced back and forth around the house, sometimes stopping and closing his eyes in deep concentration, then shaking his head and pacing some more. With a final shake of his head, he turned to me.

"I am as of yet still in a fog," he said. "But come, we shall pay a visit to the second house."

Through several blocks of the dark residential streets of

Nancy, we wandered until Holmes stopped in front of another elegant home.

This second house, the one in which another former Prussian army officer had been murdered a week earlier, was likewise a formidable obstacle for any nocturnal invasion. Instead of a fence, it was surrounded by a thick and impenetrable wall of Russian Olive trees; all planted tightly together and with horrible thorns ready to stop even the most determined of thieves or killers. There was no sign anywhere on the perimeter of the branches having been cut away to permit passage.

"The only way he could have entered," mused Holmes, "was by way of the front gate. But the structure is high and formidable. This chap must be quite the monkey to have managed such a feat."

Again, Holmes walked slowly around the house, stopping constantly to do a close examination of the impenetrable thorny hedge. Each time, he shook his head and muttered, "Impossible."

By midnight we were heading back to the hotel. Holmes walked in silence, his head cast down, his hands in his pockets, and his chin almost touching his sternum.

"Data," he said. "I am starving for data. Whenever a murder is committed, there are clues to be unearthed all over the place. So far, I have not had access to the scenes of the crimes until far too late after the fact. There are so many questions to which I need answers before I can even start to form a hypothesis."

"Very well then," I said. "Since you have conscripted me

for this undertaking, would you mind terribly telling me what data you do have. So far I am blind as a mole except for observing an ingenious method of scaling a dangerous fence."

"Oh," he said. "I must say that you have a point there, Watson. Let me tell you what I know so far from my initial investigations. I do not expect any imaginative insights from you, but your simple questions have at times been useful in directing my thoughts in a new way. So, yes. Here is what we know so far.

"All five of the victims were of about the same age, rather close to forty. All had served in Bismarck's army during the last war, the one we refer to as the Franco-Prussian conflict. I have discovered that all of them were part of the same *Kompanie* in the Prussian army when it invaded Alsace. Thus, it stands to reason that the motive for their murders is tied to something that took place during that war. But there could be a hundred possibilities. Dark secrets hidden; money or jewels squirreled away; embarrassing secrets of intrigue; revenge ... the list is long."

"Were those chaps the only young officers of their unit?" I asked.

"No, they were part of a unit that included at least three others. One, I have traced up the road to Strasbourg, a Charles Friedel, and another one now lives in England. The third cannot yet be found. I suspect that the fellow in Strasbourg is now in fear for his life and we must pay him a visit before the nimble assassin gets to him."

"When?"

Holmes appeared to ponder my question for a moment.

"If we leave in the morning, our departure will be noted by the legion of spies that infest this town, so we best depart again in the late afternoon. Strasbourg is only a few hours by train, and we should be there in sufficient time to alert the chap and advise him to vacate his house if he has been so unwise not to have already done so."

I slept soundly that night, weary from the lack of sleep the previous night and my worried travels. Once during the middle of the night, I heard footsteps going back and forth along the hallway outside my room and concluded that Holmes was pacing whilst trying to put together the pieces of the puzzle.

The following day we spent in our adjoining rooms. I used the time to review and improve my latest story about the adventures of my friend and now famous detective. Twice during the day, I checked in on my friend to make sure that he was at least eating something nourishing. On both occasions I found him in one of the armchairs, his legs folded and drawn up under him, his hands together with his fingertips touching, and his eyes closed. I knew not to disturb him with conversation but was satisfied that the bowl of fruit and platter of cold cuts appeared to have been partially diminished.

At one minute after five o'clock, he tapped quietly on my door.

"Come, Watson. The game is afoot. Off to Strasbourg. Please, quickly don your disguise, and we shall be out of Nancy long before we are missed."

I did as requested and we strolled in the fashion of unhurried French bureaucrats to the railway station and boarded the train to Strasbourg. Once on the train, we removed our disguises and became English tourists. The German border agents were suspicious of French travelers but usually welcoming to the English, what with their Kaiser being the grandson of our beloved Queen and all.

By the time we reached our destination, the sun had set. From the *Bahnhof Straßburg*, we walked a few blocks past the great Cathedral to a hotel that struck me as having been imported from Tudor England. It was quite a popular place nonetheless and Holmes and I were required to share a double room.

"Our lodgings," said Holmes, who appeared to be familiar with the establishment, "are old but very comfortable. I suspect that this city has as many spies as did Nancy but no one has followed us and we will be undetected here until we pay a visit to our monsieur first thing in the morning."

He was wrong.

At seven o'clock in the morning, we were awakened by a loud knocking on our door. I quickly leapt from the bed, pulled a dressing gown over my pajamas and started toward the door.

"Psst!" came an alert from Holmes. "Your revolver," he whispered.

I hastened back to my doctor's bag and slipped the gun into my pocket before opening the door.

"*Guten Morgan, Herr Doktor,*" said the chap in the hall. "*Bitte*, please come with *herr* Sherlock Holmes. Come quickly, please to room *dreihundert vierzehn*. We have need of your services. *Bitte, sofort*."

I turned and looked at Holmes, who shrugged and gave me instruction.

"Tell him that we will be there as soon as we dress."

"I thought you said that we were not followed," I said.

"It is possible that I underestimated the diligence of the German spies. But let us go and see what their problem is."

Chapter Three
Death in Strasbourg

Room 314 was in another wing of the hotel. Standing at the door were two rather impressive looking German chaps with *Polizei* emblazoned on their uniforms. I greeted them but, as should be expected from the Germans, they merely glared at me and said nothing. One of them opened the door and gestured to us to enter.

Several men were standing in the room and I quickly understood the reason for our having been summoned. Lying in the bed was a body and the area around the pillow was covered with blood. One did not have to be Sherlock Holmes to put together what must have taken place during the night.

A tall blond and broad-shouldered police officer approached Holmes.

"Herr Sherlock Holmes," he said. "I am Hauptkommissar Max Ballauf of the Police of Strasburg. Not coincidental is it that you are staying at this hotel? The case that of you is being investigated has to you been delivered. In the bed is Herr Charles Friedal, and dead he is. Stabbed in the eye, like all of the others. We are made aware of your reputation and welcome your assistance in the solving of this crime."

Without another word he stood back and pointed Holmes toward the bed and the body. I followed.

The unfortunate victim was a man in his mid to late forties and in rather good physical condition. If one can judge by his hair style and facial hair, one might assume that he was a former military officer. His eye socket was gory and now blackening with the dried blood. Curiously, he also had a wound to his eyebrow. There was no doubt as to how he had died. A dagger must have been inserted into his eye and pushed through to his brain. Death would have been almost immediate.

Holmes had taken out his glass and took a full half hour to examine the body, the bed, and the room. I noticed him paying close attention to several deposits of tobacco ash and some sort of German word scratched into the top of the bedside table.

"Commissar Ballauf," he said. "Did one of your men or the hotel staff open the window?"

"Nein. It was open we arrived. The maids reported hearing some disturbance being made in this room just after one o'clock in the morning, felt herself concerned, and came to knock on the door to make sure the guest was not having difficulties. There was no answer and they departed. Herr Friedal had ordered early morning coffee and strudel to be delivered at five thirty. He did not make an answer at the door when the maid arrived and she used her key to make it open. As soon as she saw what had happened she rushes out and runs to the nearest police station. I am called and, knowing that you were staying in the same hotel, I give instructions that nothing in the room be disturbed. Everything is as you see it. The window was open."

Holmes walked over to the window and leaned out. The morning sun had risen and I could see that the window opened to the courtyard below. Once Holmes had withdrawn, I also peered out and observed an entirely unobstructed wall of the building, four stories above the ground level. The only uneven features of the wall were the dark planks that had been affixed to the stucco, giving the hotel its distinctive Tudor appearance. If our killer had entered by the window, he must have been exceptionally adept at scaling walls. A *cat* indeed.

"The staff of the hotel," said the Commissar, "claim that no one suspicious comes into the hotel after eleven o'clock. He must have climbed up the wall and made the window open. No other explanation am I seeing."

I looked at Holmes and detected the familiar unmistakable faint trace of a smile on his face. "*Aha,*" I said to myself. He's on to something.

"I am honored," he said to the police officer, "to have been invited to assist in this case. I will continue my investigation and report to you tomorrow morning if that is acceptable to you. Your station, I believe, is located just east of the cathedral, is it not?"

"Ja. There it is."

"Splendid. I shall report in at eight o'clock tomorrow morning."

Holmes then turned to me, smiled and nodded and walked toward the door.

Once we were out of earshot, I demanded an explanation for the smile that had broadened into a grin.

"I was thinking how a fine cup of German coffee and a generous slice of *brötchen* would make for a delectable breakfast. Perhaps a hard-boiled egg or two. What say, Watson?"

"Enough, Holmes," I replied. "I did not come racing to the Continent to be teased."

"Oh, very well. Let us find a pleasant café, and I will be more forthcoming once breakfast is served."

After crossing over the Rhine, we found a pleasant café not far from the palace. We English consider German coffee to be a close cousin to sealant for Macadam, but in small sips it is quite palatable. We sat in silence until we had finished our breakfast and then Holmes again smiled at me in the condescending manner to which I have become accustomed even if annoyed.

"You inspected the pierced eye socket, did you not?" he said.

"I did. Obviously stabbed with a dagger through to the brain."

"And was the eye open or closed when stabbed?"

I had to stop and think about that one. "Open," I said, "there was no damage to the eyelid. But that is very odd. What man just lies on his back and looks at a dagger as his assailant is about to plunge it into his eye?"

"Very odd, indeed," said Holmes. "And the wound above the eye? What of that?"

I had taken a close look at it as well and was only a bit less perplexed.

"It did not appear to be from the dagger as it was not a single cut. Rather it was more like a triangle, as if a small chisel had been pushed into the skin."

"Excellent. And that is the first calling card left behind," said Holmes.

"What are you talking about?" I demanded.

"Come now, Watson. Where have you observed a triangle and an eye in close proximity to each other?"

I thought for a moment, and then it came to me.

"On the back of the American dollar bill?"

"Precisely. And to which fraternal organization does that symbol belong?"

"The Masons," I said.

"And they wish to let us and all other inquirers know that they are behind these killings."

"Why would they do that?" I asked.

"That, we do not yet know. But let us move on to the other evidence. How might the killer have gained entry?" he asked.

"If no one was observed coming or going past the front desk, then he must have come through the window."

"Precisely. That is exactly what the killer wishes us to believe. And even you could tell that unless we are dealing with someone with superhuman skills in scaling walls, that is impossible."

"How then?"

"Through the door."

I shook my head in disbelief. Holmes smiled at me yet again.

"I believe that I have said to you before, that once you eliminate all other …"

"Confound you, Holmes!" I said. "I know what you have said countless times. But the staff reported no one coming or going late in the evening. So that is impossible."

"No, my dear chap. The staff reported that they saw no *suspicious men* entering or leaving late in the evening or in the early hours of the morning. However, we know that in every hotel in the civilized world there are certain people who *do* enter and leave during those hours but are not considered suspicious. And who might those people be, my good man?"

The answer was obvious. "Prostitutes," I said. "Are you saying that a *woman* was the murderer?"

"There was," he said, "a faint scent of perfume on the pillow. Not something a German man would ever dream of putting on himself."

"So you believe that a woman entered the room and then stabbed these chaps? They were all former soldiers. They could have easily defended themselves against a woman."

"Of course they could if only they were thinking and behaving rationally during the seconds before one eyeball was so violently abused. And, furthermore, did you notice what the chap was wearing."

I had noticed and said that he must have been very tired to fall into bed without changing into his bedclothes.

"Tired enough not to have removed his shoes?" Holmes queried.

He did not permit me to answer but carried on.

"He had removed his suit jacket and his cravat. His shirt and his trousers were somewhat disheveled. He was obviously in a physical state that led him to momentarily close his eyes, permitting his killer to stab him with no defense having been thought necessary."

"What sort of horrible, evil woman would do such a thing?" I said.

Holmes smiled, leaned back in his chair and folded his arms across his chest.

"I have heard some rumors," he said. "Prior to this morning I considered them without credence, but my thoughts are changing. There have been stories circulating throughout the police services and press of Europe of a young woman who works in secret as a paid assassin. She is reported to be stunningly beautiful, a master of the art of seduction, irresistible to susceptible males, and utterly ruthless. These murders may be her handiwork."

"Who is she?" I asked.

"She is known as Annie Morrison and is said to come from America, but no one knows for sure. Some stories have her as French, others as German, others yet as Italian. She could easily have passed as a woman of the evening and entered and left any fine hotel along with a score of other such ladies without causing any suspicion."

"Who paid her?"

"The Masons, most likely. Or perhaps some renegade lodge of their organization. Generally, they do not engage in murder. Extortion is their preferred method of accumulating wealth, which is why so many of them own banks."

"Well then," I said, "if you know who she is and she does not yet know about you, it should not be all that difficult to track her down."

"On the contrary, my good man," replied Holmes. "She knows that I am on her trail."

"How can you say that?"

"Her calling cards."

"What are you talking about?"

"The tobacco ash."

"Holmes, enough."

"On the coffee table in the hotel room, there were four distinct little piles of tobacco ash."

"Which means," I said, "that she smokes and, being American, is not well-mannered enough to use the ash tray but drops the drops the ashes on the table."

Holmes chuckled. "Would it were only that. But each of the four deposits was a different ash. One was Virginia Gold, one from a French *Gitaines,* one was a Burley blend from Turkey, and the fourth a rather vile, rough monstrosity favored by the Australians."

Yet again, my observation was, "How very peculiar."

"And the word scratched into the lacquer on the table. Did you read what it said?"

I acknowledged that I had glanced at it but could not decipher what is said.

"It was hastily scratched," said Holmes, "but it appears that it was the word *rache.*"

I was startled. "Why that's the same word that Jefferson Hope wrote on the wall years ago. What a bizarre coincidence. So this is all about revenge as well."

He gave me yet another of his condescending smiles.

"Not at all, my friend. This brazen fiend is taunting me. Like every criminal in England or America, she has read your romanticized sensational story about our *Study in Scarlee,* and she is obviously aware of my monograph on the one hundred and forty varieties of tobacco ash. So she is rubbing my nose in it. She is utterly daring me to try to track her down and stop her."

"Can you?"

"In my entire career, I have only been bested by one woman, *the woman*, and it shall not happen again. Irene Adler was a noble woman in her own right. This woman is a cold-blooded assassin, and I will see her hang for her deeds."

The smile had long departed Holmes's face and in its place was a set jaw, eyes as hard as steel, and a furrowed brow. As he spoke, his fists slowly clenched until his knuckles whitened. The assassin who had hunted down these soldiers had become the hunted.

The pleasant interlude that we had enjoyed over coffee on at the edge of the Rhine had vanished. Without saying anything, Holmes rose from the table, left some coins beside the unfinished breakfast and turned and walked away. I hastened to follow him.

"What now?" I asked.

"Back to England."

"Pardon me if I ask why. She's killing Germans in France and Alsace. Why England?"

"Because that is where she will strike next."

"Enough, Holmes. Explain."

He immediately stopped his hurried pace and turned to me, forcing a smile.

"Forgive me, my dear chap. My manners have been terrible. I will explain. Among the young officers who were part of the battalion that occupied Metz, there were the five who are already murdered. The only other one I have identified is a fellow named Maurice Kellerman. He moved to

England immediately after leaving the Prussian army and changed his name to Morris Cunningham. He is living near Reigate in Surrey and I fully expect that he is next on the list to be assassinated. Our assassin is likely already on her way there. We need to get there as soon as possible. Our taking our time to come to Strasbourg has meant that we were not able to stop the murder of Friedal. I do not plan to make that same mistake again."

He turned and resumed his forced march back to the hotel.

"But," I protested, "you told the Commissar that you would report to him tomorrow morning."

Holmes slowed his pace. "Yes ... I suppose I did. Would you mind terribly sending him a note explaining that we were called away suddenly and that we will wire a full report from London."

"What reason can I give?"

"Good heavens, Watson. Use your imagination. Make something up. And while you are at it, please send a telegram to Mr. Cunningham in Reigate warning him to take precautions for his life and advising him that we are on our way as quickly as possible."

He resumed his near run until we reached the hotel.

Chapter Four
Return to Surrey to Stop a Murder

We departed from the hotel in full view of the desk and any spies that might have been watching us and rushed to the train station. Travel from Alsace, across France, and then back to England took two full days. This time it was Holmes who paced back and forth on the deck of the ferry whilst I scribbled away in the cabin. Upon arrival in Dover we spent the night in a local hotel and first thing the next morning we boarded a train to Surrey. By early afternoon we had arrived at the station in Reigate.

"Mr. Sherlock Holmes and Dr. Watson," spoke a voice from behind us as we entered the station. We turned to face a tall, gaunt man who was formally dressed. His face, elongated and jaundiced, was a mask of impassivity.

"Yes," replied Holmes, "and who might you be?"

"My name, sir, is William Kirwan. I am in service to the Squires Cunningham. I have been sent by him to bring you to the manor. Kindly follow me please, gentleman."

He said nothing more but reached for our valises and, taking one in each hand, turned and walked toward to roadway in front of the station. There was an elegant closed carriage standing there, attended to by a uniformed driver and a gleaming brace of black horses. Mr. Kirwan passed the luggage to the driver and then opened the carriage door.

We stepped up and inside and he followed, placing himself on the comfortable bench seat opposite Holmes and me. I heard the driver give a shout to the horses and we were underway.

"The drive," said Kirwan, "to the manor will take some twenty minutes. Since time is limited, you will forgive me if I make the most of it. I know who you are, Mr. Holmes, having read all about you in *The Strand*, and in the accounts in the press of your exceptional accomplishments."

Holmes offered a perfunctory smile and began a reply.

"Thank you ..."

"It would be," interrupted Kirwan, "a more efficient use of our time if you would not speak but listen and respond to my questions. Thank you."

Holmes stopped speaking and this time gave a nod and a genuine smile.

"I am listening."

"I assume, sir, that you are aware that over the past few years, because of the decline in the value of the pound sterling against several of the European currencies, a distressing number of fine English estates have been purchased by opportunistic foreigners."

"I am aware of that trend," replied Holmes. "It has been particularly widespread in Surrey. I was not aware, however, of its having become a bone of contention amongst the local populace. The tone of your voice leads me to suspect that it has."

"We're all fair-minded English men and women," said Kirwan. "We respect the French and the Germans and the Dutch and the rest of them, but we are perhaps a little more fond of them when they stay on their side of the Channel than on ours. And we are not at all fond of them when they come over here and take advantage of our good English families, who may have fallen on hard times."

"Are you attempting, Mr. Kirwan," said Holmes, "to allude to some aspects of your employer's undertaking. If you are, then I suggest that you come right out and say so. As you have noted, time is limited. So if you are trying to say something, sir, then say it or quit wasting my time."

The fellow appeared to be a bit taken aback by the bluntness of Holmes's statement and for a few seconds did not respond. Then he gave a nod and continued.

"You have come here because Squire Cunningham *pere* and Squire Cunningham *fils* have engaged your services. Is that correct?"

"No, that is not correct. One: I was not aware that there were two squires, a father and a son. And two: they have not yet requested my services nor have I agreed to have them as my clients."

"That is good news, Mr. Holmes. It is my understanding that you are an honorable man and I can assure you that there are no more dishonorable men in all of Surrey that Messrs. Cunningham and Cunningham."

"That, sir," replied Holmes, "is a surprising comment coming from a man who has been in their service for a long time. The fact that you are you still here leaves me highly skeptical of your probity and your motives."

"As you should be, sir. I assure you that both are above reproach and my comments are for your sake, sir, and not mine. I entered service in the manor twenty years ago. It was owned at that time by Sir Oswald Acton and a more decent man has never walked the face of this earth. It was an honor beyond words for me to be of service to him. Five years ago he entered into a promising business venture that ended up in failure, and he suffered enormous financial losses. The strain on him was so great that his heart failed. He passed away and his saintly wife was forced to sell the manor for a pittance but she needed the funds immediately to pay off debts and she took the first offer made to her. It came from a German named Kellerman. At the last minute, he demanded that, as part of the agreement, I and the rest of the staff sign contracts to serve for a minimum of five more years. We were all so devoted to Mrs. Acton, and so desirous to see her relieved of her misery, that we did not hesitate to agree to his terms. Our doing so was a terrible mistake. Should you wish me to disclose matters that are normally kept in confidence, I would agree to do so. I understand from reading Dr. Watson's stories that you are a master at getting staff to reveal confidences about their employers."

"Am I indeed?" said Holmes. "That may be true, and I recall numerous times when I had to coax and persuade the household help to take me into their confidence. I do not recall a time when it was volunteered so readily. So please proceed, and do try to be as exact as possible."

The fellow began to speak in measured tones, but with each sentence his face became progressively redder and his speech more animated.

"Quite so, sir. Both father and son are vile monsters, utterly lacking in shame, civility, or any normal degree of decency. They are, as I assume you are aware, not even Englishmen. They are immigrants from somewhere on the Continent—Germans, likely—we are not sure. They are most certainly not squires. They falsely appropriated that honorable title in order to give themselves airs. We, the staff of the manor, to a man and a maid, have put an end to that pretense. We have bruited it about the town that they are frauds and to be treated as such."

"I suspect," said Holmes, "that they were not particularly grateful to you for doing so."

"It was done in secret, sir. Were they to know the source, they would seek harsh retribution, and they are capable of exacting the same."

"Are they? How might that be so?"

"If anyone in the town dares to cross either of them, they take that person to court on completely false accusations. They use their wealth to hire some unscrupulous lawyers from London and invariably either win their cases or grind their opponents down with ruinous legal costs. They are merciless. The neighboring estate was recently sold to a chap from Leeds, another outsider with money to spare, and no sooner had the ink dried on the deeds than the Cunninghams had launched a suit claiming that they owned a prize section of pasture. They will do anything, *anything*, to have their way and line their pockets."

"They would not be the first wealthy landowners to do so. I can think of several, all Englishmen to the core, who act in the same manner, even to their own English neighbors."

"That is only the beginning of it, Mr. Holmes. Both of them are immoral, lecherous womanizers. The son has already charmed and seduced several of the young maidens in the town, promised them that they would become the lady of the manor, then tossed them aside, ruined for life. The father has acted in a similar manner with three of the widows, each of whom had been left in a financially secure position by a loving husband. But that evil man convinced them that he would be their Lord Protector, had them sign over to him authority for their affairs, drained their accounts, and tossed them aside, utterly heart-broken and impoverished."

"Are the inhabitants of Reigate complete imbeciles?" asked Holmes. "How is it that they have let this go on time after time?"

"The monsters have been brought to a complete halt, sir.

But it took time. Young women and widows are alike in the susceptibility to the false charms of a wealthy man. But now their evil deeds are known throughout, and no one in the entire town will give them the time of day. Those of us on the staff are counting the days until our years under contract have expired, and we can seek positions that afford us some degree of pride and dignity."

The man's fists had clenched as he spoke and he was near apoplectic with anger as he struggled to get the words out. Holmes remained as cool as steel.

"Very well, sir. I take your information under advisement and will govern myself accordingly. I have come to Reigate, however, because it appears that the lives of the squires might be in danger."

"That, sir," Kirwan exploded, "would be most welcomed by all and sundry. I can think of nothing more honorable for a person to do that to cut their throats. Were it not that I have a wife and children to think of, I would gladly do it myself."

With this utterance, the man suddenly seemed to realize that he might have said more than he intended to. He took a deep breath, folded his arms across his chest, and said no more. We continued in silence until we reached our destination.

The entry gate was large and stately, although not particularly fancy. The arch above the drive bore the name *Hills of Lorraine* and the grounds surrounding it were immaculate and well-groomed. The roadway to the manor house was as straight as an arrow, lined with shrubs and trees that were all planted in neat, formal rows. The house itself was large, with three full stories of near featureless walls, except for rows of unadorned windows and a central door.

William Kirwan stepped out of the carriage as soon as it stopped and reached up so that the driver could hand him our valises.

"Follow me, gentlemen," he said to us, turning and walking toward the door of the house as he spoke.

A maid opened the door and gave a slight bow and forced smile to us as we entered. She was youngish and, like so many country girls of England, rather plain, with a moon face and eyes that bulged slightly. She was not underfed.

"Maggie," said Kirwan, "please show these gentlemen to the library. The squires are expecting them. I will let them know they have arrived."

Then, turning to us, he continued, "You will most likely be made to wait for half an hour simply as a matter of arrogance on behalf of the Germans. However, the chairs are comfortable, and there are a few decent books to read. Kindly now, excuse me gentlemen, and I trust you *will* govern yourselves accordingly."

He gave a stiff bow and disappeared down a hallway that was lined with heads of various species of hunted animals. Holmes and I waited in silence in the library. I passed the time by scribbling in my notebook whilst Holmes perused the volumes and photographs on the shelves.

"Anything of interest?" I asked him, to alleviate the boredom.

389

"Interestingly," he replied without turning away from the shelves, "there is nothing of interest."

"Holmes," I said.

He gave a low chuckle. "Every single book is in English, and all appear to have been left behind by the widow who sold the house to these fellows. There is even a set of Pope's *Homer*, complete except for the fifth volume. There is not a single volume in either French or German or whatever native tongue these fellows speak. Most former soldiers have at least a few volumes of military history that they insist on taking with them as if they were their favorite pets, but these chaps are bereft of such works. There is a small framed photograph of men in uniform, but that's all. Their military experience has been all but erased."

I returned to my notebook and he to the next wall of shelves. It was a full forty-five minutes before the door opened and two men entered. Both were very casually dressed in riding clothes and bore a distinct family resemblance to each other. The older man, the father, was well into his seventies, and the younger closer to my age. Both were tall and thin, with short, cropped blond hair and neat military mustaches. Had I not been told that they were former officers in Bismarck's army, I might well have guessed.

"Good afternoon," said the younger chap. "We welcome the esteemed Messrs. Holmes and Watson to the Hills of Lorraine. I trust your journey was a comfortable one."

I had expected to hear a German accent, but there was not a trace. Using what limited skills I had acquired in my years with Holmes, I deduced that he must have had an English governess. The Germans are rather fond of their connection to our Queen and enjoy indulging in spinsters from Oxfordshire along with shortbread and Harris tweed.

Holmes did not answer the question but spoke bluntly to the man.

"Herr Kellerman, I assume you received and read the telegram we sent you."

"Yes."

"You are aware, then, that several of your fellow officers from your time in the war have been murdered."

"Yes. We know that."

"I have good reason to believe that the murderer will soon come here and attempt to murder you in the same manner. I advise both of you to vacate this place immediately and move to a safer location. I have notified Scotland Yard of my concerns, and they have agreed to provide a guarded residence in London until the murderer is apprehended."

"Really, Mister Holmes," interrupted the younger man. "You cannot expect us to go fleeing from our home every time someone tells us that there might be someone somewhere who does not like us. Really, sir, this is hardly the first time we have received threats and warnings and, I assure you, we are not cowards. Both my father and I have served with distinction in the Prussian army, where turning and running away were not options. We appreciate your apparent efforts on our behalf. However, other perspectives have come from officials in our embassy who, I assure you, have access to information far beyond that of an amateur detective."

Holmes stiffened on that one but retained his cool composure.

"I regret that I do not have the same privileged data that your embassy officials do. All I know is that five men, your former fellow officers, are now dead and I have good reason to believe that you are next on the list. I came only to apprise you of what I know and urge you to take precautions."

The younger would-be squire relaxed his expression and responded.

"We appreciate your concern for us, Mr. Holmes. It is not that we refuse to acknowledge the threat. Obviously, there is danger. But we will not run away. We have, you will be pleased to know, hired a dozen excellent men, all veterans of the Prussian army, to serve as our bodyguards and to patrol the property. They will continue to look after us until you and your friends at Scotland Yard, and all those clowns in the *gendarmes de Paris* solve this spate of crimes and catch the villain.

"Now then, gentlemen," he continued, "you have come here in good faith, and we welcome you as our guests for dinner and the evening. We will not need your offers of advice after breakfast tomorrow, and you will be free to return to London and your detective practice. Is that quite correct, father?"

"Ja."

The old fellow gave a shallow bow toward us and turned and departed from the room. His son followed. Once they had gone, Holmes and I found ourselves standing alone in the library looking quizzically at each other. The situation was relieved by the entrance of Kirwan who stood straight and announced, "Dinner will be served at half-past seven o'clock in the dining room. If you will follow me, I will show you to your rooms. You are free to enjoy the gardens until dinner time. This way, please gentlemen."

The rooms were clean and furnished in a modern fashion, albeit Spartan. The mattresses were thin and firm, and the chairs were all upright. In a way, this was satisfying to me as it confirmed my prejudices about Germans' abhorrence of creature comforts. I had hardly sat down to add to my notes than Holmes tapped on my door.

"From my window," he said, "I can see the next house along the road. I am guessing that the owner is the one referred to by Mister Kirwan."

"The chap at odds with the Cunninghams over property?" I said.

"Exactly. And as we have two and a half hours until supper is served, I suggest that we pay him a visit and have a bit of a chat. Are you up to a stiff walk?"

"I am," I said and we walked out of the manor house and along the manicured paths, through the geometric gardens and over to the neighbor's house.

This home, while of similar size and construction to the one in which we were staying, looked somewhat different. Every wall of the house was bordered by a garden bed in which were planted a limited assortment small ornamental trees. The grounds and gardens adjacent to the drive that lead up to the door were similar in their orderliness and neat geometric design to the estate in which we were staying. The walls were painted white, and the windows were unadorned with shutters, and above the front door an overly large Union Jack had been hung on a protruding flag pole. If this house could speak, I thought, it would be shouting 'Rule Britannia.'

Holmes appeared not to notice the landscaping or look of the house and was making a beeline to the front door. He gave a friendly, rhythmical knock on the door and pasted a smile on his face as it opened. The young blonde maid who answered was most assuredly not English, as no English girl engaged in service would dream of wearing a uniform that not only was suggestive of an Alpine milk maid but displayed so vast an expanse of generous bosom.

"*Guten tag*," she said pleasantly. "Please to come in. May I make announcement to *der Knappe* of our visitor?"

Holmes handed her his card, and I did likewise. She glanced at them, and her eyes widened.

"*Heiliger Strohsack!*" Sherlock Holmes and Doctor Watson. *Beeindruckend!*" She gave a smile and a stiff bow, turned and disappeared into the back of the house. We stood for several minutes in the entry hall glancing about at the variety of items mounted on the walls and side tables. There was a photograph of an impressive looking young man in uniform, a crucifix, some paintings in the recent European style that I considered smudged, a portrait of the Queen and, on the side table, a large pile of recent newspapers from the Continent and a large bust of Beethoven.

Holmes focused his gaze on the furnishings and photographs until his concentration was interrupted by the entrance of the master of the estate. A tall, broad-shouldered man of about fifty approached us. He was quite a handsome fellow, with a full head of bushy silver hair and attractive blue eyes.

"Well now, isn't this just the cat's pajamas!" he said in a refined Oxford accent as he approached us. "Is it possible? By the great detective Sherlock Holmes my humble home is visited, and the famous writer, Doctor Watson. Rather takes the egg on a sunny afternoon. To what do I owe this honor? Please, gentlemen, come in and be seated. Some brandy, perhaps. Or shall I have our Swiss miss organize a cup of tea? Please, do come in and yourselves make comfortable."

We entered a finely appointed front parlor and were seated.

"Permit me to introduce myself," he said. "I am Percy Sheridan, formerly of Leeds and London, and now of Surrey. But then, since you are Sherlock Holmes, you must have already known that, I make the assumption."

He laughed at his pleasantry, and we exchanged a minute of idle chitchat about Holmes's reputation before Holmes cut off the exchange.

"Forgive my lack of grace," he said, "but we are not here to talk about the weather. I have a more serious concern that I must address to you."

"Jolly good, then," responded Mr. Sheridan with a smile. "Then please, proceed."

"I came to Surrey because of your neighbors, the Cunninghams."

Sheridan responded with a shrug. "You don't say, Mr. Holmes. This does not surprise me. If you told me that you had investigated them and that they were about to be arrested, thrown in prison, and hanged, I could only say that it was about time. Scoundrels, both of them. Please tell me that soon they will be arrested."

"No, I cannot tell you that. What I will tell you is that it is more likely that they will be murdered if they remain in their house."

"Indeed? Well, now, quite frankly, I must say that is jolly good news. Perhaps the world would be a better place if that were to be made to happen."

Holmes gave the fellow a bit of a look. "That is not exactly a charitable thing to say about one's neighbor."

Sheridan laughed. "It is only what I would say about *these* neighbors. And it is no more than any of their neighbors would say about them. The good yeomen of this town do not like any Johnny-come-lately outsiders, myself included, but Squire Cunningham with a passion they hate, and his son even more. If some day you find them done in, you will have no fewer than a hundred local Lushingtons to suspect, every one of them the honor claiming." He laughed again.

"Let me assist you," he continued. "A start on your list of suspects. Number one," he said, extending his thumb, "would have to be our fine local constable. Forrester's his name. The younger junior squire seduced his sister and ruined her. So he's been heard saying that he'd like to kill the blackguard. Number two," he added, extending his index finger, "would be the barkeep. His dear widowed mother was swindled by the older squire, and the poor man lost his entire inheritance. And number three," he concluded, adding his middle finger, "might very well be the vicar, who has no specific complaint, but is outraged by the debauchery and misery those two have visited upon his faithful flock. There, is that enough of a start for you, Mr. Holmes?" Again, he laughed merrily.

Holmes smiled in return. "And what about you, Mr. Sheridan. Your dispute over property would give you a place on your list, would it not?"

That brought about a loud guffaw. "Aha! Our detective has been doing his homework. Jolly good. Why of course, you can add me. But in all modesty, I could not claim a post above number ten. Lawyers from both sides may be at it with both hands, but all the stake that is of me is a parcel of land, not the destruction of my honor or the theft of my inheritance. But by all means, do not leave me off your list." Again, the laughter.

Holmes did not join in the laughter or even smile. "In truth, sir, the danger is not from the local citizenry, sir. I have reason to believe that someone from the Continent may arrive and seek to do them harm."

"You don't say. The man's name, do you happen to have it? I assure you that the keys to the town he will be awarded."

We chatted for several more minutes, but it was obvious to me that Holmes had had enough of this jolly chap from the North. We excused ourselves, claiming that our dinner would be waiting and returned to The Hills of Lorraine. Holmes walked in silence, his hands thrust into the pockets of his coat and his chin nearly resting on his chest.

Our hosts did not join us for dinner, and it was served by the moon-faced English maid, who did her best to be pleasant and offer some meaningless chit-chat, but Holmes was having none of it. He glowered at the schnitzel and sauerkraut that was served to him and ate the entire meal in silence.

Chapter Five
Not Wanted, So Back to 221B

The following morning the same young maid assisted us with our departure from the manor house. She appeared to be thoroughly intimidated by Sherlock Holmes, but she stood beside me for a moment and spoke quietly.

"We're so sorry to see you leave us, Dr. Watson," she said. "When we saw the two of you arrive, all of the staff got our hopes up that something was about to change here. It is a terribly unhappy situation we are all in."

I smiled at her. "My dear, you will just have to wait it out for another few months, then your five years will be up, and you will be free to seek another position."

"I suppose so, sir," she sighed. "But if you hear of the squires' dying from drinking poisoned tea, you can have the entire lot, all twelve of us, arrested."

For a brief second, a thought flashed through my mind. Having twelve people all conspire together and jointly commit a murder would be a splendid basis for a mystery story.

I smiled again, and as I was old enough to be her father, I put my arm around her shoulder and offered some bland words of encouragement. William Kirwan loaded our valises into the carriage but did not join us on the return trip to the station. As we passed out of the gate, I noticed two large Teutonic-looking men standing guard. At the Reigate station, I saw another three of them standing and shaking hands and introducing themselves to each other. I concluded that the squires had indeed hired some of their countrymen to guard their estate.

"We have some time," said Holmes, "before the train to London departs. Let us pay a brief visit to the local constable. He's just next door."

The local constable, a friendly fellow named Stuart Forrester, welcomed us to his station. He appeared to be quite pleased to meet Sherlock Holmes but was obviously perplexed as to why Holmes would be visiting his village. Holmes explained the reasons for our visit and gave a very stern warning that a murderer would soon be making a visit to Reigate with the intent of doing in the younger Cunningham, and possibly the father as well.

"Very good, Mr. Holmes," said Constable Forrester. "But having one more person to suspect of murdering those two blackguards would extend my list to over twenty. The local folks do not like those two at all. And if a stranger comes to do the deed, I will guarantee that he will be among friends here for the rest of his life."

"So I have been led to believe," said Holmes, with a grim smile. "But please note; the person most likely to appear is not a man. It will be a young woman and a highly attractive one at that."

Forrester raised his eyebrows. "Well now, wouldn't that just take the biscuit. You say a pretty young lass might come to Reigate and murder those scoundrels. There would be a score of young local lasses and a few widows who would nominate her for sainthood if that were to happen."

"It is not my role," said Holmes, "to render judgment on the victims. I only beseech you to be vigilant so that a crime will be prevented. May I count on you to respond accordingly?"

"Of course, you may, Mr. Holmes. I will swear on my honor that should I see a beautiful young woman in town who is unknown amongst us and who may have come with murderous intent ... well ... I swear that I will declare that I am too sick to continue working for the rest of the day and will be found recovering my health at the Bull's Head."

Holmes glared at the constable who met him eye to eye and said nothing.

"Very well, Constable Forrester," said Holmes. "I believe I understand what you are telling me. Good day, sir."

"Good day, Mr. Holmes, Dr. Watson. Sorry I could not be of more use to you."

For the first half hour of the return trip to Victoria, Holmes sat in silence. As we passed Croydon, he looked up at me.

"Those Prussian veterans will most likely be useless," he muttered. "She will get past the guards and kill them both within a fortnight. Mark my words. They are as good as dead."

"Is there not anything you can do to protect them?" I asked.

He shook his head. "I cannot force anyone to become my client, least of all a couple of pig-headed Germans. If I might offer you a turn of phrase for your notebook, you could say that I predicted that both of them will become eyesores."

I chuckled at Holmes's gallows humor, and we continued the rest of the journey back to Baker Street in silence.

The next three days passed uneventfully. I tended to my patients whilst Holmes puttered away with his chemistry experiments and readings. It was not difficult for me to see that his mind was elsewhere and from time to time I observed him clenching his fists and shaking his head.

On the morning of the fourth day, as we sat quietly enjoying the delectable breakfast Mrs. Hudson had prepared for us, the bell sounded at the door on Baker Street. A minute later, Mrs. Hudson entered.

"It's the Inspector, Mr. Holmes. I told him you were still at your breakfast, but he said he was coming up anyway. Shall I show him in?"

Holmes pushed his chair back from the table and sighed. "Yes, you may. And you may as well make him a fresh cup of tea and bring him some biscuits and jam. I suspect he has been up for several hours and will not be in a good humor."

Inspector Lestrade appeared almost immediately. As predicted by Holmes, his ferret-like face was even darker than usual.

Without bothering to rise from his chair or even look up, Holmes spoke into his tea cup.

"Good morning, Inspector. Nasty business, that, down in Surrey, what say? Got them good in the old eyeball, eh."

I was looking up at Lestrade even if Holmes was not. A flush of anger spread across his face, and I heard him suck in a deep breath of self-control before speaking.

"I did not come here to endure your taunts, Holmes. I have two murders on my hands, which is bad enough, but I am informed that Sherlock Holmes met with the victims three days ago and warned the local constable that they were about to be murdered. Is that correct, Holmes?"

He sat down on the settee and folded his arms across his chest. The dutiful Mrs. Hudson handed him a cup of tea, and he graciously thanked her before returning his scowl to Holmes.

"Yes, Inspector," said Holmes. "That is correct, and I suspect that the murderer got clean away with the deed. Is that also correct?"

"No," said Lestrade. "That is wrong. We have him locked up behind bars already, but I need a statement from you. We had to lean on the carriage driver a bit hard, but he admitted that he had heard the man-servant, a Mr. William Kirwan, say that he would like to kill the two victims, and he said so in your presence. So, I need you to corroborate. Did he say that to you, Holmes? Yes, or no?"

Holmes's mouth involuntary opened and a look of shock and dismay spread across his face.

"No, Inspector, no. You have it all wrong."

"What do you mean 'No' Holmes. Are you denying that William Kirwan said that to you? Did he or didn't he?"

"That is what he said, but he is not the murderer."

"He had," said Lestrade, "the motive, the means, and the opportunity. That is what we look for, isn't it, Holmes. You've just confirmed that he said he wanted to kill them and two days later, they're dead. Other than the simple maid, he was the only person in the house when the deaths occurred. What do you mean telling me that he's not the murderer?"

Sherlock Holmes very seldom if ever loses his composure, but I had never seen him so flustered and ill at ease as he was whilst being cross-questioned by Lestrade.

"That man ... Mr. Kirwan ... he is innocent. He is a good man. You have the wrong person. He could not have done it."

"It is rather obvious to me, Holmes that he most certainly *could* have done it. You're going to have to do better than that. Now, I have a statement here that says that Sherlock Holmes acknowledges hearing Mr. William Kirwan, the man-servant of the Squires Cunningham, father and son, clearly and distinctly state that he wished to kill his masters. Kindly sign it, and I'll be on my way. And please thank Mrs. Hudson for the tea."

Holmes drew a deep breath and sat back in his chair. He seemed to have recovered his self-control and spoke in deliberate, measured tones to Lestrade.

"Inspector Lestrade," he said. "You and I have had our differences from time to time."

"That is an understatement, Holmes. Get on with it."

"I am, however, entirely certain that you know, beyond any doubt, that in spite of our differences, both of us have devoted our lives to the pursuit of justice."

"And I do not have time for a Sunday School lesson, Holmes."

"Very well then. I will tell you that I am entirely certain, beyond any doubt, that William Kirwan is innocent of the murder of the squires, and that if he is punished for the crime, you will have sent an innocent man to the gallows."

"The evidence is all stacked up against him, Holmes. If he didn't do it, then who did?"

Holmes rose from his chair and walked over to the window, slowly lit a cigarette and took two slow drafts. Lestrade was showing signs of impatience.

"Holmes, I am getting old waiting. I have two murders to deal with, and if you have evidence, then I need to hear it. Now."

"Have you ever," said Holmes, speaking to the bay window and the cloudy sky beyond, "Heard the name, Annie Morrison?"

Lestrade's glare could have burned holes into Holmes's back.

"Of course, I have heard the name, Holmes. You and I are connected to the same web of rumors. Are you suggesting that this chimera of international crime, this avenging angel who has been a nightmare on the Continent and in America, but never once appeared, even in a dream, in Britain, suddenly dropped out of the sky and into Surrey, did in two squires, and then vanished? Are you taking me for such a fool as to believe that? What's next? Dracula in Derbyshire? Beelzebub in Bucks? What sort of fool do you think I am?"

Holmes turned back, came over and sat across from him. Slowly and patiently he presented the evidence he had assembled and the conclusions he had deduced so far in this gruesome case. Lestrade interrupted him rather rudely many times and cross-questioned him quite aggressively. Holmes endured the disrespect and relentlessly piled observations and deductions on top of each other until the expression on Lestrade's face softened and began to nod his head slowly. Finally, he stood up and walked slowly toward the door, but before getting there, he reached into a pocket in his suit coat, extracted an envelope, and dropped into onto a side table.

"I reserved a cabin for the three of us on the noon train to Surrey," he said. "I told Constable Forrester to disturb nothing and keep the room chilled, and that I would be there by one thirty and would be bringing Sherlock Holmes with me."

Holmes looked positively befuddled.

"I beg your pardon?" he said.

Lestrade turned back to face him. "Look here, Holmes. I was not born yesterday. I've been in this game far too long not to know the difference between an open and shut murder case, and one that is apparently open and shut and into which Sherlock Holmes has already stuck his bloody nose. As soon as I was informed that you had been poking around, I knew jolly well that there was something rotten in the state of Denmark. I'll see you at a quarter to noon on the Victoria platform. We have rooms reserved at the inn."

Holmes, irresistibly I could tell, smiled at him. "I look forward to the excursion," he said, "But you might think about Macbeth rather than Hamlet."

Lestrade gave him one last look, shook his head, and departed.

Chapter Six
The Mysterious Maiden Appears

"Would you mind, terribly," he said to me, "making alternative arrangements for your patients for the next two days? I would be most grateful for your assistance."

"I was just scribbling a note to Dr. Ansthruser, asking him to assist me. I did the same for him a fortnight ago. I am sure he will, and I would not think of letting you return to Reigate without me, what with Dracula and Beelzebub and a murdering maiden on the loose."

"Splendid," he said. "And you might bring your service revolver along with you. It is always better to bring a gun if your assailant is bearing a dagger. Now then, we have a few hours before we have to be at the station, and I would like to enjoy the rest of my tea, which was so rudely interrupted by the dear Inspector."

He was positively beaming and smiling into his teacup. His entire body had been possessed with that unmistakable zeal that I have seen time and again when he sets out on a quest in pursuit of a villain whose machinations require the application of his most intense resolve and reasoning.

I smiled at him, fondly I admit, and again thanked heaven for my unique opportunity to assist him and chronicle his adventures.

Our brief moment of delightful anticipation did not last.

There was a soft knock at the door on Baker Street, and Mrs. Hudson soon appeared.

"It's a young lady, Mr. Holmes. I told her that you were still at breakfast, but she would not listen to me. She is terribly distraught and insists that she has been horribly wronged and that her honor is at stake, and if she cannot see you immediately she will have to throw herself into the Thames. Mind you, she is young and looks a bit the athlete, and I suspect she knows how to swim. And, she is an American. Shall I send her away?"

Holmes sighed, leaned back in his chair and rolled his eyes up toward the ceiling. His weakness for members of the fair sex in distress was the chink in his armor, and he gave a nod to Mrs. Hudson.

"Show her in. We have a few minutes still to spare, and we may as well give her a listen. Did she give you her name?"

"Yes. She said her name was Annie Morrison."

Holmes and I stared at each other in disbelief and quickly put down our tea and rose to our feet. I had a fleeting thought that I should rush to my room and fetch my service revolver but before I could move a young woman appeared in our doorway. She was of medium stature and proportions and dressed most fashionably. Her chestnut hair was perfectly arranged on top of her head but what was striking about her was her face. She was one of the most beautiful young women I had ever seen in my entire life, anywhere on earth. Her features were obviously not those of our plain English lassies, and certainly not the rugged healthy look of a typical American girl. If anything, they were French, and her brilliant smile was utterly disarming.

"Oh my," she said with an undertone of laughter and a distinctly American accent. "I do hope I am not disturbing your two wonderful gentlemen too much? Please, allow me to give you my calling card. I specially selected it just for this morning. I do understand that Mr. Sherlock Holmes is a collector of such rare and refined instruments."

She walked directly to the coffee table, reached into her handbag and placed a small dagger on the table. I did not have a clear view of it but it was unadorned and appeared to be a narrow blade, no more than five inches in length. What was odd was the metal apparatus that extended from one side of the hilt. Affixed to it was a small hollow triangle of about a half an inch along each side.

This brazen young woman then sat down on the settee and smiled beautifully but shamelessly at Sherlock Holmes.

"My dear Mr. Holmes, I am a damsel in distress and in desperate need of your services. Shall I state my case, kind sir?"

Holmes was still standing and glaring down at her.

"I do not offer my services to paid assassins. Now, either give a reason for your presence here immediately, or I shall call for the police to have to arrested."

"Oh my," she said and laughed merrily. "You do me wrong to cast me off so discourteously. But comply, I shall. In fact, kind sir, I shall give you three excellent reasons why you should refrain from calling the police."

Holmes said nothing and continued to stand and stare at her. I sat down and did the same, already, I must confess intrigued by this lovely if deadly apparition in 221B Baker Street.

"Well, Mr. Holmes, the first reason why you must not call the police is the fact that three years ago I took the gold ribbon in revolver shooting in the Rod and Gun Club of Houston, besting every one of the men who competed against me. You can read about it in the Houston Chronicle. I was listed under another name, but it is all there, I assure you, sir."

Holmes countenance did not soften. "Quit wasting my time."

"Oh my, sir. You do appear to demand haste. Such a shame. Very well then, here is my second reason. In my handbag is a Colt 45 and my hand, as you can observe, is already placed inside as well. So I am sure that you, being the brilliant detective that you are, will have deduced that my hand is firmly holding my gun and that if you rush to the window to summon the police, well, I will just have to stop you in your tracks. But I swear, sir, I would only give you a very small wound in one of your legs from which you would soon recover. I would do that, sir, out of professional courtesy since I believe in my heart of hearts that you and I truly are fighting for the same army of justice and righteousness. Now, may I give you my third reason?"

"Speak," said Holmes. I could see that the cold fury had slipped away from his face.

"Because you know, and I know, and I know that you know that I know, that your brilliant mind is burning with curiosity and very eager indeed to learn what it is that moved me to such an unexpected act as to invade your presence on such a lovely spring morning. And so you cannot resist the opportunity hear me out, knowing that it may be the only chance you will ever have for such an encounter. Would I be correct in that assumption, Mr. Holmes?" Yet again, she laughed merrily and infectiously.

Holmes shook his head but did so clearly in chagrin and resignation and sat down across from the beautiful young American.

He nodded to her. "You may proceed. But I reserve the right to send you off to the gallows once you have imparted your information."

She flashed him a brilliant smile, wriggled her bosom in a contrived attempt to become more comfortable and began.

"Well now, Mr. Holmes. You know and I know that there is a good man, a fine husband and father, in Surrey named

William Kirwan who has been falsely charged with the murder of those two terrible men, *Herr Kellerman vater* and *herr sohn*. And it would be a terrible injustice if the dear Mr. Kirwan had to suffer a minute more than necessary for a crime he did not commit."

She paused and looked sweetly at Holmes. He said nothing.

"And, of course, Mr. Holmes, you are convinced that the foul deed was carried out by none other than yours truly. That is what you think, is it not, Mr. Holmes?"

Again, Holmes said nothing.

"Well, sir. I will swear to you while standing on a stack of Bibles on top of my grandmother's grave, that I did no such thing. Now, do not get me wrong. I fully admit that I came to England with the intention of executing those two villains, but someone somehow got to them before I did. And I assure you, sir, that had I done the deed I would not be proclaiming my innocence since I would have been paid handsomely by my current employer for carrying out such a service. But my mommy and daddy—well, in truth they were my adopted mommy and daddy—made sure that I knew that no matter how hungry or desperate I might be, I was never to take anything that did not rightfully belong to me. So my income, on which I was counting, has now vanished. Now that is bad enough, but if you insist on apprehending me then the true villain will get away scot free and neither you nor I would be very pleased with that prospect, now would we Mr. Holmes? Now, sir, will you permit me to tell you the rest of my story?"

"You may," said Holmes.

"Well now, that is real good of you, kind sir. Or perhaps it would be better if I were to drop the pretense and say, *très bien, mon confrère*. Then I will explain who I am and what has led me to seek your help."

I was startled. The Texan drawl had disappeared and in its place was a very light French accent, such as one might hear from highly educated female members of a sophisticated Parisian salon. She smiled rather seductively and continued.

"Allow me to introduce myself properly, Monsieur Holmes. My true name is not Annie Morrison. I am Jeanne d'Arc Eleanor Josephine Bastien-Lepage. I was given the name of the saintly warrior because my mother was born in Domrémy-la-Pucelle, the birthplace of the maiden saint, and she gave me that name, for which I am forever honored. I was born in the town of Saint-Avold in the region of Alsace, where I lived until I was ten years old, and since then, until four years ago, I lived in the great city of Houston, in the Republic of Texas. Recently I have lived where *le Seigneur*, in his divine wisdom, has sent me.

"I assure you, Mr. Holmes, that I am not a paid assassin, as you have called me. I am an executioner, divinely called by Almighty God, through his servant, St. Michael. I have never done any harm to anyone on earth except for the execution of those evil men who have somehow managed to escape human justice and who St. Michael has told me that I must dispatch to their well-deserved eternity in hell."

Good heavens, I thought to myself. This one truly takes the biscuit. Sitting in our rooms in Baker Street was a stunningly beautiful young woman, who was not only a ruthless murderer but nuttier than a fruitcake. I was not particularly concerned for our safety, but I was surprised to see the look on Holmes's face. He appeared not to be dismissive of this lovely but insane young woman, but to be accepting and indeed intrigued.

"I have been told," she continued, "in a vision that came to me late last night, that I must set aside my other tasks and prove the innocence of Mr. Kirwan. You, sir, I have been informed by my reliable contacts at Scotland Yard, have accepted the same assignment. As we find ourselves on the same team, so to speak, I will accompany you later today to Surrey. I will see you shortly on the platform at Victoria. Permit me to bid you *adieu* until then."

She rose and smiled again in a beguiling manner at Holmes and also at me. I was speechless from her utter audacity, but Holmes responded in a most gracious voice.

"We shall look forward to your company, Mademoiselle Bastien-Lepage. But permit me to offer one small piece of advice. If you wish to lie about having a Colt 45 in your handbag, it would be useful to carry something in it that had a similar weight, a small rock perhaps, so that your bag did not ride so lightly on your arm."

Her face registered an element of surprise, and she glanced at her purse. "Oh my," she said, the Texas accent having returned, "you truly are quite observant. I so look forward to working with you. I am sure that I will be a much-improved liar as a result of our time together."

She departed, and I glared at Holmes.

"You just let her walk away," I sputtered. "If she is who

you say she is then she is responsible for a string of murders all across America and Europe. What are you thinking, Holmes?"

"I am thinking, my dear Watson, that I am aware of her trail of executions, but I also know that not one of them to date has taken place in Great Britain or anywhere in the Empire where British law would apply. And evidence against her on the Continent or in America is no more than rumor. There are no grounds on which to arrest her."

Here he paused, and then, with a trace of a smile, he added, "And, Watson, I confess that I find her quite interesting. She is as mad as a hatter and utterly deluded, but all the same is one of the most brilliant criminal minds I have ever encountered. If my information is correct, she has dispatched up to twenty men, all of whom had highly unsavory reputations, and there is not a shred of evidence against her. Observing her for as long as I am given the opportunity will be most stimulating."

He retreated then to his bedroom, turning to me only to say, "We should depart at half-past eleven. And it might be best if you brought your service revolver along with you."

Chapter Seven
Return to Surrey After the Murder

At ten minutes to noon, Holmes and I stood with Inspector Lestrade on the platform of Victoria Station. Lestrade was talking away about the puzzling murders, but Holmes was not paying close attention. His eyes were glancing up and down the platform, clearly looking to see if the divine executioner would show up. I was ready to conclude that she had lied about meeting us when, at a minute before the train was to depart, she sauntered out of the station and appeared beside us. Lestrade gave her a most peculiar visual inspection and then gave looked at Holmes that in unspoken terms demanded an explanation.

"Inspector Lestrade," said Holmes, "allow me to introduce Miss Annie Morrison. She will be accompanying us to Reigate."

The look on Lestrade's face was one of astonishment, followed quickly by anger.

"Look here, Holmes. I have neither the time nor the patience for your games. If you have no more character than to bring along a mistress half your age on official Yard business, then I have lost whatever respect I may have had for your honor. I will see you in Reigate."

He turned on his heel and walked toward a railway cabin and closed the door rather smartly behind him.

"Oh my," sighed Miss Morrison, or whoever she was. "That policeman was rather rude to you, sir, and not at all chivalrous to a young lady." She let out a trill of laughter and added, "But I do confess that being mistaken as the mistress of the illustrious Mr. Sherlock Holmes is rather flattering. I have been called much worse in the past and expect that I shall be again in the future. It is an unexpected honor to be called upon to play such a distinguished role."

Holmes gave her an angry look, but she smiled in a manner that I would have termed loving had it not come from so accomplished an actress. Holmes was disarmed and, for a passing second, I was quite sure that he blushed.

Once inside the cabin, Holmes, having recovered his composure, turned to her and said, "It will take at least an hour to get to Reigate. I believe, Miss, that you are under some degree of obligation to give a full accounting of who you are. Kindly state you case. I have no doubt that half of what you say will be falsehoods."

Again, the smile and the laugh. "How astute of you, Mr. Holmes. But do tell; which half will that be? And how will you know?"

She settled back into her seat across from us, stretched out her legs, exposing several inches of perfectly formed calf, and grinned.

"This is the account of Jeanne d'Arc Bastien-Lepage," she began, *sans* the American accent. "I am sure, Monsieur Holmes that you are aware that during the years of 1870 and 1871, there was a war fought between Prussia, or Germany as it is now called, and France. The town of Saint-Avold lies close to the German border and was quickly occupied by the invading forces of the Prussian army. Over a hundred and fifty thousand soldiers passed through our town on their way to the battle of Metz, a few kilometers to the west. But Metz held out and was besieged from August until October, when the people of the city were facing starvation, and the French forces had to surrender. Our lovely, ancient town was used by the Prussian army as a center for supplying food to the troops who were fighting in Metz. Most of our food was taken during those months, but that was a hardship we could have borne.

"The Prussian army was a perfectly disciplined fighting machine, the best in the world, and the officers had to obey a code of military conduct, and they had orders to leave the citizens in peace as long as the food quota was supplied and no resistance was given. My father was one of the leaders of our town and had a fine house. But he was passionately loyal to

La France and organized a resistance movement, a band of *francs-tireurs*, that did whatever it could to frustrate the Prussians and help our men. There was always a danger that he would be found out. The town was full of spies. Since he was a civilian, we knew that if he were caught, he would be sent to prison in Germany. But that, sir, is not what happened.

"The commanding officer of the company that occupied Saint-Avold was a man of unspeakable evil. He was not an honorable soldier, but the devil incarnate. He delighted in torture and debauchery and took every opportunity to line his own pocket by stealing from the people of the town. If they dared to object, he dealt with them in a way more cruel than can ever be imagined. Directly under his command were seven younger officers who, with one exception, followed the example of their colonel, and violated every rule of war, and did evil to any civilian they wished, beating and robbing the men, even killing them at times, and violating the women and young maidens horribly and shamelessly.

"As our town was in the border region between France and Prussia, there were many people who were loyal to France and almost as many whose allegiance fell with Prussia. Half of the population was spying on the other half. So it was not long before my father's work was revealed and our home was entered and my parents arrested. It was on the fifteenth of September in the year 1870. I ran upstairs to a closet where one of the Prussian soldiers found me. He was an honorable man, and he immediately told me to stay hidden and under no circumstances to come out, no matter how horrible might be what I heard happening. He was very insistent. I could not see his face in the darkness, but I could hear the fear in his voice. I was only seven years old, but I knew that I must do as he said.

"For three hours I hid in that closet and listened to the screams of my father as they tortured him and of my mother as they violated and beat her. I could also hear the screams of my little brother as they inflicted pain on him for no reason other than their wicked and perverse pleasure. The one officer, the man who had told me to hide, could be heard trying to get them to stop but he was laughed at and mocked.

"Then the screaming ended, and it became silent. After waiting until darkness had fallen, I came out of hiding and found the mutilated bodies of my father, mother and little brother. I walked to the neighbor's home and asked for help. They were good people who had been friends for many years and they immediately took me in. With the best of loving intentions, they arranged to have me adopted by relatives living in America in the vain hope that a new life would help me get over my tragedy. I was sent to live in Texas. I was given an American name. It did not help. Every night of my life I see the same sight and hear the same screams as I saw that evening seventeen years ago.

"Every morning, I would rise up early and walk around the corner to the church for the early mass. I would kneel and receive the sacraments and hope that the pain would go away. But on my thirteenth birthday, I stayed behind and prayed to St. Michael, just as Joan of Arc had done when she was that age. As the church bells started ringing, I saw a bright light surrounding the saint and a voice spoke to me. It was Saint

Michael, who I saw before my eyes; he was not alone, but was accompanied by many angels from Heaven. I saw them with my bodily eyes, as well as I am seeing you. At first, it appeared that his sword had left his hand and was floating down toward me. Then the sword became smaller and smaller until it was only a small dagger. And then came the voice.

"It said, 'Jeanne d'Arc, you are an instrument of divine justice and will bring God's wrath upon evil men.' In the days and weeks that followed, as I prayed for guidance, the voices came again and again, telling me that I had been called by God, just as had my namesake, to be His instrument and to be the divine executioner of those men who had done great evil but had escaped the punishment that the courts should have given them. The voices also told me that God had given me great physical beauty so that I could use it as a weapon against evil men. I kept all of these things in my heart until I was sixteen years of age and then the instruction from my voices became explicit.

"A man in Houston, where we lived, had been arrested for the murder of his wife. Everyone knew he was guilty, but he was a very rich man and managed to bribe the jury and was declared innocent. St. Michael spoke to me and told me that I was to be the instrument of justice when human justice had failed. Again, the dagger that I had seen when I was thirteen appeared before me and then vanished. But I knew what I had to do. I procured a small dagger and gave my life over to the cause of justice, believing, like Queen Esther, that *if I perish, I perish*.

"The murderer was known to be a lecher and fond of

dishonorable acts with attractive young women. I arranged to meet him, and he immediately took me to his home, where he attempted to seduce me. When he was in a fit of passion, I executed him and sent him off to hell to be punished for his evil life. No one suspected me and the police did not try very hard to solve the case, as they were quite happy to see justice done even if it were not by the courts.

"I waited before God for my next divine mission. It came a few months later. The newspapers reported that a man in Galveston had been arrested for smuggling young Mexican men and women into Texas to work on the farms. But he treated them as slaves and on the boat from Tampico these men and women had been held in the hold for two weeks. Six of them had died. But because their deaths could not be proven to have taken place in America, he was not charged. St. Michael, spoke to me and told me that this man was guilty of murder and since human justice had failed, he must be executed. I was given this mission by the voice of the saint, so at the age of seventeen, I took the train the short distance to Galveston one Saturday morning. I was back home with my adopted family by the late afternoon, and the murderer had been dispatched to hell.

"In obedience to the voices of the saints, I carried out several more missions in Texas, but when I turned eighteen, they told me that my mission was now to the world and so I departed from my home and my loving adopted family and since that day have had no home. When I hear of a great failure of justice, I ask St. Michael for the verdict of God and if it is 'guilty' I make contact through secret means with the families of the victims of the crime and inquire if they are interested in seeking justice and if they are willing to pay for it. Usually, they are. They never see my face, but they have, every one of them, compensated me for my work on behalf of divine justice.

"My greatest mission, as you may have deduced, has been the visiting of justice upon those men who murdered my family. The evil commander of the troops in Saint-Avold was Colonel Kellerman. They did great evil to many of the people of Saint-Avold and not just to my family. So the local lodge of the Masonic Order was very receptive to my offer to deliver justice and agreed to compensate me most generously for my services. I will, however, have to forego a portion of my fee since it was not I who dispatched father and son Kellerman, but some other person. I am determined to discover who this man or woman is so that together we might devote ourselves to the cause of divine justice and rid the earth of those evil men who have been able to elude the police and the courts. And that, sir, is why I have called upon you and have joined you on your quest in Surrey this afternoon."

She smiled yet again, and Holmes gave a forced smile in return.

"I assure you, Mr. Holmes, that what I have told you this afternoon is the truth. I have not lied to you."

"I have no doubt, Miss, that you believe that everything you have told me is the truth. You will forgive me if I am selective in what I choose to believe."

I also had no doubt that this young woman believed that she was speaking truthfully to us. It struck me that it was quite possible that her mind had come undone from the terrible events that happened when she was a child. It also occurred to me that everything she believed might be no more than an illusion and that she was merely a deluded American, born and raised in Texas, who quite sincerely believed herself to be someone entirely different than who she was—a latter-day Saint Joan of Arc. I was not sure if she should be committed to Broadmoor, or sent to the gallows, or considered for future beatification.

We had arrived at the Reigate Station, and we disembarked from the train. The air was brisk, and the sky was cloudless. I commented absently on the day, to which Holmes replied.

"The low temperature is fortunate. The local constable will have kept the windows of the bedrooms open so as to delay the decay of the bodies. That is always useful."

There were several cabs waiting and Mademoiselle Jeanne d'Arc and I took one whilst Holmes and Lestrade took the other. The young woman had said nothing more to us, and neither Jeanne nor Annie spoke as we drove to the Kellerman estate, although from time to time I noticed her lips moving, as if she were carrying on a conversation with persons unknown.

A constable was posted at the gate of the Hills of Lorraine, and two more stood guard at the gate of the house. Lestrade and Holmes had preceded our cab and were waiting for us to arrive. We got out and started walking towards the door, with Mademoiselle Jeanne obviously accompanying me.

The Inspector made it clear that he was having none of Holmes's nonsense with a young mistress.

"Look here, Holmes," he barked.

"My dear, Inspector," said Holmes, interrupting him. "I assure you that my relationship with this young woman is entirely honorable, as is my relationship with any woman I have even known. I am not entirely certain who she is, but have concluded that she may have some useful data and insights to offer to the investigation and that she has committed no crime on British soil. Pray, kindly indulge her presence. I will vouchsafe for her behavior."

Lestrade looked directly at me, his face demanding that I confirm Holmes's assertion. "As far as I know," I said, not entirely confident in what I did or did not know, "you may rely on what Sherlock Holmes has told you."

I gave a bit of an emphatic nod to buttress my claim, and the three of us followed the inspector into the house. For the next two hours, Holmes closely observed the courtyard, the entrance to the house, the bedrooms, and the bodies of the two victims. I followed him, making notes on what I could observe, with Holmes making the occasional comments to me regarding whatever matter he was observing.

When the close inspection of the house and the scenes of the murders had been concluded, Lestrade gave orders to the local policemen to have an undertaker remove the body and allow the household staff to re-enter the premises. The group of us then gathered back downstairs in the library.

"Very well, Holmes," said Lestrade. "Speak up. What have you *deduced*, as you like to call it?"

"The local police carefully followed your instructions and disturbed the site as little as possible. Kindly thank them for their diligence."

"I will do that," said Lestrade, "but I asked what you deduced, not what thank-you notes you wished to send."

"Yes, of course," said Holmes. "It was, however, most helpful that the soil in the courtyard had not been trampled. I observed several sets of footprints that were made by boots that are standard issue for policemen. There was, though, one set that was different from the rest. Earlier this morning, I insisted that the murderer was a woman, the same young woman who now sits in this room. I must now withdraw that accusation. It could not have been her. The length of the stride and the depth of the indentation indicate that it was a male of average height and weight. Somewhat shorter than I am, and somewhat taller than you, Inspector. About the size of Dr. Watson."

"Well now, Holmes," said Lestrade, "that is so very helpful. I'd say about half the men in the village fit that description, the vicar, the priest, the doctor and the postmaster included. In fact, so does Mr. William Kirwan, who, by the way, does not wear police footwear. Pray, continue."

"The last victim I examined, in Strasbourg, was still wearing his evening clothes, or at least most of them, and his shoes. Both of these men were in their night clothes."

"Which tells me," said Lestrade, "that we are dealing with a patient Englishman rather than an impetuous

Frenchman, or Italian, or whoever it was that did in your fellow in Alsace."

Holmes ignored the jibe and carried on. "The murderer in Europe killed her victims with a single stab of a short dagger into the brain. These men had been stabbed multiple times, again and again in the eye with a longer dagger. That was obvious from the blood that emerged from the mouth, nostrils and the other eye socket. This murderer was not at all skilled or certain of his trade. Yet there was a savagery to his actions; a rage. This man was angry, but it is possible, indeed probable, that it was the first time he had killed a man in this manner."

"You do realize," said Lestrade, "that you are doing nothing at all to dissuade me from suspecting Kirwan. Right now, he fits your description to a T. He had access to the house, and the guards have sworn that they saw no one else on the grounds last night. I know you well enough, Holmes, to respect your instincts and your reasoning, but you'll have to do a lot better that what you've done to keep Mr. Kirwan off the gallows. Now, if you have nothing else to tell me, I have a job to do. Good day."

He rose and departed from the room, leaving Holmes, Miss Whoever-she-was, and me in the library. The moon-faced maid came, asked cheerfully if we wished tea, and departed. Holmes paced back and forth for several minutes and then found an appropriately styled chair that permitted him to draw his long legs up under his body, close his eyes, and contemplate. I made some notes about the case but admit that I had very grave doubts as to whether I would ever be able to put it on record as one that Holmes solved. Our young accomplice, with nothing else to do, wandered aimlessly around the library, nonchalantly examining random books and artifacts.

I knew enough not to disturb Holmes whilst he was in his state of concentration, and so silence reigned for some fifteen minutes. It was interrupted by a loud and distressful cry from Mademoiselle Jeanne. Holmes's eyes popped open, and he glared at her, thoroughly annoyed. I stood and walked over to where she had collapsed into a large chair. She had buried her head in her hands and was visibly sobbing. In her lap was a photograph. I took the liberty of picking it up and looking at it.

It was perfectly unremarkable. It was of seven men in military uniforms. Four were seated on a bench in a park, with three more standing behind them. The clarity of the picture was poor, but I could see that none was smiling. There was nothing else in the photo to distinguish it from the thousands that soldiers have taken of themselves whilst off-duty and enjoying an afternoon out with their comrades. Yet it had brought about an anguished response from the young woman.

Chapter Eight
Come, the Game is Afoot

I was most likely not a good idea to extend a compassionate hand to her shoulder, but my years as a doctor made such an action an instinctive response.

"What is it, Miss?" I asked. "What is this photograph of?"

I watched her clench her fists until her knuckles whitened and she struggled to gain control of herself. She raised her head, her lovely face streaked with tears.

"They were in the park," she said. "The park in Saint-Avold. The town park was behind our house; the house I grew up in as a child. You can see our home in the background, behind some of the trees."

She took a deep breath and reached for the photograph.

"Here," she said, pointing at a small dark rectangle within the trees. "That is the window of my bedroom."

She stopped speaking for a full minute, then took another deep breath and continued. "That is the room I hid in when my parents and brother were killed. I have never been back to the house since that day."

The photograph was handed back to me as if it were too terrible to continue to look at. Holmes rose, came over and took it from me.

"And are these the men," he asked, "who you say visited such evil upon your family?"

Without speaking or removing her head from her hands, she nodded. "Saint Michael has said that they are."

Holmes took the photograph back to his chair, sat down, removed his glass from his pocket, and spent the next several minutes examining it. He then turned to the young woman.

"Get up!" he commanded. "If you are going to be useful to the cause of justice, you cannot indulge in whimpering and simpering."

She lifted her head. Her face betraying the shock of Holmes's rebuke. She nodded and stood.

"Come. We need to get into the village."

I was used to abrupt changes in Holmes's behavior. Inevitably it gave evidence of his having come to some insight in a case, but my curiosity could not be held back.

"Might I be so bold as to ask why?" I said.

"Because the murderer is most likely sitting in the pub enjoying his supper. With luck, Lestrade will be there as well."

The cab that had brought us to the Cunningham's estate was waiting for us and we quickly climbed in.

"The Bull's Head," shouted Holmes to the driver. "And quickly."

The old pub on the High Street was somewhat crowded with men and the occasional woman having a pint before supper or already digging into their steak and kidney pies. As I surveyed the patrons, I observed several of the chaps we had already met during our visits to Reigate as well as a couple of the recently hired German guards who would soon, I surmised, have to seek alternative employment given that they supremely failed in the job of protecting the squires.

I could see that Holmes was also looking around the room and his eyes settled on the far corner.

"Come, time to corner the prey," he said, and walked quickly toward a table at which only one man was sitting.

"Would you mind awfully, Mr. Sheridan, if we joined you at your table? This place is getting rather busy, is it not?"

Percy Sheridan looked up at Sherlock Holmes and smiled. His glance then went to me and then to Mademoiselle Jeanne. She gave him one of her radiant smiles and sat down.

"You have not met our young assistant," said Holmes. "Permit me to introduce our assistant, Mademoiselle Jeanne d'Arc Bastien-Lepage."

It was only a passing second, but a look of surprise mixed with fear passed over Sheridan's countenance as he observed her. He quickly recovered.

"It is a pleasure to meet you," said Sheridan.

"*Enchantée, monsieur,*" came the reply.

Mr. Sheridan called the waiter over and asked for two beers for the gentlemen and a shandy for the lady.

"I assume," he said, "that you have returned to Reigate to investigate the murder of the squires. Nasty business, that, eh what?"

"Yes," said Holmes, "really quite shocking. Very confusing, wouldn't you say? I hardly know where to start. So I have no choice but to ask questions of everyone and try to put some sort of theory together."

"I suppose," said Sheridan, "that is what detectives must do."

"Yes, I suppose it is. And seeing as we are sitting here, would you mind awfully if I were to start with you?"

"Me? Well, no, not at all. I fear I may not be of much use to you, but seeing as you are sitting here anyway, then you may as well get me out of the way and off the list. What would you like to know?"

"Nothing too complicated to start with," said Holmes. "Perhaps you could explain to me how it was that you managed to get past the guards, enter the house, stab two men to death and leave again without being detected. Would you mind?"

Sheridan's face went blank. For several seconds he glared

at Holmes, and then his glance traveled around the room, and finally he gazed up at the ceiling. He gave a very small nod.

"Jolly well done, Mr. Holmes. Your reputation is no doubt well-deserved. But I will only respond to your question if you agree to respond to mine. How did you come to your conclusion? I would be interested in knowing."

"I will give a full answer to your question," said Holmes. "But first, how did you get past the guards?"

"It was a trifle. I became one of them. They were all still arriving and had not even finished introducing themselves to each other. I donned my old uniform and joined them. As you have likely deduced, I speak native German and told them that I had been assigned to guard the back entrance to the house. Now they have been dismissed. I would be surprised if any of them guessed for even a second that my intent was the opposite of theirs."

I observed Holmes give a small shake to his head. Not that he doubted the truth of what he was being told, but that he never ceased to wonder at the gullibility of the members of the human race.

"And now your response to my question, Mr. Holmes," said Sheridan.

"To your credit, sir, you were somewhat more astute that those who employed the guards. What revealed your identity was, in order: First, you had recently had your gardens replanted, but without a single rose bush; something no true Englishman would ever do. And no Englishman from Leeds would ever hire Brunhilde as a housekeeper and have her prepare strudel. Your accent betrays not a single trace of the

North, something that even decades in Oxford cannot erase. You speak the English of a Junker who was raised by an English governess, although you, like all native German speakers, are so discourteous to your verbs, depositing far too many of them at the end of your sentences. An Englishman does not give a digital indication of his counting by beginning with his thumb. All of these observations make it obvious that you were not who you claimed to be. The final revelation was one for which I cannot take complete credit. Miss Bastien-Lepage brought to my attention a photograph of father and son Kellerman and some other Prussian army officers. You were not in that photograph, but in the small portrait of yourself which you display and I observed in your hallway—the one of you as a dashing young Prussian captain; one that you must find quite pleasing to look upon—you were standing in the same park as your fellow officers. There was no printing on the photographs to indicate that date and location, and the insignia on the uniforms was not easy to discern. But on close inspection, it could be seen that the uniforms were of the exact same style and cut and had identical markings. You were not only a fellow member of the Prussian army as the Kellermans, you were in the same company and the same unit. I do not know what your motive was. Revenge of some sort stemming from events that took place over a decade ago, perhaps. Nor have I discerned why you chose to take the actions you did last night. You must know that you are now on your way to the gallows, regardless of how much the Kellermans deserved to be punished. So, perhaps you will explain. And, whilst you are doing so, perhaps you could tell us just who you are."

Up to this point, the man, whoever he was, could simply have denied all of Holmes's accusations. I was bewildered as to why he had not done so. Now Holmes was asking him to incriminate himself whilst I recorded his words. I fully expected that the man would get up and walk away, knowing that there were no grounds on which to detain him. And yet, he did not move. He looked again up to the ceiling, gave a small nod, and continued.

"My name, sir, is Maxim von Witzleben. I am a member of a noble Prussian family that has a proud history of military service for the past three hundred years. As a young man, following my graduation from one of the finest gymnasia in Saarbrücken, I began my military service in the Prussian army, as my *Vater* and *Großvater* had done before me. To the rank of *Kapitän* and then *Zugführer* I was quickly promoted was honored to lead a *Zug* of fine men into the war with France. I served under Colonel Kellerman. Of all the soldiers I have even known, he was the most disgraceful and gave himself over to every form of evil, cruelty, and extortion. It is terrible to have to admit it, but several of my fellow officers went along with his vile activities. I refused to lower myself to their level and was ostracized for so doing. During the siege of Metz, our units were responsible for the provisioning of the troops and were we stationed in the village of Saint-Avold, where we organized the supply of food and ammunition so that the siege could carry on until we were victorious. It was during that time that the most terrible night of my life was experienced. It was the night of September 15 in the year 1870."

Here he stopped his account to Holmes and turned and

looked directly at Jeanne d'Arc Bastien-Lepage and spoke quietly to her.

"*Vite, ma petite. Vite, vite. Cache toi, immédiatement. Outre le fait de quoi que vous entendez, ne bougez surtout pas. Me compendez-vous? Me compendez-vous?*"

She gasped and for several seconds said nothing. Then she whispered, "C'était vous."

"Oui, ma petite, c'était moi. Forgive me, mademoiselle. Please. I should have stopped them. I should have taken out my gun and shot them to make them stop. Had I been a better man I would have done so. I am sorry."

"There is nothing to forgive," she said. "You did the best you could. Because of you, I am alive."

Her voice was no more than a whisper, and the blood had drained from her face.

"Tell these men, tell them what happened. They think I am crazy. They think I have imagined what happened. Tell them what happened."

Over the next ten minutes, Maxim von Witzleban described in dreadful detail the gruesome and horrible events that took place in the Bastien-Lepage home seventeen years earlier. The details of what he recounted are far too inhuman and depraved to be recorded in this story. Suffice it to say, I, who had been a soldier myself, could not believe that any soldier, serving under any flag, could do what these men had done.

As he spoke, I looked over at Jeanne d'Arc. She was as pale as a ghost and appeared to have entered a trance-like state. Her face was completely blank, and I realized that although she had heard what had taken place in her home and listened to the torture of her parents, she had not observed it with her eyes. Now, in her mind, these events were coming to life. She had come out of her safe hiding place in her closet and was in the room with her family, watching them die.

"The events of that night," said Maxim, "could not remain a secret. The truth will out. An account eventually made it all the way to the Chancellor. A secret tribunal was ordered. All who were present were found guilty of cowardly and unlawful conduct and dismissed from the Prussian army. We should have been brought before a firing squad and executed. But the war had just ended, and the victory over the French was being celebrated. The noble and heroic Prussian army was being hailed as the finest in the world. All of Germany was coming together to form one great country. Had our case become public, it would have spoiled the parade. So we were treated leniently and merely dismissed in disgrace.

"I defended myself, claiming that I had not participated, but the judges ruled, quite fairly, that I should have done more to stop the crimes as they were being committed, and that I should have informed our superior officers immediately afterward, which I failed to do. So I was thrown out of the army, a humiliation to my family. Generations of the von Witzleban family had served with distinction, and I alone had brought shame. But I was fortunate. My family is well-to-do, and I have an income from our properties. The other officers who were present that night somehow held on to their ill-gotten gains and have prospered.

"I vowed that I would wreak revenge on the others and bring to them the justice that they had escaped. But the days passed, and the days became weeks, and then years and the horrors of that night faded. I kept telling myself again and again that I had to do something, but I did nothing. The Kellermans ran off to England, others left Germany and lived in France, others yet changed their names and led prosperous lives in Strasbourg, Bonn, and Berlin. For a decade I did nothing. Then, last year, my life changed, and I set out on a path of action that culminated in my actions last night."

Here he paused and took a small sip of his ale. Holmes continued to observe him intensely. Jeanne d'Arc sat stone cold motionless, still in her trance. I gave in to my curiosity.

"Very well, sir. What happened?"

"You are a doctor, ja? Reach your hand up and gently touch the side of my head. Just here, behind my temple."

I did as requested and immediately recoiled.

"Merciful heavens. You have an enormous aneurism. If that were to burst, you would be dead in seconds."

"That, sir, is what my doctors told me as well. Just about nine months ago, it appeared. I was told that it could not be operated on and that I had, at most, a year to live. There is, as your English writer has said, nothing that so concentrates a man's mind as knowing he is about to die. It was bad enough for me that I had to stand before a panel of military judges and be found wanting. I did not want a repeat performance before Almighty God before being sent off into eternity. So I determined that I must set my affairs in order and must undertake to do what I should have done seventeen years ago. I needed to bring divine execution to the leaders of our evil band of officers. I needed to execute the Kellermans."

"I should have done the deed immediately but there was a part of me, my pride I admit, that wanted to torture the two villains with having to deal with me every day, knowing that I was giving news of their horrid pasts to the villagers and letting them be faced every day with the opprobrium of their neighbors. So I purchased the estate adjacent to theirs. They thought they would divert my efforts with a lawsuit over property, but I am not a poor man, and I merely hired more expensive London lawyers than they did and frustrated their efforts."

"You have owned your property now for over six months," said Holmes. "What took you so long?"

"Procrastination, indecision, perhaps even cowardice. Deciding to commit a double murder is not a decision to make quickly. So those weaknesses combined with some affairs I had to complete. I suggest that tomorrow you inquire at the offices of Wyatt Curtis, Solicitor if you wish to know more precisely what I have been up to on that score."

"Then why last night?"

"Because of you, Mr. Holmes."

Holmes said nothing but it was obvious that he was not pleased with that answer.

"You sent a warning to the Kellermans. A village has as many spies as does Alsace, especially when the villagers are united in a common cause of hatred of their would-be squires. The telegraph office duly passed along the news. Then you showed up and personally warned them. I knew that they were arrogant and stubborn, but they were not stupid. I knew that if they were convinced that danger had come too close, they would disappear. I also observed the arrival of their imperial guard of former Prussian soldiers. Those soldiers are not incompetent. It would be only a day or two before they organized themselves and began to provide impenetrable protection. Had I waited even until today, it might have been too late, and my plodding efforts would have been in vain. So I thank you, Mr. Holmes."

"Then why go to the bother of stabbing them in their sleep. You could just as easily have shot them with a rifle as they walked on the property. I am sure you have one, a Mauser most likely, and you know how to use it effectively."

"Quite correct. But I had read the accounts in the newspapers from France and Germany of the murders of the other members of the evil band of officers. Copying the method of the fellow who was doing them in, one of the local masons, I assumed, might keep you and Scotland Yard off my scent. It occurred to me that I might be able to die in bed and not in a prison cell. It seemed like a good idea at the time, until they went and arrested poor Mr. Kirwan. I was terribly upset by that news and immediately wrote out a complete confession. It is in my box at my solicitor's office. You can read it at your leisure. There is really no need for me to tell you anything else. You have all the information you need."

"Yes. I do. So you will kindly excuse me whilst I track down Inspector Lestrade and turn you over to him. I fear your wish to die in your bed and not a prison cell will not be granted."

"Ah, just one moment, if you will, please Mr. Holmes."

He then turned and spoke in a strong voice to Jeanne d'Arc.

"Mademoiselle Jeanne d'Arc Bastien-Lepage. Let my final words be a plea again for your forgiveness. May God grant you mercy and heal your pain."

The young woman startled. Her blank eyes came back to life, and she nodded in response.

"And may He be merciful to you as well, sir. I forgive you, and my saint has told me that Our Father will also."

"Merci, mademoiselle. And now, gentlemen," he said, turning to Holmes and me, "I pray that you also will forgive me if I do not accompany you to the police station. I have no desire to spend a single night in a jail cell. And please extend my apologies to my friend, the publican, for any inconvenience I cause him. And do not forget to visit the local solicitor."

He smiled serenely at each of us in turn and then, suddenly and forcefully, he struck the heel of his right hand against the side of his head.

"No!" I involuntarily shouted.

"*Ja, und Auf Wiedersehen.*" His eyes blinked several times, then they closed. His head slumped forward, and his chin rested on his cravat.

For several seconds the three of us sat in stunned silence. Then Miss Bastien-Lepage rose from her chair and walked over to Maxim von Witzleban, leaned down and planted a light kiss on is cheek. "Rest in peace, *mon capitaine*. Saint Michael told me he is waiting for you."

Chapter Nine
Where There is a Will

William Kirwan was released from police custody later that evening. The following morning, Holmes, Lestrade and I paid a visit to the offices of Mr. Wyatt Curtis, the local barrister. Jeanne d'Arc accompanied us but maintained a trance-like silence.

"Please, gentlemen and lady," said the barrister. "Do come in and be seated. And do excuse me if I seem somewhat distracted. The events of the past few days in the town have been frightfully disturbing. For ten years nothing particularly untoward took place and now were are invaded by a famous detective, Scotland Yard, and German war veterans and three men die tragically. It is a bit of a bother to our equilibrium. But enough of that, how may I be of assistance to you? I assume you are interested in the last wills and testaments recently filed by both Squires Cunningham and by Mr. Sheridan. Which one do you wish to see first?"

Not expecting this question, none of us immediately replied.

"All three," said Lestrade. "Let's have a look at them."

"Of course, Inspector. I have all three on my desk ready for you. It may come as a surprise to you to learn that neither the Cunninghams nor Mr. Sheridan were living under their legal names. The father and son are actually named Kellerman, and Mr. Sheridan was a German aristocrat, a von Witzleban."

"We were aware of that," said Holmes.

"Ah, yes. Of course. I should have expected that a Scotland Yard inspector and our famous detective had done their homework. Yes, of course. Very well. Here they are."

He handed them over to Lestrade who in turn kept one and handed the other two over to Holmes and me. As we were sitting beside each other, it was easy to glance at what the other was looking at as well as the document in our own hand. Within a few seconds, Holmes, Lestrade and I all looked up from the documents and exchanged glances with each other.

"These wills have been written in the same hand," said Holmes.

"Yes, that is obvious, isn't it?" said the solicitor. "But it is not surprising. They were neighbors and appear to have hired the same secretary. Quite practical. The wills are quite straightforward. The younger squire was the only son of the older man. Neither he nor Mr. Sheridan had any issue, and no other kin are named. The only unusual paragraphs are the specific and residual bequests. You can read them in section eighteen beginning on the fifth page. But allow me to summarize the for you."

"Go ahead," said Lestrade.

"Obviously there was a closer connection between the men than we local townspeople were aware of. Both estates have very considerable assets. There are many securities listed as well as the real properties here in Reigate, which were held free and clear of any liens or mortgages. Oddly, Mr. Sheridan leaves his entire estate to the church of St. Michael in the village of Saint-Avold in Alsace with instructions that the funds be used for the support of any local families still impoverished following the last war. Both of the Cunninghams leave the residuals to the same church with the identical instruction. However, the older Cunninghams makes several specific bequests to a short list of widows here in Reigate, and the younger has a similar list of funds to be given to five local spinsters. It is unusual, but it is all in order."

I did not have to be Sherlock Holmes to know immediately that the wills of the squires were blatant forgeries. Even my untrained eye could see the distinct similarity between the signature of Maxim von Witzleban and the handwriting of the body of the wills.

"Did you," asked Lestrade, "personally witness the signing of these documents?"

"Me? No," said the solicitor. "But they were witnessed by the postmaster, the vicar, and the constable. Their signatures appear on the final page. So there is no question that they are legitimate."

Mr. Wyatt Curtis looked at us, utterly stone-faced. It was clear to all present that the documents we were looking at were fraudulent and I waited for Holmes or Lestrade to say something.

"Very well, then," said Lestrade. "if they have reliable witnesses, then they should be put to effect as expeditiously as possible. You would agree, would you not, Holmes?"

"I would agree," Holmes replied.

"Excellent," said Lestrade. "And who are the executors?"

"Mr. William Kirwan," said the solicitor, "is named by all three parties. An excellent choice, I must say. Terrible mix-up he went through, but that is all behind him now. He will do a capital job disbursing the funds as directed and winding up the affairs of the estates."

"I have no doubt he will," said Holmes. "He is a good man."

Lestrade departed to the train station without so much as bidding us a good day. Holmes, Jeanne d'Arc and I returned to the inn and sat down for a refreshing round of morning tea.

"Well, now, mademoiselle," I said. "What now are your plans? I hope they do not involve any more executions, deserved or otherwise."

She beamed a radiant smile at me and then replied in her broad Texan accent.

"Oh my, Doctor Watson. Why, I do believe that your

Mademoiselle Jeanne d'Arc has departed. She must have gotten on the train with the terribly unpleasant policeman."

"Did she now? Well then, Miss Annie, what are *your* plans?"

"Oh my, Doctor Watson. I do believe that my gallivanting around the earth is over and done and I shall return to Houston and settle down. I will just have to find me an upright, fine young eligible gentleman with excellent prospects and a rich daddy and see to it that he marries me. I do not fancy living on a ranch with a thousand cows, but I reckon that a railway or a mining tycoon with a lovely home in the city would suit me real fine. Don't you agree, Doctor."

I laughed out loud. "I believe, miss, that you have to find that man first. The competition is quite stiff on the frontier."

"Oh my goodness gracious, doctor. That will not be at all difficult. Men really are such simple creatures. All a gal needs to do is make the poor fools feel utterly wonderful about *themselves* when they are with you, and they will never leave you. I shall send you a wedding invitation within six months. Mark my words," She laughed loudly and infectiously.

"Young lady," said Holmes. "I may not be able to fault you for your past actions, but I would hope that you would have sufficient integrity to warn whoever you plan to marry that your mind is unstable and that you are prone to hearing voices instructing you to engage in violent deeds."

The smile vanished from her face, and she looked directly at Sherlock Holmes

"Yesterday, sir, when poor Mr. Sheridan was telling you about what took place seventeen years ago, the voices inside my head were screaming until I thought my head would burst. But then they went silent. This morning I woke up and I knew that I had passed the first night in a decade in which no voice spoke to me. When I looked in the mirror, the only person who was there **was** Annie Morrison of Houston. Mademoiselle Jeanne d'Arc had departed. St. Michael has returned to heaven. He is no longer with me."

"Has he now? And your voices?"

"Mr. Holmes, my voices are gone."

Did you enjoy this story? Are there ways it could have been better? Please help the author and future readers by posting a constructive review on the site where you bought your book. Thank you.

Historical and Other Notes

The primary historical background to this story is the war between France and Germany – the Franco-Prussian War – of 1870-1871. Historians debate as to what started it. Some claim it was French foolishness; others suggest that Bismarck deliberately enticed them into a war so that he could use it as a pretext for uniting the independent German states. The Prussian army, reputed to be the best fighting machine in the world at the time, trounced the French and ended up annexing the French provinces of Alsace and Lorraine.

Metz is one of the major towns in Alsace. It was attacked by the Prussian troops early in the war, but held out for several months before surrendering, an event known as the siege of Metz. Saint-Avold is a lovely historical town in Alsace, very close to the German border. It was one of the first places in France that was occupied by the Prussian troops. Other towns and cities, including Paris, endured long sieges, resulting in high numbers of civilian deaths. An estimated 750,000 deaths, combined military and civilian, are attributed to the war.

Although the war was shorter and more contained than the world wars of the twentieth century, it was a very significant historical event for several reasons:

It demonstrated that a conscript army (the Prussians), supported by highly superior preparation and logistics, could defeat a professional army that had better arms (the French);

It was one of the first times that the Red Cross played an extensive role in the treatment of the wounded and in attempts to enforce some degree of agreed upon rules of warfare. These would later be codified into a re-draft of the Geneva Conventions;

Informal guerilla resistance units were organized by the occupied French and were somewhat effective in asymmetrical warfare. Violent and brutal reprisals against civilians were launched in response to resistance actions;

The defeat of the French and the fall of the Second Republic led to the short-lived Paris Commune. The iconic status of the Commune and the bloody crushing by the national government became seminal events in the development of world Communism;

The annexation of Alsace and Lorraine by Germany made certain that animosity between the French and Germans would continue for decades after the end of the war. It led, in part, to the chain of events that culminated in World War I;

It was the first war that was followed by the 'cult of the war dead' wherein soldiers who died in battle were buried in special cemeteries, cenotaphs erected, and remembrance ceremonies instituted.

Alsace and Lorraine remained under German control until the end of World War I. They were occupied again under Hitler and formally annexed in 1941. Over 140,000 Alsatian and Mosellian men were conscripted into the German armed forces. The territories were returned to France in 1945.

About the Author

In May of 2014 the Sherlock Holmes Society of Canada – better known as The Bootmakers – announced a contest for a new Sherlock Holmes story. Although he had no experience writing fiction, the author submitted a short Sherlock Holmes mystery and was blessed to be declared one of the winners. Thus inspired, he has continued to write new Sherlock Holmes Mysteries since and is on a mission to write a new story as a tribute to each of the sixty stories in the original Canon. He currently writes from Toronto, the Okanagan, and Manhattan.

More Historical Mysteries
by Craig Stephen Copland

www.SherlockHolmesMystery.com

Studying Scarlet. Starlet O'Halloran, a fabulous mature woman, who reminds the reader of Scarlet O'Hara (but who, for copyright reasons cannot actually be her) has arrived in London looking for her long-lost husband, Brett (who resembles Rhett Butler, but who, for copyright reasons, cannot actually be him). She enlists the help of Sherlock Holmes. This is an unauthorized parody, inspired by Arthur Conan Doyle's *A Study in Scarlet* and Margaret Mitchell's *Gone with the Wind*.

The Sign of the Third. Fifteen hundred years ago the courageous Princess Hemamali smuggled the sacred tooth of the Buddha into Ceylon. Now, for the first time, it is being brought to London to be part of a magnificent exhibit at the British Museum. But what if something were to happen to it? It would be a disaster for the British Empire. Sherlock Holmes, Dr. Watson, and even Mycroft Holmes are called upon to prevent such a crisis. This novella is inspired by the Sherlock Holmes mystery, *The Sign of the Four*.

A Sandal from East Anglia. Archeological excavations at an old abbey unearth an ancient document that has the potential to change the course of the British Empire and all of Christendom. Holmes encounters some evil young men and a strikingly beautiful young Sister, with a curious double life. The mystery is inspired by the original Sherlock Holmes story, A Scandal in Bohemia.

The Bald-Headed Trust. Watson insists on taking Sherlock Holmes on a short vacation to the seaside in Plymouth. No sooner has Holmes arrived than he is needed to solve a double murder and prevent a massive fraud diabolically designed by the evil Professor himself. Who knew that a family of devout conservative churchgoers could come to the aid of Sherlock Holmes and bring enormous grief to evil doers? The story is inspired by *The Red-Headed League*.

A Case of Identity Theft. It is the fall of 1888 and Jack the Ripper is terrorizing London. A young married couple is found, minus their heads. Sherlock Holmes, Dr. Watson, the couple's mothers, and Mycroft must join forces to find the murderer before he kills again and makes off with half a million pounds. The novella is a tribute to A Case of Identity. It will appeal both to devoted fans of Sherlock Holmes, as well as to those who love the great game of rugby.

The Hudson Valley Mystery. A young man in New York went mad and murdered his father. His mother believes he is innocent and knows he is not crazy. She appeals to Sherlock Holmes and, together with Dr. and Mrs. Watson, he crosses the Atlantic to help this client in need. This new storymystery was inspired by *The Boscombe Valley Mystery*.

The Mystery of the Five Oranges. A desperate father enters 221B Baker Street. His daughter has been kidnapped and spirited off the North America. The evil network who have taken her has spies everywhere. There is only one hope – Sherlock Holmes. Sherlockians will enjoy this new adventure, inspired by The Five Orange Pips and Anne of Green Gables.

The Man Who Was Twisted But Hip. France is torn apart by The Dreyfus Affair. Westminster needs Sherlock Holmes so that the evil tide of anti-Semitism that has engulfed France will not spread. Sherlock and Watson go to Paris to solve the mystery and thwart Moriarty. This new mystery is inspired by, *The Man with the Twisted Lip*, as well as by *The Hunchback of Notre Dame*.

The Adventure of the Blue Belt Buckle. A young street urchin discovers a man's belt and buckle under a bush in Hyde Park. A body is found in a hotel room in Mayfair. Scotland Yard seeks the help of Sherlock Holmes in solving the murder. The Queen's Jubilee could be ruined. Sherlock Holmes, Dr. Watson, Scotland Yard, and Her Majesty all team up to prevent a crime of unspeakable dimensions. A new mystery inspired by *The Blue Carbuncle*.

The Adventure of the Spectred Bat. A beautiful young woman, just weeks away from giving birth, arrives at Baker Street in the middle of the night. Her sister was attacked by a bat and died, and now it is attacking her. A vampire? The story is a tribute to *The Adventure of the Speckled Band* and like the original, leaves the mind wondering and the heart racing.

The Adventure of the Engineer's Mom. A brilliant young Cambridge University engineer is carrying out secret research for the Admiralty. It will lead to the building of the world's most powerful battleship, The Dreadnaught. His adventuress mother is kidnapped and he seeks the help of Sherlock Holmes. This new mystery is a tribute to *The Engineer's Thumb*.

The Adventure of the Notable Bachelorette. A snobbish nobleman enters 221B Baker Street demanding the help in finding his much younger wife – a beautiful and spirited American from the West. Three days later the wife is accused of a vile crime. Now she comes to Sherlock Holmes seeking to prove her innocence, This new mystery was inspired *The Adventure of the Noble Bachelor.*

The Adventure of the Beryl Anarchists. A deeply distressed banker enters 221B Baker St. His safe has been robbed, and he is certain that his motorcycle-riding sons have betrayed him. Highly incriminating and embarrassing records of the financial and personal affairs of England's nobility are now in the hands of blackmailers. Then a young girl is murdered. A tribute to *The Adventure of the Beryl Coronet.*

The Adventure of the Coiffured Bitches. A beautiful young woman will soon inherit a lot of money. She disappears. Another young woman finds out far too much and, in desperation seeks help. Sherlock Holmes, Dr. Watson and Miss Violet Hunter must solve the mystery of the coiffured bitches, and avoid the massive mastiff that could tear their throats. A tribute to *The Adventure of the Copper Beeches.*

The Silver Horse, Braised. The greatest horse race of the century, will take place at Epsom Downs. Millions have been bet. Owners, jockeys, grooms, and gamblers from across England and America arrive. Jockeys and horses are killed. Holmes fails to solve the crime until… This mystery is a tribute to *Silver Blaze* and the great racetrack stories of Damon Runyon.

The Box of Cards. A brother and a sister from a strict religious family disappear. The parents are alarmed, but Scotland Yard says they are just off sowing their wild oats. A horrific, gruesome package arrives in the post, and it becomes clear that a terrible crime is in process. Sherlock Holmes is called in to help. A tribute to *The Cardboard Box*.

The Yellow Farce. Sherlock Holmes is sent to Japan. The war between Russia and Japan is raging. Alliances between countries in these years before World War I are fragile, and any misstep could plunge the world into Armageddon. The wife of the British ambassador is suspected of being a Russian agent. Join Holmes and Watson as they travel around the world to Japan. Inspired by the *The Yellow Face*.

The Stock Market Murders. A young man's friend has gone missing. Two more bodies of young men turn up. All are tied to The City and to one of the greatest frauds ever visited upon the citizens of England. The story is based on the true story of James Whitaker Wright and is inspired by, *The Stock Broker's Clerk*. Any resemblance of the villain to a certain American political figure is entirely coincidental.

The Glorious Yacht. On the night of April 12, 1912, off the coast of Newfoundland, one of the greatest disasters of all time took place – the Unsinkable Titanic struck an iceberg and sank with a horrendous loss of life. The news of the disaster leads Holmes and Watson to reminisce about one of their earliest adventures. It began as a sailing race and ended as a tale of murder, kidnapping, piracy, and survival through a tempest. A tribute to *The Gloria Scott*.

A Most Grave Ritual. In 1649, King Charles I escaped and made a desperate run for Continent. Did he leave behind a vast fortune? The patriarch of an ancient Royalist family dies in the courtyard, and the locals believe that the headless ghost of the king did him in. The police accuse his son of murder. Sherlock Holmes is hired to exonerate the lad. A tribute to *The Musgrave Ritual*.

The Spy Gate Liars. Dr. Watson receives an urgent telegram telling him that Sherlock Holmes is in France and near death. He rushes to aid his dear friend, only to find that what began as a doctor's house call has turned into yet another adventure as Sherlock Holmes races to keep an unknown ruthless murderer from dispatching yet another former German army officer. A tribute to *The Reigate Squires*.

The Cuckold Man Colonel James Barclay needs the help of Sherlock Holmes. His exceptionally beautiful, but much younger, wife has disappeared and foul play is suspected. Has she been kidnapped and held for ransom? Or is she in the clutches of a deviant monster? The story is a tribute not only to the original mystery, *The Crooked Man*, but also to the biblical story of King David and Bathsheba.

The Impatient Dissidents. In March 1881, the Czar of Russia was assassinated by anarchists. That summer, an attempt was made to murder his daughter, Maria, the wife of England's Prince Alfred.. A Russian Count is found dead in a hospital in London. Scotland Yard and the Home Office arrive at 221B and enlist the help of Sherlock Holmes to track down the killers and stop them. This new mystery is a tribute to *The Resident Patient*.

The Grecian, Earned. This story picks up where *The Greek Interpreter* left off. The villains of that story were murdered in Budapest, and so Holmes and Watson set off in search of "the Grecian girl" to solve the mystery. What they discover is a massive plot involving the re-birth of the Olympic games in 1896 and a colorful cast of characters at home and on the Continent.

The Three Rhodes Not Taken. Oxford University is famous for its passionate pursuit of learning. The Rhodes Scholarship has been recently established and some men are prepared to lie, steal, slander, and, maybe murder, in the pursuit of it. Sherlock Holmes is called upon to track down a thief who has stolen vital documents pertaining to the winner of the scholarship, but what will he do when the prime suspect is found dead? A tribute to *The Three Students*.

A Scandal in Trumplandia. NOT a new mystery but a political. The story is a parody of the much-loved original story, *A Scandal in Bohemia*, with the character of the King of Bohemia replaced by you-know-who. If you enjoy both political satire and Sherlock Holmes, you will get a chuckle out of this new story.

Sherlock and Barack. This is NOT a new Sherlock Holmes Mystery. It is a Sherlockian research monograph.. Why did Barack Obama win in November 2012? Why did Mitt Romney lose? Pundits and political scientists have offered countless reasons. This book reveals the truth - The Sherlock Holmes Factor. Had it not been for Sherlock Holmes, Mitt Romney would be president.

From The Beryl Coronet to Vimy Ridge. This is NOT a New Sherlock Holmes Mystery. It is a monograph of Sherlockian research. This new monograph in the Great Game of Sherlockian scholarship argues that there was a Sherlock Holmes factor in the causes of World War I... and that it is secretly revealed in the *roman a clef* story that we know as *The Adventure of the Beryl Coronet*.

Reverend Ezekiel Black—'The Sherlock Holmes of the American West'—Mystery Stories.

A Scarlet Trail of Murder. At ten o'clock on Sunday morning, the twenty-second of October, 1882, in an abandoned house in the West Bottom of Kansas City, a fellow named Jasper Harrison did not wake up. His inability to do was the result of his having had his throat cut. The Reverend Mr. Ezekiel Black, a part-time Methodist minister and an itinerant US Marshall is called in. This original western mystery was inspired by the great Sherlock Holmes classic, *A Study in Scarlet*.

The Brand of the Flying Four. This case all began one quiet evening in a room in Kansas City. A few weeks later, a gruesome murder, took place in Denver. By the time Rev. Black had solved the mystery, justice, of the frontier variety, not the courtroom, had been meted out. The story is inspired by *The Sign of the Four* by Arthur Conan Doyle, and like that story, it combines murder most foul, and romance most enticing.

Collection Sets for eBooks and paperback are available at *40-50% off the price of buying them separately.*

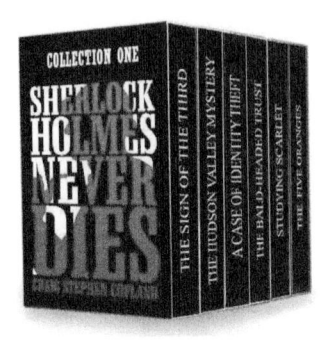

Collection One
The Sign of the Third
The Hudson Valley Mystery
A Case of Identity Theft
The Bald-Headed Trust
Studying Scarlet
The Mystery of the Five Oranges

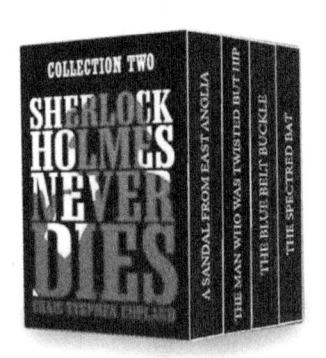

Collection Two
A Sandal from East Anglia
The Man Who Was Twisted But Hip
The Blue Belt Buckle
The Spectred Bat

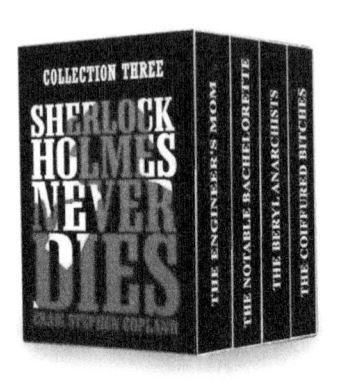

Collection Three
The Engineer's Mom
The Notable Bachelorette
The Beryl Anarchists
The Coiffured Bitches

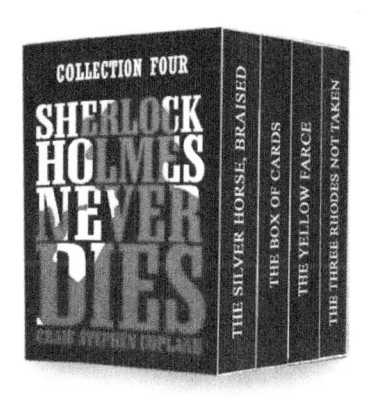

Collection Four
The Silver Horse, Braised
The Box of Cards
The Yellow Farce
The Three Rhodes Not Taken

Collection Five
The Stock Market Murders
The Glorious Yacht
The Most Grave Ritual
The Spy Gate Liars

Collection Six
The Cuckold Man
The Impatient Dissidents
The Grecian, Earned
The Three Rhodes Not Taken

Printed in Great Britain
by Amazon